Three particularly entertaining novels from Harlequin's famed Romance Library by worldwide favorite author Betty Neels

Stars through the Mist...Gerard van Doorninck asked Deborah to marry him, explaining he had found her a sensible reliable girl—one who would make an ideal hostess for his home. Love was not mentioned. But loving him, Deborah found his offer better than losing him. (#1761)

Winter of Change...Mary Jane was astounded when her dying grandfather introduced Fabian van der Blocq as her new guardian. A qualified nurse, she had proven she could take care of herself; now she was supposed to entrust her entire future to Fabian! (#1737)

Three for a Wedding...Her sister's urgent pleas persuaded Phoebe Brook to agree to assume Sybil's identity and work in a Dutch hospital under Dr. Lucius van Someren. Contrary to his sleepy appearance, he proved to be the most exciting man she'd ever met! (#1705)

**Another collection
of Romance favorites...
by a best-selling Harlequin author!**

In the pages of this specially selected
anthology are three delightfully
absorbing Romances—all by an
author whose vast readership all over
the world has shown her to be an
outstanding favorite.

For those of you who are missing
these love stories from your
Harlequin library shelf, or who wish
to collect great romance fiction by
favorite authors, these Harlequin
Romance anthologies are for you.

We're sure you'll enjoy each of the
engrossing and heartwarming stories
contained within. They're treasures
from our library...and we know
they'll become treasured additions
to yours!

The fourth anthology of 3 Harlequin Romances by

Betty Neels

Harlequin Books

TORONTO • NEW YORK • LONDON
AMSTERDAM • PARIS • SYDNEY • HAMBURG
STOCKHOLM • ATHENS • TOKYO • MILAN

These books by Betty Neels were originally published
as follows:
STARS THROUGH THE MIST
Copyright © 1973 by Betty Neels
First published in 1973 by Mills & Boon Limited
Harlequin edition (#1761) published March 1974

WINTER OF CHANGE
Copyright © 1973 by Betty Neels
First published in 1973 by Mills & Boon Limited
Harlequin edition (#1737) published December 1973

THREE FOR A WEDDING
Copyright © 1973 by Betty Neels
First published in 1973 by Mills & Boon Limited
Harlequin edition (#1705) published August 1973

ISBN 0-373-20073-0

First edition published as Harlequin Omnibus in November 1977
Second printing March 1978
Third printing May 1978
Fourth printing April 1979
Fifth printing June 1983

Contents

Stars through the Mist

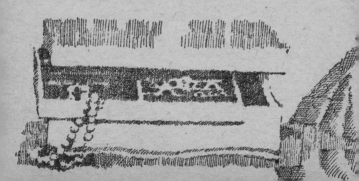

"A liking for each other, consideration, shared interests—these things make a good marriage," Gerard said when he asked Deborah to marry him. Love wasn't even a consideration.

His first marriage had been a disaster. He didn't want to repeat his mistake.

Deborah was willing to accept Gerard on any terms; but how long would she be able to suppress her own love for him?

CHAPTER ONE

THE operating theatre was a hive of industry, its usual hush giving way to sudden utterances of annoyance or impatience as the nurses went briskly to and fro about their business. Sister Deborah Culpeper, arranging her instruments with efficient speed on the trolley before her, found time to listen to the plaintive wail of her most junior nurse, who was unable to find the Langenbeck retractors she had been sent to fetch, while at the same time keeping an eye on Bob, the theatre technician, who was trying out the electrical equipment needed for the various drills which would presently be needed. She calmed the nurse, nodded approval of Bob's efforts, begged Staff Nurse Perkins to get the dressings laid out in their correct order and glanced at the clock.

One minute to nine o'clock, and as far as she could see, everything was ready. She swung the trolley round with an expert kick and then stood, relaxed and calm, behind it, knowing that in a few minutes the rest of the staff would follow suit; she never badgered them or urged them on, merely saw to it that each nurse had her fair share of the work and time enough in which to do it. She looked ahead of her now, apparently at the tiled wall opposite her, aware of every last move being made, nothing of her visible beneath the green gown which enveloped her, only her dark eyes showing above the mask. She looked the picture of calm self-assurance, and her nurses, aware of their own hurried breath and rapid pulses, envied her. A

9

quite unwarranted feeling, as it happened, for despite her outward tranquillity, Deborah's heart had quickened its pace to an alarming rate, and her breath, despite her efforts to keep it firmly under her control, had run mad. She gave her head a tiny, vexed shake, for it annoyed her very much that she should behave so stupidly whenever Mr van Doorninck was operating; she had tried every means in her power to remain uncaring of his presence and had mastered her feelings so well that she could present a placid front to him when they met and subdue those same feelings so sternly that she could scarcely be faulted as a perfect Theatre Sister; only on his operating days did her feelings get a little out of hand, something which she thanked heaven she could conceal behind her mask. She looked up now as the patient was wheeled in, arranged with nicety upon the operating table and covered with a blanket, to be followed immediately by the opening of the swing doors at the further end of the theatre and the appearance of two men.

Deborah's lovely eyes swept over the shorter, younger man—the Registrar, Peter Jackson—and rested briefly upon Mr van Doorninck. He was a very tall man with broad shoulders shrouded, as was every one else, in green theatre garb. His eyes above the mask swept round the theatre now, missing nothing as he walked to the table. His good morning to Sister Culpeper was affable if somewhat reserved, and his glance from under heavy lids was brief. She returned his greeting in a quiet, detached voice and turned at once to her trolley, wondering for the hundredth time how it was possible for a sensible woman of twenty-seven to be so hopelessly and foolishly in love with a consultant surgeon who had never uttered more than a few brief conventional phrases to her. But in love she was, and during the two years in which she had worked for him, it had strengthened into a depth of feeling which had caused her to refuse two proposals of marriage. She sighed soundlessly and began the familiar ritual of arranging the sterile sheets and towels over the unconscious form on the table.

She worked with speed and care, knowing exactly how the silent man on the other side of the table liked them arranged; in two years she had got to know quite a lot about him—that he was even-tempered but never easy-going, that when the occasion warranted it, he could display a cold anger, that he was kind and considerate and reticent about himself—almost taciturn. But of his life outside the theatre she knew very little; he was yearned over by the student nurses to whom he gave lectures, sought after by the more senior female staff, and openly laid siege to by the prettier, younger nurses. No one knew where he lived or what he did with his spare time; from time to time he let drop the information that he was either going to Holland or had just returned. The one fact which emerged from the wealth of rumour which surrounded him was that he was not married—an interesting detail which had increased the efforts of the young women who rather fancied themselves as his wife. And once or twice he had mentioned to Deborah that he had parents in Holland, as well as brothers and a sister who had been to England to visit him. Deborah had longed to ask questions and had restrained herself, knowing that if she did he would probably never tell her anything again.

She finished the preliminaries, glanced at him, and at his 'Ready, Sister?' gave her usual placid 'Yes, sir,' and handed him the towel clips which he liked to arrange for himself. After that she kept her thoughts strictly upon her job—scalpel, artery forceps, retractors, and then as he reached the bone, the lion forceps, the Langenbeck retractors, the rugines, the bone levers—she handed each in turn a second or so before he put out his hand to receive them, admiring, as she always did, his smooth technique and the sureness of his work. Not for nothing had he won a place on the top rung of the orthopaedic surgeon's ladder.

The patient was a young man with a malignant tumour of the femur; his only chance of recovery was extensive excision, a proceeding which Mr van Doorninck was undertaking now. Beyond a muttered word now and then to his registrar or a request for some special instrument, he spoke little; only when the operation was three parts completed and they were stitching up did he remark: 'There's a good chance of complete recovery here—as soon as he's fit we'll get him fitted with a leg—remind me to talk to Sister Prosser about him, Peter.'

He turned away from the table and took off his gloves to fling them into one of the bowls and walked out of the theatre, back into the scrubbing-up room, leaving Peter to supervise the removal of the patient and Deborah to organise the preparation of the theatre for the next case, reflecting as she did so that Sister Prosser, plain and plump and fifty if she was a day, was the most envied member of the nursing staff, because she saw Mr van Doorninck every day, and not only that, he took coffee with her frequently, and was known to have a great respect for her opinion of his patients' conditions.

The morning wore on; a child next with a Ewing's tumour over which the surgeon frowned and muttered to Peter, knowing that his careful surgery offered little hope of a permanent cure, then an old lady whose broken thigh was to be pinned and plated. It was like a carpenter's shop, thought Deborah, expertly changing drills and listening to the high whine of the electric equipment Bob was obediently switching on and off; what with drills and saws and mallets, it was a noisy way to spend a morning, although after five years of it she should be used to it. She had always been interested in bones and when she had finished her training and had had an opportunity of taking the post of staff nurse in the orthopaedic theatre, she had jumped at the chance, and a year later, when the Theatre Sister had retired, she had taken over her job, content with her lot—there was time enough to think about getting married in a year or two, in the meantime she would make a success of her new post, something she had done in a very short time so that there still seemed no urgency to take the idea of marriage seriously.

She was twenty-five when Mr van Doorninck walked into the theatre unit one day, to be introduced as the new orthopaedic consultant, and from that moment she had felt no desire to marry anyone at all, only him. She had realised how hopeless her wish was within a short time, and being a girl with common sense, had told herself to stop being a fool, and had accepted numerous invitations from a number of the younger doctors in the hospital. She had taken trips in fast sports cars, attended classical concerts, and visited cinemas and theatres, according to her escorts' tastes, but it hadn't helped in the least; she was left with the feeling that she had wasted her time as well as that of all the young men who had taken her out, for Mr van Doorninck's image remained clearly imprinted inside her head and refused to be budged.

She had come to realise over the last few months that there was only one way of escape from his unconscious toils; she would have to leave Clare's and start all over again somewhere else. Indeed she had already put this plan into effect, searching the *Nursing Times* for a suitable post, preferably situated at the furthest possible point from London.

They had a break for coffee after the old lady's fragile bones had been reinforced by Mr van Doorninck's expert carpentry. The talk was of the patients, naturally enough, but with their second cups, the two men began a discussion on the merits of the Registrar's new car and Deborah slipped away to scrub and relieve Staff for her own elevenses. They were still discussing cars when the theatre party reassembled around the table again to tackle a nasty shattered elbow, which Mr van Doorninck patiently fitted together like a jigsaw puzzle with Peter's help, several lengths of wire, a screw or two, and the electric drill again. That done to his satisfaction, he turned his attention to the last case, added hastily to the list at the last minute, because the patient had only been admitted early that morning with a fractured pelvis after he had crashed on his motor bike. It took longer than Deborah had expected. Half way through the operation she signed to Staff and one of the nurses to go to lunch, which left her with Bob and a very junior nurse, who, though willing and eager to please, was inclined to blunder around. It was long past two o'clock when the case left the theatre, and Mr van Doorninck, with a politely worded apology for running so far over his usual time, went too. She wouldn't see him again until Thursday; he operated three times a week and today was Monday.

The afternoon was spent doing the washdown in the theatre, and Deborah, on duty until Staff should relieve her at five o'clock, retired to her office to attend to the paper work. She had discarded her theatre gown and mask and donned her muslin cap in order to go to the dining room for her late dinner; now she spent a few moments repairing the ravages of a busy morning—not that they showed overmuch; her very slightly tiptilted nose shone just a little, her hair, which she wore drawn back above a wide forehead, still retained the smooth wings above each cheek and the heavy coil in her neck was still firmly skewered. She applied lipstick to her large, well-shaped mouth, passed a wetted fingertip across her dark brows, put her cap back on, and stared at the result.

She had been told times out of number that she was a very pretty girl, indeed, one or two of her more ardent admirers had gone so far as to say that she was beautiful. She herself, while not conceited, found her face passably good-looking but nothing out of the ordinary, but she, of course, was unaware of the delight of her smile, or the way her eyes crinkled so nicely at their corners when she laughed, and those same eyes were unusually dark,

15

the colour of pansies, fringed with long curling lashes which were the envy of her friends. She pulled a face at her reflection and turned her back on it to sit at the desk and apply herself to the miscellany upon it, but after ten minutes or so she laid down her pen and picked up the latest copy of the *Nursing Times*; perhaps there would be a job in it which might suit her.

There was—miles away in Scotland. The hospital was small, it was true, but busy, and they wanted an energetic working Sister, able to organise and teach student nurses the secrets of orthopaedics. She marked it with a cross and went back to her writing, telling herself that it was just exactly what she had been looking for, but as she applied herself once more to the delicate task of giving days off to her staff without disrupting the even flow of work, several doubts crept into her mind; not only was the hospital a satisfying distance from Mr van Doorninck, it was also, unfortunately, an unsatisfying distance from her own home. Holidays, not to mention days off, would be an almost impossible undertaking. She went home to Somerset several times a year now, and once a month, when she had her long weekend, she drove herself down in the Fiat 500 she had bought cheap from one of the housemen. She frowned, trying to remember her geography, wondering if Somerset was further away from the northern coasts of Scotland than was London. She could always spend a night with her Aunt Mary who lived on the edge of a hamlet rejoicing in the incredible name of Twice Brewed, hard by Hadrian's Wall, but even then she would have to spend another night on the road. And what was she going to tell her friends when they found out that she intended to leave? She had no good reason for doing so, she had never been anything but happy until Mr van Doorninck turned up and destroyed her peace of mind, and even now she was happy in a way because she was sure of seeing him three times a week at least. She frowned. Put like that, it sounded ridiculous—she would have to find some really sensible reason for giving in her notice. She picked up her pen once more; she would puzzle it out later, when she was off duty.

But there was no opportunity; she had forgotten that it was Jenny Reed's birthday and that they were all going out together to the cinema, so she spent the rest of the evening with half a dozen of the younger Sisters and shelved her problems.

There wasn't much time to think next day either, for the three victims of a car crash were admitted in the early hours of the morning and she was summoned early to go on duty and open up the theatre. Staff was already there when she arrived and so was the junior nurse, her eyes round with excitement as she began the humbler routine tasks which fell to her lot.

'Oh, Sister,' she breathed, 'they're in an awful bad way! Lottie Jones—she's on nights in the Accident Room, she says they've broken every bone in their bodies.'

Deborah was putting out the sharps and needles and collecting the electrical equipment. 'In which case we're going to be here for a very long time,' she remarked cheerfully. 'Where's Nurse Patterson?'

That young lady, only half awake, crept through the door as she put the question, wished her superior a sleepy good morning and went on to say: 'They're mincemeat, Sister, so rumour has it, and where's the night staff? Couldn't they have at least started . . .?'

'It's not only our three,' Deborah pointed out crisply. 'They've had a busy night, the general theatre has been on the go since midnight. Get the plaster room ready, will you, Nurse, and then see to the bowls.'

She was on the point of scrubbing up ready to start her trolleys when Mr van Doorninck walked in. She looked at him twice, because she was accustomed to seeing him either in his theatre gown and trousers, or a selection of sober, beautifully cut grey suits, and now he was in slacks and a rather elderly sweater. It made him look younger and much more approachable and it seemed to have the same effect on him as well, for he said cheerfully, 'Hullo—sorry we had to get you up early, but I wanted you here. Do you suppose they could send up some coffee—I can tell you what I intend doing while we drink it.' He glanced around him. 'These three look as though they could do with a hot drink, too,' a remark which sent Patterson scurrying to the telephone to order coffee in the consultant's name, adding a gleeful rider that it was for five people and was to be sent up at once.

Deborah led the way to her office, offered Mr van Doorninck a chair, which he declined, and sat down herself behind her desk. She had taken off her cap and had her theatre cap and mask in her hand, but she put these down now and rather absent-mindedly began to thrust the pins more securely into the great bundle of hair she had twisted

18

up in such a hurry. She did it with a lack of self-consciousness of which she was unaware and when she looked up and caught his eye, she said, 'Sorry about this—there wasn't much time, but I'm listening.'

'Three cases,' he began. 'The first is a young man —a boy, I should say, fractured pelvis, left and right fractured femurs, I'm afraid, and a fractured patella—fragmented, I shall have to remove the whole thing. The other two aren't quite so bad— fractured neck of femur, compound tib and fib and a few ribs; the third one has got off comparatively lightly with a comminuted fracture of left femur and a Potts'. I think if we work the first case off, stop for a quick breakfast, and get the other two done afterwards—have you a list for Mr Squires this morning? Doesn't he usually start at eleven o'clock?'

Deborah nodded. 'But it's a short list and I'm sure he'll agree to start half an hour later if he were asked.'

'How are you placed for staff? Will you be able to cover both theatres? You'll be running late.'

It was Staff's half day before her days off, but he wouldn't know about that. Deborah said positively: 'I can manage very well; Bob will be on at eight o'clock and both part-time staff nurses come in.'

She made a show of consulting the off-duty book before her. She wouldn't be able to go off duty herself, for she was to be relieved by one of the part-time staff nurses; she would have to telephone her now, and get her to come in at one o'clock instead.

'When would you like to start?' she wanted to know calmly.

He glanced at his watch. 'Ten minutes, if you can.'

She got up from her chair. 'We'll be ready— you'll want the Smith–Petersen nails, and shall I put out the McLaughlin pin-plate as well? And will you want to do a bone graft on the tib and fib?'

'Very probably. Put out everything we've got, will you? I'll pick what I want, we can't really assess the damage until I can get the bone fragments away.'

He followed her out of the office and they walked together down the wide corridor to the scrubbing-up room, where Peter was already at one of the basins. Deborah wished him good morning and went to her own basin to scrub—ten minutes wasn't long and she had quite a lot to do still.

The operation lasted for hours, and unlike other jobs, there was no question of hurrying it up; the broken bones had to be exposed, tidied up, blood vessels tied, tissue cut away and then the pieces brought together before they were joined by means of pins or wires, and only then after they had been X-rayed.

Mr van Doorninck worked steadily and with the absorption of a man doing a difficult jigsaw puzzle, oblivious of time or anything else. Deborah, with an eye on the clock, sent a nurse down to breakfast with the whispered warning to look sharp about it; Staff went next and when Bob came on at eight o'clock and with him the other two student nurses, she breathed more freely. She still had to telephone Mrs Rudge, the part-time staff nurse, but she lived close by and with any luck she would be able to change her duty hours; she would worry about that

20

later. She nodded to Bob to be ready with the drill, checked swabs with the junior nurse, and tidied her trolleys.

The case was wheeled away at long last, and as the patient disappeared through one door, Mr van Doorninck and Peter started off in the opposite direction. 'Twenty minutes?' said Mr van Doorninck over his shoulder as he went, not waiting for her reply.

'You must be joking,' Deborah muttered crossly, and picked up a handful of instruments, to freeze into immobility as he stopped abruptly. 'You're right, of course—is half an hour better?'

She said 'Yes, sir,' in a small meek voice and plunged into the ordered maelstrom which was the theatre. Twenty minutes later she was in her office, her theatre cap pushed to the back of her head, drinking the tea Staff had whistled up for her and wolfing down buttered toast; heaven knew when she would get her next meal....

She certainly didn't get it at dinnertime, for although the second case proved plain sailing, even if slow, the third presented every small complication under the sun; the femur was in fragments, anyone less sure of himself than Mr van Doorninck might have felt justified in amputating below the knee, but he, having made up his mind that he could save the limb, set to work to do so, and a long and tedious business it was, necessitating Deborah sending Mrs Rudge to the second theatre to take care of Mr Squires who had obligingly agreed to take his list there, and she had taken two of the nurses with her, a circumstance which had caused Staff Nurse Perkins to hesitate about taking her half day, but it was impossible to argue about it in theatre; she

21

went, reluctantly.

The operation lasted another hour. Deborah had contrived to send the nurses to their dinners, but Bob she didn't dare to send; he was far too useful and understood the electric drills and the diathermy machine even better than she did herself— besides, she was scrubbed, and at this stage of the operation there was no question of hampering Mr van Doorninck for a single second.

It was half past two when he finally straightened his back, thanked her politely for her services and walked away. She sent Bob to his belated dinner, and when Mrs Rudge arrived from the other theatre, went downstairs herself to cold beef and salad. There was certainly no hope of off-duty for her now. Mrs Rudge would go at four o'clock and that would leave herself and two student nurses when Bob went at five. She sighed, eating almost nothing, and presently went over to the Nurses' Home and tidied herself in a perfunctory manner, a little horrified at the untidiness of her appearance—luckily it had all been hidden under her cap and mask.

It had just turned four o'clock when the Accident Room telephoned to say that there was a small child coming up within minutes with a nasty compound fracture of upper arm. Deborah raced round collecting instruments, scrubbing to lay the trolley while telling the nurses, a little fearful at having to get on with it without Staff to breathe reassuringly down their necks, what to do next. All the same, they did so well that she was behind her trolley, scrubbed and threading needles when the patient was wheeled in, followed by Mr van Doorninck and Peter.

'Oh,' said Deborah, taken delightfully by surprise, 'I didn't know that it would be you, sir.'

'I was in the building, Sister,' he informed her, and accepted the towel clip she was holding out. 'You have been off duty?'

She passed him a scalpel. 'No.'

'You will be going this evening?'

She took the forceps off the Mayo table and held them ready for Peter to take. 'No,' then added hastily, in case he should think she was vexed about it, 'It doesn't matter in the least.'

He said 'Um' behind his mask and didn't speak again during the operation, which went without a hitch. All the same, it was almost six o'clock when they were finished and it would be another hour before the theatre was restored to its pristine state. It was a great pity that Peter had to put a plaster on a Potts' fracture—it was a simple one and he did it in the little plaster room, but he made a good deal of mess and Deborah, squeezing out plaster bandages in warm water for him to wind round the broken leg, found her temper wearing thin. It had been a long day, she was famished and tired and she must look a sight by now and there were still the books to write up. She glanced at the clock. In ten minutes the nurses were due off duty; she would have to stay and do her writing before she closed the theatre. She sighed and Peter cocked an eyebrow at her and asked: 'Worn out, Deb?'

'Not really, just hungry, and I haven't had time to do my hair properly or see to my face all day. I feel a fright.' She could hear her voice sounding cross, but he ignored it and agreed cheerfully:

'You look pretty awful—luckily you're so gorgeous, it doesn't matter, though the hair is a trifle

23

wild.'

She giggled and slapped a wet bandage into his outstretched hand.

'Well, it doesn't matter, there's no one to see me. I shall eat an enormous supper and fall into bed.'

'Lucky girl—I'm on until midnight.'

She was instantly sympathetic. 'Oh, Peter, how awful, but there's not much of a list for Mr Squires tomorrow afternoon and only a handful of re-plasters and walking irons—you might be able to get someone to give you a hand.'

He nodded. 'We're on call, aren't we?'

That was true; Clare's was on call until Thursday. 'I'll keep my fingers crossed,' she promised him. 'And now be off with you, I want to clear up.'

It was very quiet when the nurses had gone. Deborah tugged her cap off her dreadfully untidy hair, kicked off her shoes, and sat down at her desk. Another ten minutes or so and she would be free herself. She dragged her thoughts away from the tantalising prospect of supper and a hot bath and set to on the operation book. She was neatly pen-ning in the last name when the unit doors swung open and her tired mind registered the disturbing fact that it was Mr van Doorninck's large feet com-ing down the corridor, and she looking like some-thing the sea had washed up. She was still frantic-ally searching for her shoes when he came in the door. She rose to her stockinged feet, feeling even worse than she looked because he was, by contrast, quite immaculate—no one, looking at him now, would know that he had been bent over the operat-ing table for the entire day. He didn't look tired either; his handsome face, with its straight nose and firm mouth, looked as good-humoured and relaxed as it usually did.

Deborah spoke her thoughts aloud and quite involuntarily. 'Oh, dear—I wasn't expecting anyone and I simply....' She broke off because he was smiling nicely at her. 'I must look quite awful,' she muttered, and when he laughed softly: 'Is it another case?' He shook his head. 'You want to borrow some instruments—half a minute while I find my shoes....'

He laughed again. 'You won't need your shoes and I don't want any instruments.' He came a little further into the room and stood looking at her. She looked back at him, bewildered, her mind noting that his Dutch accent seemed more pronounced than usual although his English was faultless.

'How do you feel about marrying me?' he wanted to know blandly.

CHAPTER TWO

She was so amazed that she couldn't speak. Just for one blissful moment she savoured the delightful idea that he had fallen in love with her, and then common sense took over. Men in love, however awkward about the business, weren't likely to employ such a cool manner as his. He had sounded for all the world as though he wanted her to fit in an extra case on his next list or something equally prosaic. She found her voice at last and was surprised at its steadiness. 'Why do you ask me?' she wanted to know.

She watched his nod of approval. The light over the desk showed up the grey hair at his temples and served to highlight the extreme fairness of the rest.

His voice was unhurried as he said pleasantly:

'What a sensible girl you are—most women would have been demanding to know if I were joking. I have noticed your calm manner when we have worked together, and I am delighted to see that it isn't only in the operating theatre that you are unflurried.'

He was silent for so long that Deborah, desperate for something, anything to do, sat down again and began to stack the various notebooks and papers neatly together. That there was no need to do this, and indeed it would merely give her more work in the morning sorting them all out again, escaped her notice. He might think her sensible and calm; inside, happily concealed by her dark blue uniform, she was bubbling like a cauldron on the boil.

Presently, in the same pleasant voice, he went on: 'I will explain. I am returning to Holland to live very shortly; my father died recently and it is necessary for me to live there—there are various obligations——' he dismissed them with a wave of his hand and she wondered what they might be. 'I shall continue with my work, naturally, but we are a large family and I have a great many friends, so there will be entertaining and social occasions, you understand. I have neither the time nor the inclination to arrange such things, neither do I have the slightest idea how to run a household. I need a wife, someone who will do these things and welcome my friends.'

He paused, but she wasn't looking at him. There were some retractors on the desk, put there for repair; she had picked them up and was polishing their handles vigorously with the cloth in which they were wrapped. He leaned across the desk and

26

took them from her without a word and went on: 'I should tell you that I have been married. My wife died eight years ago and I have had no wish to become deeply involved with any woman since; I do not want to become deeply involved with you, but I see very little likelihood of this; we have worked together now for two years and I believe that I understand you very well. I would wish for your companionship and friendship and nothing more. I am aware that women set great store by marrying for love and that they are frequently unhappy as a consequence. Perhaps you do not consider what I am offering enough, and yet it seems to me that we are ideally suited, for you have plenty of common sense, a delightful manner and, I think, similar tastes to my own. I can promise you that your life will be pleasant enough.' His blue eyes stared down at her from under half-closed lids. 'You're twenty-seven,' he told her, 'and pretty enough to have had several chances of marrying and settling down with a husband and children, but you have not wanted this—am I right?'

She nodded wordlessly, squashing a fleeting, nonsensical dream of little flaxen-haired van Doornincks as soon as it had been born. Because she simply had to know, she asked: 'Have you any children?'

'No,' his voice was so remote that she wished she hadn't spoken, 'I have two brothers and a sister, all married—there are children enough in the family.'

Deborah waited for him to ask her if she liked children, but he didn't, so after a minute or two's silence she said in a quiet little voice:

'May I have some time to think about it? You see, I've always imagined that I would marry someone I...' She stopped because she wasn't sure of her voice any more.

'Loved?' he finished for her in a depressingly matter-of-fact tone. 'I imagine most girls do, but I think that is not always the best way. A liking for each other, consideration for one's partner, shared interests—these things make a good marriage.'

She stared at him, her lovely eyes round. She hadn't supposed him to be a cold man, although he was talking like one now. Either he had been unhappy in his first marriage or he had loved his wife so dearly that the idea of loving any other woman was unthinkable to him. She found either possibility unsatisfactory. With a tremendous effort she made herself be as businesslike as he was. 'So you don't want children—or—or a wife?'

He smiled. 'Shall we discuss that later? Perhaps I haven't made myself quite plain; I admire and like you, but I'm not in love with you and I believe that we can be happy together. We are sensible, mature people and you are not, I believe, a romantic girl....'

She longed to tell him how wrong he was. Instead: 'You don't believe in falling in love, then?'

He smiled so charmingly that her outraged heart cracked a little.

'And nor, I think, do you, Deborah, otherwise you would have been married long ago—you must be single from choice.'

So that was what he thought; that she cared nothing for marriage and children and a home of her own. She kept her angry eyes on the desk and said nothing at all.

Presently he said, 'I have offended you. I'm sorry, but I find myself quite unable to be anything but honest with you.'

She looked up at that and encountered his blue stare. 'I've had chances to marry,' she told him, at the same time wondering what would happen if she told him just why she had given up those same chances. 'Did you love your wife?' The question had popped out before she had been able to stop it and she watched the bleak look on his face as it slowly chilled her.

He said with a bitter little sneer which hurt her, 'All women are curious....'

'Well, I'm not all women,' she assured him sharply, 'and I'm not in the least curious'—another lie—'but it's something I should have to know— you said you wanted to be honest.'

He looked at her thoughtfully. 'You're quite right. One day we will talk about her. Will it suffice for the moment if I tell you that our marriage was a mistake?' He became his usual slightly reserved self again. 'Now that I have told you so much about myself, I do not see that you can do anything else but marry me.'

She answered his smile and was tempted to say yes at once, but common sense still had a firm place inside her lovely head; she would have to think about it. She told him so and he agreed unconcernedly. 'I shall see you on Thursday,' he observed as he went to the door. 'I'll leave you to finish your writing. Good night, Deborah.'

She achieved a calm 'Good night, Mr van Doorninck,' and he paused on the way out to say: 'My name is Gerard, by the way, but perhaps I shouldn't have told you that until Thursday.'

Deborah did no more writing; she waited until she heard the swing doors close after him and then shovelled the books and papers into a drawer, pell-mell. They could wait until tomorrow—she had far too much on her mind to be bothered with stupid matters like off-duty and laundry and instruments which needed repairing. She pinned on her cap anyhow, found her shoes at last, locked the theatre, hung the keys on the hook above the door, and went down to supper. Several of her friends were as late as she was; they greeted her with tired good nature and broke into a babble of talk to which she didn't listen until the Accident Room Sister startled her by saying, 'Deb, whatever is the matter? I've asked you at least three times what van Doorninck did with those three cases we sent up, and you just sit there in a world of your own.'

'Sorry,' said Deborah, 'I was thinking,' a remark which called forth a little ripple of weary laughter from everyone at the table. She smiled round at them all and plunged obligingly into the complexities of the three patients' operations.

'No off-duty?' someone asked when she had finished.

Deborah shook her head. 'No—I'll make it up some time.'

'He works you too hard,' said a pretty dark girl from the other side of the table. 'Cunning wretch, I suppose he turned on the charm and you fell for it.'

The Accident Room Sister said half-jokingly, 'And what wouldn't you give to have the chance of doing just that, my girl? The handsome Mr van Doorninck is a confirmed bachelor, to the sorrow of us all, and the only reason Deb has lasted so long in theatre is because she never shows the least interest in him, so he feels safe with her. Isn't that right, Deb?'

Deborah blushed seldom; by a great effort of will she prevented herself from doing so now. She agreed airily, her fingers crossed on her lap, and started on the nourishing rice pudding which had been set before her. She wouldn't have rice pudding, she promised herself. Perhaps the Dutch ... she pulled her thoughts up sharply; she hadn't decided yet, had she? It would be ridiculous to accept his offer, for it wouldn't be the kind of marriage she would want in the first place, on the other hand there was the awful certainty that if she refused him she would never see him again, which meant that she would either remain single all her days or marry someone else without loving him. So wasn't it better to marry Mr van Doorninck even if he didn't love her? At least she would be with him for the rest of her life and he need never find out that she loved him; he hadn't discovered it so far, so why should he later on?

She spooned the last of the despised pudding, and decided to marry him, and if she had regrets in the years to come she would only have herself to blame. It was a relief to have made up her mind, although perhaps it had been already made up from the very moment when he had startled her with his proposal, for hadn't it been the fulfilment of her wildest dreams?

She retired to her room early on the plea of a hard day and the beginnings of a headache, determined to go to bed and think the whole preposterous idea over rationally. Instead of which she fell sound asleep within a few minutes of putting her head on the pillow, her thoughts an uncontrollable and delicious jumble.

She had time enough to think the next day, though. Wednesday was always a slack day in theatre even though they had to be prepared for emergencies. But there were no lists; Deborah spent the greater part of the day in the office, catching up on the administrative side, only sallying forth from time to time to make sure that the nurses knew what they were about. She went off duty at five o'clock, secretly disappointed that Mr van Doorninck hadn't put in an appearance—true, he hadn't said that he would, but surely he would feel some impatience? Upon reflection she decided that probably he wouldn't, or if he did, he would take care not to let it show. She spent the evening washing her hair and doing her nails, with the vague idea that she needed to look her best when he arrived at ten o'clock the next morning.

Only he didn't come at ten. She was in theatre, on her knees under the operating table because one of the nurses had reported a small fault in its mechanism. She had her back to the door and didn't hear him enter; it was the sight of his large well-polished shoes which caused her to start up, knocking her cap crooked as she did so. He put out a hand and helped her to her feet without effort, rather as though she had been some small slip of a girl, and Deborah exclaimed involuntarily, 'Oh— I'm quite heavy. I'm too tall, you must have noticed.' Her eyes were on his tie as she babbled on: 'I'm so big . . .!'

'Which should make us a well-suited couple,' he answered equably. 'At least, I hope you will agree with me, Deborah.'

She put a hand up to her cap to straighten it, not quite sure what she should answer, and he caught her puzzled look. 'Not quite romantic enough?' he quizzed her gently. 'Have dinner with me tonight and I'll try and make amends.'

She was standing before him now, her lovely eyes on a level with his chin. 'I don't know—that is, I haven't said...'

His heavy-lidded eyes searched hers. 'Then say it now,' he commanded her gently. It seemed absurd to accept a proposal of marriage in an operating theatre, but there seemed no help for it. She drew breath:

'Yes, I'll marry you, Mr van Doorninck.' She uttered the absurd remark in a quiet, sensible voice and he laughed gently.

'Gerard, don't you think? Can you manage seven o'clock?'

Her eyes left his chin reluctantly and met his. 'Yes, I think so.'

'Good. I'll fetch you—we'll go to the Empress if you would like that.'

Somewhere very super, she remembered vaguely. 'That will be nice.' An inadequate answer, she knew, but he didn't appear to find it amiss; he took her two hands lightly in his and said: 'We'll have a quiet talk together—it is essential that we should understand each other from the beginning, don't you agree?'

It sounded very businesslike and cool to her; perhaps she was making a terrible mistake, but was there a worse mistake than letting him go away for ever? She thought not. For want of anything better to say, she repeated, 'That will be nice,' and added, 'I must go and scrub, you have a list as long as your arm.'

It stretched longer than an arm, however, by the

time they had finished. The second case held them up; the patient's unexpected cardiac arrest was a surprise which, while to be coped with, flung a decided spanner in the works. Not that Mr van Doorninck allowed it to impede his activities—he continued unhurriedly about his urgent business and Deborah, after despatching Staff to the other end of the table to help the anaesthetist in any way he wished, concentrated upon supplying her future husband's wants. The patient rallied, she heard Mr van Doorninck's satisfied grunt and relaxed herself; for a patient to die on the table was something to be avoided at all costs. The operation was concluded and the patient, still unconscious and happily unaware of his frustrated attempts to die, was borne away and it was decided that a break for coffee would do everyone some good. Deborah, crowding into her office with the three men and sharing the contents of the coffee pot with them, was less lucky with the biscuit tin, for it was emptied with a rapidity she wouldn't have prevented even if she could have done so; the sight of grown men munching Rich Tea biscuits as though they had eaten nothing for days touched her heart. She poured herself a second cup of coffee and made a mental note to wheedle the stores into letting her have an extra supply.

The rest of the morning went well, although they finished more than an hour late. Mr van Doorninck was meticulously drawing the muscle sheath together, oblivious of time. He lifted an eyebrow at Peter to remove the clamps and swab the wound ready for him to stitch and put out an outsize gloved hand for the needleholder which Deborah was holding ready. He took it without a glance and paused to straighten his back. 'Anything for this afternoon, Sister?' he enquired conversationally.

'Not until three o'clock, sir.' She glanced at Peter, who would be taking the cases. 'A baby for a gallows frame and a couple of Colles.'

'So you will be free for our evening together?'

'Yes, sir.' Hadn't she already said so? she asked herself vexedly, and threaded another needle, aware of the pricked ears and held breaths around her and Peter's swift, astonished look.

Mr van Doorninck held out his needleholder for her to insert the newly threaded needle. He said deliberately so that everyone could hear, 'Sister Culpeper and I are engaged to be married, so we are—er—celebrating this evening.'

He put out a hand again and Deborah slapped the stitch scissors into it with a certain amount of force, her fine bosom swelling with annoyance—giving out the news like that without so much as a word to her beforehand! Just wait until we're alone, she cautioned him silently, her smouldering look quite lost upon his downbent, intent head. And even if she had wanted to speak her mind, it would have been impossible in the little chorus of good wishes and congratulations. She made suitable murmurs in reply and scowled behind her mask.

But if she had hoped to have had a few words with him she was unlucky; the patient was no sooner stitched than he threw down his instruments, ripped off his gloves and made off with the long, leisurely stride which could only have been matched on her part by a frank run. She watched him go, fuming, and turned away to fob off the nurses' excited questions.

Her temper had improved very little by the time she went off duty. The news had spread, as such news always did; she was telephoned, stopped in the corridors and beseiged by the other Sisters when she went down to tea. That they were envious was obvious, but they were pleased too, for she was well liked at Clare's, and each one of them marvelled at the way she had kept the exciting news such a close secret.

'He'll be a honey,' sighed Women's Surgical Sister. 'Just imagine living with him!' She stared at Deborah. 'Is he very rich, Deb?'

'I—I don't really know.' Deborah was by now quite peevish and struggling not to show it. It was a relief, on the pretext of dressing up for the evening, when she could escape. All the same, despite her ill-humour, she dressed with care in a pinafore dress of green ribbed silk, worn over a white lawn blouse with ballooning sleeves and a fetching choirboy frill under her chin, and she did her hair carefully too, its smooth wings on her cheeks and the complicated chignon at the back of her neck setting off the dress to its greatest advantage. Luckily it was late August and warm, for she had no suitable coat to cover this finery; she rummaged around in her cupboard and found a gossamer wool scarf which she flung over her arm—and if he didn't like it, she told her reflection crossly, he could lump it.

Still buoyed up by indignation, she swept down the Home stairs, looking queenly and still slightly peevish, but she stopped in full sail in the hall because Mr van Doorninck was there, standing by the door, watching her. He crossed the polished floor and when he reached her said the wrong thing. 'I had no idea,' he commented, 'that you were such a handsome young woman.'

His words conjured up an outsize, tightly cor-
seted Titanic, when her heart's wish was to be frail
and small and clinging. She lifted pansy eyes to his
and said tartly, 'My theatre gowns are a good disguise. . . .' and stopped because she could see that he
was laughing silently.

'I beg your pardon, Deborah—you see how necessary it is for me to take a wife? I have become so
inept at paying compliments. I like you exactly as
you are and I hope that you will believe that. But
tell me, why were you looking so put out as you
came downstairs?'

She felt mollified and a little ashamed too. 'I was
annoyed because you told everyone in theatre that
we were engaged—I didn't know you were going
to.'

He chose to misunderstand her. 'I had no idea
that you wished it to remain a secret.' He smiled so
nicely at her that her heart hurried its beat.

'Well—of course I didn't.'

'Then why were you annoyed?'

An impossible question to answer. She smiled reluctantly and said:

'Oh, I don't know—perhaps I haven't quite got
used to the idea.'

His blue eyes searched hers calmly. 'You have
had second thoughts, perhaps?'

'No—oh, no.'

He smiled again. 'Good. Shall we go?'

They went through the Home door together,
and she was very conscious of the unseen eyes peering at them from the net-covered windows, but she
forgot all about them when she saw the car drawn
up waiting for them. She had wondered from time

to time what sort of car he drove, and here it was—a BMW 3 OCSL, a sleek, powerful coupé which looked as though it could do an enormous speed if it were allowed to. She paused by its door and asked: 'Yours?'

'Yes. I could use a larger car really, but once I'm in it it's O.K., and she goes like a bird. We'll change her, though, if you prefer something roomier.'

Deborah had settled herself in her seat. 'She's super, you mustn't dream of changing her.' She turned to look at him as he got in beside her. 'I always imagined that you would drive something stately.'

He laughed. 'I'm flattered that you spared even such thoughts as those upon me. I've a Citroën at home, an SM, plenty of room but not so fast as this one. I take it that you drive?'

He had eased the car into the evening traffic and was travelling westward. 'Well,' said Deborah, 'I drive, but I'm not what you would call a good driver, though I haven't had much opportunity....'

'Then we must find opportunity for you—you will need a car of your own.'

In Piccadilly, where the traffic was faster and thinner, he turned off into Berkeley Street and stopped outside the Empress Restaurant. A truly imposing place, she discovered, peeping discreetly about her as they went in—grandly Victorian with its red plush and its candelabra. When they were seated she said with disarming frankness: 'It rather takes my breath away.'

His mouth twitched. 'Worthy of the occasion, I hope.' He opened his eyes wide and she was surprised, as she always was, by their intense blue: 'For

38

it is an occasion, is it not?'

She studied him; he was really extraordinarily handsome and very distinguished in his dinner jacket. After a moment he said softly:

'I hope I pass muster?'

She blinked and smiled rather shyly. 'I beg your pardon—I didn't mean to stare. It's just that—well, you never see a person properly in theatre, do you?'

He studied her in his turn. 'No—and I made a mistake just now. I called you handsome, and you're not, you're beautiful.'

She flushed delicately under his gaze and he went on blandly: 'But let us make no mistake, I'm not getting sentimental or falling in love with you, Deborah.' His voice had a faint edge which she was quick to hear.

She forced her own voice to normality. 'You explained about that, but supposing you should meet someone with whom you do fall in love? And you might, you're not old, are you?'

'I'm thirty-seven,' he informed her, still bland, 'and I have had a number of years in which to fall in and out of love since Sasja's death.' He saw her look and smiled slightly. 'And by that I mean exactly what I said; I must confess I've been attracted to a number of women, but I didn't like them—there is a difference. I like you, Deborah.'

She sipped the drink he had ordered and studied the menu card and tried not to mind too much that he was talking to her as though she were an old friend who had just applied for a job he had going. In a way she was. She put the idea out of her head and chose Suprême de Turbot Mogador and settled for caviare for starters, then applied herself to a lighthearted conversation which gave him no opportunity of turning the talk back to themselves. But that didn't last long; with the coming of the Vacherin Glacé he cut easily into her flow of small talk with:

'As to our marriage—have you any objection if it takes place soon? I want to return to Holland as quickly as possible and I have arranged to leave Clare's in ten days' time. I thought we might get married then.'

Deborah sat with her fork poised midway between plate and mouth. 'Ten days' time?' she uttered. 'But that's not possible! I have to give a month's notice.'

'Oh, don't concern yourself with that. I can arrange something. Is that your only objection?'

'You don't know my family.'

'You live in Somerset, don't you? We might go down there and see them before we go to Holland —unless you wish to be married from your home?'

It was like being swept along a fast-moving river with not even a twig in sight. 'I—I hadn't thought about it.'

'Then how would it be if we marry quietly here in London and then go to see your parents?'

'You mean surprise them?'

'I'll be guided by you,' he murmured.

She thought this rather unlikely; all the same it was a good idea.

'Father's an historian,' she explained, 'and rather wrapped up in his work, and Mother—Mother is never surprised about anything. They wouldn't mind. I'd like a quiet wedding, but in church.'

He looked surprised. 'Naturally. I am a Calvinist myself and you are presumably Church of England.

If you care to choose your church I'll see about the licence and make the arrangements. Do you want any guests?'

She shook her head; it didn't seem quite right to invite people to a marriage which was, after all, a friendly arrangement between two people who were marrying for all the wrong reasons—although there was nothing wrong with her reason; surely loving someone was sufficiently strong grounds for marrying them? And as for Gerard, his reasons, though very different, held a strong element of practical common sense. Besides, he believed her to be in complete agreement with him over the suitability of a marriage between two persons who, presumably, had no intention of allowing their hearts to run away with their feelings. She wondered idly just what kind of a girl might steal his heart. Certainly not herself—had he not said that he liked her, and that, as far as she could see, was as far as it went.

She drank her coffee and agreed with every show of pleasure to his suggestion that they should go somewhere and dance.

He took her to the Savoy, where they danced for an hour or more between pleasant little interludes at the table he had secured well away from the dance floor. She was an excellent dancer and Gerard, she discovered, danced well too, if a trifle conservatively. Just for a space she forgot her problems and gave herself to the enjoyment of the evening, and presently, drinking champagne, her face prettily flushed, she found herself agreeing that a light supper would be delightful before he took her back to Clare's. It was almost three o'clock when he stopped the car outside the Home. He got out of the car with her and opened the heavy door with the latch key she gave him and then stood idly swinging it in his hand.

'Thank you for a delightful evening,' said Deborah, and tried to remember that she was going to marry this large, quiet man standing beside her, and in ten days, too. She felt sudden panic swamp the tenuous happiness inspired by the champagne and the dancing, and raised her eyes to his face, her mouth already open to give utterance to a variety of thoughts which, largely because of that same champagne, no longer made sense.

The eyes which met hers were very kind. 'Don't worry, Deborah,' he urged her in his deep, placid voice. 'It's only reaction; in the morning everything will be quite all right again. You must believe me.'

He bent and kissed her cheek, much as though he were comforting a child, and told her to go to bed. 'And I'll see you tomorrow before I go to Holland.'

And because she was bewildered and a little afraid and her head had begun to ache, she did as he bade her. With a whispered good night she went slowly up the stairs without looking back to see if he was watching her, undressed and got into bed, and fell at once into a dreamless sleep which was only ended by her alarm clock warning her to get up and dress, astonished to find that what Gerard had said was quite true; everything did seem all right. She went down to breakfast and in response to the urgent enquiries of her companions, gave a detailed account of her evening and then, fortified by several cups of strong tea, made her way to the theatre unit.

There wasn't much doing. Mr Squires had a couple of Smith–Petersen pins to insert, a bone graft to do, and there was a Carpal Tunnel—an easy enough list, for he kept strictly to straightforward bone work, leaving the bone tumours to Gerard van Doorninck. They were finished by one o'clock and Deborah had time to go down to dinner before sending Staff off duty. The theatre would have to be washed down that afternoon and she wanted to go through the sharps; some of the chisels needed attention, as did the grooved awl and one or two of the rugines. She would go down to the surgical stores and see what could be done. She had them neatly wrapped and was on the point of making her way through the labyrinth of semi-underground passages to the stores, when Gerard walked in. 'Hullo,' he said. 'Going somewhere?'

She explained about the sharps, and even as she was speaking he had taken them from her and put them on the desk. 'Later. I have to go again in a few minutes. I just wanted to make sure....' he paused and studied her with cool leisure. Apparently her calm demeanour pleased him, for he said: 'I told you that everything would be all right, didn't I?' and when she nodded, longing to tell him that indeed nothing was right at all, he went on: 'I've seen about the licence—there's a small church round the corner, St Joram's. Would you like to go and see it and tell me if you will marry me there?'

Her heart jumped because she still wasn't used to the idea of marrying him, although her face remained tranquil enough. 'I know St Joram's very well, I go there sometimes. I should like to be married there.'

43

He gave a small satisfied sound, like a man who had had a finicky job to do and had succeeded with it sooner than he had expected.

'I'll be back on Monday—there's a list at ten o'clock, isn't there? I'll see you before we start.'

He took her hand briefly, said goodbye even more briefly, and retraced his steps. Deborah stood in the empty corridor, listening to his unhurried stride melt into the distance and then merge into the multitude of hospital sounds. Presently she picked up the instruments and started on her way to the surgical stores.

CHAPTER THREE

THE warmth of the early September morning had barely penetrated the dim cool of the little church. Deborah, standing in its porch, peered down its length; in a very few minutes she was going to walk down the aisle with Gerard beside her and become his wife. She wished suddenly that he hadn't left her there while he returned to lock the car parked outside, because then she wouldn't have time to think. Now her head seethed with the events of the last ten days; the interview with Miss Bright, the Principal Nursing Officer, and the astonishing ease with which she found herself free to leave exactly when Gerard had wanted her to; the delight and curiosity of her friends, who even at that very moment had no idea that she was getting married this very morning; she had allowed them to think that she and Gerard were going down to her parents in Somerset. She had even allowed them to discuss her wedding dress, with a good deal of friendly bickering as to which style and material would suit her best, and had quietly gone out and shopped around for a pale blue dress and jacket and a wisp of a hat which she had only put on in the car, in case someone in the hospital should have seen it and guessed what it might be, for it was that sort of a hat. But the hat was the only frivolous thing about her; she looked completely composed, and when she heard Gerard's step behind her, she turned a tranquil face to greet him, very much at variance with her heart's secret thudding.

He had flowers in his hand, a small spray of roses and orange blossom and green leaves. 'For you,' he said. 'I know that you should have a bouquet, but it might have been difficult to hide from your friends.' He spoke easily with no sign of discomposure and proceeded to fasten them on to her dress in a matter-of-fact manner. When he had done so, he stood back to look at her. 'Very nice,' was his verdict. 'How lucky that we have such a glorious morning.' He looked at his watch. 'We're a few minutes early, shall we stroll round the church?'

They wandered off, examining the memorials on the walls and the gravestones at their feet, for all the world, thought Deborah, slightly light-headed, as though they were a pair of tourists. It was when they reached the pulpit that she noticed the flowers beautifully arranged around the chancel. She stopped before one particularly fine mass of blooms and remarked: 'How beautiful these are, and so many of them. I shouldn't have thought that the parish was rich enough to afford anything like this.'

She turned to look at her companion as she spoke and exclaimed:

45

'Oh, you had them put here. How—how thought-ful!'

'I'm glad you like them. I found the church a little bare when I came the other day—the vicar's wife was only too glad to see to them for me.'

'Thank you,' said Deborah. She touched the flowers on her dress. 'And for these too.'

They had reached the chancel at exactly the right moment; the vicar was waiting for them with two people—his wife, apparently, and someone who might have been the daily help, pressed into the more romantic role of witness.

The service was short. Deborah listened to every word of it and heard nothing, and even when the plain gold ring had been put upon her finger she felt as though it was someone else standing there, being married. She signed the register in a composed manner, received her husband's kiss with the same calm, and shook hands with the vicar and the two ladies, then walked out of the little church with Gerard. He was holding her hand lightly, talking quietly as they went, and she said not a word, only noticed every small detail about him—his grey suit, the gold cuff links in his silk shirt, the perfection of his polished shoes—who polished them? she wondered stupidly—and his imperturbable face. He turned to smile at her as they reached the door and she smiled back while hope, reinforced by her love, flooded through her. She was young still and pretty, some said beautiful, men liked her, some enough to have wanted to marry her; surely there was a chance that Gerard might fall in love with her? She would be seeing much more of him now, take an interest in his life, make herself indispensable, wear pretty clothes....

'My dear girl,' said Gerard kindly, 'how distraite you have become—quite lost in thought—happy ones, I hope?'

They were standing by the car and he had unlocked the door as he spoke and was holding it open for her, his glance as kind as his voice. She got in, strangely vexed by his kindness, and said too brightly: 'It was a nice wedding. I—I was thinking about it.'

He nodded and swung the car into the street. 'Yes, one hears the words during a simple ceremony —I have always thought that big social weddings are slightly unreal.'

It was on the tip of her tongue to ask him if his previous wedding had been just such a one, but it seemed hardly a fitting time to do so. She launched into a steady flow of small talk which lasted until they were clear of the centre of the city and heading west.

But presently she fell silent, staring out at the passing traffic as the car gathered speed, casting around in her mind for something to talk about. There was so much to say, and yet nothing. She was on the point of remarking—for the second time—about the weather when Gerard spoke. 'I think we'll lunch at Nately Scures—there's a good pub there, the Baredown. I don't know about you, Deborah, but getting married seems to have given me a good appetite.'

His manner was so completely at ease that she lost her awkwardness too. 'I'm hungry too,' she agreed, 'and I didn't realise that it was already one o'clock. We should be home by tea time.'

It was during lunch that one or two notions, not altogether pleasant, entered her head and quite unknown to her, reflected their disquiet in her face. They were sitting back at their ease, drinking their coffee in a companionable silence which Gerard broke. 'What's on your mind, Deborah?'

She put some more sugar into her cup although she didn't want it, and stirred it because it gave her something to do. She began uncertainly: 'I was just thinking—hoping that Mike, my elder brother, you know, will be home for a day or two with Helen—his wife.'

He smiled very faintly. 'Why?'

'Well, I was thinking about—about rooms. You see, the house is very old and there aren't. . . .' She tried again. 'There is Mother and Father's room and a big guest room, all the other bedrooms are small. If Mike and Helen are there they'll be in the guest room, which makes it easy for us, because then we shall have our own rooms and there won't be any need for me to make an excuse—I mean for us not sharing a room.' She gave him a determinedly matter-of-fact look which he returned with an urbane one of his own. 'I don't suppose you had thought about it?'

'Indeed I had—I thought a migraine would fill the bill.'

'Do you have migraine?'

'Good God, girl, no! You.'

She said indignantly: 'I've never had migraine in my life, I don't even know what it feels like. I really don't think. . . .'

He gave her an amused glance. 'Well, it seems the situation isn't likely to arise, doesn't it? We can hardly turn your brother and his wife out of their room just for one night.' He had spoken casually, now he changed the subject abruptly, as they got up to go.

'It was nice of you not to mind about going straight back to Holland. We'll go away for a holiday as soon as I can get everything sorted out at the Grotehof.'

She nodded. 'Oh, the hospital, yes. Have you many private patients too?'

He sent the car tearing past a lorry. 'Yes, and shall have many more, I think. I'm looking forward to meeting your family.'

She stirred in her seat. 'Father is a little absent-minded; he doesn't live in the present when he's busy on a book, and Mother—Mother's a darling. Neither of them notices much what's going on around them, but Mother never questions anything I do. Then there's Mike—and Helen, of course, and John and Billy, they're fourteen and sixteen, and Maureen who's eleven. There are great gaps between us, but it's never seemed to matter.'

They were almost at Salisbury when she ventured to remark: 'I don't know anything about your family and I'm terrified of meeting them.'

He slowed the car down and stopped on the grass verge and turned to look at her. 'My dear Deborah—you, terrified? Why? My mother is like any other mother, perhaps a little older than yours; she must be, let me see, almost sixty. My two brothers, Pieter and Willem, are younger than I, my sister Lia comes between us—she's married to an architect and they live near Hilversum. Pieter is a pathologist in Utrecht, Willem is a lawyer—he lives in den Haag.'

'And your mother, does she live with you?'

'No, she didn't wish to go on living in the house

49

after my father died—I'm not sure of the reason. She has a flat close by. We see each other often.'

'So you live alone?'

'There is Wim, who sees to everything—I suppose you would call him a houseman, but he's more than that; he's been with us for so long, and there is Marijke who cooks and keeps house and Mevrouw Smit who comes in to clean. Mother took Leen, who has been with us ever since I can remember, with her when she moved to the flat.'

'Is your house large?'

'Large?' he considered her question. 'No—but it is old and full of passages and small staircases; delightful to live in but the very devil to keep clean.' He gave her a quick, sidelong glance. 'Marijke and Mevrouw Smit see to that, of course. You will be busy enough in other ways.'

'What other ways?' asked Deborah with vague suspicion.

'I told you, did I not, that I need to entertain quite a lot—oh, not riotous parties night after night, but various colleagues who come to the hospital for one reason or the other—sometimes they bring their wives, sometimes they come on their own. And there is the occasional dinner party, and we shall be asked out ourselves.'

'Oh. How did you manage before?'

He shrugged. 'Marijke coped with the odd visitor well enough, my mother acted as hostess from time to time. Remember I have been away for two years; I spent only a short time in Amsterdam each month or so, but now I am going back to live I shall be expected to do my share of entertaining. You will be of the greatest help to me if you will deal with that side of our life.'

'I'll do my best, though it's rather different from handing instruments....'

He laughed. 'Very. But if you do it half as well you will be a great success and earn my undying gratitude.'

She didn't want his gratitude; she wanted his love, but nothing seemed further from his thoughts. Dinner parties, though, would give her the opportunity to wear pretty clothes and make the most of herself—he might at least notice her as a person. She began to plan a suitable wardrobe....

The road was surprisingly empty after they had left Salisbury behind. At Warminster they turned off on to the Frome road and then, at Deborah's direction, turned off again into the byroads, through the small village of Nunney and then the still smaller one of Chantry. Her home lay a mile beyond, a Somerset farmhouse, with its back tucked cosily into the hills behind it, and beautifully restored and tended by Mr Culpeper and his wife. It looked delightful now in the afternoon sun, its windows open as was its front door, its garden a mass of colour and nothing but the open country around it. Deborah gave a small sigh of pleasure as she saw it. 'That's it,' she told Gerard.

'Charming,' he commented. 'I hope your parents will ask us back for a visit. I can see that it is a most interesting house—those windows...' he nodded towards the side of the house, 'their pediments appear most interesting.'

He brought the car to a halt before the door and as he helped her out she said with something like relief: 'Father will be delighted that you noticed them, they're very unusual. Probably he'll talk of nothing else and quite forget that we're married.'

51

They were walking to the door. 'Do you really know something of sixteenth-century building?'

'A little.' He smiled down at her and said unexpectedly: 'You look very pretty in that blue dress. Shall I ring the bell?'

For answer she shook her head and let out a piercing whistle, answered almost immediately by an equally piercing reply followed by: 'Debby, is it really you? I'm in the sitting room. Come in, darling. I can't leave this....'

The hall was cool, flagstoned and bare of furniture save for an old oak chest against one wall and a grandfather clock. Deborah went through one of the open doors leading out of it and walked across the faded, still beautiful carpet to where her mother was kneeling on the floor surrounded by quantities of manuscript.

'Your father dropped the lot,' she began, preparing to get up. 'I simply have to get them into some sort of order.'

She was a great deal smaller than her daughter, but they shared the same lovely face and pansy eyes. She leaned up to hug her daughter with a happy: 'This is a lovely surprise. Are you on holiday or is it just a couple of days?' Her eyes lighted upon Gerard. 'You've had a lift—who's this?' She added thoughtfully, just as though he wasn't there: 'He's very good-looking.' She smiled at him and he returned her smile with such charm that she got to her feet, holding out a hand.

'Mother,' said Deborah with the kind of cheerful resignation her children had acquired over the years, 'this is Gerard van Doorninck. We got married this morning.'

Her parent remained blissfully calm and shook

hands. 'Well now,' she exclaimed, not in the least put out, 'isn't that nice? Debby always has known her own mind since she could handle a spoon. I should have loved to have been at the wedding, but since I wasn't we'll have a little celebration here.' She studied the tall quiet man before her. 'If I'm your mother-in-law, you're quite entitled to kiss me.'

And when he had: 'I hope Debby warned you about us. You see, my husband and I seldom go out, we're far too happy here and it's so quiet he can work undisturbed—and as for me, the days are never long enough. What do you do for a living?' she shot at him without pause.

'I'm an orthopaedic surgeon—I've been at Clare's for two years now. Deborah was my Theatre Sister.'

Mrs Culpeper nodded her slightly untidy head. 'Nasty places, operating theatres, but I suppose one can fall in love in one just as easily as anywhere else.' She spun round and addressed her daughter. 'Darling, how long are you staying, and when did you get married?'

'Just tonight, Mother, and we got married this morning.'

'In church, I hope?'

'Yes—that little one, St Joram's, just round the corner from Clare's.'

'Quite right too. Your brother's here with Helen —they're in the guest room, of course.' She handed Gerard the manuscript in an absentminded manner. 'Where am I to put you both?'

'Don't worry, Mother,' said Deborah in a hurry. 'I'll have my own room and Gerard can have Billy's —it's only for tonight—we couldn't think of turn-

53

ing Mike and Helen out.'

Her mother gave her a long, thoughtful look. 'Of course not, dear, and after all, you have the rest of your lives together.'

Deborah agreed with her calmly, not looking at Gerard.

'Good, that's settled—two such sensible people. Gerard, will you take these papers into the study across the hall and tell my husband that you're here? You may have to say it twice before he pays any attention; he found an interesting stone in the garden this morning—I believe it's called a shepherd's counting stone. You have a Dutch name.'

'I am Dutch, Mrs Culpeper.' And Deborah, stealing a look, was glad to see that Gerard wasn't in the least discomposed.

'I saw Queen Wilhelmina once,' Mrs Culpeper went on chattily, 'in London, during the war.' She turned to Deborah. 'Your father will be most interested, Debby. Come and put the kettle on for tea, dear.'

Deborah tucked her arm into her mother's. 'Yes, dearest, but wouldn't it be nicer if Gerard had me with him when he meets Father?'

'He looks perfectly able to introduce himself,' declared her volatile parent. 'I meant to have had tea hours ago. Come along, dear.'

Deborah looked across the room to where Gerard was standing, his arms full of papers. 'Do you mind?' she asked him.

'Not in the least. In fact it's an eminently sensible suggestion.' He smiled at her and she realized with astonishment that he was enjoying himself.

They all met again ten minutes later. She was standing at the table in the large, low-ceilinged

54

kitchen, cutting sandwiches and listening to her
mother's happy rambling talk while she arranged
the best Spode tea service on a tray, when the door
opened and the two men came in. Mr Culpeper
was a tall man, almost as tall as his new son-in-law,
with a thin upright body and a good-looking face
which wore its usual abstracted expression. He was
almost bald, but his moustache and neat Van Dyck
beard were still brown and thick. He came across
the room to where Deborah stood and flung an arm
around her shoulders and kissed her with fondness.
He said without preamble: 'I like your husband,
Debby—no nonsense about him, and thank God
I've at last found someone in the family who is interested in pediments.'

His eyes lighted upon the plate of sandwiches
before her and he helped himself to one and bit
into it with relish. 'Mike and Helen won't be back
just yet, so let's have tea.' He took the tray from his
wife and led the way to the sitting room.

Tea was a success, largely because Gerard joined
in the conversation with an ease of manner which
made him seem like an old friend of the family,
and later, when they had been left together in her
room—'for of course you will want to unpack for
Gerard', her mother had said—Deborah asked
him: 'You aren't bored? You see, we all love them
very much and we don't in the least mind when
they forget things and or start talking as though we
weren't there....'

He took her hands in his. 'No, Deborah, I'm not
bored, nor would I ever be here with your parents.
They are charming people and they have found the
secret of being happy, haven't they? I envy someone like your mother, who can cast down her tea-

cup and dash into the garden because a thrush is singing particularly sweetly—and your father . . . they are a devoted couple, I believe.'

She was very conscious of his hands. 'Yes, they are. I suppose that's why they view the world with such kindness and tolerance and at the same time when they want to, the two of them just retire into a—a sort of shell together—they're very unworldly.' She looked at him a little anxiously. 'I'm not a bit like them,' she assured him. 'We're all very practical and sensible; we've looked after them all our lives.' She smiled. 'Even little Maureen!'

He bent his head to kiss her cheek gently. 'That's why you're such a nice person, I expect. You know, I had forgotten that people could live like this. Perhaps the rest of us have our values wrong, working too hard, making money we have to worry about, going on holidays we don't enjoy—just because everyone else does.'

'But you're not like that.' She was quite certain of it.

'Thank you for saying that. I hope I'm not, but I'm often discontented with my life, though perhaps now that I have you for a companion I shall find more pleasure in it.'

She was breathless, but it would never do to let him see that. She moved her hands ever so slightly and he let them go at once. She turned away, saying lightly: 'I shall do my best, only you must tell me what you like and what you don't like—but you must never think that I shall be bored or find life dull. There's always so much to see and do and I love walking and staring round at things.'

He laughed. 'How restful that sounds—I like that too. We'll walk and stare as often as we can

56

spare the time. I have a small house in Friesland and several good friends living nearby. We must spend some weekends there.'

Deborah turned to face him again, once more quite composed. 'Another house? Gerard, I've never asked you because there hasn't been much time to talk and it didn't seem important, but now I want to know. You haven't a lot of money or anything like that, have you?'

The corners of his mouth twitched, 'As to that. Deborah, I must plead guilty, for I do have a good deal of money and I own a fair amount of land besides.' He studied her face. 'Would you have married me if you had known?'

'I don't know. Yes, I do—I should have married you just the same because you would have known that I wasn't doing it for your money—at least, I hope you would.'

She saw the bleak look erase all expression from his face and wondered what she had said to cause it. 'Oh dear, have I annoyed you?'

The look had gone; perhaps she had imagined it. 'No, Deborah, and I'm glad to hear that is how you feel about it. Now supposing I take my case to Billy's room and unpack what I need, and then do you suppose we might have a stroll in your father's delightful garden?'

A suggestion to which she agreed happily enough.

It was good to see Mike and Helen again, and even if they were surprised at her news, it was only to be expected. The evening was passed pleasantly, with some of Mr Culpeper's prized Madeira brought out to drink the bride's health and a buzz of family talk interrupted by excited telephone conversations with Maureen and her brothers. And as for Deborah, the evening had become a happy dream because when they had walked in the garden, Gerard had given her a ring with the matter-of-fact observation that she should have had it before they were married; he had gone to Holland to fetch it and had forgotten to give it to her. It was a beautiful ring, a diamond, an enormous one, in a strange old-fashioned setting of two pairs of hands supporting the stone on either side. She had exclaimed over its beauty, watching its rainbow colours as she turned her hand from side to side in order to see it better, thanking him nicely, trying to forget that he himself had forgotten.

He told her that it was the traditional betrothal ring of his family. 'At least,' he had explained, 'there are two, exactly alike. My grandmother left this one to me as I was the eldest grandson, and——' he became silent and she, anxious to help him out, said: 'What a sensible idea! The other ring will be left to—to whoever is your heir—that means,' she hurried on, 'that the wives don't have to give up their engagement rings. I wonder how that all started?'

He replied casually. 'Oh, an ancestor of mine—he had a very youthful wife, and when their son married she was still a young woman and flatly refused to give up her ring, so because he loved her to distraction he had another made just like it.'

They had laughed about it together, although secretly she thought it a charming story, and later the ring had been admired and discussed and admired again. Only when she was at last in her own room lying in her white-painted bed amidst her small, familiar possessions, did she allow herself to

58

shed a few tears because the dream would never come true, of course; she would have to be sensible and make Gerard a good wife and be thankful that he at least liked her. But at the same time, she promised herself fiercely through her tears, she would never give up trying to make him love her.

She wakened early by reason of the early morning sun shining in through the open window and was on the point of getting up when there was a tap on the door and Gerard came in. His good morning was friendly, his manner as matter-of-fact as it had been the previous evening.

'I hoped you would be awake,' he said. 'I have been wondering if you would like to pay lightning visits to your brothers and sister before we leave for Holland? The boys are at Wells, aren't they? Twelve miles, no further, and Wells to Sherborne is under twenty-five and on our way, in any case, for we can pick up the Winchester road from there. The ferry doesn't sail until midnight, so as long as we don't linger over meals, we should have ample time.' He sat down on the end of her bed. 'Would you like that?'

Deborah smiled her pleasure. 'Oh, Gerard, how kind of you to think of it! I'd simply love it—you're sure there's time?'

'Positive.' He looked at his watch. 'It's half past six—a little early perhaps ...?'

'Mother always gets up at seven. I'll go down and make the tea and tell her. We can have breakfast when we want, no one will mind. When do you want to leave?'

'Half past eight. I'll come down with you—better still,' he got off the bed, 'I'll go down and put the kettle on.'

By the time Deborah reached the kitchen he had the kettle boiling and a tray laid with cups and saucers and milk and sugar, which surprised her very much, for she hadn't supposed him to be the kind of man who would be handy about the house, indeed, even now, in need of a shave and in a dressing gown of great magnificence, he contrived to look more than elegant and the making of early morning tea seemed alien to his nature. There was, she guessed, a great deal to his character of which she knew nothing.

She took the tea upstairs, whispered their plans to her mother, who thought it a splendid idea and accepted them without demur, and then went back to the kitchen to drink her tea with Gerard, and because the morning was such a beautiful one, they wandered through the back door and strolled round the garden admiring the flowers, their tea cups in their hands, stopping to take an occasional sip.

'What a delightful way in which to start the day,' commented Gerard, back in the kitchen.

Deborah agreed. 'And one can do it almost anywhere,' she pointed out, 'provided there's a strip of grass and a few flowers, or a pleasant walk nearby ... have you a dog?'

'Yes, though he hasn't seen a great deal of me lately; Wim stands proxy for me, though. And there are two cats, but they belong to Marijke.'

'What do you call your dog?'

'Smith, he's a Jack Russell. He goes everywhere with me when I'm home.'

'I hope he'll like me; I could take him for walks.'

'You shall.' He took her cup from her and put it tidily in the sink. 'Shall we get dressed? What do we do about breakfast? Shall we get our own?'

'Everyone will be down—but we can always start if they're not.'

They left exactly on time amidst a chorus of good wishes and goodbyes and urgings to return as soon as possible, coupled with a great many messages from Mrs Culpeper for the boys and Maureen.

All of which Deborah faithfully passed on, although her listeners were all far too excited to pay any attention to them; the boys, naturally enough, were much more interested in the car than in their sister, and she was agreeably surprised to find how well Gerard got on with them. Her notions of him were sadly out, she admitted to herself as they took a boisterous leave of Billy and John and tore down the Fosse Way towards Sherborne and Maureen. She had always thought of him as being a perfect darling, of course, because she loved him, but also a little reserved as well as being a quiet man. He was still quiet, of course, but he obviously enjoyed the boys' company and she hadn't expected that.

It was mid-morning by now and Maureen came dancing out of her class to cast herself into her elder sister's embrace. 'Debby,' she shrilled, 'how lovely—tell me all about the wedding and what did you wear...?' She stopped to smile at Gerard and then throw herself with enthusiasm at him. 'Oh, you do look nice,' she assured him. 'Just wait till I tell the girls—can I come and stay with you soon?' She plucked impatiently at his arm. 'You're very good-looking, aren't you? which is a good thing because Debby's quite beautiful, isn't she, and thank heavens you're so tall because now she can wear high heels if she wants to.' She didn't wait for him to answer but turned her attention to Deborah again. 'You haven't told me what you wore.'

'This dress I'm wearing—it was a very quiet wedding, darling.'

Deborah smiled at her small sister; she and the boys were all so large, but Maureen took after her mother in her smallness, although at the moment she had no looks at all, only a great deal of charm.

'Shall I come and have lunch with you?' she wanted to know.

It was Gerard who answered her. 'Sorry, Maureen. We're on our way home to Holland, but how about paying us a visit in the holidays? We'll come over and fetch you.'

She flung her arms around him. 'Oh, will you? Will you really? Promise?'

'Promise.' He bent and kissed her small elfin face and looked at Deborah. 'We must go, my dear,' and he smiled half-humorously over the child's head.

They had time and to spare when they reached Dover, for the big car had eaten up the miles and they had stopped only briefly on the way. Gerard parked the car in the queue and invited Deborah to get out.

'There's an hotel just outside the dock gates,' he told her. 'We have ample time to have dinner before we go on board.'

When they reached the hotel it was long past the time that dinner was served, but Gerard seemed to have little difficulty in persuading the waiter that just this once he might stretch a point. They dined simply, watching the harbour below from their table in the window.

Deborah was surprised to find that there was a

cabin booked for her when they got on board; the crossing was barely four hours and she wasn't in the least tired, but when she said so, Gerard merely smiled and told her that it would be a good idea if she were to get some sleep. 'It can be very noisy,' he explained. 'Even if you don't sleep, you can read— I'll get you some magazines. And my cabin is next to yours, so you have only to knock if you want anything.'

She thanked him, wishing that they could have spent the time together talking, for she suspected that once they got to his home he would be swallowed up in his work almost at once and she might see very little of him. He was going to take up the appointment which had been waiting for him in the hospital where he had been a consultant for some years; she felt sure that he would want to start at once.

She lay down on her bunk and pulled a blanket over her and opened the first of the magazines. Long before the ferry sailed, she was asleep.

CHAPTER FOUR

DEBORAH was called with a cup of tea and a polite request from the steward that she would join her husband in the lounge as soon as she was ready. Gerard was waiting for her, looking, at four-fifteen in the morning, quite immaculate, so that she was glad that she had taken trouble with her own appearance; her face nicely made up, her hair as neat as it always was, her blue outfit fresh and creaseless from its careful hanging while she slept.

It was still dark when they landed, but Gerard

shot away as though he knew the road blindfold, which, she conceded, was probably the case. But although he drove fast he didn't allow it to interfere with the casual conversation which he carried on, explaining in which direction they were going, pointing out the towns as they passed through them and warning her when they approached the frontier between Belgium and Holland.

It was growing lighter now. They passed through the small town of Sluis with its narrow, twisting streets, still so quiet in the early morning and then out again on to the straight tree-lined road, making for the ferry at Breskens. 'There is another route,' he told her, 'through Antwerp and Breda, but it's usually loaded with traffic. Even with a possible delay on the ferry I find this way shorter now that the new bridges and roads are open to Rotterdam.'

It was light enough to see by now and Deborah, wide awake, asked endless questions and could barely wait to drink the coffee he fetched for her on board the ferry, because she wanted to see everything at once as they crossed the great river. She thought Flushing disappointingly dull, although the sea-front, which she could see in the distance, was probably delightful with its long line of hotels facing the beach. But she had little enough chance to do more than glimpse it, for Gerard skirted the town and took the motorway to Goes, past factories and shipyards and a great deal of dreary flat country. She would have liked to have commented upon this, for after Somerset she found it depressing, but she held her tongue, and presently, once they were past Goes, on the fine road crossing the islands, speeding towards Rotterdam, she cheered up, for here the country was green and pretty in the morning sunlight and the houses with their steep red roofs and the solid farms looked delightful enough. Even Rotterdam, even though there was little to see but towering flats and factories and docks, was interesting and bustling with early workers, and the more so because Gerard told her a great deal about it as he eased the car through the ever-increasing traffic with a patience and good humour she was sure she would never have had.

Once through the city and on the motorway once more, Gerard remarked: 'We could have crossed the river lower down and gone through Europoort on the new road to Delft, but you have already seen so many factories and blast furnaces—this way is more interesting and we can stop in Delft and have breakfast. Reyndorp's Prinsenhof will be open by now.'

Delft, Deborah discovered at once, was quite a different kettle of fish. Gerard parked the car in one of the main streets of the picturesque little town and led her across the road to the restaurant, where they obligingly served them with an ample breakfast at a table in a window overlooking the street. There were already plenty of people going to work on their bicycles, milk carts, bread carts, carts loaded with vegetables and weaving in and out of them, hordes of schoolchildren on their motorised bikes.

'Everything seems to start very early,' Deborah exlaimed. 'Look, there's a shop open already.'

'A good many open at eight o'clock, sometimes earlier. I suppose we breakfast earlier than they do in England—we lunch at midday, and most people have an evening meal about six o'clock.'

'That makes a very long evening.'

His blue eyes twinkled. 'Ah, yes—but the Dutchman likes to sit at home reading his paper, drinking his glass of gin and surrounded by his wife and children. Perhaps you find that dull, but we don't think so.'

Deborah shook her head; it didn't sound dull at all. She enjoyed for a fleeting moment a vivid picture of Gerard and herself on either side of the hearth with a clutch of small van Doornincks between them. She brushed the dream aside briskly; he had told her that he had a great many friends and entertained quite frequently and that they would go out fairly often, and perhaps, as there were to be no little van Doornincks, that was a very good thing.

They were less than forty miles from Amsterdam now and once back on the motorway it seemed even less. They seemed to come upon the city suddenly, rising abruptly from the flat fields around it and Gerard had perforce to slow down, turning and twisting through narrow streets and along canals which looked so charming that she wished that they might stop so that she might take a better look. Presently he turned into a busy main street, only to cross it and turn down another narrow street bordering a canal.

'Where are we now?' she ventured to ask.

'The Keizersgracht. It's a canal which runs almost in a full circle round the city. There are other canals which follow its line exactly, rather like a spider's web. All of them contain beautiful old houses, most of which are embassies or warehouses or offices now.'

She peered around her; the houses were large, tall and built on noble lines with big square windows and great front doors, and despite this they contrived to look homelike. She said so and heard him laugh. 'I'm glad you like them, for here we are at my—our home.'

He had slowed the car and stopped outside a double-fronted, red brick house, its front door reached by a double row of steps, its windows, in orderly rows, large and square, its roof, Deborah could see, craning her pretty neck, ended in a rounded gable which leaned, very slightly, forward. She would have liked to have stood and stared, just as she would have paused by the canals, but Gerard was waiting for her. He took her hand as she got out of the car and drew it under his arm and mounted the steps to the door which opened as they reached it.

This would be Wim, she guessed, a short, thick-set man with grizzled hair and blue eyes set in a round, cheerful face. He shook Gerard's proffered hand with pleasure and when Gerard introduced him to Deborah, took her hand too and said in heavily accented, difficult English:

'I am happy, Mevrouw. It is a moment to rejoice. My felicitations.'

She thanked him, and without knowing it pleased him mightily by remarking on his knowledge of English, adding the rider that she hoped that her Dutch would be as good. Upon this small wave of mutual friendliness they entered the hall, while Wim closed the door behind them.

The hall was narrow, although it had two deep alcoves, each with a wall table and a mirror hanging above. Along one side, between them, was a double door, carved and arched, and beyond them a carved wooden staircase. On the other side of the hall there were three doors and an arched opening reached by several descending steps, coming up which now was a tall, thin, middle-aged woman, with pale hair which could have been flaxen or equally well grey. She wore a rather old-fashioned black dress and a large print apron and although her face seemed severe she was smiling broadly now. She broke at once into speech and then turned to Deborah, her hand held out, and began all over again. When she finally stopped Deborah smiled and nodded and asked Gerard urgently: 'Please will you tell Marijke that I'll learn Dutch just as soon as I can, so that we can have the pleasure of talking to each other?'

She watched him as he repeated what she had said in his own language. It sounded like nonsense to her, but she supposed that if she worked hard enough at it, she would at least learn the bare bones of it in a few weeks, and anyway, it seemed that she had said the right thing, for Marijke was smiling more broadly than ever. She shook Deborah's hand again, said something to Gerard in which the word coffee was easily recognisable, and went back down the steps while Wim opened the first of the doors in the hall for them to enter.

The room had a very high ceiling of ornamental plaster work and panelled walls ending in a shelf two thirds of the way up, upon which rested a collection of china which Deborah supposed was Delft. The furniture was comfortable, upholstered in a russet velvet which went well with the deep blues and greens and ambers of the vast carpet. The lampstands were delicate china figures holding aloft cream and russet shades. She found the room delightful, although it was a good deal more splendid than she had expected.

They had their coffee sitting side by side upon a small settee covered in exquisite needlework, and somehow the sight of the old, beautifully simple silver coffee service on its heavy tray flanked by cups which should by rights have been in some museum, so old and fragile were they, depressed her; she had expected comfort, certainly, but this was more than comfort, it was an ageless way of life which she would have to learn to live. She shivered a little, thinking of the dinner parties; possibly the guests would dislike her....

'It's all strange, isn't it?' Gerard was at his most placid, 'but it's home. All this'—he waved a large, square hand—'has been handed down from one son to the next, whether we have wanted it or not, though to be honest, I love every stick and stone of the place, and I hope that you will too.' He put down his coffee cup. 'You will be tired. Would you like to go to bed?'

She was quite taken aback. 'Oh, no, thank you, I'm not in the least tired. If I might just go to my room, I could unpack and change my clothes. I expect you have a great deal to do.'

She saw at once that she had said the right thing, for the relief on his face, quickly suppressed, was real enough. 'Yes, I have. Shall we meet again for lunch? I've asked Mother round.' He smiled nicely. 'You'll feel better once you have met her.'

She got to her feet and he walked with her to the door, opened it and called for Marijke. Even as Deborah started up the staircase in the wake of the older woman, she heard him cross the hall to the front door.

Her room was at the back of the house and her

luggage was already in it. As soon as Marijke had left her she went to the window, to discover a small garden below, with a fountain in its centre and tubs of flowers grouped round it. There was grass too, only a very small circle of it, but it looked green and fresh, and brooding over the cheerful little plot was a copper beech, rustling faintly in the wind.

Deborah turned her back on the pleasant scene presently to survey the room: large and airy and furnished in the style of Chippendale, probably genuine pieces, she thought, caressing the delicate lines of the dressing table. There was a vast cupboard along one wall with a door beside it and on the opposite wall a tallboy. The bed was wide and covered with the same pastel pale chintz as the curtains, the carpet was a deep cream and the lamps and small armchair were covered in pink striped silk. A beautiful room. She sighed her content and hastened to open the first of its three doors. A bathroom with another door leading back on to the landing, she glanced quickly at its luxury and crossed the room. The second door opened on to a short corridor lined with cupboards and lighted by a window on its other side; there was a door at its end and she opened that too and went in. Gerard's luggage was there, so this was his room, smaller than her own and a little severe but just as comfortable. It, too, had a door leading on to the landing and a bathroom built into a deep alcove.

She went back the way she had come and had a bath and put on a plain cotton jersey dress the colour of apricots, then sat down at the dressing table and did her face with great care and arranged her hair in its smooth wings with the chignon at the back, put her engagement ring back on her finger and, after a long look at herself in the handsome mirror, made her way downstairs.

There were voices in the sitting room and she heard Gerard's laugh. His mother had arrived. She trod firmly down the staircase and had almost reached the bottom when he appeared in the sitting room doorway.

'I thought I heard you,' he greeted her smilingly, and whistled briefly. A small dog scampered past him and across the hall. 'Here's Smith, I've just fetched him from the vet.'

Smith had halted in front of her and she sat down on the stairs and put out a gentle hand. 'Hullo, Smith,' she said, 'I hope we're going to be friends.' The dog stared at her with bright black eyes, and after a moment wagged his tail and allowed her to stroke him, and when she got to her feet, walked quite soberly beside her to where Gerard was waiting.

He took her arm as they went into the sitting room and led her over to the window where his mother sat. She wasn't at all what Deborah had imagined she would be; small for a start, almost as small as her own mother, and her eyes were brown and kind. Her nose was an autocratic little beak, but the mouth below it was as kind as the eyes. She stood up as they reached her and said in excellent English:

'Deborah, my dear, welcome to the family. You do not know how happy I am to see Gerard married, and to such a lovely girl. I must say that he described you very well, but I have been longing to meet you. Gerard, bring a chair over here so that I can talk to Deborah—and pour us all a drink.'

And when Deborah was seated and he had gone to the other end of the room where the drinks were laid out on a Pembroke table: 'You must not think that I order him about, my dear. Indeed, I would not dream of doing any such thing, but just now and again I pretend to do so and he pretends to do as I wish. It works very well for us both. And now tell me, what do you think of this house?'

'I've only seen a very little of it; Gerard had things to do.... What I have seen I find quite beautiful.'

The older lady nodded complacently. 'I knew you would like it—love it, I hope. I did, still do, but my husband and I were devoted and without him it doesn't seem the same—besides, I was determined to leave it the moment Gerard told me about you.' She smiled faintly. 'I think I guessed before that.' She gave Deborah a long, thoughtful look and Deborah looked back at her, her eyes quiet.

'Then he lived in a huge flat,' his mother explained, taking it for granted that Deborah knew what she was talking about. She shuddered delicately. 'He loathed it, although he never said so....' she broke off as Gerard came towards them.

'Champagne,' he announced, 'as befits an occasion,' and he lifted his glass to Deborah.

They lunched without haste, although the moment they had finished Gerard excused himself on the pretext of a visit to the hospital as well as his consulting rooms to see what his secretary had got for him. 'Mother will love to show you the house,' he told Deborah as he prepared to leave. 'Don't wait tea—I don't expect to be back much before six.'

She smiled and nodded because that was what

she would have to learn to do cheerfully from now on; watch him go through the front door and then wonder where he had gone to and what he was doing and who he was with ... it didn't bear thinking about. She turned to her mother-in-law with a too-bright smile and professed herself eager to explore the house.

Gerard had been right when he had described it as being full of narrow passages and old staircases, and some of the rooms were very small, although all were charmingly furnished. Deborah wandered up and down with Mevrouw van Doorninck, stopping to peer at family portraits or admire a mirror or one of the trifles of silver or china with which the house was filled. When they had finally completed their tour, she said: 'I feel as though I had turned you out, Mevrouw van Doorninck. How could you bear to leave?'

'It was a wrench, Deborah, but I have some of the furniture in the flat and all my personal treasures. I had made up my mind before Gerard's father died that I would leave, although Gerard didn't want it. You see, I wanted him to marry again, and if I had stayed here, he might never have done so. But living on his own, without a wife to greet his guests and arrange his dinner parties and run the house ... that sounds all wrong, my dear, but I don't mean it to be. He talked about you several times when he came home from Clare's, you know. He told me what a quiet, sensible girl you were and how capable and charming, and I hoped that he would ask you to marry him, and you see that I have my wish.' She patted Deborah's hand. 'You must come and see me very soon—tomorrow if Gerard can spare the time, and then in a day or so I shall give a small dinner party for you so that you can meet the family. You will feel a little strange at first, but I'm sure that Gerard will arrange for you to have Dutch lessons and show you round Amsterdam and show you off to his friends. Very soon you will settle down quite nicely.'

And indeed, to all intents and purposes Deborah did settle down. To the world around her she presented a calm, unruffled face, charming manners and a smiling acceptance of her new way of life. True to her promise, Mevrouw van Doorninck had given her dinner party, where she had met Gerard's sister and brothers; three nice people anxious to make her feel at home. They were considerably younger than he and she liked them at once. She met the children too; Lia had two boys, and Pieter and Willem had a boy and a girl each, all rather alike with pale flaxen hair and blue eyes and just as willing as their parents to absorb her into the family, the older ones trying out their school English on her, the toddlers not caring what language she spoke.

And because Gerard had done nothing about it, she had asked Wim's advice and found herself an old dry-as-dust professor, long retired from his university chair at Leiden, and applied herself assiduously to her Dutch—a disheartening task, she soon discovered, what with the verbs coming at the end of a sentence instead of the middle and the terrible grammar, but at least she had learned a few dozen words, correctly pronounced—the old professor had seen to that. It was amazing the amount one could learn when one applied oneself and one had, sadly enough, time idle on one's hands.

But there was one person amongst the many

whom she met whom she could not like—Claude van Trapp, a man younger than Gerard and a friend of the family since their boyhood days: He was good-looking, and what she would suppose could be described as good fun. He was certainly an intelligent man, and yet Deborah mistrusted him; she found his charm false, and the snide remarks he let fall from time to time seemed to her to be spiteful more than witty. It surprised her that Gerard tolerated him with a careless good humour which annoyed her, and when the opportunity occurred she had, in a roundabout way, tried to discover the reason for this. But he had only laughed and shrugged his great shoulders. 'A little sharp in the tongue, perhaps,' he conceded, 'but we have known each other since our pram days, you know.'

She hadn't pursued the subject, for it was apparent that Gerard was so tolerant of Claude's comings and goings to the house that he hardly noticed him and indeed probably believed him to be the boy he had known. She knew him to be incapable of pettiness or meanness himself, so he certainly wouldn't expect it or look for it in his friends. He was, in fact, blinded by familiarity and she could do nothing about it. But after the first few meetings, she contrived to slip away on some pretext or other when Claude came to the house; easily enough done, for she was taking her duties seriously and there was always something to do around the house, and when his company was unavoidable she behaved with an impeccable politeness towards him, meeting his malicious titbits of gossip and innuendoes with a charming vagueness, ignoring his thinly veiled contempt for her apparent dimness, just as she ignored his admiring glances and sly looks.

It was after she had been in Holland a bare three weeks that Claude called one afternoon. She was in the little garden with Smith, sitting under the shade of the copper beech while she learned the lesson Professor de Wit had set her. It was a beautiful day and she felt a little drowsy, for the night before they had given their first dinner party, quite a small one but nerve-racking. All the same, it had been a success and she had been elated by Gerard's pleased comments afterwards; she had even allowed herself the satisfaction of knowing that he had admired her in the new dress she had bought for the occasion, a pale green silk sheath. She had worn the thick gold chain his mother had given her and of course, her lovely ring. After the guests had gone home, he had followed her into the drawing room and leaned against the wall, watching her as she went round plumping up cushions, restoring chairs to their original places and moving the small tables carefully. It was a room she already loved, its grandeur mitigated by a pleasant homeliness, brought about, she was sure, by the fact that it was lived in. She moved a priceless Rockingham vase to a place of safety and said with satisfaction: 'There, now it looks like itself again—I think your friends must love coming here, Gerard.'

'I daresay.' He sauntered across the pale Aubusson carpet towards her. 'A pleasant and successful evening, Deborah, and you were a perfect hostess. I knew that you would make me an excellent wife—you are also a very charming and beautiful one.' He bent and kissed her. 'Thank you, my dear.'

She had waited, hoping foolishly that he might

say more; that he found her attractive, even that he was falling a little in love with her, but his bland: 'What a wise choice I have made,' gave her little consolation. She had said a little woodenly that she was pleased that she was living up to his good opinion of her and wished him a good night, to go to her room and lie very wide awake in her vast bed until the early hours of the morning. Three weeks, she had reminded herself. and that was only a fraction of the lifetime ahead of her, playing the hostess to Gerard's friends, helping him in every way she could, keeping his home just as he wanted it, taking an interest in his work on those all too rare occasions when he talked about it.

She remembered that she didn't even know where the hospital was, nor for that matter, his consulting rooms, and when she had asked him he had said kindly that he imagined she had enough to fill her days without bothering her head about such things, and then, sensing her hurt, had offered to take her to the hospital and show her round.

It was almost as though he were keeping her at arms' length ... and yet he had been good to her and very kind; she had a more than generous allowance, and true to his promise, Maureen was to visit them in a week's time and when Deborah had admired a crocodile handbag he had bought it for her without hesitation. He had bought her a car too—a Fiat 500—and opened accounts at all the larger shops for her. He was generous to a fault, and she repaid him in the only ways she knew how; by breakfasting with him each morning even though he was immersed in his post which she opened for him, and after he had gone, sorted for his secretary to attend to when she came during the morning. And she was always waiting for him when he got home in the evenings, sitting with Smith in the garden or reading in the sitting room. She wasn't sure if this was what he wanted her to do, and it was difficult to tell because he was unfailingly courteous to her, but at least she was there if he should want to talk. In a week or two, when she knew him a little better, she would ask him.

She applied herself to her Dutch grammar again and twiddled Smith's ears gently. There was still an hour before Wim would bring the tea and Gerard had said that he would be late that evening. She sighed and began to worry her way through the past tense of the verb *to be*.

Her earnest efforts were interrupted by the appearance of Claude. She looked up in some surprise as he lounged across the little plot of grass.

'Oh, hullo, Claude,' she forced her voice to politeness. 'I didn't hear the bell.'

'I walked in,' he told her coolly. 'A lovely afternoon and nothing to do—I thought I might invite myself to tea.'

She closed her book. 'Why, of course,' and felt irritated when he sat down beside her and took it from her.

'What's this? Dutch grammar—my goodness, you are trying hard, aren't you? Does Gerard know, or did he fix it up for you?'

She became evasive. 'I have lessons from a dear old professor—it's a difficult language, but I know quite a few words already, as well as one or two sentences.'

'"I love you," for instance, or should it be "do you love me?", he asked, and added: 'Oh, I've annoyed you—I must apologise, but the idea of Gerard loving anyone is so amusing that I can't help wondering.'

Deborah turned to look at him, amazed at the fury of the rage she was bottling up. 'I know that you are a very old friend of Gerard's, but I don't care to discuss him with anyone: I hope you understand that.'

'Lord, yes,' he said easily. 'You have my fullest admiration, Debby—it must be hellishly difficult.'

'I prefer you not to call me Debby,' she told him austerely, and then, her curiosity getting the better of her good sense: 'What must be difficult?'

He grinned. 'Why, to be married to Gerard, of course. Everyone knows what a mess he made of his first marriage—no wonder the poor girl died. . . .'

She had had enough; if he had intended to anger her, he had succeeded; her fury bubbled over as she got up, restraining herself with difficulty from slapping his smiling face. She said in a voice which shook with anger: 'I was told you were Gerard's friend, but you aren't behaving like a friend! I haven't the least idea what you're talking about, and I don't want to know. I think you should go— now!'

He didn't budge, but sat looking up at her, grinning still. 'If only I knew you better there would be a number of interesting questions I should like to ask, though I daresay you wouldn't answer them. I had no idea that you had such a nasty temper. Does Gerard know about it, I wonder?'

'Does Gerard know what?' asked Gerard from the shadow of the door, and Deborah jumped at the sound of his quiet voice, hating herself for doing it, whereas Claude didn't move, merely said: 'Hullo, there— early home, aren't you? The newly married man and all that?'

Deborah suddenly didn't care if Claude was an old family friend or not; she said hotly: 'I was just asking Claude to leave the house, but now you're here, Gerard, I think he should tell you why.'

'No need, my dear.' Gerard sounded almost placid. 'I'm afraid I have been guilty of eavesdropping—it was such an interesting conversation and I couldn't bring myself to break it up.'

He strolled across the grass to join them. 'Get up,' he ordered Claude, and his voice was no longer placid, but cold and contemptuous. 'It is a strange thing,' he commented to no one in particular, 'how blind one becomes to one's friends, though perhaps friends isn't quite the operative word. Deborah is quite right, I think you should leave my house— this instant, Claude, and not come back.'

Claude had got to his feet. 'You're joking....'

'No.'

'Just because I was going to tell Debby....' he turned to look at her, 'Deborah—about Sasja? Don't be ridiculous, Gerard, if I don't tell her someone else will.'

'Possibly, but they would tell the truth. What were you going to tell her, Claude?' The coldness of his voice was tinged with interest.

'I——? Only that....'

Deborah had had enough; she interrupted sharply: 'I'm going to my room.'

Her husband put out a hand and took her arm in a gentle grip which kept her just where she was, but he didn't look at her.

'Get out,' he advised Claude softly, 'get out before I remember that you were once a friend of mine, and if you come here again, annoying my

80

wife, I'll make mincemeat of you.'

Deborah watched Claude go, taking no notice of his derisive goodbye. She didn't look at Gerard either, only after the faint slam of the front door signalled the last of Claude van Trapp did she say once more: 'If you don't mind—I've a headache.... I'll get Wim to bring you out some tea.'

'Wait, Deborah.' Gerard had turned her round to face him, his hands on her shoulders. 'I'm sorry about this—I had no idea that Claude ... thank you for being loyal, and in such circumstances. You have every right to be angry, for I should have told you the whole sorry story before our marriage, but it is one I have tried to forget over the years, and very nearly succeeded—the idea of digging it all up again....'

'Then I don't want to hear it,' declared Deborah. 'What possible difference could it make anyway? It isn't as though we're—we're....'

'In love?' he finished for her. 'No, but we are friends, companions if you like, sharing our lives, and you have the right to know—and I should like to tell you.' He had pulled her close and his arms were very comforting—but that was all they were. She leaned her head against his shoulder and said steadily: 'I'm listening.'

'I married Sasja when I was twenty-eight. She was nineteen and gay and pretty and so young. I was studying for my fellowship and determined to be a success because I loved—still love—my work and nothing less than success would do. It was my fault, I suppose, working night after night when we should have been out dancing, or going to parties or the theatre. Perhaps I loved her, but it wasn't the right kind of love, and I couldn't understand why she hadn't the patience to wait until I had got my feet on the bottom rung of the ladder, just as she couldn't understand why I should choose to spend hour after hour working when I could have been taking her out.' He sighed. 'You see, I had thought that she would be content looking after our home—we had a modern flat in Amsterdam—and having our children.' His even voice became tinged with bitterness. 'She didn't want or like children and she had no interest in my work. After a year she found someone else and I, God forgive me, didn't discover it until she was killed, with the other man, in a plane crash.'

Deborah said into the superfine cloth of his shoulder: 'I'm sorry, Gerard, but I'm glad I know.' She lifted her face to meet his. 'I wanted to slap Claude—I wish I had!'

She was rewarded by his faint smile. 'He was right in a way, you know—I was really responsible for Sasja's death.'

'He was not! He made it sound underhand and beastly—quite horrible—and it wasn't like that, nor was it your fault.'

'Yes, it was, Deborah—I married the wrong girl just because I was, for a very short time, in love with her. Now you know why I don't want to become involved again—why I married you.'

'And if that's a compliment, it's a mighty odd one,' she told herself silently, and swallowed back the tears tearing at her throat.

Out loud, she said matter-of-factly: 'Well, now you've told me, we won't talk about Sasja again.' She took a heartening breath. 'You don't still love her?'

His voice was nicely reassuring. 'Quite sure. My

love wore thin after a very few months—when she died I had none left.'

And Deborah's heart gave a guilty skip of joy; she was sorry about Sasja, but it was a long time ago, and she hadn't treated Gerard very well. She registered a mental resolve to find out more about her from her mother-in-law when the occasion was right, for it seemed to her that Gerard was very likely taking a blame which wasn't his. She drew away from him and said briskly: 'I'll get the tea, shall I? Would you like it out here?'

She was glad of the few minutes' respite to compose herself once more into the quiet companion he expected when he came home; she and Wim took the tea out between them and when she sat down again under the copper beech she saw that Gerard was leafing through her Dutch grammar.

She poured the tea and waited for him to speak. 'Something I forgot,' he said slowly. 'I should have arranged lessons for you.'

'As a matter of fact,' she began carefully, sugaring his tea and handing him the cup, 'I do have lessons. I asked around and I go to a dear old man called Professor de Wit four times a week. He's very good and fearfully stern. I've had eight lessons so far. He gives me a great deal of homework.'

Gerard put the book down. 'I have underestimated you, Deborah,' he observed wryly. 'Tell me, why are you going to all this trouble?'

She was taken aback. 'Trouble? It's no trouble, it's something to do. Besides, how can I be a good wife if I can't even understand my husband's language? Not all your friends speak English.'

He was staring at her, frowning a little. 'You regard our marriage as a job to be done well—is that how you think of it, Deborah?'

She took a sandwich with a hand which trembled very slightly; it would never do for him to get even an inkling. 'Yes,' she declared brightly. 'Isn't that what you wanted?' and when he didn't reply, went on: 'Maureen will be here next week. I know you won't have any time to spare, but will you suggest the best outings for her? I thought I'd take her to Volendam in the Fiat—all those costumes, you know—and then we can go to the Rijksmuseum and the shops and go round the canals in one of those boats. I'm longing to go—and the Palace, if it's open.'

'My poor Deborah, I've neglected you.'

'No. I knew that you were going to be busy, you told me so. Besides, I've had several weeks in which to find my own feet.'

He smiled. 'You're as efficient a wife and hostess as you were a Theatre Sister,' he told her. And because she thought he expected it of her, she laughed gaily and assured him that that had been her ambition.

Presently he got to his feet. 'I've a couple of patients to see at my consulting rooms,' he told her, 'but I'll be back within the hour. Are we doing anything this evening?'

She shook her head. Perhaps he would take her out—she would wear the new dress....

'Good. Could we dine a little earlier? I've a mass of work to do; a couple of quiet hours in the study would be a godsend to me.'

Deborah even managed a smile. 'Of course—half past six? That will give you a lovely long evening.'

He hesitated. 'And you?'

84

She gave him a calm smiling look from her lovely eyes. 'I've simply masses of letters to write,' she lied.

CHAPTER FIVE

THEY fetched Maureen the following week, travelling overnight to arrive at Sherborne in the early morning, picking up an ecstatic child beside herself with excitement, and driving on to Deborah's home for lunch. The boys were home for the half-term holiday too and it was a noisy hilarious meal, with the whole family talking at once, although Mr Culpeper confined his conversation to Gerard, because, as he remarked a little severely to the rest of his family, he appeared to be the only calm person present. He had, it was true, greeted his various children with pleasure, but as he had just finished translating an Anglo-Saxon document of some rarity, and wished to discuss it with someone intelligent, he took little part in the rather excited talk. Deborah could hear various snatches of her learned parent's rambling dissertation from time to time and wondered if Gerard was enjoying it as much as he appeared to be. She decided that he was; he was even holding his own with her father, something not many people were able to do. They exchanged brief smiles and she turned back to Maureen's endless questions.

They left shortly afterwards, driving fast to catch the night ferry, and Maureen, who had sat in front with Gerard, had to be persuaded to go to the cabin with Deborah when they got on board; the idea of staying up all night, and on a boat, was an alluring one, only the pleasures in store in the morning, dangled before her sleepy eyes by Gerard, convinced her that a few hours of sleep was a small price to pay for the novelty of driving through a foreign country at half past four in the morning.

The weather was fine, although it was still dark when they landed. Maureen, refreshed by a splendid nap, sat beside Gerard once more, talking without pause. Deborah wondered if he minded, although it was hard to tell from his manner, which was one of amused tolerance towards his small sister-in-law. Once or twice he turned to speak to her and she thought that there was more warmth in his voice when he spoke, but that could be wishful thinking, for after the unpleasant business with Claude and all that he had told her about his marriage to Sasja, she had hoped that perhaps his feelings might have deepened from friendship to even the mildest of affection.

She was to think that on several occasions during the next few days, but never with certainty. Gerard, it seemed, could spare the time to take his small relative round and about where he had not found it possible with herself, and Deborah caught herself wondering if he was seizing the opportunity to get upon a closer footing with herself. He drove them to Volendam, obligingly helped Maureen purchase postcards and souvenirs, admired the costumed villagers, standing ready to have their photos taken by the tourists, and when Maureen wished that she had a camera so that she could take her own pictures, purchased one for her. And what was more, he showed nothing but pleasure when she flung her arms around him and thanked him extravagantly for it.

They lunched that day at Wieringerwerf, after the briefest of visits to Hoorn. The restaurant was on the main road, a large, bustling place, colourful with flags and brightly painted chairs and tables on its terraces; not at all the sort of place Gerard would choose to go to for himself, Deborah suspected, but Maureen, eyeing the coloured umbrellas and the comfortable restaurant, pronounced it super. She chose her lunch from an enormous menu card and told Gerard that he was super too, and when he laughed, said:

'But it's true, you are super. I'm not surprised that Debby married you. If you could have waited a year or two, I'd have married you myself. Perhaps you have some younger brothers?'

'Married, I'm afraid, my dear—but I have a number of cousins. I'll arrange for you to meet them next time you come and you can look them over.' Deborah saw no mockery in his face and loved him for it.

Maureen agreed to this. 'Though I don't suppose you'll want me again for a little while. I mean, there are so many of us, aren't there? You'll only want a few at a time.'

Gerard glanced at Deborah. 'Oh, I don't know,' he said easily. 'I think it would be rather fun if all of you were to come over and spend Christmas. There's plenty of room.'

She beamed at him. 'I say, you really are the greatest! I'll tell Mother, so's she can remind Father about it, then it won't come as a surprise to him—he forgets, you know.'

She polished off an enormous icecream embellished with whipped cream, chocolate, nuts and fruit, and sighed blissfully. 'Where do we go next?' she wanted to know.

Gerard glanced at his watch. 'I'm afraid back home. I have a list this afternoon at four o'clock.'

'You won't be home for dinner?' asked Deborah, trying to sound casual.

'I very much doubt it. Can you amuse your-selves?'

'Of course.' Had she not been amusing herself times without number all these weeks? 'Shall I get you something cooked when you come in?'

'Would you? It could be any time.'

It was late when he got back, Marijke had gone to bed, leaving Wim to lay a tray for his master. So it was Deborah who went down to the kitchen and heated soup and made an omelette and a fresh fruit salad and carried them up to the dining room.

She arranged everything on the table and when Gerard was seated went to sit herself in one of the great armchairs against the wall.

'I hope it was successful,' she essayed, not know-ing if he was too tired to talk or if he wanted to talk about it.

He spooned his soup. 'Entirely successful. You're referring to the case this afternoon—I had no idea that you knew about it.'

'I didn't. You always have a list on Thursday afternoons, but you have never been later than eight o'clock, so I guessed. . . .'

He laughed. 'I keep forgetting that you've worked for me for two years. It was an important patient and he had come a long way in the hope that I could help him, but he refused utterly to allow me to begin the operation until his wife had arrived.'

88

'Was it a chondroma?'

'Yes.'

'Poor man, but I'm glad you could help him. His wife must be so thankful.'

Gerard began on the omelette. 'I imagine so,' and when he didn't say anything else she said presently: 'Thank you for spending so much time with us today. Maureen loved it.'

'And you?'

'I loved it too; it's all foreign to me, even though I live here now.'

He frowned. 'I keep forgetting that too. I shan't have a minute to spare tomorrow, but I'll manage an afternoon the day after—have you any plans?'

'Could we go somewhere for tea? Maureen loves going out to tea, especially if it's combined with sightseeing. I could take her on a round of the canals tomorrow.'

He speared the last of the omelette, complimented her upon her cooking and observed: 'I know I'm booked up for tomorrow, but how would it be if you both came to the hospital and had a look round? I'll get one of the housemen to take you round. Go to the—no, better still, I'll come home and pick you up, only you mustn't keep me waiting. Paul van Goor can look after you and see you into a taxi afterwards. Would you like that?'

She said very quietly: 'Enormously,' wondering if he was being kind to Maureen or if he was allowing her to share his life just a little at last. 'If you'll tell us what time you want us to be ready, we'll be waiting.' She got up. 'Would you like the brandy? I'm going to fetch the coffee.'

'Shall we go into the sitting room and share the pot between us?'

She loathed coffee so late at night, but she would gladly swallow pints of it if he wanted her to talk to. Perhaps the operation had been a bit of a strain —she had no idea who the important patient might be and she had too much sense to ask. All the same, when she had poured coffee for them both she asked him: 'I'd love to hear about the op if it wouldn't bore you—which method did you use?'

She had done the right thing, she could sense that. He told her, using terms he had no need to explain, describing techniques she understood and could comment upon with intelligence. It was very late when he had finished, and when he apologised for keeping her up she waved a careless hand and said in a carefully matter-of-fact voice: 'I enjoyed it.'

She took the tray back to the kitchen, wished him goodnight and went quickly upstairs, because she couldn't trust herself to preserve her careful, tranquil manner any longer.

She and Maureen were to be ready at half past one on the following afternoon, and at exactly that time Gerard came for them. He was preoccupied but, as always, courteous during the short drive. The Grotehof hospital was in the centre of the city, tucked away behind some of its oldest houses. The building was old too, but had been extended and modernized until it was difficult to see where the old ended and the new began. The entrance was in the old part, through a large, important door leading to a vast tiled hall. It was here that Gerard, with a muttered word of apology, handed them over with a hasty word of introduction to a young and cheerful houseman, Paul van Goor, who, obviously primed as to his task, led them through a labyrinth of corridors to the children's ward, talking all the time in excellent English.

From there they went to the surgical block, the medical block, the recreation rooms, the Accident Room, the dining room for the staff and lastly the theatre block, the newest addition to the hospital, he told them proudly. It consisted of six theatres, two for general surgery, one for E.N.T., one for cardio-thoracic work and two for orthopaedics. They couldn't go inside, of course, although Deborah longed to do so, and when she peered through the round window in the swing doors she felt a pang of regret that it was no longer her world; she amended that—the regret was because it was still Gerard's world and she no longer had a share in it, for at least at Clare's she worked with him. Now she was a figurehead in his house, running it smoothly and efficiently, dressing to do him credit, living with him and yet not sharing his life.

She sighed, and Paul asked her if she was tired and when she said no, suggested that they might like to go back through the hospital garden, very small but lovingly tended. They returned via lengthy staircases and roundabout passages, Deborah deep in thought, Maureen and Paul talking earnestly. They were passing a great arched doorway when a nurse flung it open and coming towards them from the other side was Gerard, a different Gerard, surrounded by a group of housemen and students, his registrar, the Ward Sister and a handful of nurses. If he saw them he took no notice; Deborah hadn't expected him too. She managed to snatch at Maureen's hand as she lifted it to wave to him.

'No, you can't, darling,' she said urgently. 'Not here, it wouldn't do. I'll explain later.'

She had done her best to do so on their way to Mevrouw van Doorninck's flat in the taxi Paul had got for them, but all Maureen said was: 'Oh, Debby, how stuffy you are—he's my brother-in-law, and you're married to him, of course he can wave to us if he wants to; important people do just what they like and no one minds.'

She was inclined to argue about it; fortunately she was kept too occupied for the rest of the afternoon, for Gerard's mother had gathered the family together to meet Maureen and the party was a merry one. 'Only,' as Mevrouw van Doorninck declared to Deborah, as they drank their tea and nibbled the thin sugary biscuits, 'it's such a pity that Gerard can't be here too. I had hoped now that he was married ... it is as though he is afraid to be happy again.' She glanced at Deborah, who said nothing at all, and went on presently: 'He seems very fond of Maureen, such a sweet child. I look forward to meeting the rest of your family, my dear.'

'I'm sure they're just as eager to meet you, Mevrouw van Doorninck.' Deborah was relieved that they had left the subject of Gerard. 'They're all coming over to spend Christmas.'

'Christmas?' Her companion gave her another sharp look. 'A great deal could happen by then.'

Deborah would have liked to ask her mother-in-law what, in heaven's name, could happen in this well-ordered, well-organised world in which she now lived. A flaming row, she told herself vulgarly, would relieve the monotony, but Gerard was difficult to quarrel with—he became at once blandly courteous, placidly indifferent, a sign, she had decided forlornly, that he didn't consider her of sufficient importance in his life to warrant a loss of temper.

She and Maureen got up to go presently, walking back to the house in the Keizersgracht, to curl up in the comfortable chairs in the sitting room and discuss the delights of Christmas and the not so distant pleasures of the next day when Gerard had promised to take them out.

He telephoned just before dinner, to say that he was detained at the hospital and would dine with a colleague and she wasn't to wait for him. All the same she sat on, long after Maureen had gone to bed and Wim and Marijke had gone to their rooms. But when the clock struck midnight and there was no sign of him, she went to bed too, but not to sleep. She heard his quiet steps going through the quiet house in the early hours of the morning and lay awake until daylight, wondering where he had been and with whom.

He was at breakfast when she got down in the morning, looking, Deborah thought, a little tired but as impeccably dressed as he always was, and although she wanted very much to ask him why he had come home so very late the night before, she held her tongue, remarked on the pleasant morning and read her letters. She was rewarded for this circumspect behaviour by him saying presently:

'I promised to take you both out this afternoon. I'm sorry, but it won't be possible. Could you find something to do, do you suppose?'

She wouldn't let him see her disappointment. 'Of course—there are a hundred and one things on Maureen's list. She'll be disappointed, though.'

'And you.' His glance was thoughtful.

'Oh, I'll be disappointed too; I love sightseeing. As it's her last day, I'll take her to Schevingenen. She'll love it there, and your mother was telling me of a lovely tea-room near the sea.'

She smiled at him, a friendly, casual smile, to let him see that it was of no importance whatever that he had had to cry off, and picked up the rest of her post, only to put it down again as a thought struck her.

'Gerard, would you rather not take Maureen back tomorrow? I can easily take her in the Fiat. Rather a comedown for her after the BMW and the Citroën, I know, but I've been on the road several times now and you said yourself that my driving had improved....'

He frowned at her across the table. 'I don't like the idea of you going that distance, though I must confess that it would be awkward for me to leave.'

'That's settled, then,' she said briskly. 'Only if you don't mind, I think I'll spend a night at home; I don't think I'd be much good at turning round and coming straight back.'

'An excellent idea.' He was still frowning. 'I wonder if there's someone who could drive you— Wim's taking Mother up to Friesland or he could have gone; there may be someone at the hospital.'

'Don't bother,' said Deborah quickly, 'you've enough to do without that. I'll be quite all right, you know, you don't need to give it another thought.'

'Very well, I won't, though if it had been anyone else but you ...'

She was left to decide for herself if he had intended that as a compliment or not.

They were on their way back from Schevingenen that afternoon when she found herself behind her husband's car. He was driving the Citroën, and seated beside him was a small, dark, and very attractive woman, a circumstance which made Deborah thankful that Maureen was so taken up with a large street organ in the opposite direction that she saw nothing.

Presently the traffic allowed her to slip past him. Without looking she was aware of his sudden stare as she raced the little car ahead of the Citroën while Maureen chattered on, still craning her neck to see the last of the organ. Deborah answered her small sister's questions mechanically while her thoughts were busy. So Gerard couldn't spare the time to take them out, though seemingly he had leisure enough to drive around with a pretty woman during an afternoon which was to have been so busy. She had, she told herself savagely, two minds to stay home for a good deal longer than one night. There were, if her memory served her right, several social engagements within the next week or so—let him attend them alone, or better still, with his charming companion. She frowned so fiercely at the very idea that Maureen, turning to speak to her, wanted to know if she had a headache.

Gerard was home for dinner. Deborah greeted him with her usual calm friendliness, hoped that his day hadn't been too busy and plunged into an account of their outing that afternoon, pausing at the end of it to give him time to tell her that he had seen her, and explain his companion. But he said nothing about it at all, only had a short and lively conversation with Maureen and joined her in a game with Smith before shutting himself up in his study.

Deborah exerted herself to be entertaining during dinner, and if her manner was over-bright, her companions didn't seem to notice. After the meal, when Gerard declared himself ready to take Maureen on a boat tour of the lighted canals, even though it was almost dark and getting chilly, she pleaded a headache and stayed at home, working pettishly at a petit-point handbag intended for her mother-in-law's Christmas present.

She and Maureen left after breakfast the next morning to catch the midday ferry from Zeebrugge and Gerard had left the house even earlier; over breakfast he had had very little to say to her, save to advise her to take care and wish her a pleasant journey, but with Maureen he had laughed and joked and given her an enormous box of chocolates as a farewell present and responded suitably to her uninhibited hugs.

They made good time to the ferry, and once on board, repaired to the restaurant where, over her enormous lunch, Maureen talked so much that she didn't notice that Deborah was eating almost nothing.

The drive to Somerset was uneventful. By now the little girl was getting tired; she dozed from time to time, assuring Deborah that she did so only to ensure that she would be wide awake when they reached home. Which left Deborah with her thoughts, running round and round inside her head like mice in a wheel. None of them were happy and all of them were of Gerard.

They reached home at about midnight, to find her parents waiting for them with hot drinks and sandwiches and a host of questions.

Deborah was answering them rather sleepily when the telephone rang and Mr Culpeper, annoyed at the interruption, answered it testily. But his sharp voice shouting, 'Hullo, hullo' in peremptory tones changed to a more friendly accent. 'It's Gerard,' he announced, 'wants to speak to you, Deb.'

She had telephoned the house in Amsterdam on their arrival at Dover, knowing very well that he wouldn't be home and leaving nothing but a brief message with Wim. She picked up the receiver now, schooling her voice to its usual calm and said: 'Hullo, Gerard.'

His voice was quiet and distinct. 'Hullo, Deborah. Wim gave me your message, but I wanted to hear for myself that you had got home safely. I hope I haven't got you out of bed.'

'No. You're up late yourself.'

His 'Yes' was terse. He went on quickly: 'I won't keep you. Have a good night's sleep and drive carefully tomorrow. Good night, Debby.'

She said good night and replaced the receiver. He had never called her Debby before; she wondered about it, but she was really too tired to think. Presently they all went to bed and she slept without waking until she was called in the morning.

She was to take Maureen back to school after breakfast and then continue on her return journey. It seemed lonely after she had left her little sister, still talking and quite revived by a good night's sleep. There hadn't been much time to talk to her mother while she had been home, and perhaps that was a good thing; she might have let slip some small thing ... all the same, it had been a cheerful few hours. Her parents, naturally enough, took it for granted that she was happy and beyond asking after Gerard and agreeing eagerly to the Christmas visit they had said little more; there had been no chance because Maureen had so much to talk about. It would have been nice to have confided in someone, thought Deborah, pushing the little car hard along the road towards the Winchester by-pass, but perhaps not quite loyal to Gerard. The thought of seeing him again made her happy, but the happiness slowly wilted as the day wore on. There had been brilliant sunshine to start with, but now clouds were piling up behind her and long before she reached Dover, it was raining, and out at sea the sky showed a uniform greyness which looked as though it might be there for ever.

She slept for most of the crossing, sitting in a chair in the half-filled ship; she was tired and had been nervous of getting the car on board. Somehow with Maureen she hadn't found it frightening, but going up the steep ramp to the upper car deck she had quaked with fright; it was a relief to sit down for a few hours and recover her cool. She fetched herself a cup of coffee, brought a paperback and settled back. They were within sight of land when she woke and feeling tired still, she tidied herself and after a hasty cup of tea, went to the car deck.

Going down the ramp wasn't too bad, although her engine stalled when she reached the bottom. Deborah found herself trembling as she followed the cars ahead of her towards the Customs booth in the middle of the docks road. Suddenly the drive to Amsterdam didn't seem the easy journey she had made it out to be when she had offered to take Maureen home. It stretched before her in her mind's eye, dark and wet, with the Breskens ferry to negotiate and the long-drawn-out, lonely road across the islands, and Rotterdam ... she had forgotten what a long way it was; somehow she hadn't noticed that when she was with Gerard, or even when she had taken Maureen back, but then it had been broad daylight.

She came to a halt by the Customs, proffered her passport and shivered in the chilly night air as she wound down the window. The man smiled at her. 'You will go to the left, please, Mevrouw.' He waved an arm towards a road leading off from the main docks road.

Deborah was puzzled; all the cars in front of her were keeping straight on. She said slowly so that he would be sure to understand: 'I'm going to Holland—don't I keep straight on to the main road?'

He was still smiling but quite firm. 'To the left, Mevrouw, if you will be so good.'

She went to the left; possibly they were diverting the traffic; she would find out in good time, she supposed. She was going slowly because the arc lights hardly penetrated this smaller side road and she had no idea where it was leading her, nor was there a car in front of her. She was on the point of stopping and going back to make sure that she hadn't misunderstood the Customs man, when her headlights picked out the BMW parked at the side of the road and Gerard leaning against its boot. In the bad light he looked enormous and very reassuring too; she hadn't realized just how much she had wanted to be reassured until she saw him there, standing in the pouring rain, the collar of his Burberry turned up to his ears, a hat pulled down over his eyes. She pulled up then and he walked over to her and when she wound down the window, said: 'Hullo, my dear. I thought it might be a good idea to come and meet you and drive you back—the weather, you know....'

She was still getting over her surprise and joy at seeing him. Her 'hullo' was faint, as was her protesting: 'But I can't leave the Fiat here?'

She became aware that Wim was there too, standing discreetly in the background by his master's car. Gerard nodded towards him. 'I brought Wim with me, he'll take the Fiat back.' He opened the car door. 'Come along, Deborah, we shall be home in no time at all.'

She got out silently and allowed herself to be tucked up snugly beside him in the BMW, pausing only to greet Wim and hope that he didn't mind driving the Fiat home.

'A pleasure, Mevrouw,' grinned Wim cheerfully, 'but I think that you will be there first.' He put out a hand to take the car keys from her and raised it in salute as he walked back to her car.

As Gerard reversed his own car and swept back the way she had come Deborah asked: 'Oh, is that why he told me to come this way and not out of the main gate?'

'Yes—I was afraid that we might miss you once you got past the Customs. Did you have a good trip back?'

For a variety of reasons and to her great shame her voice was drowned in a sudden flood of tears. She swallowed them back frantically and they poured down her cheeks instead. She stared out of the window at the outskirts of the town—flat land, dotted here and there with houses, it looked untidy even in the dim light of the overhead street lamps —and willed herself to be calm. After a minute Gerard said 'Deborah?' and because she would have to say something sooner or later she managed a 'Yes, thank you,' and spoilt it with a dreary snivel.

He slid the car to the side of the road on to a patch of waste land and switched off the engine. He had tossed off his hat when he got into the car; now he turned his handsome head and looked down at her in the semi-dark. 'What happened?' he asked gently, and then: 'Debby, I've never seen you cry before.'

She sniffed, struggled to get herself under control and managed:

'I hardly ever do—n-nothing's the m-matter, it's just that I'm tired, I expect.' She added on a small wail: 'I was t-terrified—those ramps on the ferry, they were ghastly—I thought I'd never reach the top and I didn't notice with Maureen, but when I was by m-myself it was awful, and the engine stalled and it was raining and when I got off the ferry it s-seemed s-such a long way to get home.' She hiccoughed, blew her nose and mopped her wet cheeks.

'I should never have let you go alone, I must have been mad. My poor girl, what a thoughtless man I am! You see, you are—always have been—so calm and efficient and able to cope, and then last night when I telephoned you, you sounded so tired —I rearranged my work to come and meet you. I remembered this long dark road too, Deborah, and in the Fiat it would be even longer. Forgive me, Deborah.'

She sniffed. His arm, flung along the back of the seat and holding her shoulders lightly, was comforting, and she was rapidly regaining her self-control. Later, she knew, she would be furious with herself for breaking down in this stupid fashion. She said in a voice which was nearly normal: 'Thank you very much, Gerard. It was only because it was raining and so very dark.'

She felt his arm slide away. 'I've some coffee here —Marijke always regards any journey more than ten miles distant from Amsterdam as being fraught with danger and probable starvation and provides accordingly. Sandwiches, too.'

They ate and drank in a companionable silence and presently Gerard began to talk, soothing nothings about her parents and her home and Smith— perhaps he talked to his more nervous patients like that, she thought sleepily, before he told them that he would have to operate. He took her cup from her presently and said: 'Go to sleep, Deborah, there's nothing to look at at this time of night—I'll wake you when we reach Amsterdam.'

She started to tell him that she wasn't tired any more, and fell asleep saying it.

She wakened to the touch of his hand on her arm. 'A few minutes,' he told her, and she was astonished to see the still lighted, now familiar streets of the city all around them. But the Keizers-gracht was only dimly lit, its water gleaming dimly through the bare trees lining the road. It was still raining, but softly now, and there were a few lights from the houses they passed. As they drew up before their own front door, she saw that the great chandelier in the hall was beaming its light through the glass transom over the door and the sitting room was lighted too so that the wet pavement glistened in its glow. Gerard helped her out of the car and took her arm and they crossed the cobbles together as the front door was flung open and Marijke, with a wildly barking Smith, stood framed within it.

Going through the door Deborah knew at that moment just how much she loved the old house; it welcomed her, just as Marijke and Smith were welcoming her, as though she had returned from a long and arduous journey. She smiled a little mistily at Marijke and bent to catch Smith up into her arms. They went into the sitting room and Gerard took her coat, then Marijke was there almost at once with more hot coffee and a plate of paper-thin sandwiches. She talked volubly to Gerard while she set them out on the silver tray and carried it over to put on the table by Deborah's chair. When she had gone, Deborah asked: 'What was all that about?'

He came to sit opposite her and now she could see the lines of fatigue on his face, so that before he could answer she asked: 'Have you had a hard day?'

He smiled faintly. 'Yes.'

'You've been busy—too busy, lately.'

'That is no excuse for letting you go all that way alone.'

She said firmly: 'It was splendid for my driving. I'll not mind again.'

'There won't be an again,' he told her briefly, 'and Marijke was talking about you.'

'Oh—I recognised one word—stomach.'

It was nice to see him laugh like that. 'She said that you look tired and that beautiful women should never look other than beautiful. She strongly advised nourishment for your—er—stomach so that you would sleep like a rose.'

Deborah said softly: 'What a charming thing to

103

say, about the rose, I mean. Dear Marijke—she and Wim, they're like the house, aren't they?' And was sorry that she had said it, because he might not understand. But he did; the look he gave her was one of complete understanding. She smiled at him and then couldn't look away from his intent gaze. 'You saw me the other afternoon,' he stated the fact simply. 'You have been wondering why I couldn't find the time to take you and Maureen on a promised trip and yet have the leisure to drive around with a very attractive woman—she was attractive, did you not think so?'

'Yes.'

'I don't discuss my patients with you, you know that, I think—although I must confess I have frequently wished to do so—but I do not wish you to misunderstand. The patient upon whom I operated the other evening was. . . .' he named someone and Deborah sat up with a jerk, although she said nothing. 'Yes, you see why I have been so worried and—secretive. The lady with me was his wife. She had been to Schiphol to meet her daughter, who was breaking her journey on her way home to get news of her father. At the last moment his wife declared that she was unable to tell her and asked me to do it. We were on our way back to the hospital when you saw us. I should have told you sooner. I'm not sure why I didn't, perhaps I was piqued at the way you ignored the situation. Any other woman—wife—would have asked.'

'It was none of my business,' she said stiffly. 'I didn't know. . . .'

'You mean that you suspected me of having a girl-friend?' He was smiling, but she sensed his controlled anger.

There was no point in being anything but honest with him. 'Yes, I think I did, but it still wouldn't be my business, and it shouldn't matter, should it?'

He hadn't taken his eyes off her. 'I believe you said that once before. You think that? But do you not know me well enough to know that I would have been quite honest with you before I married you?'

Her head had begun to ache. 'Oh, yes, indeed, but that wasn't what I meant. What I'm trying to say is that I've no right to mind, have I?'

Gerard got to his feet and pulled her gently to hers. 'You have every right in the world,' he assured her. 'I don't think our bargain included that kind of treatment of each other, Deborah. I don't cheat the people I like.'

She didn't look at him. 'No, I know that, truly I do. I'm sorry I was beastly. I think I'm tired.'

They walked together out of the room and in the hall he kissed her cheek. 'I'll wait for Wim, he shouldn't be much longer now. And by the way, I've taken some time off. In a couple of days I'll take you to the house in Friesland, and we might go and see some friends of mine who live close by—she's English, too.'

Deborah was half way up the stairs. 'That sounds lovely,' she told him and then turned round to say: 'Thank you for coming all that way, it must have been a bind after a hard day's work.'

He didn't answer her, but she was conscious of his eyes on her as she climbed the stairs.

CHAPTER SIX

BUT before they went to Friesland Deborah met some other friends of Gerard's. She had spent a quiet day after her return, arranging the menu for a dinner party they were to give during the following week, paying a morning visit to her mother-in-law, telephoning her own mother and writing a few letters before taking Smith for a walk. She was back home, waiting for Gerard's return from the Grotehof after tea, when the telephone rang.

It was a woman's voice, light and sweet, enquiring if Mijnheer van Doorninck was home. 'No,' said Deborah, and wondered who it was, 'I'm sorry —perhaps I could take a message?' She spoke in the careful Dutch the professor had taught her, and hoped that the conversation wasn't going to get too involved.

'Is that Gerard's wife?' asked the voice, in English now, and when Deborah said a little uncertainly: 'Why, yes——' went on: 'Oh, good. I'm Adelaide van Essen. My husband's paediatrician at the Grotehof and a friend of Gerard. We got back from England last night and Coenraad telephoned me just now and told me about you. You don't mind me ringing you up?'

'I'm delighted—I don't know any English people here yet.'

'Well, come and meet me—us, for a start. Come this evening. I know it's short notice, but I told Coenraad to ask Gerard to bring you to dinner— you will come?'

'I'd love to.' Deborah paused. 'I'm not sure about Gerard, he works late quite a lot and often works at home.'

She had the impression that the girl at the other end of the line was concealing surprise. Then: 'I'm sure he'll make time. We haven't seen each other for ages and the men are old friends. We live quite near you, in the Herengracht—is seven o'clock too early? Oh, and here's our number in case you want to ring back. Till seven, then. I'm so looking forward to meeting you.'

Deborah went back to her chair. The voice had sounded nice, soft and gentle and friendly. She spent the next ten minutes or so in deciding what she should wear and still hadn't made up her mind when Gerard came in.

His hullo was friendly and after he had enquired about her day, he took a chair near her. 'I met a friend of mine at the Grotehof this afternoon,' he told her, 'Coenraad van Essen—he's married to an English girl. They're just back from England and they want us to go round for dinner this evening. Would you like to go? It's short notice and I don't know if it will upset any arrangements you may have made?'

She chose a strand of silk and threaded her needle. 'His wife telephoned a few minutes ago. I'd like to go very much. She suggested seven o'clock, so I had better go and talk to Marijke.'

Marijke hadn't started the cutlets and the cheese soufflé; Deborah, in her laborious Dutch and helped by a few words here and there from Wim, suggested that they should have them the following day instead and apologised for the short notice. To which Marijke had a whole lot to say in reply, her face all smiles. Deborah turned to Wim. 'I don't quite understand....'

'Marijke is saying that it is good for you to see a lady of your own age and also English. She wishes you a merry evening.' He beamed at her. 'Me, I wish the same also, Mevrouw.'

She wore the pink silk jersey dress she had been unable to resist the last time she had visited Metz, the fashionable dress shop within walking distance of the house, and went downstairs to find Gerard waiting for her. 'I'm not late?' she asked anxiously as she crossed the hall.

'No—I wanted a few minutes with you. Shall we go into the sitting room?'

Deborah's heart dropped to her elegant shoes. What was he going to tell her? That he was going away on one of his teaching trips—that he wouldn't be able to take her to Friesland after all? She arranged her face into a suitable composure and turned to face him.

'Did you never wonder why I had not given you a wedding gift?' he asked her. 'Not because I had given no thought to it; there were certain alterations I wanted done, and only today are they finished.'

He took a small velvet case from his pocket and opened it. There were earrings inside on its thick satin lining; elaborate pearl drops in a diamond setting. She looked at them with something like awe. 'My goodness,' she uttered, 'they're—they're beautiful! I've never seen anything like them.'

He had taken them from their box. 'Try them on,' he invited her. 'They're very old, but the setting was clumsy; I've had them re-set to my own design. You are tall enough to take such a style, I think.'

She had gone to the mirror over the sofa table and

hooked them in and stood looking at them. They were exquisite, and he was right, they suited her admirably. She turned her lovely head and watched the diamonds take fire. 'I don't know how to thank you,' she began. 'They're magnificent!'

Thanking him didn't seem quite enough, so she went to him and rather hesitantly kissed his cheek. 'Do you suppose I might wear them this evening?' she asked.

'Why not?' He had gone over to the small secretaire by one of the windows and was opening one of its drawers. He returned with another, larger case in his hand. 'This has been in the family for quite some time too,' he observed as he gave it to her. 'I've had it re-strung and the clasp re-set to match the earrings.'

Deborah opened the case slowly. There were pearls in it, a double row with a diamond and pearl clasp which followed the exact pattern of the earrings. She stared at it and all she could manage was an ecstatic 'Oh!' Gerard took them from her and fastened them round her neck and she went back to the mirror and had another look; they were quite superb. 'I don't know how to thank you,' she repeated, quite at a loss for words. 'It's the most wonderful wedding present anyone could dream of having.'

He was standing behind her, staring at her reflection. After a moment he smiled faintly. 'You are my wife,' he pointed out. 'You are entitled to them.' He spoke lightly as he turned away.

He need not have said that, she thought unhappily, looking at her suddenly downcast face in the mirror. It took her a few moments to fix a smile on to it before she turned away and picked up her coat.

'Do we walk or go in the car?' she asked brightly.

He helped her into her coat and she could have been his sister, she thought bitterly, for all the impression she made upon him. 'The car,' he told her cheerfully. 'It's almost seven, perhaps we had better go at once.'

The house in the Herengracht was bigger than Gerard's but very similar in style. Its vast front door was opened as they reached it and an elderly man greeted them with a 'Good evening, Mevrouw —Mijnheer.'

Gerard slapped him on the shoulder. 'Tweedle, how are you? You haven't called me Mijnheer for many a long day.' He looked at Deborah, smiling. 'This is Tweedle, my dear, who has been with Coenraad since he was a toddler. I daresay you will meet Mrs Tweedle presently.'

'Indeed, she will be delighted,' Tweedle informed them gravely, adding: 'The Baron and Baroness are in the small sitting room, Mr Gerard.'

He led the way across the panelled hall and opened a door, announcing them as he did so, and Deborah, with Gerard's hand under her elbow urging her gently on, went in.

The room was hardly small and she saw at a glance that it was furnished with some magnificent pieces worthy of a museum, yet it was decidedly lived in; there was a mass of knitting cast down carelessly on a small drum table, a pile of magazines were tumbled on to the sofa table behind the big settee before the chimneypiece, and there was a pleasant scent of flowers, tobacco and—very faint— beeswax polish. There were two people in the room, a man as tall as Gerard but somewhat older, his dark hair greying at the temples, horn-rimmed glasses astride his handsome beaky nose. It was a kind face as well as a good-looking one, and Deborah decided then and there that she was going to like Gerard's friend. The girl who got up with him was small, slim and very pretty, with huge dark eyes and a mass of bright red hair piled high. She was wearing a very simple dress of cream silk and some of the loveliest sapphires Deborah had ever set eyes on. She felt Gerard's hand on her arm again and went forward to receive the baron's quiet welcome and the charming enthusiasm of his small wife, who, after kissing Gerard in a sisterly fashion, led her to a small sofa and sat down beside her.

'You really are a dear to come at a moment's notice,' she declared. 'You didn't mind?'

Deborah shook her head, smiling. She was going to like this small vivid creature. 'It was kind of you to ask us. I'm so glad to meet another English girl. Gerard has been so busy and—and we haven't been married very long. I've met a great many of his colleagues, though.'

Her companion glanced at her quickly. 'Duty dinners,' she murmured, 'and the rest of the time they're immersed in their work. Coenraad says you were Gerard's Theatre Sister.'

'Yes. I worked for him for two years while he was at Clare's.' She felt she should have been able to say more about it than that, but she could think of nothing. There was a pause before her hostess asked: 'Do you like Amsterdam? I love it. We've a house in Dorset and we go there whenever we can, and to my parents, of course. The children love it.'

She didn't look old enough to have children.

111

'How many have you?' Deborah asked.

'Two.' Adelaide turned to take the drink her husband was offering her and he corrected her smilingly: 'Two and a half, my love.'

Deborah watched him exchange a loving glance, full of content and happiness, and swallowed envy as she heard her host say: 'Do you hear that, Gerard? You're going to be a godfather again—some time in the New Year.' And when Gerard joined them, he added: 'We'll do the same for you, of course.'

Everyone laughed; this was the sort of occasion, Deborah told herself bitterly, that she hadn't reckoned with. She made haste to ask the children's names and was at once invited to visit them in their beds.

'They won't be asleep,' their doting mother assured her, 'at least Champers won't. Lisa's only eighteen months old and drops off in seconds. Champers likes to lie and think.'

She led the way up the curving staircase and into the night nursery where an elderly woman was tidying away a pile of clothes. She was introduced as Nanny Best, the family treasure, before she trotted softly away with a bright nod. The two girls went to the cot first; the small girl in it was a miniature of her mother, the same fiery hair and preposterous lashes, the same small nose. She was asleep, her mother dropped a kiss on one fat pink cheek and crossed the room to the small bed against the opposite wall. There was no doubt at all that the small boy in it was the baron's son. Here was the dark hair, the beaky nose and the calm expression. He grinned widely at his mother, offered a hand to Deborah and after kissing them both good night, declared his intention of going to sleep.

They went back downstairs and were met in the hall by the Labrador dogs. 'Castor and Pollux,' Adelaide introduced them, and tucked an arm into Deborah's. 'Call me Adelaide,' she begged in her sweet voice. 'I'm going to call you Deborah.' She paused to look at her companion. 'You're quite beautiful, you know, no wonder Gerard married you.' Her eyes lingered on the earrings. 'I like these,' she said, touching them with a gentle finger, 'and the pearls, they suit you. How lucky you are to be tall and curvy, you can wear all the jewels Gerard will doubtless give you, but look at me—one pearl necklace and I'm smothered!'

They laughed together as they entered the room and the two men looked up. Coenraad said: 'There you are, darling—do you girls want another drink before dinner?'

The meal was a splendid one. Deborah, looking round the large, well appointed dining room, reflected how well the patrician families lived with their large old houses, their priceless antique furniture, their china and glass and silver and most important of all, their trusted servants who were devoted to them and looked after their possessions with as much pride as that of their owners.

She was recalled to her surroundings by Adelaide. 'So you're going to Friesland,' she commented. 'I expect Gerard will take you to see Dominic and Abigail—she's English, too—they live close by. They're both dears. They've a house in Amsterdam, of course, but they go to Friesland when they can. Abigail is expecting a baby in about six months.' She grinned happily. 'Won't it be fun, all of us living near enough to pop in and visit, and so nice for the children—they can all play together.'

Deborah agreed, aware that Gerard had stopped talking and was listening too. 'What are the schools like?' she heard herself ask in a voice which sounded as though she really wanted to know.

They stayed late; when they got back home the house was quiet, for Wim and Marijke had long since gone to bed, but the great chandelier in the hall still blazed and there were a couple of lamps invitingly lighting the sitting room. Deborah wandered in and perched on the side of a chair.

'You enjoyed the evening?' Gerard wanted to know, following her.

'Very much—what a nice person Adelaide is, and so is Coenraad. I hope I did the right thing, I asked them to join our dinner party next week.'

'Splendid. Coenraad and I have known each other for a very long time.' He went on: 'He and Addy are very devoted.'

'Yes.' Deborah didn't want to talk about that, it hurt too much. 'I'm looking forward to meeting Abigail too.'

'Ah, yes, on Saturday. We'll leave fairly early in the morning, shall we, go to the house first and then go on to Dominic's place in the afternoon. Probably they'll want us to stay for dinner, but as I'm not going in to the Grotehof in the morning, it won't matter if we're late back.'

She got up. 'It sounds delightful. I think I'll go to bed.' She put a hand up to the pearl necklace. 'Thank you again for my present, Gerard. I'll treasure it, and the earrings.'

He was switching off the lamps. 'But of course,' he told her blandly. 'They have been treasured for generations of van Doorninck brides, and I hope will continue to be treasured for a long time to come.'

She went upstairs wondering why he had to remind her so constantly that married though they were, she was an—she hesitated for a word—outsider.

Deborah half expected that something would turn up to prevent them going to Friesland, but it didn't. They left soon after eight o'clock, travelling at a great pace through Hoorn and Den Oever and over the Afsluitdijk and so into Friesland. Once on the land again, Gerard turned the car away from the Leeuwarden road, to go through Bolsward and presently Sneek and into the open country beyond. Deborah was enchanted with what she saw; there seemed to be water everywhere.

'Do you sail at all?' she wanted to know of Gerard.

He slowed the car and turned into a narrow road running along the top of a dyke. He looked years younger that morning, perhaps because he was wearing slacks and a sweater with a gay scarf tucked in its neck, perhaps because he had a whole day in which to do as he liked.

'I've a small yacht, a van der Stadt design, around ten tons displacement—she sails like a dream.'

She wasn't sure what ten tons displacement meant. 'Where do you keep her?'

'Why, at Domwier—I can sail her down the canal to the lake. I've had no time this summer to do much sailing, though, and it's getting late in the year now, though with this lovely autumn we might have a chance—would you like to come with me?'

'Oh, please, if I wouldn't be a nuisance; I don't know a thing about boats, but I'm willing to learn.'

'Good—that's a dare, if the weather holds. We're almost at Domwier—it's a very small village; a church, a shop and a handful of houses. The house is a mile further on.'

The sun sparkled on the lake as they approached it, the opposite shore looked green and pleasant with its trees and thickets, even though there weren't many leaves left. They drove through a thick curtain of birch and pine and saw the lake, much nearer now, beyond rough grass. She barely had time to look at it before Gerard turned into a short sandy lane and there was the house before them. It looked like a farmhouse without the barn behind it, built square and solid with no-nonsense windows and an outsize door surmounted by a carving of two white swans. The sweep before the house was bordered by flower beds, still colourful with dahlias and chrysanthemums, and beyond them, grass and a thick screen of trees and bushes through which she glimpsed the water again. Smith tumbled out of the car to tear round the garden, barking ecstatically, while they made their way rather more soberly to the front door. It stood open on to a tiled hall with a door on either side and another at its end through which came a stout woman, almost as tall as Gerard. That she was delighted to see them was obvious, although Deborah could discover nothing of what she was saying. It was only when Gerard said: 'Forgive us, we're speaking Fries, because Sien dislikes speaking anything else,' that she realised that they were speaking another language altogether. Her heart sank a little; now she would have to learn this language too! As though he had read her thoughts, Gerard added: 'Don't worry, you won't be expected to speak it, though Sien would love you for ever if you could learn to understand just a little of what she says.'

'Then I'll do that, I promise. Do you come up here often?'

He corrected her gently: 'We shall, I hope, come up here often. Once things are exactly as I want them at the hospital, I shall have a good deal more time. I have been away for two years, remember, with only brief visits.'

'Yes, I know, but must you work so hard every day? I mean, you're not often home...' She wished she hadn't said it, for she sensed his withdrawal.

'I'm afraid you must accept that, Deborah.' He was smiling nicely, but his eyes were cool. He turned back to Sien and said something to her and she shook Deborah's hand and, still talking, went back to the kitchen.

Gerard flung an arm round Deborah's shoulders and led her to the sitting room. 'Coffee,' he invited her, 'and then we'll go round the place.' His manner was friendly, just as though he had forgotten their slight discord.

The room was simply furnished in the traditional Friesian style, with painted cupboards against the walls, rush-seated chairs, a stove with a tiled surround and a nicely balanced selection of large, comfortable chairs. There was a telephone too and a portable television tucked discreetly in a corner. 'It's simple,' Gerard had seen her glance, 'but we have comfort and convenience.'

Most decidedly, she agreed silently, as Sien came in with a heavy silver tray with its accompanying silver pot and milk jug and delicate cups. The coffee was delicious and so was the spiced cake which accompanied it. They sat over it and Deborah, determined to keep the conversation on safe ground, asked questions about the house and the furniture and the small paintings hung each side of the stove. She found them enchanting, just as beautiful in their way as the priceless portraits in the Amsterdam house; the ancestors who had sat for Paulus Potter, the street scene by Hendrik Sorgh and the two by Gerrit Berckheyde; she had admired them greatly, almost nervous of the fact that she was now in part responsible for them. But these delicate sketches and paintings were much smaller and perfect to the last hair and whisker—fieldmice mostly, small animals of all kinds, depicted with a precise detail which she found amazing.

'They're by Jacob de Gheyn,' Gerard told her. 'An ancestress of mine loved small animals, so her husband commissioned these for her, and they have been there ever since. I agree with you, they're quite delightful. Come and see the rest of the house.'

The dining room was on the other side of the hall, with a great square bay window built out to take in the view of the lake beyond, comfortably furnished with enormous chairs covered in bright patterned damask. There was a Dutch dresser against one wall, decked with enormous covered tureens and rows of old Delftware. There was a similar dresser in the kitchen too which Deborah could see was as up-to-date as the latest model at the Ideal Home Exhibition, and upstairs the two bathrooms, tiled and cosily carpeted, each with its pile of brightly coloured towels and a galaxy of matching soaps and powders, rivalled the luxury of the town house. By contrast the bedrooms were simply furnished while still offering every comfort, even the two small attic rooms, reached by an almost perpendicular flight of miniature stairs, were as thickly carpeted and as delightfully furnished as the large rooms on the floor below.

As they went downstairs again she said a little shyly: 'This is a lovely house, Gerard—how wonderful to come here when you want peace and quiet. I love the house in Amsterdam, but I could love this one as much.'

He gave her an approving glance. 'You feel that? I'm glad, I have a great fondness for it. Mother too, she comes here frequently. It's quiet in the winter, of course.'

'I think I should like it then—does the lake freeze over?'

They had strolled into the dining room and found Sien busy putting the finishing touches to the lunch table. 'Yes, though not always hard enough for skating. 1 can remember skating across to Dominic's house during some of the really cold winters, though.'

'But it's miles. . . .'

He poured her a glass of sherry. 'Not quite. Round about a mile, I should suppose. We shall have to drive back to the road presently, of course, and go round the head of the lake. It's no distance.'

They set off after a lunch which Deborah had thoroughly enjoyed because Gerard had been amusing and gay and relaxed; and she had never felt so close, and she wondered if he felt it too. It was on the tip of her tongue to try and explain a little to him of how she felt—oh, not to tell him that she loved him; she had the good sense to see that such a statement would cook her goose for ever, but to let him see, if she could, that she was happy and contented and anxious to please him. But there was no chance to say any of these things; they left immediately after lunch and the journey was too short to start a serious talk.

Dominic's house, when they reached it, was a good deal larger than their own but furnished in a similar style. Dominic had come to meet them as they got out of the car, his arm around his wife's shoulders. He was another large man. Deborah found him attractive and almost as good-looking as Gerard, and as for his wife, she was a small girl who would have been plain if happiness hadn't turned her into a beauty. She shook hands now and said in a pretty voice:

'This is a lovely surprise—we heard that Gerard had married and we had planned to come and see you when we got back to Amsterdam. We were returning this week, but the weather's so marvellous, and once the winter starts it goes on and on.'

Inside they talked until tea came, and presently when Gerard suggested that they should go, there was no question of it. 'You'll stay to dinner,' said Abigail. 'Besides,' and now she was smiling, 'I mustn't be thwarted, because of my condition.' There was a general laugh and she turned to Deborah. 'Well, I'm not the only one, I hear Adelaide van Essen is having another baby—isn't she a dear?'

Deborah agreed. 'It's wonderful to find some

other English girls living so close by.' She added hastily, 'Not that I'm lonely, but I find Dutch rather difficult, though I am having lessons.'

'Professor de Wit?' asked Abigail. 'Adelaide went to him. I nursed his brother before I married Dominic.' The two girls plunged into an interesting chat which was only broken by Dominic suggesting mildly that perhaps Abigail should let Bollinger know that there would be two more for dinner.

Abigail got up. 'Oh, darling, I forgot. Deborah, come and meet Bolly—he came over from England with me, and he's part of the household now.'

She smiled at her husband as they left the room, and Deborah, seeing it, felt a pang of sadness. It seemed that everyone else but herself and Gerard was happily married. Walking to the kitchen, half listening to Abigail's happy voice, she wondered if she had tried hard enough, or perhaps she had tried too much. Perhaps she annoyed him in some way, or worse, bored him. She would have to know. She resolved to ask him.

She did so, buoyed up by a false courage induced by Dominic's excellent wine. They were half way home, tearing along the Afsluitdijk with no traffic problems to occupy him.

'Do I bore you, Gerard?' she asked, and heard the small sound he made. Annoyance? Impatience? Surprise, perhaps.

But when he answered her his voice was as cool and casually friendly as usual. 'Not in the least. What put such an idea into your head?'

'N-nothing. I just wondered if you were quite satisfied—I mean with our marriage; if I'm being the kind of wife you wanted. You see, we're not much together and I don't know a great deal about you—perhaps when you get home in the evening and you're tired you'd rather be left in peace with the paper and a drink. I wouldn't mind a bit. . . .'

They were almost at the end of the dyke, approaching the great sluices at its end. Gerard slowed down and gave her a quick look in the dark of the car.

He said on a laugh: 'I do believe you're trying to turn me into a Dutchman with my gin and my paper after a hard day's work!' His voice changed. 'I'm quite satisfied, Deborah. You are the wife I wanted, you certainly don't bore me, I'm always glad to see you when I get home, however tired I am.' His voice became kind. 'Surely that is enough to settle your doubts?'

Quite enough, she told him silently, and quite hopeless too. An irrational desire to drum her heels on the floorboards and scream loudly took possession of her. She overcame it firmly. 'Yes, thank you, Gerard,' and began at once to talk about the house in Friesland. The subject was threadbare by the time they reached Amsterdam, but at least she had managed not to mention themselves again.

It was late and she went straight to bed, leaving Gerard to take Smith for his last perambulation and lock up, and in the morning when she came down it was to hear from Wim that he had been called to the hospital in the very early morning and hadn't returned. It was almost lunchtime when he did, and as his mother had been invited for that meal, it was impossible to ask him about it; in any case, even if they had been alone, he would probably not have told her anything. She applied herself to her mother-in-law's comfort and after lunch sat in the drawing room with her, listening to tales of the family and making suitable comments from time to time, all the while wondering where Gerard had got to. He had gone to his study—she knew that, because he had said that he had a telephone call to make, but that was more than two hours ago. The two ladies had tea together and Deborah had just persuaded the older lady to stay to dinner when Gerard joined them with the hope that they had spent a pleasant afternoon and never a word about his own doings.

He told her the reason for his absence that evening after he had driven his mother back to her flat.

'Before you ask me any of the questions I feel sure are seething inside your head, I'll apologise most humbly.'

'Apologise? Whatever for?' She put down the book she had been reading and stared at him in astonishment.

'Leaving you with Mother for the entire afternoon.'

'But you had some calls to make—some work to do, didn't you?'

He grinned suddenly and her heart thumped against her ribs because he looked as she knew he might look if he were happy and carefree and not chained to the hospital by chains of his own forging. 'I went to sleep.' And when she goggled at him: 'I know, I'm sorry, but the fact is, I had some work to do after we got home last night and I stayed up until two o'clock or thereabouts, and I had to go to the Grotehof for an emergency op at five.'

'Gerard, you must have been worn out! Why on earth didn't you tell me, why won't you let me help you....' That wouldn't do at all, so she went on briskly: 'And there was I telling your mother that you never had a minute to call your own, working at your desk even on a Sunday afternoon.'

He was staring hard at her. 'You're a loyal wife,' he said quietly, and she flushed faintly under his eyes.

'I expect all wives are,' she began, and saw the expression on his face. It had become remote again; he was remembering Sasja, she supposed, who hadn't been loyal at all. 'Shall we have dinner early tomorrow evening so that you can get your work done in good time? Have you a heavy list in the morning?'

'That was something I was going to tell you. I've changed the list to the afternoon—two o'clock, because I thought we might go for a run in the morning.'

A little colour crept into her cheeks again, but she kept her voice as ordinary as possible. 'That sounds nice. Where shall we go?'

'Not too far. The river Vecht, perhaps—we could keep off the motorway and there won't be much traffic about this time of the year.'

Deborah agreed happily, and later, in bed, thinking about it, she dared to hope that perhaps Gerard's first rigid ideas about their marriage weren't as rigid as they had been. She slept peacefully on that happy thought.

They were out of Amsterdam by nine o'clock the next morning, driving through the crisp autumn air. Gerard took the road to Naarden and then turned off on to the narrow road following the Vecht, going slowly so that Deborah could inspect the houses on its banks, built by the merchant princes in the eighteenth century, and because she found them so fascinating he obligingly turned the car at the end of the road and drove back again the same way, patiently answering her questions about them. They had coffee in Loenen and because there was still plenty of time before they had to return to Amsterdam he didn't follow the road to Naarden again, but turned off into the byroads which would lead them eventually back to the city.

The road they were on stretched apparently unending between the flat fields, and save for a group of farm cottages half a mile away, and ahead of them the vague outline of a farmhouse, there was nothing moving except a farm tractor being driven across a ploughed field. Deborah watched the driver idly as they came level with him. 'He must be lonely,' she said idly, and then urgently: 'Gerard, that tractor's going to turn over!'

She was glad that he wasn't one of those men who asked needless questions; they weren't travelling fast, so he slid to a halt and had the door open as the tractor, some way off, reared itself up like an angry monster and crashed down on to its hapless driver.

Even in his hurry, it warmed Deborah's heart when Gerard leaned across her to undo her door and snap back her safety belt so that she could get out quickly. There was a narrow ditch between the road and the field; he bridged it easily with his long legs and then turned to give her a hand before they started to run as best they might across the newly turned earth.

The man had made no sound. When they reached him he was unconscious, trapped by the bonnet of the tractor, its edge biting across the lower half of his body.

It was like being back in theatre, thought Deborah wildly, working in a silent agreed pattern which needed no speech. She found a pulse and counted it with care while Gerard's hands began a careful search over the man's body.

'Nasty crack on his head on this side,' she offered, and peered at the eyes under their closed lids. 'Pupil reaction is equal.'

Gerard grunted, his fingers probing and feeling and probing again.

'I'm pretty sure his pelvis is fractured, God knows what's happened to his legs—how's his pulse?' She told him and he nodded. 'Not too bad,' and examined more closely the wound on the man's head. 'Can't feel a fracture, though I think there may be a crack. We've got to get this thing eased off him, even if it's only a centimetre.'

He slid a powerful arm as far as it would go and heaved with great caution and slowness. 'Half an inch would do it.' He was talking to himself. 'Your belt, Debby—if we could budge this thing just a shade and stuff your belt in. . . .'

She had her belt off while he was still speaking. 'How about trying to scoop the earth from under him and slip the belt in?'

He had understood her at once. He crouched beside the man, the belt in his hand, his arm ready to thrust it between the bonnet's rim and the man's body. Deborah dug with speedy calm; there was nothing to use but her hands. She felt the nails crack and tear and saw, in a detached way, the front of her expensive tweed two-piece gradually disappear under an encrustation of damp earth, but presently she was able to say: 'Try now, Gerard.'

It worked, albeit the pressure was eased fractionally and wouldn't last long. Gerard withdrew his arm with great care and said: 'We have to get help.' His voice was as calm as though he was commenting upon the weather. 'Take the keys and drive the car to that farm we saw ahead of us and ask ... no, that'll take too long, I'll go. Stay here—there's nothing much you can do. Push the belt in further if you get the chance.' He got to his feet. 'Thank heaven you're a strapping girl with plenty of strength and common sense!'

He started to run back towards the car, leaving her smouldering; did he really regard her as strapping? He had made her sound like some muscly creature with no feminine attributes at all! Deborah chuckled and the chuckle changed to a sob which she sternly swallowed; now was no time to be feminine. She took the man's pulse once more and wondered how long she would have to wait before Gerard got back.

Not long—she saw the car racing down the road and prayed silently that there would be nothing in the way. The next minutes seemed like eternity. Deborah turned her head at length to see Gerard with four or five men, coming towards her. They were carrying ropes and when he was near enough she said in the matter-of-fact voice he would expect of her: 'His pulse is going up, but it's steady. What are you going to do?'

'Get ropes round this infernal thing and try and drag it off.'

'You'll get double hernias,' she warned him seriously.

Gerard gave a crack of laughter. 'A risk we must all take. I fear, there's no other tractor for miles around.'

He turned away from her and became immersed in the task before him. They had the ropes in place and were heaving on them steadily when the first police car arrived, disgorging two men to join the team of sweating, swearing men. The tractor shuddered and rolled over with a thud, leaving the man free just as the second police car and an ambulance arrived.

Gerard scarcely heeded them; he was on his knees, examining the man's legs. 'By some miracle,' he said quietly to Deborah, 'they're not pulped. I may be able to do something about them provided we can get at him quickly enough. Get me some splints.'

She went to meet the ambulance men making all the speed they could over the soft earth. She had no idea what the word splint was in Dutch, but luckily they were carrying an armful, so she took several from one rather astonished man, smiled at him and raced back to Gerard. He took them without a word and then said: 'Good lord, girl, what am I supposed to tie them with?'

She raced back again and this time the ambulance man ran to meet her and kept beside her as she ran back with the calico slings. There was help enough now, she stood back and waited patiently. It took a long time to get the man on to the stretcher and carry him, with infinite caution across the field to the waiting ambulance. She waited until the little procession had reached it before following it and when she reached the car there was no sign of Gerard, so she got in and sat waiting with the patience she had learned during her years of nursing. The ambulance drove off presently and one of the policemen leaned through the car window and proffered her a note—from Gerard, scribbled in his almost undecipherable scrawl. 'I must go with the ambulance to the Grotehof,' he had written on a sheet torn out of his pocket book. 'Drive the car back and wait in the hospital courtyard.' He had signed it 'G' and added a postscript: 'The BMW is just like the Fiat, only larger.'

All the same, reading these heartening words, Deborah felt a pang of nervousness; she had never driven the BMW; if she thought about it for too long she would be terrified of doing so. She thanked the policeman who saluted politely, and happily ignorant of the fact that she was almost sick with fright, drove away. It was quite five minutes before she could summon up the courage to press the self-starter.

She was still shaking when she stopped the car cautiously before the entrance to the hospital, wondering what she was supposed to do next. But Gerard had thought of that; Deborah was sitting back in her seat, taking a few calming breaths when the Medical Ward Sister, whom she had already met, popped her head through the window. 'Mevrouw van Doorninck, you will come with me, please.'

'Hullo,' said Deborah, and then: 'Why, Zuster?'

'It is the wish of Mijnheer van Doorninck.' Her tone implied that there was sufficient reason there without the need for any more questions.

'Where is he?' asked Deborah, sitting stubbornly where she was.

'In theatre, already scrubbed. But he wishes most

earnestly that you will come with me.' She added plaintively: 'I am so busy, Mevrouw.'

Deborah got out of the car at once, locked it and put the keys in her handbag. She would have to get them to Gerard somehow; she had no intention of driving through Amsterdam in the BMW—getting to the hospital had been bad enough. She shuddered and followed the Sister to the lift.

They got out on the Medical floor and she was bustled through several corridors and finally through a door. 'So—we are here,' murmured the Sister, said something to whoever was in the room, gave Deborah a smile and tore away. Deborah watched her go, knowing just how she felt; probably she was saying the Dutch equivalent of 'I'll never get finished,' as she went; even the simple task of escorting someone through the hospital could make a mockery of a tight and well-planned schedule of work.

It was Doctor Schipper inside the room waiting for her. Deborah had met him before; she and Gerard had had dinner with him and his wife only the week before. She wished him a good afternoon, a little puzzled, and he came across the little room to shake her hand.

'You are surprised, Mevrouw van Doorninck, but Gerard wishes most urgently that you should have a check-up without delay. He fears that you may have strained yourself in some way—even a small cut....'

'I'm fine,' she declared, aware of sore hands. 'Well, I've broken a few fingernails and I was scared stiff!'

A young nurse had slid into the room, so Deborah, submitting to the inevitable, allowed herself to be helped out of her deplorable dress and examined with thoroughness by Doctor Schipper. He stood back at length. 'Quite O.K.,' he assured her. 'A rapid pulse, but I imagine you had an unpleasant shock—the accident was distressing. . . .'

'Yes, but I think it was having to drive the car which scared me stiff. I only drive a Fiat 500, you know—there's quite a difference. Can I go home now?'

'Of course. Nurse will arrange for you to have a taxi, but first she will clean up your hands, and perhaps an injection of A.T.S. to be on the safe side —all that earth. . . .'

She submitted to the nurse's attentions and remembered the car keys just as she was ready to go. 'Shall I leave them at the front door?' she asked Doctor Schipper.

He held out a hand. 'Leave them with me—I'll get them to Gerard. He won't want them just yet, I imagine.'

Deborah thanked him, reminded him that he and his wife were dining with them in a few days' time and set off for the entrance with the nurse, where she climbed into a taxi and went home to find Wim and Marijke, worried about their non-appearance for lunch, waiting anxiously.

She was herself again by the evening, presenting a bandbox freshness to the world marred only by her deplorable nails and an odd bruise or two. She had deliberately put on a softly clinging dress and used her perfume with discreet lavishness; studying herself in the mirror, she decided that despite her height and curves, she looked almost fragile. She patted a stray wisp of hair into position, and much comforted by the thought, went downstairs to wait for Gerard.

He came just before dinner, gave her a brief greeting and went on: 'Well, we've saved the legs and I've done what I could with the pelvis—he's in a double hip spica.' He poured their drinks and handed hers, at the same time looking her over with what she could only describe to herself as a professional eye. 'Schipper told me that you were none the worse—you've recovered very well. Thank heaven you were with me!'

'Yes,' she spoke lightly without looking at him. 'There's nothing like beef and brawn....'

His eyes strayed over her, slowly this time and to her satisfaction, not in the least professionally. 'Did I say that? I must have been mad! Anyone less like beef and brawn I have yet to see—you look charming.'

Deborah thanked him in a level voice while her heart bounced happily. When he asked to see her hands she came and stood before him, holding them out. There were some scratches and the bruises on her knuckles were beginning to show, and the nails made her shudder. He put his drink down and stood up and surprised her very much by picking up first one hand and then the other and kissing them, and then, as if that wasn't enough, he bent his head and kissed her cheek too.

CHAPTER SEVEN

DEBORAH had gone to sleep that night in a state of mind very far removed from her usual matter-of-factness. She wakened after hours of dreaming, shreds and tatters with no beginning and no end and

132

went downstairs with the remnants of those same dreams still in her eyes. Nothing could have brought her down to earth more quickly than Gerard's brief good morning before he plunged into a list of things he begged her, if she had time, to do for him during the day—small errands which she knew quite well he would have no time to see to for himself, but it made her feel like a secretary, and from his businesslike manner he must think of her as that, or was he letting her know that his behaviour on the previous evening was a momentary weakness, not to be taken as a precedent for the future?

She went round to see her mother-in-law in the afternoon. The morning had been nicely filled with Gerard's commissions and a lesson with the professor, and now, burdened with her homework, she made her way to Mevrouw van Doorninck's flat, walking briskly because the weather, although fine, was decidedly chilly. She paused to look at one or two shops as she went; the two-piece she had worn the day before was a write-off; the earth had been ground into its fine fabric and when she had shown it to Marijke that good soul had given her opinion, with the aid of Wim, that no dry-cleaner would touch it. She would have to buy another outfit to replace it, Deborah decided, and rang the bell.

Mevrouw van Doorninck was pleased to see her. They got on very well, for the older woman had accepted her as a member of the family although she had never invited Deborah's confidence. She was urged to sit down now and tell all that had happened on the previous day.

'I didn't know you knew about it,' observed Deborah as she accepted a cup of tea.

'Gerard telephoned me in the evening—he was

so proud of you.'

Deborah managed to laugh. 'Was he? I only know that he thanked heaven that I was a strong young woman and not a—a delicate feminine creature.'

She turned her head away as she spoke; it was amazing how that still hurt. Her mother-in-law's reply was vigorous. 'You may not be delicate, my dear, but you are certainly very feminine. I can't imagine Gerard falling in love with any other type of woman.'

Deborah drank some tea. 'What about Sasja?' she asked boldly. 'Gerard told me a little about her, but what was she really like—he said that she was very pretty.'

'Very pretty—like a doll, she was also a heartless and immoral young woman and wildly extravagant. She made life for Gerard quite unbearable. And don't think, my dear,' she went on dryly, 'that I tried to interfere or influence Gerard in any way, although I longed to do so. I had to stand aside and watch Gerard make the terrible mistake of marrying her. Infatuation is far worse than love, Deborah, it blinds one to reality; it destroys ... fortunately he had his work.' She sighed. 'It is a pity that work has become such a habit with him that he hardly knows how to enjoy life any more.' She looked at Deborah, who stared back with no expression at all. 'You have found that, perhaps?'

'I know he's very busy getting everything just as he wants it at the Grotehof—I daresay when he is satisfied he'll have more time to spare.'

'Yes, dear.' Mevrouw van Doorninck's voice had that same dryness again, and Deborah wondered uneasily if she had guessed about Gerard and herself. It would be unlikely, for he always behaved beautifully towards her when there were guests or family present—he always behaved beautifully, she amended, even when they were alone. Her mother-in-law nodded. 'I'm sure you are right, my dear. Tell me, who is coming to the dinner party tomorrow evening?'

Deborah recited the names. She had met most of the guests already, there were one or two, visiting specialists, whose acquaintance she had yet to make; one of them would be spending the night. She told her mother-in-law what she intended wearing and got up to go. When she bent to kiss the older lady's cheek she was surprised at the warmth of the kiss she received in return and still more surprised when she said: 'If ever you need help or advice, Deborah, and once or twice I have thought ... no matter. If you do, come to me and I will try and help you.'

Deborah stammered her thanks and beat a hasty retreat, wondering just what Gerard's mother had meant.

She dressed early for the dinner party because she wanted to go downstairs and make sure that the table was just so, the flowers as they should be and the lamps lighted. It was to be rather a grand occasion this time because the Medical Director of the hospital was coming as well as the *Burgemeester* of the city, who, she was given to understand, was a very important person indeed. She was wearing a new dress for the occasion, a soft lavender chiffon with long full sleeves, tight cuffed with a plunging neckline discreetly veiled by pleated frills. There was a frill round the hem of the skirt too and a swathed belt which made the most of her waist. She had added the pearls and the earrings and hoped that she looked just as a successful consultant's wife should look.

'Neat but not gaudy,' she told herself aloud, inspecting her person in the big mirror on the landing, not because she hadn't seen it already in her room where there were mirrors enough, but because this particular mirror, with its elaborate gilded frame somehow enhanced her appearance.

'That's a decidedly misleading statement.' Gerard's voice came from the head of the stairs and she whirled round in a cloud of chiffon to face him.

'You're early, how nice! Everything's ready for you—I'm going down to see about the table.'

'This first.' He held out a large old-fashioned plush casket. 'You told me the colour of your dress and it seemed to me that Great-aunt Emmiline's garnets might be just the thing to go with it.'

Deborah sat down on the top tread of the staircase, her skirts billowing around her, and opened the box. Great-aunt Emmiline must have liked garnets very much; there were rings and brooches and two heavy gold bracelets set with large stones, earrings and a thick gold necklace with garnets set in it.

'They're lovely—may I really borrow them? I'll take great care. . . .'

He had come to sit beside her. 'They're yours, Deborah. I've just given them to you. I imagine you can't wear the whole lot at once, but there must be something there you like?'

'Oh, yes—yes. Thank you, Gerard, you give me so much.' She smiled at him shyly and picked out one of the bracelets and fastened it round a wrist. It looked just right; she added the necklace, putting the precious pearls in her lap. She wasn't going to take off her engagement ring; she added two of the simpler rings to the other hand and found a pair of drop earrings. She added her pearl earrings to the necklace in her lap and hooked in the garnets instead and went to look in the mirror. Gerard was right, they were exactly right with the dress. 'Have I got too much on?' she asked anxiously.

'No—just right, I should say. That's a pretty dress. What happened to the one you spoilt?'

'It's ruined. I showed it to Marijke—the stain has gone right through.'

'I'm sorry. Buy yourself another one. I'll pay for it.'

Deborah was standing with the casket clasped to her breast. 'Oh, there's no need, I've got heaps of money from my allowance.'

'Nevertheless you will allow me to pay for another dress,' he insisted blandly.

'Well—all right, thank you. I'll just put these away.'

When she came out of her room he had gone. There was nothing to do downstairs, she had seen to everything during the day and she knew that Marijke and Wim needed no prompting from her. She went and sat by the log fire Wim had lighted in the drawing room and Smith, moving with a kind of slow-motion stealth, insinuated himself on to her silken lap. But he got down again as Gerard joined them, pattering across the room when his master went to fetch the drinks and then pattering back again to arrange himself on Gerard's shoes once he had sat down. A cosy family group, thought Deborah, eyeing Gerard covertly. He looked super in a black tie—he was a man who

137

would never lose his good looks, even when he was old. She had seen photos of his father, who in his mid-seventies had been quite something—just like his son, sitting there, stroking Smith with the toe of his shoe and talking about nothing in particular. It was a relief when the doorbell signalled the arrival of the first of their guests, because she had discovered all at once that she could not bear to sit there looking at him and loving him so much.

The evening was a success, as it could hardly have failed to have been, for Deborah had planned it carefully; the food was delicious and the guests knew and liked each other. She had felt a little flustered when the *Burgemeester* had arrived, an imposing, youngish man with a small, plump wife with no looks to speak of but with a delightful smile and a charming voice. She greeted Deborah kindly, wished her happiness upon her recent marriage and in her rather schoolgirl English wanted to know if she spoke any Dutch. It was a chance to pay tribute to the professor's teaching; Deborah made a few halting remarks, shocking as to grammar but faultless as to accent. There was a good deal of kindly laughter and when the *Burgemeester* boomed: 'Your Dutch is a delight to my ear, dear lady,' her evening was made.

She had had no time to do more than say hullo to Coenraad and Adelaide, but after dinner, with the company sitting around the drawing room, the two girls managed to get ten minutes together.

'Very nice,' said Adelaide at once, 'I can see that you're going to be a wonderful wife for Gerard— it's a great drawback to a successful man if he hasn't got a wife to see to the social side. When I first married I thought it all rather a waste of time,

138

but I was wrong. They talk shop—oh, very discreetly, but they do—and arrange visits to seminars and who shall play host when so-and-so comes, and they ask each other's advice.... I like your dress, and the garnets are just the thing for it—another van Doorninck heirloom, I expect? I've got some too, only I have to be careful—my hair, you know.' She grinned engagingly. 'Did you go to Friesland?'

Deborah nodded. 'Yes, I loved the house, we had lunch there and then we went to see Dominic and Abigail. It's lovely there by the lake.'

'And what's all this about an accident? The hospital was positively humming with it. Coenraad told me about it, but you know what men are.'

They spent five minutes more together before Deborah, with a promise to telephone Adelaide in a few days, moved across the room to engage her mother-in-law in conversation.

It was after everyone had gone, and Doctor de Joufferie, their guest for the night, had retired to his room, that Gerard, on his way to let Smith out into the garden, told her that Claude was back in Amsterdam after a visit to Nice. 'I hear he's sold his house here and intends to live in France permanently.'

'Oh.' She paused uncertainly on her way to bed. 'He won't come here?'

'Most unlikely—if he does, would you mind?'

Deborah shook her head. 'Not in the least,' she assured her husband stoutly, minding very much.

Her answer was what he had expected, for he remarked casually 'No, you're far too sensible for that and I have no doubt that you would deal with him should he have the temerity to call.' He turned away. 'That's a pretty dress,' he told her for the second time that evening.

She thanked him nicely, wishing that he had thought her pretty enough to remark upon that too; apparently he was satisfied enough that she was sensible.

She ruminated so deeply upon this unsatisfactory state of affairs that she hardly heard his thanks for the success of the evening, but she heard him out, murmured something inaudible about being tired, and went to bed.

Doctor de Joufferie joined them for breakfast in the morning, speaking an English almost as perfect as Gerard's. The two men spent most of the time discussing the possibility of Gerard going to Paris for some conference or other: 'And I hope very much that you will accompany your husband,' their visitor interrupted himself to say. 'My wife would be delighted to show you a little of Paris while we are at the various sessions.'

Deborah gave him a vague, gracious answer; she didn't want to hurt the doctor's feelings, but on the other hand she wasn't sure whether Gerard would want her to go with him; he had never suggested, even remotely, such a possibility. She led the conversation carefully back to the safe ground of Paris and its delights, at the same time glancing at her husband to see how he was reacting. He wasn't, his expression was politely attentive and nothing more, but then it nearly always was; even if he had no wish to take her, he would never dream of saying so.

The two men left together and she accompanied them to the door, to be pleasantly surprised at the admiration in the Frenchman's eyes as he kissed her hand with the hope that they might meet again soon. She glowed pleasantly under his look, but the glow was damped immediately by Gerard's brief, cool kiss which just brushed her cheek.

She spent an hour or so pottering round the house, getting in Wim's way, and then went to sit with her Dutch lesson, but she was in no mood to learn. She flung the books pettishly from her and went out. Gerard had told her to buy a new dress— all right, so she would, and take good care not to look too closely at the price tag. She walked along the Keizersgracht until she came to that emporium of high fashion, Metz, and once inside, buoyed up by strong feelings which she didn't bother to define, she went straight to the couture department. She had in mind another tweed outfit, or perhaps one of the thicker jersey suits. She examined one or two, a little shocked at their prices, although even after so short a time married to Gerard, she found that her shock was lessening.

It was while she was prowling through the thickly carpeted alcove which held the cream of the Autumn collection that she saw the dress—a Gina Fratini model for the evening—white silk, high-necked and long-sleeved, pin-tucked and gathered and edged with antique lace. Deborah examined it more closely; it wouldn't be her size, of course, and even if it were, when would she wear it, and what astronomical price would it be? She circled round it once more; it would do very well for the big ball Gerard had casually mentioned would take place at the hospital before Christmas, and what about the *Burgemeester's* reception? But the size? The saleswoman, who had been hovering discreetly, pounced delicately. She even remembered Deborah's name, so that she felt like an old and valued customer, and what was more, her English was good.

'A lovely gown, Mevrouw van Doorninck,' she said persuasively, 'and so right for you, and I fancy it is your size.' She had it over her arm now, yards and yards of soft silk. 'Would you care to try it on?'

'Well,' said Deborah weakly, 'I really came in for something in tweed or jersey.' She caught the woman's eye and smiled. 'Yes, I'll try it on.'

It was a perfect fit and utterly lovely. She didn't need the saleswoman's flattering remarks to know it. The dress did something for her, although she wasn't sure what. She said quickly, before she should change her mind: 'I'll take it—will you charge it to my husband, please?'

It was when she was dressed again, watching it being lovingly packed, that she asked the price. She had expected it to be expensive, but the figure the saleswoman mentioned so casually almost took her breath. Deborah waited for a feeling of guilt to creep over her, and felt nothing; Gerard had insisted on paying for a dress, hadn't he? Declining an offer to have it delivered, she carried her precious box home.

She would have tried it on then and there, but Wim met her in the hall with the news that Marijke had a delicious soufflé only waiting to be eaten within a few minutes. But eating lunch by herself was something quickly done with, so she flew upstairs to her room and unpacked the dress. It looked even more super than it had done in the shop. She put it on and went to turn and twist before the great mirror—she had put on the pearls and the earrings and a pair of satin slippers; excepting for the faint untidiness of the heavy chignon, she looked ready

142

for a ball.

'Cinderella, and more beautiful than ever,' said Claude from the stairs.

Deborah turned round slowly, not quite believing that he was there, but he was, smiling and debonair, for all the world as though Gerard had never told him not to enter the house again.

'What are you doing here?' she asked, and tried to keep the angry shake from her voice.

'Why, come to pay you a farewell visit. I'm leaving this city, thank heaven, surely you've heard that? But I couldn't go until I had said goodbye to you, but don't worry, I telephoned the hospital and they told me that Gerard was busy, so I knew that it was safe to come, and very glad I am that I did. A ball so early in the day? Or is the boy-friend coming?'

Her hand itched to slap his smiling face. 'How silly you are,' she remarked scathingly. 'And you have no right to walk into the house as though it were your own. Why didn't you ring the bell?'

'Ah, I came in through the little door in the garden. You forget, my lovely Deborah, that I have known this house since many years; many a time I've used that door.' He was lounging against the wall, laughing at her, so that her carefully held patience deserted her.

'Well, you can go, and out of the front door this time. I've nothing to say to you, and I'm sure Gerard would be furious if he knew that you had come here.'

He snapped his fingers airily. 'My dear good girl, let us be honest, you have no idea whether Gerard would be annoyed or not; you have no idea about anything he does or thinks or plans, have you? I don't suppose he tells you anything. Shall I tell you what I think? Why, that you're a figurehead to adorn his table, a hostess for his guests and a competent housekeeper to look after his home while he's away—and where does he go, I wonder? Have you ever wondered? Hours in the Grotehof—little trips to Paris, Brussels, Vienna, operating here, lecturing there while you sit at home thinking what thoughts?'

He stopped speaking and stared at her pinched face. 'I'm right, aren't I? I have hit the nail on its English head, have I not? Poor beautiful Deborah.' He laughed softly and came closer. 'Leave him, my lovely, and come to Nice with me—why not? We could have a good time together.'

She wasn't prepared for his sudden swoop; she was a strong girl, but he had hold of her tightly, and besides, at the back of her stunned mind was the thought that if she struggled too much her beautiful dress would be ruined. She turned her face away as he bent to kiss her and brought up a hand to box him soundly on the ear. But he laughed the more as she strained away from him, her head drawn back. So that she didn't see or hear Gerard coming up the stairs, although Claude did. She felt his hold tighten as he spoke.

'Gerard—hullo, *jongen,* I knew you wouldn't mind me calling in to say goodbye to Deborah, and bless her heart, she wouldn't let me go without one last kiss.'

She felt him plucked from her, heard, as in a dream, his apology, no doubt induced by the painful grip Gerard had upon him, and watched in a detached way as he was marched down the stairs across the hall to disappear in the direction of the front door, which presently shut with some force. Gerard wasn't even breathing rapidly when he rejoined her, only his eyes blazed in his set face.

'You knew he was coming?' His tone was conversational but icy.

'Of course not.' She was furious to find that she was trembling.

'How did he get in? Doesn't Wim open the door?'

'Of course he does—when the bell rings. He—he came in through the door in the garden. I had no idea that he was in the house until he spoke to me here.' She essayed a smile which wavered a little. 'I'm glad you came home.'

'Yes?' His eyebrows rose in faint mockery. 'You didn't appear to be resisting Claude with any great show of determination.'

She fired up at that. 'He took me by surprise. I slapped his cheek.'

'Did you call Wim?'

Deborah shook her head. Truth to tell, it hadn't entered her head.

Her husband stared at her thoughtfully. 'A great strapping girl like you,' he commented nastily. 'No kicking? No struggling?'

She hated him, mostly because he had called her a strapping girl. She wanted to cry too, but the tears were in a hard knot in her chest. She said sullenly: 'I was trying on this dress—it's new....' He laughed then and she said desperately: 'You don't believe me, do you? You actually think that I would encourage him.' Her voice rose with the strength of her feelings. 'Well, if that's what you want to believe, you may do so!'

She swept to her bedroom door and remembered

something as she reached it. 'I bought this dress because you told me to and I've charged it to you— it's a model and it cost over a thousand gulden, and I'm glad!' She stamped her foot. 'I wish it had cost twice as much!'

She banged the door behind her and locked it, which was a silly action anyway, for when had he ever tried the door handle?

She took the dress off carefully and hung it away and put on a sober grey dress, then combed her hair and put on too much lipstick and went downstairs. She was crossing the hall when Gerard opened his study door and invited her to join him in a quiet voice which she felt would be wiser to obey. She went past him with her head in the air and didn't sit down when he asked her to.

'I came home to pack a bag,' he told her mildly, all trace of ill-humour vanished. 'There is an urgent case I have to see in Geneva and probably operate on. I intend to catch the five o'clock flight and I daresay I shall be away for two days. I'm sorry to spring it on you like this, but there's nothing important for a few days, is there?'

'Nothing.' Wild horses wouldn't have dragged from her the information that it was her birthday in two days' time. She had never mentioned it to him and he had never tried to find out.

He nodded. 'Good——' he broke off as Wim came in with a sheaf of flowers which he gave to Deborah. 'Just delivered, Mevrouw,' he told her happily, and went away, leaving a heavy silence behind him.

Deborah started to open the envelope pinned to its elaborate wrapping and then stopped; supposing it was from Claude? It was the sort of diabolical joke he would dream up. . . .

She looked up and found Gerard watching her with a speculative eye and picked up the flowers and walked to the door. 'I'll pack you a case,' she told him. 'Will you want a black tie, or is it to be strictly work?'

His eyes narrowed. 'Oh, strictly work,' he assured her in a silky voice, 'and even if it weren't, a black tie isn't always essential in order to—er—enjoy yourself.'

He gave her a look of such mockery that she winced under it; it was almost as if Claude's poisoned remarks held a grain of truth.

Outside she tore open the little envelope and read the card; the flowers were from Doctor Joufferie. She suppressed her strong desire to run straight back to Gerard and show it to him, and went to pack his bag instead.

It was quiet in the house after he had gone. Deborah spent the long evening working at her Dutch, playing with Smith and leafing through magazines, and went to bed at last with a bad headache. She had expected Gerard to telephone, but he didn't, which made the headache worse. There was no call in the morning either; she hung around until lunchtime and then went out with Smith trotting beside her on his lead. She walked for a long time, and it was on her way back, close to the house, that she stopped to pick up a very small child who had fallen over, the last in a line of equally small uniformed children, walking ahead of her. She had seen them before, and supposed that they went to some nursery school or other in one of the narrow streets leading from the Keizersgracht. She comforted the little girl, mopped up a

147

grazed knee and carried her towards the straggling line of her companions. She had almost reached it when a nun darted back towards them, breaking into voluble Dutch as she did so.

Deborah stood still. 'So sorry,' she managed, 'my Dutch is bad.'

The nun smiled. 'Then I will speak my bad English to you. Thank you for helping the little one—there are so many of them and my companion has gone on to the Weeshuis with a message.'

Deborah glanced across the road to where an old building stood under the shadow of the great Catholic church. 'Oh,' she said, and remembered that a Weeshuis was an orphanage. 'They're little orphans.'

The nun smiled again. 'Yes. We have many of them. The older ones go to school, but these are still too small. We go now to play and sing a little after their walk. Once we had a lady who came each week and told them stories and played games with them. They liked that.' She held out her arms for the child and said: 'I thank you again, Mevrouw,' and walked rapidly away to where the obedient line of children waited. Deborah watched them disappear inside the orphanage before she went home.

It was after her lonely tea that she had an idea. Without pausing to change her mind, she left the house and went back to the orphanage and rang the bell, and when an old nun came to peer at her through the grille, she asked to see the Mother Superior. Half an hour later she was back home again after an interview with that rather surprised lady; she might go once a week and play with the children until such time as a permanent helper could be found. She had pointed out hesitantly that she wasn't a Catholic herself, but the Mother Superior didn't seem to mind. Thursday evenings, she had suggested, and any time Deborah found the little orphans too much for her, she had only to say so.

The morning post brought a number of cards and parcels for her. She read them while she ate her breakfast and was just getting up from the table when Wim came in with a great bouquet of flowers and a gaily tied box.

'Mijnheer told me to give you these, Mevrouw,' he informed her in a fatherly fashion, 'and Marijke and I wish you a very happy birthday.' He produced a small parcel with the air of a magician and she opened it at once. Handkerchiefs. dainty, lace-trimmed ones. She thanked him nicely, promised that she would go to the kitchen within a few minutes so that she could thank Marijke, and was left to examine her flowers. They were exquisite; roses and carnations and sweet peas and lilies, out of season and delicate and fragrant. She sniffed at them with pleasure and read the card which accompanied them. It bore the austere message: With best wishes, G. So he had known all the time! She opened the box slowly; it contained a set of dressing table silver, elegantly plain with her initials on each piece surmounted by the family crest. There was another card too, less austere than its fellow. This one said: 'To Deborah, wishing you a happy birthday.'

She went upstairs and arranged the silver on her dressing table, and stood admiring it until she remembered that she had to see Marijke. She spent a long time arranging the flowers so that she was a

149

little late for her lesson and Professor de Wit was a little put out, but she had learnt her lesson well, which mollified him sufficiently for him to offer her a cup of coffee when they had finished wrestling with the Dutch verbs for the day. She went back home presently to push the food around her plate and then go upstairs to her room. Her mother-in-law was in Hilversum, she could hardly telephone Adelaide and tell her that it was her birthday and she was utterly miserable. Thank heaven it was Thursday; at least she had her visit to the orphans to look forward to.

There was still no word from Gerard. Deborah told Wim that she was going for a walk and would be back for dinner at half past seven as usual, and set out. The evenings were chilly now and the streets were crowded with people on their way home or going out to enjoy themselves, but the narrow street where the orphanage was was quiet as she rang the bell.

The orphans assembled for their weekly junketings in a large, empty room overlooking the street, reached through a long narrow passage and a flight of steps, and one of the dreariest rooms Deborah had ever seen, but there was a piano and plenty of room for twenty-eight small children. It was when she had thrown off her coat and turned to survey them that she remembered that her Dutch was, to say the least, very indifferent. But she had reckoned without the children; within five minutes they had discovered the delights of 'Hunt the Slipper' and were screaming their heads off.

At the end of the hour they had mastered Grandmother's Steps too as well as Twos and Threes, and for the last ten minutes or so, in order that they might calm down a little, she began to tell them a story, mostly in English of course, with a few Dutch words thrown in here and there and a great deal of mime. It seemed to go down very well, as did the toffees Deborah produced just before the nun came to fetch them away to their supper and bed. An hour had never gone so quickly. She kissed them good night, one by one, and when they had gone the empty room seemed emptier and drearier than ever. She tidied it up quickly and went home.

Indoors, it was to hear from Wim that Gerard had telephoned, but only to leave a message that he would be home the following evening. Deborah thanked him and went to eat her dinner, choking it down as best she could because Marijke had thought up a splendid one for her birthday. Afterwards, with Smith on her lap, she watched T.V. It was a film she had already seen several times in England, but she watched it to its end before going to bed.

Gerard came home late the following afternoon. Deborah had spent the day wondering how to greet him. As though nothing had happened? With an apology? She ruled this one out, for she had nothing to apologize for—with a dignified statement pointing out how unfair he had been? She was still rehearsing a variety of opening speeches when she heard his key in the door.

There was no need for her to make a speech of any kind; it riled her to find that his manner was exactly as it always was, quiet, pleasant—he was even smiling. Taken aback, Deborah replied to his cheerful hullo with a rather uncertain one followed by the hope that he had had a good trip and that everything had been successful. And would he like something to eat?

He declined her offer on his way to the door. 'I've some telephoning to do,' he told her. 'The post is in the study, I suppose?'

She said that yes, it was and as he reached the door, said in a rush: 'Thank you for the lovely flowers and your present—it's quite super—I didn't know that you knew....'

'Our marriage certificate,' he pointed out briefly. 'I'm sorry I was not here to celebrate it in the usual Dutch manner—another year, perhaps.'

'No, well—it didn't matter. It's a marvellous present.'

Gerard was almost through the door. He paused long enough to remark:

'I'm glad you like it. It seemed to me to be a suitable gift.' He didn't look at her and his voice sounded cold. He closed the door very quietly behind him.

Deborah threw a cushion at it. 'I hate him,' she raged, 'hate him! He's pompous and cold and he doesn't care a cent for me, not one cent—a suitable present indeed! And just what was he doing in Geneva?' she demanded of the room at large. She plucked a slightly outraged Smith from the floor and hugged him to her. 'None of that's true,' she assured him fiercely, and opened the door and let him into the hall. She heard him scratching on the study door and after a few moments it was opened for him.

They dined together later, apparently on the best of terms; Deborah told Gerard one or two items which she thought might interest him, but never a word about the orphans, The van Doornincks were Calvinists; several ancestors had been put to death rather nastily by the Spaniards during their occupation of the Netherlands. It was a very long time ago, but the Dutch had long memories for such things. She didn't think that Gerard would approve of her helping, even for an hour, in a convent. Her conscience pricked her a little because she was being disloyal to him; on the other hand, she wasn't a Catholic either, but that hadn't made any difference to her wish to help the children in some small way. She put the matter out of her mind and asked him as casually as possible about his trip to Geneva.

She might have saved her breath, for although he talked about Switzerland and Geneva in particular, not one crumb of information as to his activities while he was there did he offer her. She rose from the table feeling frustrated and ill-tempered and spent the rest of the evening sitting opposite him in the sitting room, doing her embroidery all wrong. Just the same, when she went to bed she said quite humbly: 'I'm really very sorry to have bought such an expensive dress, Gerard—I'll pay you back out of my next quarter's allowance.'

'I offered you a new dress,' he reminded her suavely. 'I don't remember telling you to buy the cheapest one you saw. Shall we say no more about it?'

Upon which unsatisfactory remark she went to bed.

It didn't seem possible that they could go on as before, with no mention of Claude, no coolness between them, no avoiding of each other's company, but it was. Deborah found that life went on exactly as before, with occasional dinner parties, drinks with friends, visits to her mother-in-law and Gerard's family and an occasional quiet evening at home with Gerard—and of course the weekly visit to the orphans.

It was getting colder now, although the autumn had stretched itself almost into winter with its warm days and blue skies. But now the trees by the canal were without leaves and the water looked lifeless; it was surprising what a week or so would do at that time of year, and that particular evening, coming home from the convent, there was an edge of winter in the air.

Deborah found Gerard at home. He was always late on Thursdays and when she walked into the sitting room and found him there she was surprised into saying so.

'I've been out,' she explained a little inadequately. 'It was such a nice evening,' and then could have bitten out her tongue, for there was a nasty wind blowing and the beginnings of a fine, cold rain. She put a guilty hand up to her hair and felt its dampness.

'I'll tell Marijke to serve dinner at once,' she told him, 'and change my dress.'

That had been a silly thing to say too, for the jersey suit she was wearing was decidedly crumpled from the many small hands which had clung to it. But Gerard said nothing and if his hooded eyes noticed anything, they gave nothing away. She joined him again presently and spent the evening waiting for him to ask her where she had been, and when he didn't, went to bed in a fine state of nervous tension.

Several days later he told her that he would be going away again for a day and possibly the night as well.

'Not Geneva?' asked Deborah, too quickly.

He was in the garden, brushing Smith. 'No— Arnhem.'

'But Arnhem is only a short distance away,' she pointed out, 'surely you could come home?'

He raised his eyes to hers. 'If I should come home, it would be after ten o'clock,' he told her suavely. 'That is a certainty, so that you can safely make any plans you wish for the evening.'

She stared at him, puzzled. 'But I haven't any plans—where should I want to go?'

He shrugged. 'Where do you go on Thursday evenings?' he asked blandly, and when she hesitated, "That was unfair of me—I'm sorry. I only learned of it through overhearing something Wim said. Perhaps you would rather not tell me.'

'No—that is, no,' she answered miserably. 'I don't think so.'

Gerard flashed her a quizzical glance. 'Quid pro quo?' he asked softly.

She flushed and lifted her chin. 'When I married you, you made it very clear what you expected of me. Maybe I've fallen short of—of your expectations, but I have done my best, but I wouldn't stoop to paying you back in your own coin!'

She flounced out of the room before he could speak and went to her room and banged the door. They were going out that evening to dinner with a colleague of Gerard's. She came downstairs at exactly the moment when it was necessary to leave the house, looking quite magnificent in the pink silk jersey dress and the pearls and with such a haughty expression upon her lovely face that Gerard, after the briefest of glances, forbore from speaking. When she peeped at him his face was impassive, but she had the ridiculous feeling that he was laughing at her.

He had left the house when she got down in the morning. She had breakfast, did a few chores around the house and prepared to go out. She was actually at the front door when the telephone rang and when she answered it, it was to hear Sien's voice, a little agitated, asking for Gerard.

'Wim,' called Deborah urgently, and made placating noises to Sien, and when he came: 'It's Sien —I can't understand her very well, but I think there's something wrong.'

Sien had cut her hand, Wim translated, and it was the local doctor's day off and no one near enough to help; the season was over, the houses, and they were only a few, within reach were closed for the winter. She had tied her hand up, but it had bled a great deal. Perhaps she needed stitches? and would Mevrouw forgive her for telephoning, but she wasn't sure what she should do.

'Ask her where the cut is,' commanded Deborah, 'and if it's still bleeding.' And when Wim had told her, gave careful instructions: 'And tell her to sit down and try and keep her arm up, and that I'm on my way now—I'll be with her in less than two hours.'

She was already crossing the hall to Gerard's study where she knew there was a well-stocked cupboard of all she might require. She chose what she needed and went to the front door. 'I don't know how long I shall be, Wim,' she said. 'You'd better keep Smith here. I expect I may have to take Sien to hospital for some stitches and then try and find someone who would stay a day or two with her —she can't be alone.'

'Very good, Mevrouw,' said Wim in his fatherly fashion, 'and I beg you to be careful on the road.'

She smiled at him—he was such an old dear. 'Of course, Wim, I'll be home later.'

'And if the master should come home?'

Deborah didn't look at him. 'He said after ten this evening, or even tomorrow, Wim.'

She drove the Fiat fast and without any hold-ups, for the tourists had gone and the roads were fairly empty; as she slowed to turn into the little lane leading to the house she thought how lovely it looked against the pale sky and the wide country around it, but she didn't waste time looking around her; she parked the car and ran inside.

Sien had done exactly as she had been told. She looked a little pale and the rough bandage was heavily bloodstained, but she greeted Deborah cheerfully and submitted to having the cut examined.

'A stitch or two,' explained Deborah in her threadbare Dutch, knowing that it would need far more than that, for the cut was deep and long, across the palm.

'Coffee,' she said hearteningly, and made it for both of them, then helped Sien to put on her coat and best hat—for was she not going to hospital to see a doctor, she wanted to know when Deborah brought the wrong one—locked the door and settled her companion in the little car. It wasn't far to Leeuwarden and Sien knew where the hospital was.

She hadn't known that Gerard was known there too. She only had to give her name and admit to being his wife for Sien to be given V.I.P. treatment. She was stitched, given A.T.S., told when to come again and given another cup of coffee while Deborah had a little talk with the Casualty Officer.

'Can I help you at all?' he wanted to know as he handed her coffee too.

She explained thankfully about Sien being alone. 'If someone could find out if she has a friend or family nearby who would go back with her for a day or two, I could collect them on the way back. If not, I think I should take her back with me to Amsterdam or stay here myself.'

She waited patiently while Sien was questioned. 'There's a niece,' the young doctor told her, 'she lives at Warga, quite close to your house. Your housekeeper says that she will be pleased to stay with her for a few days.'

'You're very kind,' said Deborah gratefully. 'It's a great hindrance not being able to speak the language, you know. My husband will be very grateful when he hears how helpful you have been.'

The young man went a dusky red. 'Your husband is a great surgeon, Mevrouw. We would all wish to be like him.'

She shook hands. 'I expect you will be,' she assured him, and was rewarded by his delighted smile.

Sien's niece was a young edition of her aunt, just as tall and plump and just as sensible. Deborah drove the two of them back to the house, gave instructions that they were to telephone the house at Amsterdam if they were in doubt about anything, asked them if they had money enough, made sure that Sien understood about the pills she was to take if her hand got too painful, wished them goodbye, and got into the Fiat again. It was early afternoon, she would be home for tea.

CHAPTER EIGHT

But she wasn't home for tea; it began to rain as she reached the outskirts of the city, picking her careful way through streets which became progressively narrower and busier as she neared the heart of the city. The cobbles glistened in the rain, their surface made treacherous; Deborah had no chance at all when a heavy lorry skidded across the street, sweeping her little car along with it. By some miracle the Fiat stayed upright despite the ominous crunching noises it was making. Indeed, its bonnet was a shapeless mass by the time the lorry came to a precarious halt with Deborah's car inextricably welded to it.

She climbed out at once, white and shaking but quite unhurt except for one or two sharp knocks. The driver of the lorry got out too to engage her immediately in earnest conversation, not one word of which did she understand. Dutch, she had discovered long since, wasn't too bad provided one had the time and the circumstances were favourable. They were, at the moment, very unfavourable. She looked round helplessly, not at all sure what to do—there were a dozen or more people milling about them, all seemingly proffering advice.

'Can't anyone speak English?' she asked her growing audience. Apparently not; there was a short pause before they all burst out again, even more eager to help. It was a relief when Deborah glimpsed the top of a policeman's cap above the heads, forging its way with steady authority towards her. Presently he came into full view, a grizzled man with a harsh face. Her heart sank; awful visions of spending the night in prison and no one any the wiser were floating through her bemused brain. When he spoke to her she asked, without any hope at all: 'I suppose you don't speak English?'

He smiled and his face wasn't harsh any more. 'A little,' he admitted. 'I will speak to this man first, Mevrouw.'

The discussion was lengthy with a good deal of argument. When at length the police officer turned to her she hastened to tell him:

'It wasn't anyone's fault—the road was slippery —he skidded, he wasn't driving fast at all.'

The man answered in a laboured English which was more than adequate. 'He tells me that also, Mevrouw. You have your papers?'

She managed to open the car's battered door and took them out of her handbag. He examined her licence and then looked at her. 'You are wife of Mijnheer Doorninck, *chirurg* at the Grotehof hospital.'

She nodded.

'You are not injured, Mevrouw?'

'I don't think so—I feel a little shaky.' She smiled. 'I was scared stiff!'

'Stiff?' He eyed her anxiously.

'Sorry—I was frightened.'

'I shall take you to the hospital in one moment.' He was writing in his notebook. 'You will sit in your car, please.'

Deborah did as she was told and he went back to talk some more to the lorry driver, who presently got into his cab and drove away.

'It will be arranged that your car'—his eye swept

over the poor remnant of it—'will be taken to a garage. Do not concern yourself about it, Mevrouw. Now you will come with me, please.'

'I'm quite all right,' she assured him, and then at his look, followed him obediently to the police car behind the crowd, glad to sit down now, for her legs were suddenly jelly and one arm was aching.

They were close to the hospital. She was whisked there, swept from the car and ushered into the Accident Room where Gerard's name acted like a magic wand; she barely had time to thank the policeman warmly before she was spirited away to be meticulously examined from head to foot. There was nothing wrong, the Casualty Officer decided, save for a few painful bruises on her arm and the nasty shock she had had.

'I will telephone and inform Mijnheer van Doorninck,' he told her, and she stifled a giggle, for Gerard's name had been uttered with such reverence. 'He's not home,' she told him, 'not until late this evening or tomorrow morning—he's in Arnhem. In any case, I'm perfectly all right.'

She should have suspected him when he agreed with her so readily, suggesting that she should drink a cup of tea and have a short rest, then he would come back and pronounce her fit to go home.

She drank the tea gratefully. There was no milk with it, but it was hot and sweet and it pulled her together and calmed her down. She lay back and closed her eyes and wondered what Gerard would say when he got back. She was asleep in five minutes.

She slept for just over an hour and when she wakened Gerard was there, staring down at her, his blue eyes blazing from a white face. She wondered, only half awake, why he looked so furiously angry, and then remembered where she was.

She exclaimed unhappily: 'Oh, dear—were you home after all? But I did tell them not to telephone the house. . . .'

'I was telephoned at Arnhem. How do you feel?'

Deborah ignored that. 'The fools,' she said crossly, 'I told them you were busy, that there was no need to bother you.'

'They quite rightly ignored such a foolish remark. How do you feel?' he repeated.

She swung her legs off the couch to let him see just how normal she was. 'Perfectly all right, thank you—such a fuss about nothing.' She gulped suddenly. 'I'm so sorry, Gerard, I've made you angry, haven't I? You didn't have to give up the case or anything awful like that?'

His grim mouth relaxed into the faintest of smiles. 'No—I had intended returning home this evening, anyway. And I am not angry.'

She eyed him uncertainly. 'You look. . . .' She wasn't sure how he looked; probably he was tired after a long-drawn-out operation. She forced her voice to calm. 'I'm perfectly able to go home now, Gerard, if that's convenient for you.'

He said slowly, studying his hands: 'Is that how you think of me? As someone whose wishes come before everything else? Who doesn't give a damn when his wife is almost killed—a heartless tyrant?'

She was sitting on the side of the couch, conscious that her hair was an untidy mop halfway down her neck and that she had lost the heel of a shoe and her stockings were laddered. 'You're not a heartless tyrant,' she protested hotly. 'You're not—

you're a kind and considerate husband. Can't you see that's why I hate to hinder you in any way? It's the least I can do—I'd rather die. ...'

She had said too much, she realized that too late.

'Just what do you mean by that?' he asked her sharply.

Deborah opened her mouth, not having any idea what to say and was saved from making matters worse by the entry of the Casualty Officer, eager to know if she felt up to going home and obviously pleased with himself because he had come under the notice of one of the most eminent consultants in the hospital and treated his wife to boot. He was a worthy young man, his thoughts were written clearly on his face, Deborah thanked him cordially and was pleased when Gerard added his own thanks with a warmth to make the young man flush with pleasure. She hadn't realized that Gerard was held in such veneration by the hospital staff; the things she didn't know about him were so many that it was a little frightening—certainly they were seen to the entrance by an imposing number of people.

The BMW was parked right in front of the steps; anyone else, she felt sure would have been ordered to move their car, for no one could get near the entrance, but no one seemed to find anything amiss. Gerard helped her in and she sat back with a sigh. As he drove through the hospital gateway she said apologetically: 'The police said they would take the Fiat away and they'd let you know about it. It—it's a bit battered.'

'It can be scrapped.' His voice was curt. 'I'll get you a new car.'

That was all he said on the way home and she

could think of nothing suitable to talk about herself. Besides, her head had begun to ache. Wim and Marijke were both hovering in the hall when they got in. Gerard said something to them in Dutch and Marijke came forward, talking volubly.

'Marijke will help you to bed,' Gerard explained. 'I suggest that you have something to eat there and then get a good sleep—you'll feel quite the thing by the morning.' His searching eyes rested for a brief, professional minute on her face. 'You have a headache, I daresay, I'll give you something for that presently. Go up to bed now.'

She would have liked to have disputed his order, but when she considered it, bed was the one place where she most wanted to be. She thanked him in a subdued voice and went upstairs, Marijke in close attendance.

She wasn't hungry, she discovered, when she was tucked up against her pillows and Marijke had brought in a tray of soup and chicken. She took a few mouthfuls, put the tray on the side table and lay back and closed her eyes, to open them at once as Gerard came in after the most perfunctory of knocks. He walked over to the bed, took her pulse, studied the bruises beginning to show on her arm, and then stood looking down at her with the expression she imagined he must wear when he was examining his patients—a kind of reserved kindliness. 'You've not eaten anything,' he observed.

'I'm not very hungry.'

He nodded, shook some pills out of the box he held, fetched water from the carafe on the table and said: 'Swallow these down—they'll take care of that headache and send you to sleep.'

She did as she was bid and lay back again against

the pillows.

'Ten minutes?' she wanted to know. 'Pills always seem to take so long to work.'

'Then we might as well talk while we're waiting,' he said easily, and sat down on the end of the bed. 'Tell me, what is all this about Sien? Wim tells me that you went up to Domwier because she had cut her hand.'

'Yes—the doctor wasn't there and it sounded as though it might have needed a stitch or two—she had six, actually. I—I thought you would want me to look after her as you weren't home.'

He took her hand lying on the coverlet and his touch was gentle. 'Yes, of course that was exactly what I should have wanted you to do, Deborah. Was it a bad cut?'

She told him; she told him about their visit to the hospital at Leeuwarden too, adding: 'They knew you quite well there—I didn't know....' There was such a lot she didn't know, she thought wearily. 'I got the doctor there to find out if Sien had any friends or family—I fetched her niece, they seemed quite happy together.' She blinked huge, drowsy eyes. 'I forgot—I said I would telephone and make sure that Sien was all right. Could someone...?'

'I'll see to it. Thank you, my dear. What a competent girl you are, but you always were in theatre and you're just as reliable now.'

She was really very sleepy, but she had to answer that. 'No, I'm not. I bought that terribly expensive dress just to annoy you—and what about Claude? Have you forgotten him? You thought I was quite unreliable with him, didn't you?'

She was aware that her tongue was running away

with her, but she seemed unable to help herself. 'Don't you know that I... ?' She fell asleep, just in time.

She was perfectly all right in the morning except for a badly discoloured arm. All the same, Marijke brought her breakfast up on a tray with the injunction, given with motherly sternness, to eat it up, and she was closely followed by Gerard, who wished her a placid good morning and cast a quick eye over her. 'I've told Wim,' he said as he was leaving after the briefest of stays, 'that if anyone telephones about the Fiat that he is to refer them to me. And by the way, Sien is quite all right. I telephoned last night and again this morning. She sends her respects.'

Deborah smiled. 'How very old-fashioned that sounds, and how nice! But she's a nice person, isn't she? I can't wait to learn a little of her language so that we can really talk.'

He smiled. 'She would like that. But first your Dutch—it's coming along very nicely, Deborah—your grammar is a little wild, but your accent is impeccable.'

She flushed with pleasure. 'Oh, do you really mean that? Professor de Wit is so loath to praise. I sometimes feel that I'm making no headway at all.' She smiled at him. 'I'm glad you're pleased.'

He opened the door without answering her. 'I shouldn't do too much today,' was all he said as he went.

If he had been there for her to say it to, she would have told him that she didn't do too much anyway because there was nothing for her to do, but that would have sounded ungrateful; he had given her everything she could possibly want—a lovely home, clothes beyond her wildest dreams, a car, an allowance which she secretly felt was far too generous—all these, and none of them worth a cent without his love and interest. She had sometimes wondered idly what the term 'an empty life' had meant. Now she knew, although it wouldn't be empty if he loved her; then everything which they did would be shared—the dinner parties, the concerts, the visits to friends, just as he would share the burden of his work with her. Deborah sighed and got out of bed and went to look out of the window. It was a cold, clear morning. She got dressed and presently telephoned Adelaide van Essen and invited her round for coffee.

It was two days later that Deborah mentioned at breakfast that she had never seen Gerard's consulting rooms and, to her surprise, was invited to visit them that very day.

'I shan't be there,' he explained with his usual courtesy. 'I don't see patients there on a Thursday afternoon—it's my heavy afternoon list at the Grotehof, but go along by all means. Trudi, my secretary, will be there—her English is just about as good as your Dutch, so you should get on very well together.'

He had left soon afterwards, leaving her a prey to a variety of feelings, not the least of which was the sobering one that he had shown no visible regret at not being able to take her himself. Still, it would be something to do.

She went after lunch, in a new tweed suit because the sun was shining, albeit weakly. She was conscious that she looked rather dishy and consoled herself with the thought that at last she was being allowed to see another small, very small, facet of

Gerard's life.

The consulting rooms were within walking distance, in a quiet square lined with tall brick houses, almost all of which had brass plates on their doors—a kind of Dutch Harley Street, she gathered, and found Gerard's name quickly enough. His rooms were on the first floor and Deborah was impressed by their unobtrusive luxury; pale grey carpet, solid, comfortable chairs, small tables with flowers, and in one corner a desk where Trudi sat.

Trudi was young and pretty and dressed discreetly in grey to match the carpet. She welcomed Deborah a little nervously in an English as bad as her Dutch and showed her round, leaving Gerard's own room till last. It too was luxurious, deliberately comfortable and relaxing so that the patient might feel at ease. She smiled and nodded as Trudi rattled on, not liking to ask too many questions because, as Gerard's wife, she should already know the answers. They had a cup of tea together presently and because Trudi kept looking anxiously at the clock, Deborah got up to go. Probably the poor girl had a great deal of work to do before she could leave. She was halfway across the sea of carpet when the door opened and Claude came in. She was so surprised that she came to a halt, her mouth open, but even in her surprise she saw that he was taken aback, annoyed too. He cast a lightning glance at Trudi and then back to Deborah. 'Hullo, my beauty,' he said.

She ignored that. 'What are you doing here?' she demanded, 'I'm quite sure that Gerard doesn't know. What do you want?'

He still looked shaken, although he replied airily enough. 'Oh, nothing much. Trudi has something for me, haven't you, darling?'

The girl looked so guilty that Deborah felt sorry for her. 'Yes—yes, I have. It's downstairs, I'll get it.'

She fled through the door leaving Deborah frowning at Claude's now smiling face. 'What are you up to?' she wanted to know.

'I?' he smiled even more widely. 'My dear girl, nothing. Surely I can come and see my friends without you playing the schoolmarm over me?'

'But this is Gerard's office....'

'We do meet in the oddest places, don't we?' He came a step nearer. 'Jealous, by any chance? Gerard would never dream of looking for us here....'

'You underestimate my powers,' said Gerard in a dangerously quiet voice. 'And really, this time, Claude, my patience is exhausted.'

He had been standing in the open doorway. Now he crossed the room without haste, knocked Claude down in a businesslike fashion, picked him up again and frogmarched him out of the room. Deborah, ice-cold with the unexpectedness of it all, listened to the muddle of feet going down the stairs. It sounded as though Claude was having difficulty in keeping his balance. The front door was shut with quiet finality and Gerard came back upstairs. He looked as placid as usual and yet quite murderous.

'Is this why you wanted to visit these rooms?' he asked silkily.

She had never seen him look like that before. 'No, you know that.'

'Why is Trudi not here?'

'Trudi?' She had forgotten the girl, she hadn't the least idea where she had gone. 'She went to fetch something for Claude—he didn't say what it was.'

'She is downstairs, very upset,' he informed her coldly. 'She told me that she hadn't been expecting anyone else—only you.'

Deborah gaped at him. 'She said that? But....' But what, she thought frantically—perhaps what Trudi had said was true, perhaps she hadn't expected Claude. But on the other hand he had told her that he had come to fetch something and that Trudi was an old friend.

'Oh, please, do let me try and explain,' she begged, and met with a decided: 'No, Deborah—there is really no need.'

She stared at him wordlessly. No, she supposed, of course there was no need; his very indifference made that plain enough. It just didn't matter; she didn't matter either. She closed her eyes on the bitter thought, all the more bitter because she had thought, just once or twice lately, that she was beginning to matter just a little to him.

She opened her eyes again and went past him and down the stairs. Trudi was in the hall. Deborah gave her a look empty of all expression and opened the door on to the square. It looked peaceful and quiet under the late afternoon sky, but she didn't notice that; she didn't notice anything.

Once in the house, she raced up to her room and dragged out a case and started to stuff it with clothes. There was money in her purse, enough to get her to England—she couldn't go home, not just yet at any rate, not until she had sorted her thoughts out. She would go to Aunt Mary; her remote house by Hadrian's Wall was exactly the sort of place she wanted—a long, long way from Amsterdam, and Gerard.

She was on her way downstairs with her case when the front door opened and Gerard came in. He shut it carefully and stood with his back to it.

'I must talk to you, Deborah,' his voice was quiet and compelling. 'There's plenty of time if you're going for the night boat train. I'll drive you to the station—if you still want to go.'

Deborah swept across the hall, taking no notice, but at the door, of course, she was forced to stop; only then did she say: 'I'll get a taxi, thank you— perhaps you will let me pass.'

'No, I won't, my dear. You'll stay and hear what I have to say. Afterwards, if you still wish it, you shall go. But first I must explain.' He took the case from her and set it on the floor and then went back to lean against the door. 'Deborah, I have been very much at fault—I'm not sure what I thought when I saw Claude this afternoon. I only know that I was more angry than I have ever been before in my life, and my anger blinded me. After you had gone Trudi told me the truth—that Claude had come to see her. She is going to Nice with him, but they had planned it otherwise—I was to know nothing about it until I arrived in the morning and found a letter from her on my desk.' He smiled thinly. 'It seems that since Claude could not have my wife, he must make do with my secretary. None of this is an excuse for my treatment of you, Deborah, for which I am both ashamed and sorry. What would you like to do?'

'Go away,' said Deborah, her voice thick with tears she would rather have died than shed. 'I've an aunt—if I could go and stay with her, just for a little while, just to—to ... I've not been much of a

171

success—I'd do better to go back to my old job.'

He said urgently: 'No, that's not true. No man could have had a more loyal and understanding wife. It is I who have failed you and I am only just beginning to see ... perhaps we could start again. You really want to go?' He paused and went on briskly: 'Come then, I'll take you to the station.'

If only he would say that he would miss her— She thought of a dozen excuses for staying and came up with the silliest. 'What about your dinner, and Wim—and Sien?'

'I'll see to everything,' he told her comfortably. 'You're sure that you have enough clothes with you?'

Deborah looked at him in despair; he was relieved that she was going. She nodded without speaking, having not the least idea what she had packed and not caring, and followed him out to the car. At the station he bought her ticket, stuffed some money into her handbag and saw her on to the train. She thought her heart would break as it slid silently away from the platform, leaving him standing there.

By the time she reached Aunt Mary's she was tired out and so unhappy that nothing mattered at all any more. She greeted her surprised relation with a story in which fact and fiction were so hopelessly jumbled together that they made no sense at all, and then burst into tears. She felt better after that and Aunt Mary being a sensible woman not given to asking silly questions, she was led to the small bedroom at the back of the little house, told to unpack, given a nourishing meal and ordered with mild authority to go to bed and sleep the clock round. Which she did, to wake to the firm conviction that she had been an utter fool to leave Gerard—perhaps he wouldn't want her back; he'd positively encouraged her to go, hadn't he? Could he be in love with some girl at long last and wish to put an end to their marriage and she not there to stop, if she were able, such nonsense? The idea so terrified her that she jumped out of bed and dressed at a great speed as though that would help in some way, but when she got downstairs and Aunt Mary took one look at her strained face, she said: 'You can't rush things, my dear, nor must you imagine things. Now all you need is patience, for although I'm not clear exactly what the matter is, you can be certain that it will all come right in the end if only you will give it time. Now go for a good long walk and come back with an appetite.'

Aunt Mary was right, of course. After three days of long walks, gentle talk over simple meals and the dreamless sleep her tiredness induced, Deborah began to feel better; she was still dreadfully unhappy, but at least she could be calm about it now. It would have been nice to have given way to tears whenever she thought about Gerard, which was every minute of the day, but that would not do, she could see that without Aunt Mary telling her so. In a day or two she would write a letter to him, asking him—she didn't know what she would ask him; perhaps inspiration would come when she picked up her pen.

The weather changed on the fourth day; layers of low cloud covered the moors, the heather lost its colour, the empty countryside looked almost frightening. There was next to no traffic on the road any more and even the few cottages which could be seen from Aunt Mary's windows had somehow merged themselves into the moorland around them so that they were almost invisible. But none of these things were reasons to miss her walk. She set off after their midday meal, with strict instructions to be back for tea and on no account to go off the road in case the mist should come down.

Sound advice which Deborah forgot momentarily when she saw an old ruined cottage some way from the road. It looked interesting, and without thinking, she tramped across the heather towards it. It was disappointing enough when she reached it, being nothing but an empty shell, but there was a dip beyond it with a small dewpond. She walked on to have a closer look and then wandered on, quite forgetful of her aunt's words. She had gone quite a distance when she saw the mist rolling towards her. She thought at first that it must be low-lying clouds which would sweep away, but it was mist, creeping forward at a great rate, sneaking up on her, thickening with every yard. She had the good sense to turn towards the road before it enveloped her entirely, but by then it was too late to see where she was going.

Shivering a little in its sudden chill, she sat down; probably it would lift very shortly. If she stayed where she was she would be quite safe. It would be easy to get back to the road as soon as she could see her way. It got too cold to sit after a time, so she got to her feet, stamping them and clapping her hands and trying to keep in one spot. And it was growing dark too; a little thread of fear ran through her head—supposing the mist lasted all night? It was lonely country—a few sheep, no houses within shouting distance, and the road she guessed to be a good mile away. She called herself a fool and stamped her feet some more.

It was quite dark and the mist was at its densest when she heard voices. At first she told herself that she was imagining things, but they became louder as they drew closer—children's voices, all talking at once.

'Hullo there!' she shouted, and was greeted by silence. 'Don't be frightened, I'm by myself and lost too. Shall we try and get together?'

This time there was a babble of sound from all around her. 'We're lost too.' The voice was on a level with her waist. 'Miss Smith went to get help, but it got dark and we started to walk. We're holding hands.'

'Who are you, and how many?' asked Deborah. Someone small brushed against her and a cold little hand found her arm. 'Oh, there you are,' it said tearfully. 'We're so glad to find someone—it's so dark. We're a school botany class from St Julian's, only Miss Smith lost the way and when the mist came she thought it would be quicker if she went for help. She told us to stay where we were, but she didn't come back and we got frightened.' The voice ended on a sob and Deborah caught the hand in her own and said hearteningly: 'Well, how lucky we've met—now we're together we've nothing to be afraid of. How many are there of you?'

'Eight—we're still holding hands.'

'How very sensible of you. May I hold hands too, then we can tell each other our names.'

There was a readjustment in the ranks of the little girls; the circle closed in on her. Deborah guessed that they were scared stiff and badly needed her company. 'Who's the eldest of you?' she enquired.

'Doreen—she's eleven.'

'Splendid!' What was so splendid about being eleven? she thought, stifling a giggle. 'I expect the mist will lift presently and we shall be able to walk to the road. It's not far.'

'It's miles,' said a plaintive voice so that Deborah went on cheerfully, 'Not really, and I can find it easily. My name's Deborah, by the way. How about stamping our feet to keep warm?'

They stamped until they were tired out. Deborah, getting a little desperate, suggested: 'Let's sit down. I know it's a bit damp, but if we keep very close to each other we shall keep warm enough. Let's sing.'

The singing was successful, if a little out of tune. They worked their way through 'This old man, he played one', the School Song, 'Rule Britannia' and a selection of the latest pop tunes. It was while they were getting their breath after these musical efforts that Deborah heard a shout. It was a nice, cheerful sound, a loud hullo in a man's voice, answered immediately by a ragged and very loud chorus of mixed screams and shouts from the little girls.

'Oh, that won't do at all,' said Deborah quickly. 'He'll get confused. We must all shout together at the same time. Everyone call "Here" when I've counted three.'

The voice answered them after a few moments, sometimes tantalizingly close, sometimes at a distance. After what seemed a long time, Deborah saw a faint glow ahead of them. A torch. 'Walk straight ahead,' she yelled, 'you're quite close.'

The glow got brighter, wavering from side to side and going far too slowly. 'Come on,' she shouted, 'you're almost here!'

The faint glow from the torch was deceptive in the mist, for the next thing she knew Gerard was saying from the gloom above her head, 'A fine healthy pair of lungs, dear girl—I've never been so glad to hear your voice, though I'm glad you don't always bellow like that.'

Surprise almost choked her. 'Gerard! Gerard, is it really you? How marvellous—how could you possibly know. . . .'

'Your Aunt Mary told me that you had gone for a walk and it seemed a good idea to drive along the road to meet you. When the mist got too thick I parked the car, and then it was I heard these brats squealing,' there were muffled giggles to interrupt him here, 'and I collected them as I came.'

'You haven't got the botany class from St Julian's too?' she gasped. 'You can't have—I've got them here.'

'Indeed I have—or a part of it. A Miss Smith went for help and left them bunched together, but being the little horrors they are, they wandered off.'

'There aren't any missing?'

'No—we counted heads, as it were. Seven young ladies—very young ladies.'

Deborah had found his arm and was clutching it as though he might disappear at any moment. 'I've got eight of them here. What must we do, Gerard?'

'Why, my dear, stay here until the mist goes again. The car is up on the road, once we can reach it I can get you all back to Twice Brewed in no time at all.' He sounded so matter-of-fact about it that she didn't feel frightened any more. 'Your aunt has got everything organised by now, I imagine. She seemed to be a remarkably resourceful

177

woman.' His hand sought and found hers and gave it a reassuring squeeze. 'In the meantime, I suggest that we all keep together, and don't let any of you young ladies dare to let go of hands. Supposing we sit?'

There was a good deal of giggling and a tremendous amount of shuffling and shoving and pushing before everyone was settled, sitting in a tight circle. Deborah, with Gerard's great bulk beside her, felt quite light-hearted, and the children, although there was a good deal of whining for something to eat, cheered up too, so that for a time at least, there was a buzz of talk, but gradually the shrill voices died down until there was silence and, incredibly, she dozed too, to wake shivering a little with the cold despite the arm around her shoulders. She whispered at once in a meek voice: 'I didn't mean to go to sleep, I'm sorry,' and felt the reassuring pressure of Gerard's hand.

'Not to worry. I think they have all nodded off, but we had better have a roll-call when they wake to be on the safe side.'

'Yes. I wonder what the time is, it's so very dark.'

'Look up,' he urged her, quietly. 'Above our heads.'

By some freak of nature the mist had parted itself, revealing a patch of inky sky, spangled with stars. 'Oh, lovely!' breathed Deborah. 'Only they don't seem real.'

'Of course they're real,' his whisper was bracing. 'It's the mist which isn't real. The stars have been there all the time, and always will be, only sometimes we don't see them—rather like life.' He sighed and she wondered what he meant. 'You see that bright one, the second star from the right?'

178

She said that yes, she could see it very well.

'That's our star,' he told her surprisingly, and when she repeated uncertainly 'Ours?' he went on: 'Do you not know that for every star in the heavens there is a man and a woman whose destinies are ruled by it? Perhaps they never meet, perhaps they meet too late or too soon, but just once in a while they meet at exactly the right moment and their destinies and their lives become one.'

In the awful, silent dark, anything would sound true; Deborah allowed herself a brief dream in which she indeed shared her destiny with Gerard, dispelled it by telling herself that the mist was making her fanciful, and whispered back: 'How do you know it's our star—it's ridiculous.'

'Of course it's ridiculous,' he agreed affably, and so readily that she actually felt tears of disappointment well into her eyes. 'But it's a thought that helps to pass the time, isn't it? Go to sleep again.'

And such was the calm confidence in his voice that she did as she was told, to waken in the bitter cold of the autumn dawn to an unhappy chorus of little girls wanting their mothers, their breakfasts, and to go home. Deborah was engulfed in them with no ears for anything else until she heard watery giggles coming from Gerard's other side, and his voice, loud and cheerful, declaring that they were all going to jump up and down and every few minutes bellow like mad. 'It's getting light; there will be people about soon.' He sounded quite positive about that. So they jumped and shouted, and although the mist was as thick as it ever was, at least they got warm, and surely any minute now the mist would roll away.

It did no such thing, however. They shouted

themselves hoarse, but there was no reply from the grey blanket around them. First one child and then another began to cry, and Deborah, desperately trying to instil a false cheer into her small unhappy companions, could hear Gerard doing the same, with considerably more success so that she found herself wondering where she had got the erroneous idea that he wasn't particularly keen on children. She remembered all at once what he had said about Sasja who hadn't wanted babies—the hurt must have gone deep. It seemed to her vital to talk about it even at so unsuitable a time and she was on the point of doing so when the mist folded itself up and disappeared. It was hard not to laugh; the little girls were still gathered in a tight circle, clutching each other's hands. They were white-faced and puffy-eyed, each dressed in the school uniform of St Julian's—grey topcoats and round grey hats with brims, anchored to their small heads by elastic under their chins. Some of them even had satchels over their shoulders and most of the hats were a little too large and highly unbecoming.

There was an excited shout as they all stood revealed once more and a tendency to break away until Gerard shouted to them to keep together still. 'A fine lot we would look,' he pointed out good-naturedly, 'if the mist comes back and we all get lost again.' He looked round at Deborah and smiled. 'We'll hold hands again, don't you think, and make for the road.'

They were half way there when they saw the search party—the local police, several farmers and the quite distraught Miss Smith who, when they met, burst into tears, while her botany class, with a complete lack of feeling for her distress and puffed up with a great sense of importance, told everyone severally and in chorus just how brave and resourceful they had been. It took a few minutes to sort them into the various cars and start the short journey to St Julian's.

Deborah found herself sitting beside Gerard, with four of the smallest children crammed in the back. She was weary and untidy, but when he suggested he should drop her off at Aunt Mary's as they went past, she refused.

On their way back from the school she began. 'How did...?' and was stopped by a quiet: 'Not now, dear girl, a hot bath and breakfast first.'

So it was only when they had breakfasted and she was sitting drowsily before a roaring fire in Aunt Mary's comfortable sitting room that she tried again. 'How did you know that I was here?'

'I telephoned your mother.'

'Oh—did she ask—that is, did she wonder....'

'If she did, she said nothing. Your mother is a wise woman, Deborah.'

'Why did you come?'

He was lying back, very much at his ease, in a high-backed chair, his eyes half shut. 'I felt I needed a break from work, it seemed a good idea to bring the car over and see if you were ready to come back.' He added: 'Smith is breaking his heart—think about it. Why not go to bed now, and get a few hours' sleep?'

Deborah got up silently. Smith might be breaking his doggy heart, but what about Gerard? There was no sign of even a crack; he was his usual calm, friendly self again, and no more. She went up to her little room and slept for hours, and when she came downstairs Aunt Mary was waiting for her.

'I told you to have patience, Debby,' she remarked with satisfaction. 'Everything will come right without you lifting a finger, mark my words.'

So when Gerard came in from the garden presently, she told him that she was ready to go back with him when he wished. She woke several times in the night and wondered, despite Aunt Mary's certainty, if she had made the right decision.

CHAPTER NINE

It was two days before they returned to Amsterdam, two days during which Gerard, who had become firm friends with Aunt Mary, dug the garden, chopped wood and did odd jobs around the house, as well as driving the two ladies into Carlisle to do some shopping.

They left after lunch, to catch the Hull ferry that evening, and Deborah, who had been alternately dreading and longing for an hour or so of Gerard's company, with the vague idea of offering to part with him and the even vaguer hope that he would tell her how much he had missed her, was forced to sit beside him in the car while he sustained a conversation about aunt Mary, the beauties of the moors, the charm of the small girls they had met and the excellence of his hostess's cooking. Each time Deborah tried to bring the conversation round to themselves he somehow baulked her efforts; in the end, she gave up, and when they reached Hull, what with getting the car on board, arranging to have dinner and their cabins, there wasn't much need to talk. Quite frustrated, she pleaded a headache directly they had finished dinner and retired to her cabin. She joined him for an early breakfast, though, because he had asked her to; he had, he told her, an appointment quite early in the morning at the hospital and didn't wish to waste any time.

He talked pleasantly as they took the road to Amsterdam and Deborah did her best to match his mood, but at the house he didn't come in with her, only unloaded her case and waited until Wim had opened the door before he drove away. She followed Wim inside. Gerard hadn't said when he would be home, nor had he spoken of themselves. She spent a restless day until he came home soon after tea and, as usual, went to his study. But before he could reach the door she was in the hall, a dozen things she wanted to say buzzing in her head. In the end she asked foolishly: 'What about Trudi? Did you get someone to take her place?'

He had halted and stood looking at her with raised eyebrows. 'Oh, yes—a middle-aged married woman, very sober and conscientious. You must go and see her for yourself some day.'

Deborah was left standing in the hall, her mouth open in surprise. Did he suppose her to be jealous of something absurd like that? She mooned back into the sitting room, Smith at her heels. Of course she was jealous; he filled her with rage, he was exasperating and indifferent, but she was still jealous. She would have to cure that, she told herself sternly, if she was to have any peace of mind in the future—the uncertain future, she had to allow, and wondered why Gerard had wanted her back. But if she had hoped to see a change in his manner towards her, she was doomed to disappointment. He was a quiet man by nature, he seemed to her to be

183

even quieter now, and sometimes she caught him staring at her in a thoughtful manner; it was a pity that his habit of drooping the lids over his eyes prevented her from seeing their expression. There was no hint of a return of those few strange moments on the moor; they had been make-believe, she told herself, and took pains to take up the smooth, neat pattern of their life together as though it had never been ruffled out of its perfection.

She visited his family, arranged a dinner party for a medical colleague who was coming from Vienna and bought yet another new dress to wear at it. It was a very pretty dress, fine wool in soft greens and pinks, with a wide skirt. It would go very well with Tante Emmiline's garnets and perhaps, she hoped wistfully, Gerard might notice it. She hung it carefully in her clothes cupboard and went to get ready for the orphans' hour and for a number of muddled but sincere reasons, took almost every penny of her remaining allowance and when she reached the orphanage gate, stuffed the money into the alms box hung upon it, accompanying the action with a hotch-potch of wordless prayers—and later, when one of them was answered, took fresh heart. For Gerard noticed the new dress; indeed, he stood looking at her for so long that she became a little shy under his steady gaze and asked in a brittle little voice: 'Is there something wrong? Don't you like my dress?' She achieved a brittle laugh too. 'A pity, because it's too late to change it now.'

His eyes narrowed and a little smile just touched the corners of his mouth. 'Far too late, Deborah,' he said quietly, 'and I wouldn't change a single....' his voice altered subtly. 'The dress is delightful and you look charming.' He turned away as he spoke and the old-fashioned door bell tinkled through the house. 'Our guests, my dear. Shall we go and meet them?'

The other prayers must have become mislaid on the way, thought Deborah miserably as she got ready for bed later that evening, for when their guests had gone Gerard had told her that he would be going to Vienna for a five-day seminar in a day's time. When he had asked her if she would like him to bring back anything for her she had replied woodenly that no, there was nothing, thank you, and made some gratuitous remark about a few days of peace and quiet and now was her chance to take the new Fiat and go and see Abigail, who was still in Friesland.

Gerard had paused before he spoke. 'Why not?' he agreed affably, and looked up from the letters he was scanning. 'When is the baby due—several months, surely.'

'Almost six. I've knitted a few things, I'll take them with me.'

He nodded and went to open the door for her. 'Good idea.' He patted her kindly on the shoulder as she passed him. 'Sleep well, my dear,' and as an afterthought: 'I had no idea that you could knit.'

The pansy eyes smouldered. 'It's something I do while you're away or working in your study. I get through quite an amount.' Her voice was very even and she added a pleasant: 'Good night, Gerard.'

She didn't see him at breakfast, although he had left a scribbled note by her plate saying that he would be home for lunch—not later than one o'clock.

But it was later than that, it was six in the evening. She had eaten her lunch alone, telling herself that was what being a surgeon's wife meant; something she had known about and expected; it happened to all doctors' wives—the young houseman's bride, the G.P.'s lady, the consultant's wife, they all had to put up with it and so would she, only in their cases, a shared love made it easier. Deborah sighed, and loving him so much, hoped with all her heart that he, at least, was satisfied with their marriage. Apparently no more was to be said about Claude or any of the events connected with him, and in any case it was too late for recriminations now—besides, she wasn't sure if she had any; living with him, in the house he loved and which she had come to love too, was infinitely better than never seeing him again.

She was in the garden playing with Smith when he joined her. He looked weary and a little grim and she said at once: 'I've a drink ready for you—come inside,' and then because she couldn't bear to see him looking like that: 'Must you go tomorrow, Gerard? Is it important?'

He took the glass from her and smiled in a way which somehow disturbed her. 'Yes, Deborah, I think it's very important—I have to be sure of something, you see. It involves someone else besides myself.'

An icy finger touched her heart and she turned away from him. 'Oh, well, I'll telephone Abigail.'

'I thought you had already arranged to visit her.'

'No—it had quite slipped my mind,' she improvised hastily, because the reason she hadn't telephoned was because she had hoped, right until this last moment, that he might suggest her going with him, but he wouldn't do that now. Hadn't he said that there was someone else? She wondered if he had meant a patient and very much doubted it. She telephoned Abigail there and then, being very gay about it.

She wished Gerard a cheerful goodbye after breakfast the next morning and after a fine storm of weeping in her room afterwards, dressed herself and drove the car to Friesland where she received a delighted welcome from Abigail and Dominic. They had come out to meet her, walking together, not touching, but so wrapped together in happiness so secure and deep that she could almost see it. For a moment she wished she hadn't come, but later, laughing and talking in their comfortable sitting room, it wasn't so bad. Indeed the day went too quickly. Driving back Deborah contemplated the four days left before Gerard should come back. There was, of course, the orphans' hour, but that wasn't until Thursday. She would have to fill the days somehow. She spent the rest of the journey devising a series of jobs which would keep her occupied for the next day or two.

She was a little early when she got to the orphanage on Thursday evening, but although it still wanted five minutes to the hour, the children were already assembled in the long, bare room, At least, thought Deborah, as she took off her coat and prepared for the next hour's boisterous games, the evening would pass quickly, and the next day Gerard would be back. She longed to see him, just as she dreaded his return, wondering what he would have to tell her, or perhaps he would have nothing to say, and that would be even harder to bear.

She turned to the task in hand, greeting the children by name as they milled around her, separating the more belligerent bent on the inevitable fight, picking up and soothing those who, just as inevitably, had fallen down and were now howling their eyes out. Within five minutes, however, she had a rousing game of 'Hunt the Slipper' going—a hot favourite with the orphans because it allowed a good deal of legitimate screaming and running about. This was followed by 'Twos and Threes'. A good deal of discreet cheating went on here; the very small ones, bent on getting there first, were prone to fall on their stomachs and bawl until Deborah raced to pick them up and carry them in triumph to the coveted place in the circle.

There was a pause next, during which she did her best to tidy her hair which had escaped most of its pins and hung most untidily around her shoulders. But it took too long, besides, there was no one to see—the children didn't care and she certainly didn't. 'Grandmother's Steps' was to be the final game of the evening, and Deborah, her face to the wall, listened to the stampede of what the orphans imagined were their creeping little feet and thanked heaven that there was no one below them or close by. She looked over her shoulder, pretending not to see the hasty scramble of the slower children to achieve immobility, and turned to the wall again. Once more, she decided, and then she would declare them all out and bring the game to a satisfactory conclusion.

She counted ten silently and turned round. 'All of you,' she began in her fragmental Dutch which the children understood so well. 'You're out ... I saw you move....' Her voice died in her throat and her breath left her; behind the children, half way down the room, stood Gerard.

He came towards her slowly, pausing to pat a small tow-coloured head of hair or lift the more persistent hangers-on out of his way. When he reached her he said with a kind of desperate quietness: 'I thought I should never find you—such a conspiracy of silence....'

Her hand went to cover her open mouth. 'Wim and Marijke, they knew—they discovered. They were sweet about it—don't be angry with them.' She searched his calm face for some sign; his eyes were hooded, there was the faintest smile on his mouth; she had no idea what his true feelings were. She went on earnestly: 'You see, it's a Catholic convent and you—your family are Calvinists.' Her look besought him to understand. 'You—you don't mix very well, do you? Separate schools and hospitals and....'

'Orphanages?' he offered blandly.

She nodded wordlessly and lapsed into thought, to say presently:

'Besides, you're home a day early.'

'Ah,' the lids flew open revealing blue eyes whose gleam made her blink. 'Am I to take it that that is a disappointment to you?'

'Disappointment?' Her voice rose alarmingly. There were small hands tugging at her skirt, hoarse little voices chanting an endless 'Debby' at her, but she hardly noticed them; she had reached the end of her emotional tether.

'Disappointment? Disappointment? This week's been endless—they always are when you go away. I'm sick and tired—I won't go on like this, being a kind of genteel housekeeper and wondering all the time—every minute of every day—where you are and what you're doing and pretending that I don't care. . . .'

She was in full spate, but the rest of it never got said; she was gripped in an embrace which bade fair to crack her ribs, and kissed with a fierceness to put an end to all her doubts.

'How can a man be so blind?' Gerard spoke into her ear and the children's voices faded quite away from her senses. 'The star was there, only I didn't want to see it. I wanted to stay in the mist I had made—the nice safe mist which wouldn't allow anything to interfere with my work, because that was all I thought I had left. And yet I suppose I knew all the time. . . .' He loosed his hold for the fraction of a minute and looked down into her face. 'I love you, my darling girl,' he said, and kissed her again; a pleasant state of affairs which might have gone on for some time if it hadn't been for the insistent pushes, tugs and yells from the orphans—it was story time and they knew their rights.

It was Deborah who broke the spell between them. 'My darling, I have to tell them a story—just until seven o'clock.' She smiled at him, her pansy eyes soft with love; he kissed her once more, a gentle kiss this time, and let her go. 'A fairy story,' she told him. ' "Rose Red and Rose White" . . .'

His mouth twitched into a faint smile. 'In which language, dear heart?' he asked.

'Both, of course—I don't know half the words.' She smiled again. 'Heaven knows what they're thinking of us at this moment!'

'Nor I, though I'm very sure of what I'm thinking about you, but that can wait.'

He pulled up the tattered old music stool so that she could sit on it and the children jostled happily against each other, getting as close as they could.

'Rose Red and Rose White,' began Deborah in a voice lilting with not quite realized happiness, and the children fell silent as she plunged into the story, using a wild mixture of Dutch and English words and a wealth of gestures and mime and never doubting that the children understood every word, which, strangely enough, they did. They sat enrapt, their small mouths open, not fidgeting, and two of them had climbed on to Gerard's knees where he sat on one of the low window seats, listening to his wife's clear voice mangling the Dutch language. She had reached a dramatic point in her narrative when the room shook and trembled under the tones of the great bell from the church across the road.

'Seven o'clock,' said Deborah, very conscious of Gerard's look. 'We'll finish next week,' and added, 'Sweeties!' at the top of her voice, producing at the same time the bag of toffees which signalled the end of play hour.

She was marshalling her small companions into a more or less tidy line when the faint dry tinkle of the front door bell whispered its way along the passage and up the stairs. It was followed almost at once by the Mother Superior, who greeted Deborah warmly, the children with an all-embracing smile, and an extended hand for Gerard, admirably concealing any surprise she might have felt at finding him there.

'The little ones have been good?' she asked Deborah.

'They always are, Mother. Do you want me to come on Friday next week, or is it to be Thursday again?'

The nice elderly face broke into a smile. 'You

will have the time?' The pale blue eyes studied Gerard, the hint of a question in their depths.

'I approve of anything my wife does,' he told her at once, 'even though you and I are in—er—opposite camps.'

She answered him gravely, although her eyes were twinkling. 'That is nice to know, Mijnheer van Doorninck. You like children?'

He was looking at Deborah. 'Yes, Mother, although I'm afraid I've not had much to do with them.'

'That will arrange itself,' the old lady assured him, 'when you have children of your own.' She glanced at Deborah, smiling faintly. 'Thank you for your kind help, my child. And now we must go.'

The line of orphans stirred its untidy ranks; they hadn't understood anything of what had been said, and they wanted their supper, but first of all they wanted to be kissed goodnight by Debby, who always did. A small sigh went through the children as she started at the top of the line, bending over each child and hugging it, until, the last one kissed, they clattered out of the room and down the stairs. Deborah stood in the middle of the room, listening to the sound of their feet getting fainter and fainter until she could hear it no longer. Only then did she turn round.

Gerard was still by the window. He smiled and opened his arms wide and she ran to him, to be swallowed up most comfortably in their gentle embrace.

'My adorable little wife,' he said, and his words were heaven in her ears; she was five foot ten in her stockings and no slim wand of a girl; no one had

192

ever called her little before. Perhaps Gerard, from his vantage point of another four inches, really did find her small. She lifted a glowing face for his face, and presently asked:

'You're not angry about the orphans?'

'No, my love. Indeed, they are splendid practice for you.'

She leaned back in his arms so that she could see his face. 'You're not going to start an orphanage?'

'Hardly that, dear heart—I hope that our children will always have a home.'

'Oh.' She added idiotically: 'There are twenty-eight of them.'

He kissed the top of her head. 'Yes? It seemed like ten times that number. Even so, I would hardly expect ...!' She felt his great chest shake with silent laughter. 'A fraction of that number would do very nicely, don't you agree?' And before she could answer: 'Don't you want to know why I have come back early?'

'Yes—though it's enough that you're here.' She leaned up to kiss him.

'Simple. I found myself unable to stay away from you a moment longer. At first, I wanted to keep everything cool and friendly and impersonal between us, and then, over the weeks, I found it harder and harder to leave you, even to let you out of my sight, and yet I wouldn't admit that I loved you, although I knew in my heart—I could have killed Claude.'

'But you let me go away—all the way to Aunt Mary's....'

'My darling, I thought that I had destroyed any chance of making you love me.'

'But I did love you—I've loved you for years....'

193

He held her very close. 'You gave no sign, Debby —but all the same I had to follow you, and then I found you in the mist with all those little girls in their strange round hats.'

Deborah laughed into his shoulder. 'You showed me our star,' she reminded him.

'It's still there,' he told her. 'We're going to share it for the rest of our lives.'

He turned her round to face the window. 'There —you see?'

The sky was dark, but not as dark as the variegated roofs pointing their gables into it, pointing, all of them, to the stars. The carillon close by played its little tune for the half hour and was echoed a dozen times from various parts of Amsterdam. It was all peaceful and beautiful, but Deborah was no longer looking at it. She had turned in her husband's arms to face him again, studying his face.

'Are we going home?' she asked, when he had kissed her just once more, she said, 'Our home, darling Gerard.'

'Our home, my love, although for me, home will always be where you are.'

There was only one answer to that. She wreathed her arms round his neck and kissed him.

WINTER OF CHANGE

Winter
of Change

Mary Jane was indignant. What had her grandfather been thinking of? A guardian... at her age! At their first meeting she took an instant dislike to Fabian van der Blocq.

And when she learned that Fabian intended taking his duties seriously, matters became worse.

"You...mean," she stammered, almost bereft of words, "that if anyone wants to marry me he'll have to ask your permission? But that's absurd!"

CHAPTER ONE

SISTER THOMPSON made her slow impressive way down Women's Surgical, bidding her patients a majestic good morning as she went, her sharp eyes behind their glasses noticing every small defect in the perfection she demanded on her ward—and that applied not only to the nursing and care of the ladies lying on either side of her, but also to the exact position of the water jugs on the lockers, the correct disposal of dressing gowns, the perfection of the bedspreads and the symmetry of the pillows. The nurses who worked for her held her in hearty dislike, and when posted to her ward quickly learned the habit of melting away out of her sight whenever their duties permitted. Something which Mary Jane Pettigrew, her recently appointed staff nurse, was, at that particular time, quite unable to do. She watched her superior's slow, inevitable progress with a wary eye as she changed the dressing on Miss Blake's septic finger; she had no hope of getting it done before Sister Thompson arrived, for Miss Blake was old and shaky and couldn't keep her hand still for more than ten seconds at a time. Mary Jane, watching Nurse Wells and Nurse Simpson disappear, one into the sluice room, the other into the bathrooms at the end of the ward, wondered how long it would be before they were discovered—in the meantime, perhaps she could sweeten Sister Thompson's temper.

She fastened the dressing neatly and wished her superior a cheerful good morning which that good lady didn't bother to answer, instead she said in an arbitrary manner: 'Staff Nurse Pettigrew, you've been on this ward for two weeks and not only do you fail to maintain discipline amongst the nurses; you seem quite incapable of keeping the ward tidy. There are three pillows—and Miss Trump's top blanket, also Mrs Pratt's water jug is in the wrong place...'

Mary Jane tucked her scissors away in her pocket and picked up the dressing tray. She said with calm, 'Mrs Pratt can't reach it unless we put it on that side of her locker, Sister, and Miss Trump was cold, so I unfolded her blanket. May the nurses go to coffee?'

Sister Thompson cast her a look of dislike. 'Yes— and see that they're back before Mr Cripps' round.' She turned on her heel and went back up the ward and into her office, to appear five minutes later with the information that Mary Jane was to present herself to the Chief Nursing Officer at once, 'and,' added Sister Thompson, 'I suggest that you take your coffee break at the same time, otherwise you will be late for the round.'

Which meant that unless the interview was to be a split-second, monosyllabic affair, there would be no coffee. Mary Jane skimmed down the ward, making a beeline for the staff cloakroom. Whatever Sister Thompson might say, she was going to take a few minutes off in order to tidy her person. The room was small, nothing more than a glorified cupboard, and in order to see her face in the small mirror she was forced to rise on to her toes, for she was a small girl, only a little over five feet, with delicate bones and a tiny waist. She took one look at her reflection now, uttered a sigh and whipped off her cap so that she might smooth her honey-brown hair, fine and straight and worn in an old-fashioned bun on the top of her head. The face which looked back at her was pleasant but by no means pretty; only her eyes, soft and dark, were fine under their thin silky arched brows, but her nose was too short above a wide mouth and although her teeth were excellent they tended to be what she herself described as rabbity. She rearranged her cap to her satisfaction, pinned her apron tidily and started on her journey to the office.

Her way took her through a maze of corridors, dark passages and a variety of staircases, for Pope's Hospital was old, its ancient beginnings circumvented by more modern additions, necessitating a conglomeration of connecting passages. But Mary Jane, her thoughts busy, trod them unhesitatingly, having lived with them for more than three years. She had no idea why she was wanted, but while she was in the office it might be a good idea to mention that she wasn't happy on Women's Surgical. She had been aware, when she took the post, that it would be no bed of roses; Sister Thompson was notorious for her ill-temper and pernickety ways, but Mary Jane, recently State Registered, had felt capable of moving mountains ... She would, she decided as she sped down a stone-flagged passage with no apparent ending, give in her notice at the end of the month and in the meantime start looking for another job. The thought of leaving Pope's was vaguely worrying, as she had come to regard it as her home, for indeed she had no home in the accepted sense. She had been an orphan from an early age, brought up, if one could call it that, by her grandfather, a retired Army colonel, who lived in a secluded house near Keswick and seldom left it. She had spent her holidays there all the while she was at the expensive boarding school to which he had sent her, and she had sensed his relief when she had told him, on leaving that admirable institution, that she wished to go to London and train to be a nurse, and in the three years or more in which she had been at Pope's she had gone to see him only once each year, not wishing to upset his way of living, knowing that even during the month of her visit he found her youthful company a little tiresome.

Not that he didn't love her in his own reserved, elderly fashion, just as she loved him, and would have loved him even more had he encouraged her to do so. As it was she accepted their relationship with good sense because she was a sensible girl, aware too that she would probably miss a good deal of the fun of life because she would need to work for the rest of it; even at the youthful age of twenty-two she had discovered that men, for the most part, liked good looks and failing that, a girl with a sound financial background, and she had neither, for although her grandfather lived comfortably enough, she had formed the opinion over the years that his possessions would go to some distant cousin she had never seen, who lived in Canada. True, old Colonel Pettigrew had educated her, and very well too, provided her with the right clothes and given her handsome presents at Christmas and on her birthday, but once she had started her training as a nurse, he had never once offered to help her financially—not that she needed it, for she had the good sense to keep within her salary and although she liked expensive clothes she bought them only when she saved enough to buy them. Her one extravagance was her little car, a present from her grandfather on her twenty-first birthday; it was a Mini and she loved it, and despite her fragile appearance, she drove it well.

The office door was firmly closed when she reached it and when she knocked she was bidden to enter at once the outer room, guarded by two office Sisters, immersed in paper work, one of whom paused long enough to wave Mary Jane to a chair before burying herself in the litter of papers on her desk. Mary Jane perched on the edge of a stool, watching her two companions, feeling sorry for them; they must have started out with a desire to nurse the sick, and look where they were now —stuck behind desks all day, separated from the patients by piles of statistics and forms, something she would avoid at all costs, she told herself, and was interrupted in her thoughts by the buzzer sounding its summons.

The Chief Nursing Officer was quite young, barely forty, with a twinkling pair of eyes, a nice-looking face and beautifully arranged hair under her muslin cap. She smiled at Mary Jane as she went in.

'Sit down, Staff Nurse,' she invited. 'There's something I have to tell you.'

'Oh lord, the sack!' thought Mary Jane. 'Old Thompson's been complaining...' She was deep in speculation as to what she had done wrong when she was recalled to her surroundings by her companion's pleasant voice.

'It concerns your grandfather, Nurse Pettigrew. His housekeeper telephoned a short time ago. He isn't very well and has asked for you to go to his home in order to look after him. Naturally you will wish to do so, although I've been asked to stress the fact that there's no'—she paused—'no cause for alarm, at least for the moment. I believe your grandfather is an old man?'

Mary Jane nodded. 'Eighty-two,' she said in her

rather soft voice, 'but he's very tough. May I go at once, please?'

'As soon as you wish. I'll telephone Sister Thompson so that there's no need for you to go back to the ward. Perhaps when you get to your grandfather's, you'll let me know how things are.'

She was dismissed. She made her way rapidly to the Nurses' Home, thankful that she wouldn't have to face Sister Thompson, her mind already busy with the details of her journey. It was full autumn, it would be cold in Cumberland, so she would take warm clothes but as few as possible—she could pack a case in a few minutes. She was busy doing that when her bedroom door was flung open and her dearest friend, Janet Moore, came in. 'There's a rumour,' she began, 'someone overheard that you'd been sent to the Office.' Her eyes lighted on the little pile of clothes on the bed. 'Mary Jane, you've never been ... no, of course not, you've never done anything really wicked in your life. What's up?'

Mary Jane told her as she squeezed the last sweater into her case, shut the lid and started to tear off her uniform. She was in slacks and a heavy woolly by the time she had finished, and without bothering to do more than smooth her hair, tied a bright scarf over it, pushed impatient feet into sensible shoes, caught up her handbag and the case and made for the door, begging her friend to see to her laundry for her as she went. 'See you,' she said briefly, and Janet called after her:

'You're not going now—this very minute? It's miles away—it'll be dark ...'

'It's ten o'clock,' Mary Jane informed her as she made off down the corridor, 'and it's two hundred and ninety miles—besides, I know the way.'

It seemed to take a long time to get out of London, but once she was clear of the suburbs and had got on to the A1, she put a small, determined foot down on the accelerator, keeping the little car going at a steady fifty-five, and when the opportunity occurred, going a good deal faster than that.

Just south of Newark she stopped for coffee and a sandwich and then again when she turned off the A1 at Leeming to cross the Yorkshire fells to Kendal. The road was a lonely one, but she knew it well, and although the short autumn afternoon was already dimming around her, she welcomed its solitude after the rush and bustle of London. At Kendal she stopped briefly before taking the road which ran through Ambleside and on to Keswick. The day was closing in on her now, the mountains around blotting out the last of a watery sun, but she hardly noticed them. At any other time she would have stopped to admire the view, but now she scarcely noticed them, for her thoughts were wholly of her grandfather. The last few miles of the long journey seemed endless, and she heaved a sigh of relief as she wove the car through Keswick's narrow streets and out again on to the road climbing to Cockermouth. Keswick was quickly left behind; she was back in open country again and once she had gone through Thronthwaite she slowed the car. She was almost there, for now the road ran along-side the lake with the mountains crowding down to it on one side, tree-covered and dark, shutting out the last of the light, and there was only an odd cottage or two now and scattered along the faint gleam of the water, larger houses, well away from each other. The road curved away from the lake and then returned and there, between it and the water, was her grandfather's house.

It stood on a spit of land running out into the lake, its garden merging into the grass alongside the quiet water. It was of a comfortable size, built of grey stone and in a style much favoured at the beginning of the nineteenth century, its arched windows fitted with leaded panes, its wrought-iron work a little too elaborate and a turret or two ornamenting its many-gabled roof. All the same it presented a pleasing enough picture to Mary Jane as she turned the car carefully into the short drive and stopped outside the front porch. Its door stood open and the woman standing there came to meet her with obvious relief.

'Mrs Body, how lovely to see you! I came as quickly as I could—how's Grandfather?'

Mrs Body was pleasant and middle-aged and housekeeper to the old Colonel for the last twenty years or more. She took Mary Jane's hand and said kindly, 'There, Miss Mary Jane, if it isn't good to see you, I must say. Your grandfather's not too bad—a heart attack, as you know, but the doctor's coming this evening and he'll tell you all about it. But now come in and have tea, for you'll be famished, I'll be bound.'

She led the way indoors as she spoke, into the dim, roomy hall. 'You go up and see the Colonel, he's that anxious for you to get here—and I'll get the tea on the table.'

Mary Jane nodded and smiled and ran swiftly up the uncarpeted staircase, past the portraits of her ancestors and on to the landing, to tap on a door in its centre. The room she was bidden to enter was large and rather over-full of ponderous furniture, but cheerful enough by reason of the bright fire burning in the grate and the lamps on either side of the bed.

The Colonel lay propped up with pillows, an old man with a rugged face which, to Mary Jane's discerning eye, had become very thin. He said now in a thin thread of a voice, 'Hullo, child—how long did it take you this time?' and she smiled as she bent to kiss him; ever since he had given her the car, he had made the same joke about the time it took her to drive up from London. She told him now, her head a little on one side as she studied him. She loved him very much and he was an ill old man, but none of her thoughts showed on her calm, unremarkable features. She sat down close to the bed and talked for a little while in her pretty voice, then got up to go to her tea, telling him that she would be back later.

'Yes, my dear, do that. I daresay Morris will be here by then, he knows all about me.' He added wistfully, 'You'll stay, Mary Jane?'

She retraced her steps to his bed. 'Of course, Grandfather. I've no intention of going back until you're well again—I've got unlimited leave from Pope's,' she grinned engagingly at him, 'and you know how much I love being here in the autumn.'

Tea was a substantial meal; a huge plate of bacon and eggs, scones, home-made bread and a large cake, as well as a variety of jams and a dish of cream. Mary Jane, who was hungry, did justice to everything on the table while Mrs Body, convinced that she had been half starved in hospital, hovered round, urging her to make a good meal.

She did her best, asking questions while she ate, but Mrs Body's answers were vague, so it was with thankfulness that she went to meet the doctor when he rang the bell. She had known him since she was a little girl

207

and held him in great affection, as he did her. He gave her an affectionate kiss now, saying, 'I knew you would come at once, my dear. You know your grandfather's very ill?'

They walked back to the sitting room and sat down. 'Yes,' said Mary Jane. 'I'll nurse him, of course.'

'Yes, child, I know you will, but that won't be for long. He'll rally for a few days, perhaps longer, but he's not going to recover. He was most anxious that you should come.'

'I'll stay as long as I can do anything to help, Uncle Bob—who's been looking after him?'

'Mrs Body and the district nurse, but he wanted you —there's something he wishes to talk to you about. I suggest you let him do that tomorrow morning when he's well rested.' He smiled at her. 'How's hospital?'

She told him briefly about Sister Thompson. 'It's not turning out quite as I expected, perhaps I'm not cut out to make a nurse...'

He patted her shoulder. 'Nonsense, there's nothing wrong with you, Mary Jane. I should start looking for another job and leave as soon as you can—at least...' He paused and she waited for him to finish, but he only sat there looking thoughtful and presently said: 'Well, I'll go and take a look—you'll be around when I come downstairs?'

He went away, and Mary Jane went along to the kitchen and spent some time helping Mrs Body and catching up on the local news until Doctor Morris re-appeared. In the hall he said briefly: 'He's fighting a losing battle, I'm afraid,' then went on to give her his instructions, 'and I'll be in some time tomorrow morning,' he concluded.

There was a dressing room next to the Colonel's

208

room. Mary Jane, who usually slept in one of the little rooms, moved her things into it, had a brief chat with her grandfather, settled him for the night and went down to the kitchen where the faithful Mrs Body was waiting with cocoa. They sat at the table, drinking it, with Major, the Colonel's middle-aged dog, sitting at their feet, and discussed the small problems confronting them. Mary Jane finished her cocoa and put down her cup. 'Well, now I'm here,' she said in her sensible way, 'you must have some time to yourself—these last few days must have been very tiring for you. If I'd known, I'd have come sooner.'

Mrs Body shook her head. 'Your grandfather wouldn't hear of it, not at first, but when Doctor Morris told him—he couldn't get you here fast enough,' she concluded, and sighed. 'All the same, I'll admit I'll be glad of an hour or so to myself. Lily comes up each morning as she always does, she's a good girl, and now you're here, I could get away for a bit.'

Mary Jane agreed. 'Supposing you take the Mini for a couple of hours each day? You could go to Keswick or Cockermouth if you want to do some shopping. I'll be quite all right here—I can go for a walk when you get back.'

The housekeeper gave her a grateful smile. 'That's kind of you, Miss Mary Jane, I'd like that. I want my hair done and one thing and another—you don't mind me using the Mini?'

'Heavens, no. Now I think I'll go to bed, it's been a long day. Will you be all right? I'll be in the dressing room and I've fixed Grandfather's bell and I shall leave the door open—besides, he's had a sedative. You will sleep? or shall I bring you something?'

'Bless you, child, I've never taken any of those nasty

pills yet, and don't intend to. I'll sleep like a baby.'

It was a bright, clear morning when Mary Jane woke the next morning and her grandfather was still sleeping; he had wakened once in the small hours and she had gone and sat with him for an hour until he dozed off again; now he would probably sleep for another hour or more. She put on slacks and a sweater, tied her hair back and went downstairs. Mrs Body was already up, so they drank their early morning tea together and then Mary Jane took Major into the garden and across the grass to the lake's edge. The water was calm and as smooth as silk, the mountains reflected in it so that it took on their colour, grey and green. Across the lake Skiddaw loomed above the other peaks, the sun lending it a bronze covering for its granite slopes.

Mary Jane looked about her with pleasure as she threw sticks for Major, a pleasure tinged with sadness because the Colonel was ill, and although he was an old man, and didn't, she suspected, mind dying, she would miss him very much. He had been all the family she had known; now she would be alone, save for the cousin in Canada. She had never met him and her grandfather seldom mentioned him. She supposed that after her grandfather died, this cousin would inherit the house and whatever went with it. She knew nothing of the Colonel's affairs; he had encouraged her to earn her own living when she had left school and she had always imagined that he had done so because he couldn't afford to keep her idle at home, for although the house was a comfortable one and well furnished and there was no evidence of poverty, common sense told her that the old man and his housekeeper could live economically enough, whereas if she lived with them, she would need clothes and pocket money and holidays.... She went back into the house, and after a reassuring peep at the Colonel, went to eat her breakfast.

Mrs Body left soon after Lily arrived and Mary Jane went upstairs to make her grandfather comfortable for the day. He seemed better, even demanding his razor so that he might shave himself, a request which she refused in no uncertain manner. Indeed, she fetched the old-fashioned cut-throat razor which he always used, and wielded it herself without a qualm, an action which caused him to ask her somewhat testily exactly what kind of work she did in hospital. There seemed no point in going too deeply into this; she fetched the post, opened his letters for him, and when he had read them, offered to read *The Times* to him. Perhaps it was her gentle voice, perhaps it was the splendid sports news, one or other of them sent him off into a sound sleep. She put the bell by his hand and went downstairs. It was barely eleven o'clock. Mrs Body wouldn't be back until the afternoon, Lily was bustling around the sitting room—Mary Jane went into the garden, round to the front of the house where she would be able to hear her grandfather's bell; there was a lot of weeding which needed doing in the rose beds which bordered the drive.

She had been hard at it for fifteen minutes or so when she became aware that a car had stopped before the gate, and when she looked round she saw that it was a very splendid car—a Rolls-Royce Corniche convertible, the sober grey of its coachwork gleaming against the green of the firs bordering the road behind it. Its driver allowed the engine to idle silently while he looked at Mary Jane, who, quite unable to recognise the car or its occupant, advanced to the gate, tossing back her mousey hair as she did so. 'Are you lost?' she wanted to know. 'Cockermouth is only...'

'Thank you, but no, I am not lost,' said the man. 'This is Colonel Pettigrew's house.' It was, she realised, a statement, not an enquiry.

She planted her fork in between the roses, dusted off her grubby hands and advanced a few steps. 'Yes, it is.' She eyed him carefully; she had never seen him before and indeed, she wouldn't have forgotten him easily if she had, for he was a handsome man, not so very young any more, but the grey hair at his temple served to emphasise the intense blackness of the rest, and his eyes were as dark as his hair, under thick straight brows. His nose was a commanding one and his mouth was firm above an angular jaw. Oh, most definitely a face to remember.

'I've come to see Colonel Pettigrew.' He didn't smile as he spoke, but looked her up and down in a casual uninterested fashion.

She ignored the look. 'Well, I'm not sure that you should,' she offered calmly. 'He's ill, and at the moment he's asleep. Doctor Morris will be here presently, and I think he should be asked first, but if you like to come in and wait—you'll have to be quiet.'

The eyebrows rose. 'My dear good young woman, you talk as though I were a pop group or a party of schoolchildren! I'm not noisy by nature and I don't take kindly to being told what I may and may not do.'

'Oh, pooh,' said Mary Jane, a little out of patience, 'don't be so touchy! Come in, do.' She added, 'Quietly.'

The car whispered past her and came to a silent halt at the door, and the man got out. There was a great deal of him; more than six foot, she guessed, and largely built too. She wondered who he was, and was on the point of asking when she heard the bell from her grandfather's room. 'There,' she shot at her companion, a little unfairly, 'you've woken him up,' and flew upstairs.

The Colonel looked refreshed after his nap. He said at once, 'I heard a car and voices. I'm expecting someone, but there's hardly been time...'

Mary Jane shook up a pillow and slipped it behind his head. 'It's a man,' she explained unhurriedly. 'He's got beetling eyebrows and he's got rather a super Rolls. He says he wants to see you, but I told him he couldn't until Uncle Bob comes.'

A faint smile lighted up her grandfather's face. 'Did you, now? And did he mind?'

'I didn't ask him.'

Her grandfather chuckled. 'Well, my dear, if it won't undermine your authority too much, I should like to see him—now. We have important business. Morris knows he's coming and I don't suppose he'll object. Tell him to come up.'

'All right, Grandfather, if you say so.'

She found the stranger in the sitting room, sitting in one of the comfortable old-fashioned chairs. He got to his feet as she went in and before she could speak, said: 'All right, I know my way,' and was gone, taking the stairs two at a time. She followed him into the hall just in time to hear the Colonel's door shut quietly on the old man's pleased voice. After a moment she went slowly into the garden again.

She was still there when Doctor Morris arrived, parked his elderly Rover beside the Rolls, greeted her cheerfully and added in a tone of satisfaction, 'Ah, good, so he's arrived—with your grandfather, I suppose?'

Mary Jane pulled a weed with deliberation. 'Yes, he is—and very high-handed, whoever he is, too. I asked him to wait until you came, but Grandfather heard us talking and wanted to see him at once—he said it was business. He seems better this morning, so I hope you don't mind?'

The doctor shook his head. 'No, I'm pleased. You're both here now—your grandfather was worrying. I'll go up now.'

He left her standing there. She stared after him; he hadn't told her who the stranger was, but he obviously knew him. She went indoors, tidied herself and went along to get a tray of coffee ready, to find that Lily had already done so. 'And lunch, miss—I suppose the gentleman will be staying like last time. I'd better do some extra potatoes, hadn't I?'

Mary Jane agreed, desiring at the same time to question Lily about the probable guest, but if her grandfather had wanted to tell her, he could have done so, so too could Uncle Bob. If they wanted to have their little secrets, she told herself a trifle huffily, she for one didn't care. Probably the visitor was a junior partner to her grandfather's solicitor, but surely he wouldn't be able to afford a Rolls-Royce? She went outside again and had a good look at the car—it had a foreign number plate and it came from Holland, a clue which she immediately seized upon; the man was someone from her grandfather's oldest friend, Jonkheer van der Blocq, an elderly gentleman whom she had never met but about whom she knew quite a bit, for her grandfather had often mentioned him. Relieved that she had solved the mystery, she went back indoors in time

214

to meet the doctor coming downstairs.

'There you are,' he remarked for all the world as though he had spent the last hour looking for her. 'Your grandfather wants you upstairs.' He eyed her thoughtfully. 'He's better, but you know what I mean by that, don't you? For the time being. Now run up, like a good girl. I'll be in the sitting room.'

She started up the stairs, remembering to call over her shoulder:

'There's coffee ready for you—would you ask Lily?' and sped on to tap on the Colonel's door and be bidden to enter.

The stranger was standing with his back to the window, his hands in his pockets, and the look he cast her was disconcerting in its speculation; there was faint amusement too and something else which she couldn't place. Mary Jane turned her attention to her elderly relative.

'Yes, Grandfather?' she asked, going up to the bed.

He eyed her lovingly and with some amusement on his tired old face.

'You're not a pretty girl,' he observed, and waited for her to answer.

'No, I know that as well as you—you didn't want me up here just to remind me, did you?' She grinned engagingly. 'I take after you,' she told him.

He smiled faintly. 'Come here, Fabian,' he commanded the man by the window.

And when he had stationed himself by the bed: 'Mary Jane, this is Fabian van der Blocq, the nephew of my old friend. He is to be your guardian after my death.'

Her eyes widened. 'My guardian? 'But I don't need a guardian, Grandfather! I'm twenty-two and I've never met Mr—Mr van der Blocq in my life before, and—and . . .'

'You're not sure if you like me?' His voice was bland, the smile he gave her mocking.

'Since you put the words into my mouth, I'm not sure that I do,' Mary Jane said composedly. 'And what do you have to be the guardian of?'

'This house will be yours, my dear,' explained her grandfather, 'and a considerable sum of money. You will be by no means penniless and there must be someone whom I can trust to keep an eye on you and manage your business affairs.'

'But I——' She paused and glanced across the bed to the elegant figure opposite her. 'Oh, you're a lawyer,' she declared. 'I wondered if you might be.'

Mr van der Blocq corrected her, still bland. 'You wondered wrongly. I'm a surgeon.'

She was bewildered. 'Are you? Then why . . .?' she went on vigorously, 'Anyway, Grandfather isn't going to die.'

The old gentleman in the bed made a derisive sound and Mr van der Blocq curled his lip. 'I am surprised that you, a nurse, should talk in such a fashion —you surely don't think that the Colonel wishes us to smother the truth in a froth of sickly sentiment?'

Mary Jane drew her delicate pale eyebrows together. 'You're horrible!' she told him in her gentle voice. It shook a little with the intensity of her feelings and she gave him the briefest of glances before turning back to her grandfather, whom she discovered to be laughing weakly.

'Don't you mind,' she demanded, 'the way this—this Mr van der Blocq talks?'

Her grandfather stopped laughing. 'Not in the least,

my dear, and I daresay that when you know him better you won't mind either.'

She tossed her untidy head. 'That's highly unlikely. And now you're tired, Grandfather—you're going to have another nap before lunch.'

To her surprise he agreed quite meekly. 'But I want you back in the afternoon, Mary Jane—and Fabian.'

She agreed, ignoring the man staring at her while she rearranged blankets, shook up pillows and made her grandfather comfortable. This done to her satisfaction, she made for the door. Mr van der Blocq, beating her to it by a short head, opened it with an ironic little nod of his handsome head, and without looking at him she went through it and down the stairs to where Doctor Morris was waiting.

They drank their coffee in an atmosphere which was a little tense, and when the doctor got up to go, Mary Jane got up too, saying, 'I'll see you to your car, Uncle Bob,' and although he protested, did so. Out of their companion's hearing, however, she stopped.

'Look,' she said urgently, 'I don't understand—why is he to be my guardian? He doesn't even live in England, does he? and I don't know him—besides, guardians are old. . . .'

The doctor's eyes twinkled. 'At a rough guess I should say he was nudging forty.'

'Yes? But he doesn't look . . .' She didn't finish the sentence. 'Well, it all seems very silly to me, and Grandfather . . .' She lifted her eyes to her companion. 'He's really not going to get any better? Not even if we do everything we possibly can?'

'No, my dear, and it will be quite soon now. I'll be back this evening. You know where to find me if you want me.'

She went back slowly to the sitting room and Mr Van der Blocq, lounging by the window, turned round to say: 'I don't suppose you got much help from Doctor Morris, did you?' He went on conversationally, 'If it is of any comfort to you, I dislike the idea of being your guardian just as much—probably more—than you dislike being my ward.'

Mary Jane sat down and poured more coffee for them both. 'Then don't. I mean, don't be my guardian, there's no need.'

'You heard your grandfather. You will be the owner of this house and sufficient money to make you an attractive target for any man who wants them.' He came across the room and sat down opposite her. 'I shall find my duties irksome, I dare say, but you can depend upon me not to shirk them.' He sat back comfortably. 'Do you mind if I smoke my pipe?'

She shook her head, and suddenly mindful of her duties as a hostess, asked, 'Where are you staying? Or are you perhaps only here for an hour or two?' She added hastily, 'You'll stay to lunch?'

A muscle twitched at the corner of his mouth. 'Thank you, I will—and I'm not staying anywhere,' his dark eyes twinkled. 'I believe the Colonel expected that I would stay here, but if it's too much trouble I can easily go to a hotel.'

'Oh no, not if Grandfather invited you. I'll go and see about lunch and get a room ready.' She got to her feet. 'There's sherry on the sofa table, please help yourself.'

Lily, she discovered when she got to the kitchen, had surpassed herself with Duchesse potatoes to eke out the cold chicken and salad, and there was a soup to start with; Mary Jane, feverishly opening tins to make a fruit salad, hoped that their guest wouldn't stay too long; she found him oddly disquieting and she wasn't even sure if she liked him, not that that would matter overmuch, for she supposed that she would see very little of him. She wasn't sure what the duties of a guardian were, but if he lived in Holland he was hardly likely to take them too seriously.

Ten minutes later, making up the bed in one of the guest rooms, she began to wonder for how long she was to have a guardian—surely not for the rest of her life? The idea of Mr van der Blocq poking his arrogant nose into her affairs, even from a distance, caused her to shudder strongly. She went downstairs, determined to find out all she could as soon as possible.

CHAPTER TWO

HER intention met with no success however. At lunch, her questions, put, she imagined, with suitable subtlety, were parried with a faint amusement which annoyed her very much, and when in desperation she tried the direct approach and asked him if, in the event of his becoming her guardian, it was to last a lifetime, he laughed and said with an infuriating calm:

'Now, why couldn't you have asked that in the first place? I have no intention of telling you, however. I imagine that your grandfather will explain everything to you presently.'

Mary Jane looked down her unassuming little nose. 'How long are you staying?' she asked with the icy politeness of an unwilling hostess. A question which met with an instant crack of laughter on the part of her companion. 'That depends entirely upon your grandfather's wishes, and—er—circumstances.'

She eyed him levelly across the table. 'You don't care tuppence, do you?' she declared fiercely. 'If Grandfather dies. . . .'

She was unprepared for the way in which his face changed, and the quietness of his voice. 'Not if, when. And why pretend? Your grandfather knows that he is dying. He told me this morning that his one dread as he got older was that he would be stricken with some lingering complaint which would compel him to lie for months, dependent on other people. We should be glad that he is getting his wish, as he is.' His eyes swept over her. 'Go and do your face up, and look cheerful, he expects us in a short while, and don't waste time arguing that he must have another nap; I happen to know that he won't be happy until he has had the talk he has planned.'

Mary Jane got to her feet. 'You've no right to talk to me like this,' she said crossly, 'and I have every intention of tidying myself.'

She walked out of the room, and presently, having re-done her face and brushed her hair until it shone, she put it up as severely as possible, under the impression that it made her look a good deal older, and went back downstairs, having first peeped in on the Colonel, to find him dozing. So she cleared away the lunch dishes and was very surprised when Mr van der Blocq carried them out to the kitchen, and because Lily had gone home, washed up, looking quite incongruous standing at the sink in his beautifully cut suit.

The Colonel was awake when they went upstairs;

Mary Jane sat him up in his bed, arranging him comfortably with deft hands and no fuss while Mr van der Blocq looked on, his hands in his pockets, whistling softly under his breath.

'And now,' said the Colonel with some of his old authority, 'you will both listen to me, but first I must thank you, Fabian, for coming at once without asking a lot of silly questions—it must have caused you some inconvenience, though I suppose you are now of sufficient consequence in your profession to be able to do very much as you wish. Still, the journey is a considerable one—did you stop at all?'

His visitor smiled faintly. 'Once or twice, but I enjoy long journeys and the roads are quiet at night.'

Mary Jane cast him a surprised look. 'You've been travelling all night?' she wanted to know. 'You haven't slept?'

He gave her an impatient glance, his 'no' was nonchalant as he turned back to the old man in the bed. 'Enough that I'm here, I'm sure that Doctor Morris wouldn't wish us to waste your strength in idle chatter.' A remark which sent the colour flaming into Mary Jane's cheeks, for it had been so obviously directed against herself.

Her grandfather closed his eyes for a moment. 'You're quite right. Mary Jane, listen to me—this house and land will be yours when I die, and there is also a considerable amount of money which you will inherit—that surprises you, doesn't it? Well, my girl, your mother and father wouldn't have thanked me if I had reared a feather-brained useless creature, depending upon me for every penny. As it is, you've done very well for yourself, and as far as I'm concerned you can go on with your nursing if you've set your mind on it, though I would rather that you lived here and made it home,' he paused, a little short of breath. 'You're not a very worldly young woman, my dear, and I've decided that you should have a guardian to give you help if you should need it and see to your affairs, and cast an eye over any man who should want to marry you—you will not, in fact, be able to marry without Fabian's consent.' He paused again to look at her. 'You don't like that, do you? but there it is—until you're thirty.'

Mary Jane swallowed the feelings which could easily have choked her. She said, keeping her voice calm and avoiding Mr van der Blocq's eye, 'And your cousin in Canada, Grandfather? I always thought that he was— that he would come and live—I didn't know about the money.'

Her grandparent received this muddled speech with a frown and said with some asperity, 'Dead. His son's dead too, I believe—there was a grandson, I believe, but no one bothered to let me know. Besides, you love the place, don't you, Mary Jane?'

She swallowed the lump in her throat. If he was going to be coolly practical about his death, she would try her best to be the same.

'Yes, Grandfather, you know I do, but I don't need the money—I've my salary. . . .'

'Have you any idea what a house like this costs in upkeep? Mrs Body, Lily, the rates, the lot—besides, you deserve to have some spending money after these last three years living on the pittance you earn.'

He closed his eyes and then opened them again, remembering something.

'You witness what I've said, Fabian? You understand your part in the business, eh? And you're still willing? I would have asked your uncle, but that's not possible any more, is it?'

Mr van der Blocq agreed tranquilly that he was perfectly willing and that no, it was not possible for his uncle to fulfil the duties of a guardian. 'And,' he concluded, and his voice now held a ring of authority and firmness, 'if you have said all you wished to say, may I suggest that you have a rest? We shall remain within call. Rest assured that your wishes shall be carried out when the time comes.'

Mary Jane, without quite knowing how, found herself propelled gently from the room, but halfway down the stairs she paused. 'It's so unnecessary!' she cried. 'Surely I can run this house and look after my own money—and it's miles for you to come,' she gulped. 'And talking about it like this, it's beastly....'

He ignored that, merely saying coolly, 'I hardly think you need to worry about my too frequent visits.' He smiled a small, mocking smile and she felt vaguely insulted so that she flushed and ran on down the stairs and into the kitchen, where she found Mrs Body, unpacking her shopping. She looked up as Mary Jane rushed in and said: 'Hullo, Miss Mary Jane, what's upset you? The Colonel isn't...?'

'He's about the same. It's that man—Mr van der Blocq—we don't seem to get on very well.' She stood in front of the housekeeper, looking rather unhappily into her motherly face. 'Do you know him?'

'Lor', yes, my dear—he's been here twice in the last few months, and a year or two ago he came with that friend of your grandfather's, the nice old gentleman who lives in Holland—he's ill too, so I hear.'

Mary Jane waved this information on one side. 'He's staying,' she said. 'I don't know for how long. I made

223

up a bed in the other turret room. Ought we to do something about dinner?'

'Don't you worry about that, Miss Mary Jane—the Colonel told me that he'd be coming, so I've a nice meal planned. If you'll just set the table later on—but time enough for that. Supposing you go for a little walk just down to the lake and back. You'll hear me call easily enough and a breath of air will do you good before tea.'

Mary Jane made for the door and flung it open. She had a great deal to think about; it was a pity she had no one to confide in; she hadn't got used to the fact that her grandfather was dying, nor his matter-of-fact attitude towards that fact, and the strain of matching his manner with her own was being a little too much for her. She wandered down the garden, resolutely making herself think about the house and the future. She didn't care about the money, just as long as there was enough to keep everything going as her grandfather would wish it to be. She stopped to lean over a low stone wall, built long ago for some purpose or other but now in disuse. The Colonel, a keen gardener, had planted it with a variety of rock plants, but it had no colour now. She leaned her elbows on its uneven surface and gazed out to the lake and Skiddaw beyond, not seeing them very clearly for the tears which blurred her eyes. It was silly to cry; her grandfather disliked crying women, he had told her so on various occasions. She brushed her hand across her face and noted in a detached way that the mountains had a sprinkling of snow on their tops while the rest of them looked grey and misty and sad. She wished, like a child, that time might be turned back, that somehow or other today could have been avoided. Despite herself, her eyes filled with tears again; she wasn't a crying girl, but just for once she made no attempt to stop them.

Major had followed her out of the house, and sat close to her now, pressed against her knee, and when he gave a whispered bark she wiped her eyes hastily and turned round. Mr van der Blocq was close by, just standing there, looking away from her, across the lake. He spoke casually. 'You have had rather a shock, haven't you? You must be a little bewildered. May I venture to offer you a modicum of advice?' He went on without giving her a chance to speak. 'Don't worry about the future for the moment. It's not a bad idea, in circumstances such as these, to live from one day to the next and make the best of each one.'

He was standing beside her now, still not looking at her tear-stained face, and when she didn't reply he went on, still casually:

'Major hasn't had a walk, has he? Supposing we give him a run for a short while?'

Mary Jane, forgetful of the deplorable condition of her face, looked up at him. 'I don't like to go too far away....'

'Nor do I, but Mrs Body has promised to shout if she needs us—she's sitting with your grandfather now, and I imagine we could run fast enough if we needed to.' He smiled at her and just for a moment she felt warmed and comforted.

'All right,' she agreed reluctantly, 'if you say so,' and started off along the edge of the lake, Major at her heels, not bothering to see if Mr van der Blocq was following her.

They walked into the wind, not speaking much and then only about commonplace things, and as they turned to go back again Mary Jane had to admit to herself that she felt better—not, she hastened to remind herself, because of her companion but probably because she had needed the exercise and fresh air. She went straight to her grandfather's room when they got back to the house, but he was still sleeping, so obedient to Mrs Body's advice she went to the sitting room and had tea with her visitor. They spoke almost as seldom as they had done during their walk; indeed, she formed the opinion that her companion found her boring and hardly worthy of his attention, for although his manners were not to be faulted she had the strongest feeling that they were merely the outcome of courtesy; in other circumstances he would probably ignore her altogether. She sighed without knowing it and got up to feed Major.

When she got back to the sitting room, Mr van der Blocq got to his feet and with the excuse that he had telephone calls to make and letters to write, went away to the Colonel's study, which, he was careful to explain, his host had put at his disposal, leaving Mary Jane to wander out to the kitchen to help Mrs Body and presently to lay the table in the roomy, old-fashioned dining room before going up to peep once more at her sleeping grandfather before changing from her slacks and sweater into a grey wool dress she had fortuitously packed, aware as she did so of the murmur of voices from the Colonel's room.

She frowned at her reflection as she smoothed her hair into its neat bun and did her face. If Mr van der Blocq had wakened her grandfather in order to pester him with more papers, then she would have something to say to him! He came out of the adjoining room as she left her own, giving her a wordless nod and standing aside for her to go down the stairs. She waited until they were both in the hall before she said: 'I think you must be tiring Grandfather very much. I don't think he should be disturbed any more today—there's surely no need.'

He paused on his way to the study. 'My dear good girl, may I remind you that I am a qualified physician as well as a surgeon, and as such am aware of your grandfather's condition—better, I must remind you, than you yourself.' He looked down his long nose at her. 'Be good enough not to interfere.'

Mary Jane's bosom heaved, her nice eyes sparkled with temper. 'Well, really it's not your business....'

He interrupted her. 'Oh, but it is, unfortunately. I am here at your grandfather's request to attend to his affairs—at his urgent request, I should remind you, before he should die, and here you are telling me what to do and what not to do. You're a tiresome girl.'

With which parting shot, uttered in his perfect, faintly accented English, he went into the study, closing the door very gently behind him.

Mary Jane, a gentle-natured girl for the most part, flounced into the sitting room, and quite beside herself with temper, poured herself a generous measure of whisky. It was a drink she detested, but now it represented an act of defiance, she tossed off a second glass too. It was unfortunate that Mr van der Blocq chose to return after five minutes, by which time the whisky's effects upon her hungry inside were at their highest; by then her head was feeling decidedly strange and her feet, when she walked to a chair, didn't quite touch the floor. It was unfortunate too that he saw this the moment he entered the room and observed coldly, 'Good God, woman, can't I turn my back for one minute without you reaching for the whisky bottle—you reek of it!' An exaggeration so gross that she instantly suspected that he had been spying upon her.

She said carefully in a resentful voice, 'You're enough to drive anyone to drink,' the whisky urging her to add, 'Are you married? If you are, I'm very sorry for your wife.'

He took her glass from her and set it down and poured himself a drink. 'No, I'm not married,' he said blandly, 'so you may spare your sympathy.' He sat down opposite her, crossed his long legs and asked, 'What did you do before you took up nursing? Were you ever here, living permanently?'

She cleared her fuzzy mind. 'No, I went to a boarding school, although I came here for the holidays, and then when I left school—when I was eighteen—I asked Grandfather if I might take up nursing and I went to Pope's. I've only been home once a year since then.'

'No boy-friends?' She hesitated and he added, 'I shall be your guardian, you know, I have to know a little about you.'

'Well, no.' Her head was clearer now. 'I never had much chance to meet any—only medical students, you know, and the housemen, and of course they always went for the pretty girls.' She spoke without self-pity and he offered no sympathy, nor did he utter some empty phrase about mythical good looks she knew she hadn't got, anyway. He said merely, 'Well, of course—I did myself, but one doesn't always marry them, you know.'

She agreed, adding in a matter-of-fact voice, 'Oh, I know that, I imagine young doctors usually marry where there's some money—unless they're brilliant with an assured future, and you can't blame them—how else are they to get on?'

'A sensible opinion with which I will not argue,' he assured her, his tone so dry that her slightly flushed face went slowly scarlet. It was fortunate that Mrs Body created a diversion at that moment by telling them that dinner would be ready in fifteen minutes and would Mary Jane like to take a quick peep at the Colonel first?

She was up in his room, pottering around because she sensed that he wanted company for a few minutes. When Doctor Morris arrived she waited while he examined his patient, adjusted his treatment, asked if he was through with his business, nodded his satisfaction at the answer and wished him a good night. Downstairs again, he accepted the drink offered him, muttered something to Mr van der Blocq and turned to Mary Jane.

'Your grandfather's happy; he's put his affairs in order, it's just a question of keeping him content and comfortable. You'll do that, I know, Mary Jane.' He stood up. 'I must be off, I've a couple more visits. Fabian, come to the car with me, will you?'

They talked very little over their meal and anything which they said had very little to do with the Colonel or what he had told them that day—indeed, Mr van der Blocq kept the conversation very much in his own hands, seeming not to notice her long silences and monosyllabic replies. She went to bed early, leaving him sitting by the fire, looking quite at home, with Major at his feet and still more papers on the table before him.

Once ready for bed, she went through to her grandfather's room, to find him awake, so she pulled up a chair to the dim lamp and made herself comfortable, declaring that she wasn't sleepy either. After a while he dozed off and so did she, to waken much later to find Mr van der Blocq standing looking down at her. She wasn't sure of the expression on his face, but whatever it was it changed to faint annoyance as she got silently to her feet. He said briefly, 'Go to bed,' and sat down in the chair she had vacated.

She was awakened by his hand on her shoulder. She sat up at once with an urgent whispered 'Grandfather?' and when he nodded and handed her her dressing gown from a chair, she jumped out of bed, thrust her arms into its sleeves anyhow and was halfway to the door in her bare feet when he reminded her, 'Your slippers—it's cold.' Before she quite reached the door he caught her by the arm. 'Your grandfather wants to say something to you—don't try and stop him; he's quite conscious and as comfortable as he can be. I've sent for Morris.'

The Colonel was wide awake and she went straight to the bed and took his hand with a steady smile. He squeezed her fingers weakly.

'Plenty of guts—like me,' he whispered with satisfaction. 'Can't abide moaning women. Something I want you to do. Always wanted you to meet my friend—Fabian's uncle—he's ill too. Go and look after him—bad-tempered fellow, can't find a nurse who'll stay. Promised Fabian you'd go.' He looked at her. 'Promise?'

She said instantly, 'Yes, Grandfather, I promise. I'll look after him.'

'Won't be for long—Fabian will see to everything.'

She glanced across at the man standing on the other side of the bed, looking, despite pyjamas and dressing gown, as impassive and withdrawn as he always did.

She wondered, very briefly, if he had any feelings at all; if so, they were buried deep. He returned her look with one of his own, unsmiling and thoughtful, and then went to the door. 'That's Morris's car—I'll let him in and wake Mrs Body.'

The Colonel died a couple of hours later, in his sleep, a satisfied little smile on his old face so that Mary Jane felt that to cry would be almost an insult—besides, had he not told her that she had guts? She did all the things she had to do with a white set face, drank the tea Mrs Body gave her, then had a bath and dressed to join Mr van der Blocq at the breakfast table, where she ate nothing at all but talked brightly about the weather. Afterwards, thinking about it, she had to admit that he had been a veritable tower of strength, organising a tearful Mrs Body and a still more tearful Lily, arranging everything without fuss and a minimum of discussion, telephoning the newspapers, old friends, the rector. . . .

She came downstairs from making the beds just as he came out of the study and Mrs Body was coming from the kitchen with the coffee tray. He poured her a cup, told her to drink it in a no-nonsense voice, and when she had, marched her off for a walk, Major at their heels. It was a fine morning but cold, and Mary Jane, in her sweater and slacks and an old jacket snatched from the back porch, was aware that she looked plainer than even she thought possible—not that she cared. She walked unwillingly beside her companion, not speaking, but presently the soft air and the quiet peace of the countryside soothed her; she even began to feel grateful to him for arranging her day and making it as easy as he could for her. She felt impelled to tell him this, to be told in a brisk impersonal way that as her guardian it was his moral obligation to do so.

He went on: 'We need to talk; there is a good deal to be arranged. You will have to leave Pope's—you realised that already, I imagine. I think it may be best if I wrote to your Matron or whatever she is called nowadays, and explain your circumstances. Your grandfather's solicitor will come here to see you—and me, but there should be no difficulties there, as everything was left in good order. I think it may be best if you return to Holland with me on the day after the funeral; there's no point in glooming around the house on your own, and I can assure you that my uncle needs a nurse as soon as possible—his condition is rapidly worsening and extremely difficult.' He paused to throw a stone for Major. 'He was a good and clever man, and I am fond of him.'

Mary Jane stood still and looked at him. 'You've thought of everything,' she stated, and missed the gleam in his eyes. 'I only hope I'll be able to manage him and that he'll like me, because I promised Grandfather...'

Her voice petered out and although she gulped and sniffed she was quite unable to stop bursting into tears. She was hardly aware of Mr van der Blocq whisking her into his arms, only of the nice solid feel of his shoulder and his silent sympathy. Presently she raised a ruined face to his. 'So sorry,' she said politely. 'I don't cry as a general rule—I daresay I'm tired.'

'I daresay you are. We'll walk back now, and after lunch, which you will eat, you shall lie on the sofa in the study and have a nap while I finish off a few odd jobs.'

He let her go and strolled down to the water's edge

while she wiped her eyes and blew her nose and re-tied her hair, and when they started back, he took her arm, talking, deliberately, of the Colonel.

Under his eye she ate her lunch, and still under it, tucked herself up in front of the study fire and fell instantly asleep. She awoke to the clatter of the tea tray as Mrs Body set it on the table beside the sofa and a moment later Doctor Morris came in.

The two men began at once to talk, and gradually, as she poured the tea and passed the cake, Mary Jane joined in. Before the doctor got up to go she realised with surprise that she had laughed several times. The surprise must have shown on her face, for Mr van der Blocq said with uncanny insight: 'That's better—your grandfather liked you to laugh, didn't he? Now, if you feel up to it, tell me how you stand at Pope's. A month's notice is normal, I suppose—have you any holidays due? Any commitments in London?'

'I've a week's holiday before Christmas, that's all, and I'm supposed to give a month's notice. There's nothing to keep me in London, but all my clothes and things are at Pope's.'

'We will pick them up as we go. What is the name of your matron?'

'Miss Shepherd—she's called the Principal Nursing Officer now.'

'Presumably in the name of progress, but what a pity. I shall telephone her now.' Which he did, with a masterly mixture of authority and charm. Mary Jane listened with interest to his exact explanations, which he delivered unembellished by sentiment and without any effort to enlist sympathy. It didn't surprise her in the least that within five minutes he had secured her resignation as from that moment.

When he had replaced the receiver, she remarked admiringly, 'My goodness, however did you manage it? I thought I would have to go back.'

'Manage what?' he asked coolly. 'I made a reasonable request and received a reasonable reply to it—I fail to see anything extraordinary in that.'

He returned to his writing, leaving her feeling snubbed, so that her manner towards him, which had begun to warm a little, cooled. It made her feel cold too, as though he had shut a door that had been ajar and left her outside. She went to the kitchen presently on some excuse or other, and sat talking to Mrs Body, who was glad of the company anyway.

'You've not had time to make any plans, Miss Mary Jane?' she hazarded.

'No, Mrs Body. You know that Grandfather left me this house, don't you? You will go on living here, won't you? I don't think I could bear it if you and Lily went away.'

The housekeeper gave her a warm smile. 'Bless you, my dear, of course we'll stay—it would break my heart to go after all these years, and Lily wouldn't go, I'm sure. But didn't I hear Doctor van der Blocq say that you would be going back to Holland with him?'

Mary Jane explained. 'It won't be for long, I imagine—if you wouldn't mind being here—do you suppose Lily would come and live in so that you've got company? I'm not sure about the money yet, but I'm sure there'll be enough to pay her. Shall I ask her?'

'A good idea, Miss Mary Jane. Supposing I mention it to her first, once everything's seen to? I must say the doctor gets things done—everything's going as smooth as silk and he thinks of everything. That reminds me, he told me to move your things back to your old room.'

Mary Jane looked surprised. 'Oh, did he? How thoughtful of him,' and then because she was young and healthy even though she was sad: 'What's for dinner—I'm hungry.'

Mrs Body beamed. 'A nice bit of beef. For a foreign gentleman the doctor isn't finicky about his food, is he? and I always say there's nothing to beat a nice roast. There's baked apples and cream for afters.'

'I'll lay the table,' Mary Jane volunteered, and kept herself busy with that until Mr van der Blocq came out of the study, when she offered him a drink, prudently declining one herself before going upstairs to put on the grey dress once more. The sight of her face, puffy with tears and tense with her stored-up feelings, did little to reassure her, and when she joined Mr van der Blocq in the sitting room, the brief careless glance he accorded her deflated what little ego she had left. Sitting at table, watching him carving the beef with a nicety which augured well for his skill at his profession, she found herself wishing that he didn't regard her with such indifference—not, she told herself sensibly, that his opinion of her mattered one jot. He wasn't at all the sort of man she ... He interrupted her thoughts.

'It seems to me a good idea if you were to call me Fabian. I do not like being addressed as Mr van der Blocq—inaccurately, as it happens. Even Mrs Body manages to address me, erroneously, as Doctor dear.' He smiled faintly as he looked at her, his eyebrows raised.

She studied his face. 'Well, if you want me to,' her voice was unenthusiastic, 'only I don't know you very well, and you're ...'

'A great deal older than you? Indeed I am.'

It annoyed her that he didn't tell her how much older, but she went on, 'I was going to say that I find it a little difficult, because Grandfather told me that you were an important surgeon and I wouldn't dream of calling a consultant at Pope's by his first name.'

The preposterous idea made her smile, but he remained unamused, only saying in a bored fashion, 'Well, you are no longer a nurse at Pope's—you are Miss Pettigrew with a pleasant little property of your own and sufficient income with which to live in comfort.'

She served him a baked apple and passed the cream. 'What's a sufficient income?' she wanted to know.

He waved a careless, well kept hand. 'Four—five thousand a year.'

She had been on the point of sampling her own apple, but now she laid down her spoon and said sharply, 'That's nonsense—that's a fortune!'

'Not in these days, it will be barely enough. There's your capital, of course, but I shall be in charge of that.' His tone implied that he was discussing something not worthy of his full attention, and this nettled her.

'You talk as though it were chicken feed!'

'That was not my intention. I'm sure you are a competent young woman and well able to enjoy life on such a sum. The solicitor will inform you as to the exact money.'

'Then why do I have to have you for a guardian?'

He put down his fork and said patiently, 'You heard your grandfather—I shall attend to any business to do with investments and so forth and have complete control of your capital. I shall of course see that your income is paid into your bank until you assume full control over your affairs when you are thirty. It will also be necessary for me to give my consent to your marriage should you wish to marry.'

She was bereft of words. 'Your consent—if I should choose——' She almost choked. 'It's not true!'

'I am not in the habit of lying. It is perfectly true, set down in black and white by your grandfather, and I intend to carry out his wishes to the letter.'

'You mean that if anyone wants to marry me he'll have to ask you?'

He nodded his handsome head.

'But that's absurd! I never heard such nonsense ... how could you possibly know—have any idea...?'

His voice had been cool, now it was downright cold. 'My dear good girl, let me assure you that I find my duties just as irksome as you find them unnecessary.'

This shook her. 'Oh, will you? I suppose they'll take up some of your time. I'll try not to bother you, then— I daresay there'll be no need for us to see much of each other.'

His lips twitched. 'Probably not, although I'm afraid that while you are at my uncle's house you will see me from time to time—he's too old to manage his own affairs, and my cousin, who lives with him, isn't allowed to do more than run the house.'

They were in the sitting room drinking their coffee when she ventured: 'Will you tell me a little about your uncle? I don't know where he lives or anything about him, and since I am to stay there...'

Mr van der Blocq frowned. 'Why should I object?' he wanted to know testily. 'But I must be brief; I'm expecting one or two telephone calls presently. He lives in Friesland, a small village called Midwoude. It is in fact on the border between Friesland and Groningen. The country is charming and there is a lake

237

close by. The city of Groningen is only a few miles away; Leeuwarden is less than an hour by car. You may find it a little lonely, but I think not, for you are happy here, aren't you? My uncle, I have already told you, is difficult, but my cousin Emma will be only too glad to make a friend of you.'

'And you—you live somewhere else?'

'I live and work in Groningen.' He spoke pleasantly and with the quite obvious intention of saying nothing more. She had to be content with that, and shortly after that, when he went to answer his telephone call, Mary Jane went into the kitchen, helped Mrs Body around the place, laid the table for breakfast and went up to bed.

Now if I were a gorgeous creature with golden hair and long eyelashes, she mused as she wandered up the staircase, we might be spending the evening together— probably he had some flaxen-haired beauty waiting for him in Groningen. For lack of anything better to do and to keep her thoughts in a cheerful channel, she concocted a tale about Mr van der Blocq in which the blonde played a leading part, and he for once smiled frequently and never once addressed the creature as 'my dear good girl'.

The next few days passed quickly; there was a good deal to attend to and Major had to be taken for his walk, and time had to be spent with the Colonel's friends who called in unexpected numbers. The lawyer came too and spent long hours in the study with her guardian, although he had very little to say to her.

It wasn't until after the funeral, when the last of the neighbours and friends had gone, that old Mr North asked her to join him in the study and bring Mrs Body and Lily with her. Mary Jane half listened while he read the legacies which had been left to them both, it wasn't until they had gone and she was sitting by the fire with Fabian at the other end of the room that Mr North gave her the details of her own inheritance. The money seemed a vast sum to her; she had had no idea that her grandfather had had so much, even the income she was to receive seemed a lot of money. Mr North rambled on rather, talking about stocks and shares and securities and ended by saying:

'But you won't need to worry your head about this, Mary Jane, Mr van der Blocq will see to everything for you. I understand that you will be travelling to Holland tomorrow. That will make a nice change and you will return here ready to take your place in local society. I take it that Mrs Body will remain?'

She told him that yes, she would, and moreover Lily had agreed to live in as well, so that the problem of having someone to look after the house and Major was solved.

'You have no idea how long you will be away?' asked Mr North.

'None,' she glanced at Fabian, who took no notice at all, 'but I'm sure that Mrs Body will look after everything beautifully.'

The old gentleman nodded. 'And you? You will be sorry to leave your work at the hospital, I expect.'

She remembered Sister Thompson. 'Yes, though I was thinking of changing to another hospital.' She smiled at him. 'Now I shan't need to.'

He went shortly afterwards and she spent the rest of the day packing what clothes she had with her and making final arrangements with Mrs Body before taking Major for a walk by the lake. It was a clear evening with the moon shining. Mary Jane shivered a little

239

despite her coat, not so much with cold as the knowledge that she would miss the peace and quiet even though she had it to come back to.

She went indoors presently and into the study to wish Fabian good night. He stood by her grandfather's desk while she made a few remarks about their journey and then said a little shyly, 'You've been very kind and—and efficient. I don't know what we should have done without your help. I'm very grateful.'

He rustled the papers in his hand and thanked her stiffly, and she went to her room, wondering if he would ever unbend, or was he going to remain coldly polite and a little scornful of her for the rest of their relationship? Eight years, she told herself as she got into bed, seemed a long time. She would be thirty and quite old, and Fabian would be ... she started to guess and fell asleep, still guessing.

CHAPTER THREE

MARY JANE had never travelled in a Rolls-Royce—she found it quite an experience. Fabian was a good driver and although he spoke seldom he was quite relaxed, she sat silently beside him, thinking about the last two weeks—such a lot had happened and there had been so much to plan and arrange; she hoped she had forgotten nothing—not that it would matter very much, for her companion would not have overlooked the smallest detail. He had told her very little about the journey, beyond asking her to be ready to start at eight o'clock in the morning.

They were on the motorway now, doing a steady seventy, and would be in London by early afternoon, giving her ample time in which to pack her things at the hospital before they left for the midnight ferry.

'Anything you haven't time to see to you can leave,' he had told her, 'and arrange to send on the things you don't want—Mrs Body can sort them out later. You can buy all you need when we get to Holland.'

'Oh no, I can't, I've only a few pounds.'

'I will advance you any reasonable sum—do you need any money now?'

'No, thank you, but what about my fare?'

'Mr North and I will take care of such details.'

They had settled into silence after that. Mary Jane stared through the window as the Rolls crept up behind each car in turn and passed it. Presently she closed her eyes against the boredom of the road, the better to think. But her thoughts were muddled and hazy; she hadn't slept very well the night before, and fought a desire to doze off, induced by the extreme comfort of the car, and had just succeeded in reducing her mind to tolerable clarity when her efforts were shattered by her companion's laconic, 'We'll stop for coffee.'

She glanced at her watch; they had been on the road for just two hours and Stafford wasn't far away. 'That would be nice,' she agreed pleasantly, and was a little surprised when he left the motorway, taking the car unhurriedly down side roads which led at last to a small village.

'Stableford,' read Mary Jane from the signpost. 'Why do we come here?'

'To get away from the motorway for half an hour. There's a place called The Cocks—ah, there it is.' He pulled up as he spoke.

The coffee was excellent and hot, and Mary Jane ate a bun because breakfast seemed a long time ago, indeed, a meal in another life.

'What time shall we get to London?' she wanted to know.

'A couple of hours, I suppose. We will have a late lunch before I take you to Pope's. I'll call for you there at seven o'clock.'

'The boat doesn't go until midnight, does it?'

'We shall dine on the way.'

'Oh.' She felt somehow deflated; if he had said something nice about dining together, or even asked her—obviously he was performing a courteous duty with due regard to her comfort and absolutely no pleasure on his part. She followed him meekly out to the car and for the remainder of the journey only spoke when she was spoken to and that not very often. Only when they were driving through London's northern suburbs did he remark: 'We'll go to Carrier's, it's an easy run to Pope's from there.'

The restaurant was down a passage, double-fronted and modern, and Mary Jane, by now famished, chose fillet of beef in shirtsleeves, because it sounded quaint and filling at the same time. She was given a dry sherry to drink before they ate; she would have preferred a sweet one, but somehow Fabian looked the kind of man who would wish to order the drinks himself and she felt certain that he knew a great deal more about them than she ever would; she might be a splendid nurse, a tolerable cook and handy in the garden, but the more sophisticated talents had so far eluded her. It surprised her when he suggested, after she had disposed of the beef in its shirtsleeves and he had eaten his carpet bag steak, that she might like to sample Robert's Chocolate Fancy.

'Women like sweet things,' he told her tolerantly, and asked for the cheese board for himself.

Pope's looked greyer, more old-fashioned and more hedged in by the towering blocks of flats around it than ever before. 'You'll have to see the Matron—you had better do that first,' said Fabian as he helped her out of the car. 'Do you want me to come with you?'

She declined politely and with secret regret; it would have been a pleasure to have walked through the hospital with Fabian beside her; she could just imagine the curious and envious glances that would have been cast at her.

He nodded. 'Good. I've one or two things to do. I'll be here at seven exactly.'

There was a greal deal for her to do too. After the interview with Miss Shepherd, which was unexpectedly pleasant, there was a brief visit to Women's Surgical, where Sister Thompson wasn't pleasant at all, and then a long session of packing in her room. It was amazing what she had collected over the years! After due thought she packed a trunk with everything she judged might be unsuitable in a Dutch winter, which left her with some thick tweeds in a pleasing shade of brown, a variety of sweaters, a couple of jersey dresses and a rather nice evening dress she couldn't resist taking, although she saw no chance of wearing it. It was pale blue and green organza with long tight sleeves and a pie-frill collar, and it suited her admirably.

When she had finished packing she went along to the sitting room, where most of her friends were having tea, and found so much to talk about that she had to hurry to complete the tiresome chores of handing in her uniform to the linen room and waiting while it was checked, and then running all over the home to hand in the key of her room, both tasks requiring patience while the appropriate persons were found, the right forms filled in and signed and the farewells made, but she was at the hospital entrance by seven o'clock, wearing the brown tweeds and a felt hat which did nothing for her at all. All the same, she looked nice; her handbag and gloves and shoes were good and the tweed suit and coat suited her small slender person.

She reached the door just as Fabian drew up and got out of the car. He gave her a laconic 'Hullo', put her case in the boot and enquired about the rest of the luggage.

'It's in my trunk—one of my friends will send it on to Mrs Body.'

'Good. And Miss Shepherd—any difficulties?'

'No, thank you. None.'

'Get in, then.'

She didn't much like being ordered about, she was on the point of saying so when those of her closer friends who were off duty or who had been able to escape from their wards for a few minutes arrived in a chattering bunch to see her off. They embraced her in turn and with some warmth, at the same time taking a good look at Mr van der Blocq, who bore their scrutiny with a faint smile and complete equanimity, even when Penny Martin, the prettiest and giddiest of the lot of them, darted forward and caught him by the arm.

'Take care of Mary Jane,' she begged him with the faint lisp which most of the housemen found irresistible, 'and if you want another nurse at any time, I'd love to come.'

He smiled down at her, and Mary Jane, glimpsing the charm of it, felt quite shaken by some feeling she had no time to consider. He had never smiled at her like that; he must dislike her very much. The supposition caused her to be very quiet as they drove away from the cheerful little group on the steps, in fact, she didn't speak at all until they had crossed the river, gone through Southwark and joined the A2.

'You'll miss your friends,' commented her companion, slowing down for the traffic lights, 'and hospital life.' The car swept ahead again. 'There's no reason why you shouldn't go back to work there later on—you could spend your holidays in Cumberland.'

'Oh, I wouldn't do that,' declared Mary Jane, startled out of her silence. 'I shall like living in Grandfather's house and I shall find plenty to do. I shall miss Pope's, of course, but not the ward I was on.'

He shot her a brief, amused glance. 'Oh? Tell me about it.'

She did, rather haltingly at first, but he seemed interested and she found herself saying more than she intended.

'There is certainly no point in you going back to Women's Surgical,' he agreed. 'It sounds a joyless place, and your Sister Thompson needs to go on the retirement list.'

'But she's quite young, only forty.'

'You think that forty is quite young?'

'Heavens, yes.' She broke off as he turned the car down a side road. 'Where are we going? I thought this led to the M2.'

'There's a good place at Hollingbourne, and we have plenty of time.'

245

The restaurant was pleasantly quiet and the food exceptional. Mary Jane was beginning to think that Fabian wouldn't go anywhere unless the food and the service were near perfection. She remembered the simple meals she and Mrs Body had cooked and wondered, as she ate her Kentish roast duckling, if he had enjoyed them. Probably not.

They kept up a desultory conversation as they ate— the kind of conversation, she told herself hopelessly, that one sustained with fellow patients in a dentist's waiting room. Before she could stop the words, they popped out of her mouth. 'What a pity we don't get on.'

If she had hoped to take him by surprise, she had failed. His expression didn't change as he answered in the pleasantest of voices.

'Yes, it is. Probably as we get to know each other better, our—er—incompatibility will lessen.' He smiled briefly and changed the subject abruptly. 'Tell me, do you ride? If so, there is a good stables near my uncle's house—they could let you have a mount.'

'Oh, could they? I should like that. I'm not awfully good, but I enjoy it.'

'In that case you had better not go out alone.'

Which remark compelled her to say, 'Oh, I can ride well enough, you needn't worry about that—it's just that I'm not a first-class horsewoman.'

They sipped coffee in silence until she said defiantly, 'I shall buy a horse when I get back home,' and waited to see what he would say. She was disappointed when he replied blandly, 'Why not? Shall we go?'

They were at Dover with time to spare. They left the car in the small queue and had coffee in the restaurant and Fabian bought her an armful of magazines. Once on board he suggested that she should go to her cabin. 'We berth very early,' he warned her, 'half past four or thereabouts. We'll stop for breakfast on the way to Friesland.'

His advice was sound. Mary Jane slept for a few hours, and fortified by tea, joined him on deck as the boat docked, and then followed him down to the car deck. There was no delay at all as they landed; they were away in a few minutes, tearing down the cobbled street towards the Dutch border.

The Rolls bored through the motorway from Antwerp towards the frontier and Breda, going through the town without stopping. It was quiet and dark, although a slow dawn was beginning to lighten the sky; by the time they reached Utrecht there was a dim, chilly daylight struggling through the clouds. Mary Jane shivered in the warm car and Fabian spoke after miles of silence. 'We'll stop here and have breakfast.'

It seemed a little early for there to be anywhere open, but he stopped the car outside Smits Hotel, said, 'Stay where you are,' and went inside to return very quickly and invite her inside, where she was welcomed by the hall porter with a courtesy she would have found pleasant in broad daylight, let alone at that early hour of the morning, but Fabian seemed to take it all very much for granted, as he did the breakfast which was presently set before them. They ate at leisure, lingering over a final cup of coffee while he explained the route they were to follow. 'Less than a hundred miles,' he told her. 'We shall be at my uncle's house for coffee.'

And they were, after a drive during which Mary Jane, after several efforts at polite conversation, had become progressively more and more silent, staring out

247

at the flat, frost-covered fields on either side of the road, observing with interest the cows in their coats, the large churches and the small villages so unlike her own home, and wishing with all her heart that she was back there—she even wished she was back at Pope's, coping with Sister Thompson's petty tyranny, but when her companion said, 'Only a few more miles now,' she pulled herself together; self-pity got one nowhere, and if Grandfather could know what she was thinking now he would be heartily ashamed of her show—even to herself—of weakness.

She sat up straight, rammed the unbecoming hat firmly upon her head and said, 'I'm glad, and I'm sure you must be too—travelling with someone you dislike can be very tiresome.'

Mr van der Blocq allowed a short sharp exclamation to leave his lips. 'Does that remark refer to myself or to you?' he queried silkily.

'Both of us.' She spoke without heat and lapsed into silence, a silence she would have liked to break as he took the car gently through a very small village—a cluster of one-storied cottages, a shop and an over-sized church—and turned off the road through massive iron gates and a tree-lined drive, and pulled up before his uncle's house. She would have liked to exclaim over it, for it was worthy of comment; built of rose brick with a steep slate roof and an iron balcony above its massive front door. It had two stories, their windows exactly matching, and all with shutters. It reminded her of some fairy tale, standing there silent, within the semi-circle of sheltering trees, most of them bare now. She was impressed and longed to say so.

Fabian got out, came round to help her out too and walked beside her up the shallow steps to the opening door. A white-haired man stood there, neatly dressed in a dark suit and looking so pleased to see them that she deduced, quite rightly, that this wasn't Jonkheer van der Blocq. Fabian quickly put her right, explaining as he shook the old man's hand, 'This is Jaap, he has been in the family for forty years—he sees to everything and will be of great help to you.'

Mary Jane put out a hand and had it gently wrung while Jaap made her welcome—presumably—in his own language. She nodded and smiled and followed him into a handsome lobby and through its inner glass doors to the hall, an imposing place, its walls hung with dark, gilt-framed portraits, vicious-looking weapons and a variety of coats of arms. It needed flowers, she decided as she glanced about her, something vivid to offset the noble plastered ceiling and marble floor with its dim Persian rugs. She was arranging them in her mind's eye when Fabian said: 'The sitting room, I suppose—the first door on the left.'

She followed Jaap through a double door into a room whose proportions rivalled those of the hall—the ceiling was high, the walls, painted white and ornamented at their corners with a good deal of carved fruit and flowers, carried a further selection of paintings. The furniture was massive and she had the feeling that excepting for the easy chairs flanking the large open fire, and the Chesterfield drawn up before it, the seating accommodation would be uncomfortable—an opinion which Fabian probably shared, for he advised her to take a chair by the fire, taking her coat and tossing it to Jaap.

'My cousin will be here in a moment,' he told her, and went to look out of the windows, while Mary Jane, left to herself, rearranged the furniture in her mind, set a few floral arrangements on the various tables and regarded with awe a large cabinet on the opposite wall; it was inlaid, with a good deal of strapwork, and she considered it hideous.

'German?' she asked herself aloud.

'You're right,' agreed Fabian from the window. 'The Thirty Years' War or thereabouts, I believe, and frankly appalling.'

She turned to look at him. 'Now isn't that nice, we actually agree about something!' She added hastily, 'I don't mean to be rude—I have no business to pass an opinion . . .'

He shrugged his wide shoulders. 'I'm flattered that we should share even an opinion.'

'Now that's a . . .' She was saved from finishing the forceful remark she was about to make by the entry of a lady into the room. The cousin, without doubt—fortyish, tall and thin and good-looking, her face marred by the anxious frown between her brows and the look of harassment she wore. Indeed, she appeared to be so hunted that Mary Jane expected to see her followed by Fabian's uncle in one of his more difficult moods. But no one else appeared; the lady trod across the room to Fabian, crying his name in a melodramatic fashion, and flung her arms around him. He received her embrace with a good-humoured tolerance, patted her on the shoulder and said in English: 'Now, Emma, you can stop behaving like a wet hen. Here is Mary Jane come to nurse Oom Georgius.'

He turned round and went to Mary Jane's side. 'This is my cousin Emma van der Blocq—I'm sure you will be good friends, and I know she is delighted to have you here to lighten her burden.'

'Indeed yes,' his cousin joined in, shaking Mary

Jane's hand in an agitated way. 'I'm quite worn out, for my father thinks I am a very poor nurse and I daresay I am—I'm sure you will be able to manage him far better than I.' She sighed deeply. 'The nurses never stay.'

It sounded as though the old gentleman was going to be a handful, Mary Jane thought gloomily, but she had promised her grandfather, and in a way she was glad, because she would be too occupied to brood over his death. She said in her pleasant voice, 'I'll do my best. Perhaps when you have the time, you will tell me what you would like me to do.'

Cousin Emma became more agitated than ever. 'Oh yes, of course, but first you shall see your room and we will have lunch.' She looked at Fabian. 'You will go and see Father?'

He nodded and followed them out of the room and up the elegant staircase at one side of the hall, but on the landing they parted, he going to the front of the house while Mary Jane and her hostess entered a room at the head of the stairs. It was a large room, but not, she was relieved to see, nearly as large as the sitting room. It was furnished with a quantity of heavy Mid-Victorian furniture, all very ornate, carved and inlaid. The bed was a ponderous affair too, but the curtains and coverlet were pretty and the carpet was richly thick under her feet.

Here she was left alone to tidy herself before going downstairs again, something she was about to do when she was halted by a thunderous voice from behind a pair of handsome doors across the landing, bellowing something in Dutch, and a moment later Fabian appeared, to lean over the balustrade as she went down the stairs and ask if she would be good enough to visit

251

his uncle.

The room they entered was vast, with a fourposter bed dwarfed against one wall and a great many chests and tallboys and massive cupboards. In the centre of this splendour sat Jonkheer van der Blocq, facing a roaring fire. And a handsome old man he was too, with white hair, a little thin on top, and Fabian's features. He didn't wait for his nephew to speak but began at once in a stentorian voice.

'Hah—so my good old friend died, and you are the Mary Jane he wrote so much of.' He produced a pair of spectacles and planted them upon his nose and stared at her. 'A dab of a girl, too. He promised me that if I should outlive him, he would send you to me. Nurses,' he went on in a triumphant voice, 'don't stay. Do you suppose you will?'

Mary Jane walked up to his chair, not in the least put out. 'I don't see why not,' she said in a reasonable voice, 'and anyway, I promised Grandfather I would. I'm not easily upset, you know.' She gave him a kind smile and he croaked with laughter. 'We'll see about that! At any rate you will be a change from that fool daughter of mine, always fussing around.'

'I daresay she wants to help you, but some people— and you, I suspect, aren't easy to do things for; they find fault all the time.'

He sat back against his cushions and she thought that he might explode; instead he burst out laughing. 'Dammit, if you're not like your grandfather!' he declared. 'No looks but plenty of spirit. I shall come down to lunch.' He turned to Fabian. 'And you, what do you think of her, eh?'

'I have no doubt that Mary Jane is an excellent nurse.'

'That wasn't what I meant. However, you may give me an arm and we'll go down. I rather fancy a glass of *Genever* before we lunch.'

'You'll not get it,' observed his nephew good-humouredly. 'A glass of white wine is all that Trouw allows you, and that's what you will have.'

The old man, far from being annoyed at this arbitrary remark, chuckled, and the three of them went down to the dining room in the friendliest possible way. The old gentleman's good humour lasted throughout the meal, and when Fabian got up to go, saying that he had an appointment that afternoon in Groningen, begged him to come again as soon as he could. 'Though I daresay you have a good deal of work to catch up on. How long have you been away?'

And when Fabian told him he continued: 'It will take you a week or two to work everything off, I daresay. Well, come when you can, Fabian.'

His thunderous voice sounded wistful and Mary Jane guessed that he was fond of his nephew, though probably nothing on earth would make him admit to it. Bidden by her host to see Fabian into his car, she walked a little self-consciously to the door and stood in the lobby while he spoke to Jaap, but presently he turned to her and said:

'Doctor Trouw will be here this evening, I believe. He speaks English and will explain all there is to know about my uncle. I hope it has been made clear to you that you are a guest here as well as a nurse, although you will doubtless find yourself called upon frequently enough if my uncle becomes particularly difficult.'

She raised surprised eyes to his. 'A guest? But I understood Grandfather to say that I was to take care

253

of your uncle. I know he's not in bed, but he needs someone, and he's a lot more ill than he allows, isn't he? And he said himself that nurses don't stay. Does he really dislike your cousin looking after him?'

He gave a short laugh. 'I assure you that he does, nor does she like looking after him. Do as you think fit, but I for one shall not hold you to your promise, for you had no idea what it might entail when you gave it, and nor, I believe, did your grandfather. Uncle Georgius is going to get worse very soon now, and he will be what you so aptly describe in your language as a handful.'

'Look,' said Mary Jane patiently, 'you came over to Grandfather when he sent for you and it must have been inconvenient, but I don't think you would have refused, would you? Well, neither shall I.'

She gave him a determined little nod and the corner of his mouth twitched a little. 'Very well,' he said blandly, and turned to go.

'Just a minute,' she was self-conscious again, 'I want to thank you for making my journey so comfortable and for doing so much for us.' She looked at him earnestly. 'You didn't know any of us well, you could so easily have refused—you had every right. I—I heard what your uncle said about your backlog of patients.'

'Like you, I keep my word,' he told her. 'Goodbye.'

She watched the Rolls slip away between the trees and told herself that she was well rid of such a cold, disagreeable man, and the feeling which she ascribed to relief at his going was so strong that she very nearly burst into tears.

Mary Jane slipped into the life of the big, silent house quite easily. She was an adaptable girl and her training had made her more so. In only a few days she had taken over all the tiresome chores which Emma van der Blocq disliked so much; the persuading of the old gentleman to rise in the morning when he flatly refused, the coaxing of him to go to bed at a reasonable hour—more, the battle of wills which was fought daily over the vexed question as to whether his pills were to be taken or not. But at least he slept well once he was in his bed and she had turned out the lights save for one small lamp, turned his radio to a thread of sound, arranged the variety of odds and ends he insisted upon having on his bedside table and wished him a cheerful goodnight, however grumpy he was. She was free then, but too tired to do anything other than write an odd letter or so or leaf through a magazine. She was free during the day too, as she was frequently told, both by Jonkheer van der Blocq and his daughter, but somehow it was difficult to get away, for if the old gentleman didn't want her, Emma van der Blocq did, even if only for a gossip. It wasn't until several days after her arrival that Mary Jane, during the course of one of these chats, asked her hostess why Jaap always referred to her as Freule—a question which kept Emma van der Blocq happy for an entire afternoon, explaining the intricacies of the Dutch nobility. She added a wealth of information regarding their titles, their houses and lands to a fascinated Mary Jane, who at the end of this dissertation, asked, 'So what do I call Fabian? He's a surgeon—is he Mister or Doctor?'

Cousin Emma looked slightly taken aback. 'But of course you have not fully understood. He is also Jonkheer, he is also a professor of surgery, you comprehend? Therefore he is addressed as Professor Jonkheer van der Blocq.'

'My goodness,' observed Mary Jane, 'what a mouthful!' Now she knew why he had looked so amused when she had addressed him as Mister. It had been nice of him not to say anything, though it surprised her that he hadn't taken the opportunity of discomfiting her. Her companion went on earnestly, 'I am old-fashioned enough to set great store upon these things, but I believe that the young people do not. Fabian may not be young any more, but he does not care in the least about his position, he . . .' She was interrupted by the entry of Corrie, the maid, begging her to ask Miss to go at once to the master of the house, and as Mary Jane got obediently to her feet, she said: 'What a blessing you are to us all. You do not know the relief I feel at not having to answer every call from Papa's room.'

And Mary Jane, skipping up the stairs for the tenth time that day, could well believe her. She was a little puzzled that nobody had offered to relieve her of her duties from time to time—it would be all right for a week or so, but she began to feel the need for a little relaxation and exercise and for some other distraction other than card games and Cousin Emma's rather theatrical conversation.

It was the next afternoon, when after a fruitless effort on her part to escape for a walk, she was playing cards with her patient, that he wanted to know what she thought of Fabian.

'I don't know him well enough to form an opinion,' she told him in a matter-of-fact way. 'He saw to everything very nicely—we couldn't have managed without him, and Grandfather liked him.' She paused and searched her memory. 'Everyone liked him,' she said in surprise.

'But not you?'

Until that moment she hadn't realised that she had never analysed her feelings towards Fabian. 'I've not thought about it.'

The old gentleman persisted, 'Perhaps he doesn't like you?'

She shuffled the cards and dealt them. 'Probably not. One gets on better with some people than others.'

'You're not much to look at.'

'No—it's your turn.'

He slammed down a card. 'Men fall for a pretty face.'

'So I should imagine.' She smiled at him across the card table and he glowered back.

Presently he went on, 'A pretty face isn't everything. You're delightful company, Mary Jane; it was good of your grandfather to let me share you. You don't mind staying a little while?'

She shook her head. 'Not in the least. I'll stay as long as you want me to.'

He snorted. 'Don't let us wrap up our words. You know as well as I do that I shall probably be dead in a week or so. You're not bored?'

It was difficult to answer that, because she was, just a little. She longed to get away for an hour or so each day; she had known that she would spend some time with Jonkheer van der Blocq each day, but even private nurses were entitled to their free periods, and she wasn't a private nurse—Fabian had told her that. He had spoken of trips to Groningen and getting a mount from the nearby stables; so far she had had no time for either, indeed she had no idea where the stables were, and when, on the previous day, she had mentioned going for a walk to Freule van der Blocq, that good lady had reacted quite violently to the suggestion; it seemed that the idea of being left with her father was more than she could bear, so Mary Jane had said no more about it. When Doctor Trouw paid his next visit, she would have a little talk with him and see what could be done.

She had hoped that Fabian would have come, even for half an hour to see how she was managing, but although the telephone rang frequently, she had no means of knowing if any of the calls were from him; it was really rather mean of him, and she decided that she liked him even less than she had supposed, and told herself forcefully that she didn't care if she never saw him again.

He came the very next morning, while Mary Jane, after a protracted argument between her host and his daughter, was in church. Emma went to church each Sunday, driven by Jaap in the Mercedes Benz which was housed, along with a Mini, in the garage at the back of the house, and she had seen no reason why Mary Jane shouldn't accompany her. 'Jaap will be here,' she had pointed out to her enraged parent, 'he can help you dress and we shall be back very shortly.'

Her father pointed out testily that if Jaap drove them to church, there would be no one to dress him, and he certainly wasn't going to wait while Jaap drove around the countryside just because she wanted to go to church.

Mary Jane, feeling a little like a bone between two dogs, felt her patience wearing thin round the edges. 'Look,' she offered when she could make herself heard, 'can't I drive the Mini? It's no distance, and that would leave Jaap free.'

So they had gone to church and on the return journey when she turned the little car carefully into the drive once more, it was to find a silver-grey pre-war Jaguar SS 100 parked before the door. She got out and went to inspect it with a good deal of interest; it wasn't an original but a modern version of it, she discovered as she prowled around its chassis, wondering to whom it belonged, and when Cousin Emma cried happily: 'Oh, good, Fabian's here—this is his car,' Mary Jane, her inquisitive person bent double over the dashboard, remarked:

'I don't believe it.'

'Why not?' It was Fabian who spoke and startled her so much that she turned round in a kind of jump, and when she didn't speak, he repeated impatiently, 'Why not?'

'Well,' she said slowly, 'it's unexpected—I hardly thought that you...'

'I'm too old for it?' His voice was suave.

'What nonsense, of course not, it's just that...' She gave up, staring at him silently. After a moment he laughed and turned to his cousin.

'Well, Emma, how are you? I've been with Oom Georgius. He seems in fine shape, considering all things, though a little annoyed because Mary Jane wasn't at home.'

He looked at Mary Jane as he spoke, and she, aware of his faintly accusing tone, went red, just as though, she thought crossly, she were in the habit of tearing off for hours at a time, whereas the morning's outing, if it could be called that, had been the first since she had arrived. She turned on her heel and walked into the house as Cousin Emma burst into voluble speech.

She was in Jonkheer van de Blocq's room fighting her usual battle over his pills when Fabian came in.

He sat down by the fire without speaking, watching her while, with cunning and guile, she persuaded the old man to swallow them down. He still said nothing as she prepared to leave them, only walking to the door to open it for her. She barely glanced at him as she passed through.

They all lunched together in the dining room, and Jonkheer van der Blocq, a little excited at Fabian's visit, talked a great deal, repeating himself frequently and forgetting his words and showing little flashes of splendid rage when he did. The meal took some time and when it was at last finished he was tired, so that for once, when Mary Jane suggested that he might like to lie down for half an hour, he agreed meekly. She accompanied him upstairs again, tucked him up on the chaise-longue in his room, thoughtfully provided him with a book, his spectacles, the bell and the tin of fruit drops he liked to suck, bade him be a good boy in a motherly voice, and went downstairs.

She was crossing the hall when she heard Fabian's voice, usually so quiet and measured in its tones, raised in anger and as she reached the door she could hear Cousin Emma doing what she described to herself as a real Sarah Bernhardt. Her hand on the heavy brass knob, she wondered if she should go in, and had her mind made up for her by a particularly loud squawk. At any moment, she thought to herself vexedly, she would have strong hysterics to deal with, thanks to Fabian. She flung open the door to find Freule van der Blocq standing in a tragic pose in the middle of the room, and Fabian lounging against one of the Corinthian pillars which supported the vast fireplace. He spoke sharply.

'There you are! Perhaps you can answer my questions without weeping and wailing. Have you been out at all since you arrived here?'

'Oh yes—to church.'

'Don't infuriate me, I beg of you, you know very well what I mean. Have you had time to yourself each day, to go out, to ride, to visit Groningen?'

'Well I ...'

'Yes or no?' he ground out.

'You see ...'

'I see nothing, largely owing to your inability to answer my questions.' He frowned at her. 'There seems to be some gross misunderstanding; you are here as a guest, to give some time and company to Uncle Georgius at your grandfather's request. That does not mean that you have to spend each day cooped up in the house at everyone's beck and call.'

'Don't exaggerate,' Mary Jane told him calmly, 'just because you're annoyed. It's your fault anyway. You should have explained exactly what I was supposed to do—you didn't tell me much, did you, and I dare say you didn't tell Freule van der Blocq anything either. I refuse to be blamed, and I won't allow you to blame her either.'

He gave her a hard stare. 'Oh? Am I supposed to apologise to you, then?' his voice was silky and very quiet.

'No, I don't suppose any such thing, because I can't imagine you apologising to anyone, though you could at least say you're sorry to your cousin. It's unkind of you to make her cry.'

His eyes had become black, he was still staring at her, rather as though he had never seen her before, she thought uneasily. She shook off the feeling and prompted him, 'Well, go on—or perhaps you would rather

261

not do with me here.'

She whisked out of the room before he could reply and crossed the hall to the long drawing room, a very much gilded apartment, with a wealth of grand furniture and huge display cabinets full of silver and porcelain. Not at all to her taste; she hurried over the vast carpeted floor and into the verandah room beyond where there was a piano. With the doors shut she was sure no one could hear her playing, and really, she had to do something to take her mind off things. It was a beautiful instrument. She sat down on the stool before it and tried a scale with the soft pedal down and then went on to a rambling mixture of tunes, just as they came into her head. She played tolerably well, disregarding wrong notes and forgetting about the soft pedal but putting in a good deal of feeling. Halfway through a half remembered bit of *Eine Kleine Nachtmusik*, Fabian stalked in, taking her by surprise because he entered by the garden door behind her. She stopped at once, folded her hands tidily in her lap and waited to hear what he had to say.

'You are the most infuriating girl!' he began in a pleasantly conversational tone. 'I have apologised to my cousin; if I apologise to you will you be kind enough to listen to what I have to say?'

'Of course—though why...'

'Just listen. I apologise for a start, and now to the other matter. It seems that Cousin Emma was so glad to have someone in the house who could handle my uncle that she took advantage of that fact. Unintentionally, I should add. In future you are to take what time you wish for yourself. I know that I can depend upon you to do what you can for Uncle Georgius if and when he becomes worse—I imagine Trouw will give you good warning of that, if it is possible. You are free to go where you wish, is that understood? Have you any money?'

'Not much.'

'I will arrange for you to have sufficient for your needs. I will also see Uncle Georgius and explain to him.'

Mary Jane got up and closed the piano. 'You won't upset him? He's such a dear, I like him.'

He gave her a considering look. 'So do I. If you care to do so, I will drive you over to the riding stables in half an hour and arrange for you to hire a mount.'

'I should like that—are we going in that Jag?'

Fabian looked surprised. 'Of course.' He opened the door and they went through together. 'You play well.'

'Thank you—I hope no one minds.'

'No one will mind.' They were in the hall again, where he left her to go to his uncle's room, and she went into the sitting room where his cousin greeted her in a melodramatic manner and a fresh flood of tears. She was still eulogising Fabian, Mary Jane and then Fabian again when the object of her praise walked in, bidding Mary Jane to fetch her coat and go with him—something she was glad to do, for much as she liked Cousin Emma, a little of her went a long way, especially when she was upset.

It was cold in the car, but she had tied her head in a scarf and Fabian had tucked a rug around her. She sat, exhilarated by the fresh air and their progress through the narrow country roads. The stables were a mile or so away; the journey seemed too short; for once Fabian was being pleasant—she allowed him to choose a quiet mare for her use with the secret resolve to pick out something a little more lively once he was safely back in Groningen—there was no use in annoying him over such a small matter, especially as he seemed disposed to be friendly, indeed he seemed in such a good frame of mind that she was emboldened to ask him how his work was going and whether he was still busy.

'Yes, just at the moment, but I shall be able to come over from time to time—in any case, there will be some papers for you to sign in a few days—some stocks I am transferring.' She looked a little blank and he went on smoothly, 'It seems to me to be somewhat of a paradox that you should trust me without question to attend to your affairs while at the same time you dislike me.'

She bit her lip and wished he wouldn't say things she couldn't answer. After a little thought, she said carefully, 'Well, I haven't much choice, have I?' and was annoyed when he laughed.

He went away after tea and she spent most of the evening trying to convince Jonkheer van der Blocq that just because she wanted to go out sometimes it didn't mean that she didn't like his company. She played three games of Racing Demon with him to prove her point.

The best time to go riding was in the morning. Mary Jane had an early breakfast and took the Mini over to the stables and rode for an hour. By the time she got back to the house, her host was awake and clamouring for her and his daughter was wanting her company. It worked very well, for they hardly noticed her absence, and she, refreshed by her morning exercise, felt prepared to be at their disposal for the rest of the day. And Fabian had telephoned each day too, to make sure that she was doing as he had asked, and she had answered truthfully enough that she was riding each day. Time enough to go to Groningen—at present the old gentleman needed her company, so did his daughter. She had no great opinion of herself, but she could see that the two of them rubbed each other up the wrong way, and a third party was necessary for peaceful living.

It was on her third morning's ride that she decided to ask for another horse; the mare was a nice beast, but a little slow. Without actually telling any fibs she managed to imply that Fabian had told her that she might make another choice if she wasn't quite pleased with the mare, and chose a bay, a spirited animal with a rolling eye and a little too big for her. But he went well and now that she had got the lie of the country she knew just where to take him—along the shore of the Leekstermeer, where there were trees and a good deal of undergrowth on either side of the unmade road. It was a dull morning, with the threat of rain— she had put on two sweaters and plaited her hair so that it would be out of the way, not caring at all if she should get wet. She reached the road to the lake and began to pick a way along the path she saw running beside it, looking about her as she did so. It was pretty there—not a patch on her own lake at home, but still charming and peaceful, even though the trees were bare of leaves and the grass was rough. She and the bay ambled along, for there was time enough; she could canter back along the road presently, there would be no traffic to speak of and there was an ample grass verge if he should get restive.

They were on the point of turning to go back when she became aware of horse's hooves behind her and when she turned to look it was to see Fabian astride a great roan, coming towards her at a canter. He rode well, she noted. He also looked very angry, she noted that too, and pulled in the bay with a resigned sigh.

His 'good morning' was icy, so she merely nodded in reply and waited silently for him to speak.

'I picked out a good little mare for you. Why aren't you riding her?' Mary Jane considered him thoughtfully. 'Well, I'm capable of choosing a mount, for one thing. I'm sick to death of you treating me as though I were a half-witted old maid you can barely bring yourself to be civil to!' She drew a swelling breath. 'And another thing, you may be my guardian, but you don't own me. I've a mind of my own.'

'And a temper, I see,' he observed dampingly. 'You forget that I had no notion of how you rode. If I had allowed you to choose for yourself and you could barely sit the beast and had taken a tumble, I should have done less than my duty to you as your guardian.'

'Oh, pooh!' she tossed her head and the pigtail swung over her shoulder.

'You look about ten years old,' he said unexpectedly, and smiled at her, 'Shall we cry a temporary truce? I came out to see you; I have those papers ready for you to sign and I wondered if you would like to come to Groningen for an hour or so.'

She eyed him with surprise. 'You mean you actually want me to go with you to Groningen?'

His voice was tinged with impatience. 'Yes. You see I'm being civil. We might even manage not to quarrel for a couple of hours.' He spoke without smiling now, his face turned away.

'Oh, very well,' she told him, knowing that her voice sounded ungracious, 'then I'd better go back.'

They rode back in silence. Only when they reached the stables did Fabian tell her quietly, 'I was mistaken, Mary Jane. You ride well.'

CHAPTER FOUR

Fabian had come in the Jaguar, so that Mary Jane, with an eye to the weather, tied a silk scarf over her head in place of the unbecoming hat, wishing she had had the sense to bring her sheepskin jacket with her. It was barely November but already cold, and an open car, although great fun, needed suitable clothes, but once they were on their way, she didn't feel cold at all; she glowed with excitement and pleasure. An outing would be delightful, especially if they could remain friends for an hour.

Her patient, in a mellow mood, had agreed to his daughter keeping him company for a short time, only begging Mary Jane to return at the earliest possible moment. His daughter had been rather more urgent in her request not to be left for longer than was absolutely necessary with her irascible parent; she had also given Mary Jane a shopping list of things which she declared she urgently needed. It was a miscellany of knitting wool, embroidery silks, Gentlemen's Relish, chocolate biscuits and a particular brand of bottled peach which could only be obtained at a certain shop in the city. Mary Jane accepted it obligingly, to have it taken from her at once by Fabian, who put it in his pocket with a brisk 'I'll see to these,' and an injunction to hurry herself up. So here she was, sitting snugly beside Fabian, who was making short work of the few miles to Groningen.

She found the city very fine, with its two big squares and its old buildings. Fabian, going slowly through the traffic, pointed out the imposing, towering spire of

St Martin's church before he turned off the main street and into a tree-lined one, bisected by a canal. The houses here were patrician, flat-faced and massive, each of them with its great front door reached by a double flight of steps. The sound of the traffic came faintly down its length so that it was easy to hear the rustle of the wind in the trees' bare branches.

'This is beautiful,' declared Mary Jane with satisfaction.

Fabian stopped before one of the houses. 'Yes, I think so too. I'm glad you like it.'

'Is this the lawyer's house?' she asked him.

'No, it's mine. We'll go inside and get those papers dealt with.'

She hadn't thought much about where he lived and when she had, it had been a vague picture of some smallish town house. This mansion took her by surprise, and she was still more surprised when they went inside. The hall was long and narrow and panelled waist high, with rich red carpeting on its floor to cover the black and white of its marble. The wall chandeliers were exquisite and there were flowers on the wall table. She wanted to take a more leisurely look, but an elderly woman appeared from the back of the house, was introduced as Mevrouw Hol and swept her away to an elegantly appointed cloakroom, where she tidied her hair, did things to her face and left her outdoor things before being led to a room close by where Fabian was waiting for her.

She took it to be a study, as it was lined with bookshelves and its main furniture was a massive desk and an equally massive chair, but the chairs by the fire were of a comfortably normal size. Mary Jane took the one offered her and sighed with content; the room was warm and light and airy and quite, quite different from the over-furnished house in which Fabian's uncle lived.

He sat down at the desk now, saying: 'You won't mind having coffee here? We can see to these papers at the same time, they'll not take long.'

She drank her coffee and then, under his direction, signed the papers, each one of which he carefully explained to her before asking her to do so. When she had finished she said with faint apology, 'I'm sorry you've had all this extra work, but I suppose once it's seen to, you won't need to bother any more.'

'On the contrary.' He didn't smile as he spoke and she felt chilled. 'If you have finished your coffee perhaps you would like to come with me and get Emma's shopping—and by the way, I believe that I promised you some money for your own use.' He opened a drawer in the desk and handed her a little bundle of notes. 'There are a thousand gulden there—about seventy-five pounds. If you need more, please ask me.'

She looked at him round-eyed. 'Whatever should I want with all that money?'

He smiled faintly. 'I imagine that you will find things to buy with it.'

She became thoughtful. 'Well, yes—there are one or two things...'

He went back to his desk and silently handed her a pad and pencil. A few minutes later she looked up. 'You know,' she informed him in surprise, 'I've made quite a list.'

'I thought maybe you would. Would a store suit you or do you want a boutique?'

She shot him a suspicious glance which she countered with a grave detachment. How did he know about boutiques? she wondered, and assured him that a large store would be much easier. 'I'll be as quick as I can,' she assured him.

'No need—I told Cousin Emma that we shouldn't be back until after tea. We'll lunch out and you will have hours of time.'

Mary Jane had forgotten how pleasant it was to go shopping with plenty of money to spend. By the time Fabian had worked his way through the list Emma had given them, it was burning a hole in her purse, and when Fabian left her outside a large store, assuring her that most of the assistants spoke English and she had nothing to worry about and that he would be waiting for her in an hour's time, she could hardly wait to start on a tour of inspection. Fabian had been right, there was no difficulty in making herself understood; everyone seemed to speak English. She bought everything which she had written on her list and a good deal besides, and when, strolling through the hat department, she saw a velvet beret which would go very well with her coat, she bought that too and, a little drunk with the success of her shopping, put it on.

She was only ten minutes late at the store entrance and when she would have apologised to Fabian for keeping him waiting he said to surprise her, 'Late? Are you? I never expected you back within the hour and a half—we agreed upon an hour, if you remember. We'll have lunch and if you have anything else to buy you can get it later.

They lunched at the Hotel Baulig, and as they were both hungry they started the meal with *erwtensoep*—a thick pea soup enriched with morsels of bacon and ham and sausage, went on to a dish of salmon with asparagus tips and quenelles of sole, and having finished this delicacy, agreed upon fresh fruit salad to round off their lunch. They sat a considerable time over their coffee, for rather to Mary Jane's surprise, they found plenty to talk about, and although she thought Fabian rather reserved in his manner, at least he was agreeable.

They did a little more shopping after they left the hotel, for it seemed sense to her to buy one or two presents while she had the opportunity. It was when she had declared herself satisfied with her purchases that Fabian remarked, 'But you have bought nothing for yourself.'

'Yes, I have, lots of things—and a hat.' She waited for him to notice the beret and was deeply mortified when he said: 'Oh, did you? why don't you wear it, then?' He glanced at their parcels. 'It must be a very small one, there's nothing here which looks like a hat bag.'

She boiled, but silently. She wasn't sure if he was teasing her or if he took so little notice of her that he hadn't even noticed what she was wearing. Neither of these ideas were very complimentary to herself. She answered with a sweetness which any of her closer friends would have suspected, 'I know where it is. I think I've finished, thank you. I expect you would like to be getting back to Midwoude.'

He gave her a searching look. 'Why?'

'Well, you've done your good deed for today, haven't you?' Her voice was light despite his look.

'Indeed yes, and it's made me thirsty. Shall we have tea somewhere?'

She kept her voice light. 'No, thank you. I think I should like to go back now. I'm most grateful to you...'

His tone was curt. 'Spare the thanks,' he begged her coldly, and thereafter sustained an ultra-polite conversation during their short journey back to Midwoude, where he handed her and her packages over to Jaap, wished her a distant good evening, got back into his car and drove away, a great deal too fast.

Emma van der Blocq, pouring a late tea in the small room at the back of the house where the two of them sometimes sat, professed surprise as Mary Jane joined her. 'I didn't expect you back until much later,' she declared happily, 'but surely Fabian could have stayed for tea—even for dinner?' She interrupted herself, 'No, perhaps not for dinner—he goes out a good deal, you know. Where did you have lunch, Mary Jane?'

She remembered the name of the hotel and felt rather pleased with herself about it, and Cousin Emma nodded, her interest aroused.

'A very nice place. Of course he really prefers the Hotel at Warffrum—Borg de Breedenburg—but that is for his more romantic outings.' She smiled at Mary Jane. 'He has girl-friends, as you can imagine—I wonder why he didn't take you there?'

'I imagine,' said Mary Jane in a dry little voice, 'that I don't qualify for a romantic background.'

'No, perhaps not,' agreed her companion with disconcerting directness. 'Fabian only takes out very pretty girls, you know—and always beautifully dressed, as you can imagine.' She smiled again, quite oblivious of any feelings Mary Jane might possess. 'He's a most observant man.'

'You surprise me,' said Mary Jane waspishly, thinking of the lovely velvet beret he hadn't even noticed. 'And now I'll just go up and see how Jonkheer van der

Blocq is. Did he have a quiet day?'

Her companion's face crumpled ominously. 'Oh, my dear, however did I manage before you came? He was so cross, and he refused to take his pills. Doctor Trouw will be here presently and he will be so annoyed.' She sounded so upset that Mary Jane paused on her way to the door.

'He's far too nice to get cross with you,' she assured her, 'and he knows that it isn't always easy ...'

Emma's face broke into a simper. 'Oh yes, he is so good ... I've known him for years, you know, long before he married. His wife died last year. She was a quiet little thing—no looks at all. You remind me of her.'

To which remark Mary Jane could think of no answer at all. She escaped through the door and spent the rest of the evening with the old gentleman, who seemed delighted to see her again and to her great relief made no remarks at all about her face or her lack of looks.

It turned a great deal colder the next day, but Mary Jane went riding just the same, bundled in several sweaters against the wind, and returning to the house with glowing cheeks and a sparkle in her eyes. Of Fabian there was no sign, but that didn't surprise her —why should he come anyway? He had only visited the house because he needed some papers signed—it certainly wasn't for her company. Let him use his leisure escorting the beauties of Groningen to romantic dinners, she thought, her lip curling, and then her mood changed and she fell to thinking how very satisfactory it would be if she could be escorted to this hotel Emma had been so enthusiastic about, wearing the organza dress. She sighed and prodded her mount to quicken his pace. Chance was a fine thing, she told him, as they turned for home.

She had her chance the very next day, as it turned out, for when Doctor Trouw called he brought his son with him. A pleasant young man in his twenties, he had recently qualified and was about to join his father's practice. Over coffee he remarked, 'You are a stranger here, I don't suppose you go out very much. I should like to take you out to dinner one evening.'

Mary Jane accepted with alacrity, and when, to her delight, he suggested that he should take her to Hotel Borg de Breedenborg on the following evening, she agreed with flattering speed.

She spent the intervening time imagining herself sweeping into the restaurant while Fabian, already there with some girl, would be bowled over by the sight of her in the organza, prettied up for the evening. The urge to shake him out of his cool, casual attitude towards herself was growing very strong, it caused her to take twice as long as usual in her preparations for the evening, which were so effective that when she went along to see her patient before they left, he was constrained to remark upon her changed appearance, as indeed was Cousin Emma, who rather tactlessly remarked that she hardly recognised Mary Jane in her finery.

Willem was rather nice and she was determined to have a pleasant evening. As they drove to the hotel she set herself to draw him out with a few well-chosen questions about his work. It wasn't until they reached the hotel that she was struck by the thought that her chance of seeing Fabian was small indeed. Even if he had a host of girl-friends, he surely didn't dine there every evening. He had his work—presumably that kept him busy, and surely he must spend some of his evenings at home, catching up on his reading, writing, even operating when it was necessary. She left her coat, patted the hair which had taken so long to put up and determinedly dismissed him from her head as she rejoined Willem.

The restaurant was full and she realized with something of a shock that it was already Saturday again—a whole week since she had seen Fabian. She sat down opposite her companion, gave him a brilliant smile and glanced around her. Fabian was sitting quite near their table, and the girl he was with was just as lovely as she had imagined she would be. Mary Jane turned the brilliance of her smile into a polite, tight-lipped one as she caught his eye and turned her attention to Willem, who, once they had ordered, launched into an earnest description of his days, hour by hour, almost minute by minute. She strove to keep an interested expression on her face, and when it was possible, laughed gaily, so that Fabian, whom she hadn't looked at again, would see how much she was enjoying herself. It was a pity that Fabian and his companion should go while they themselves were only half way through dinner. He paused as they passed the table, his hand on the girl's arm. He said austerely, 'I'm glad to see that you are enjoying yourself, Mary Jane,' nodded briefly to Willem and went on his way. Mary Jane watched him smile down at the girl as they went through the door and wondered briefly where they were going, and then concentrated on Willem, who had started to tell her at great length about a girl he had met at his hospital. She obviously occupied his thoughts to a large extent; by the time he had finished, Mary Jane even knew the size of her shoes.

They went back to the house at a reasonable hour because, as Willem reminded her, his father, who was dining with Cousin Emma and keeping an eye on her father at the same time, needed a good night's sleep. He took his farewell of her half an hour later with the hope that they might spend another evening together before she returned to England, and Mary Jane, thanking him nicely, wondered how she could possibly have been interested in him, even for such a short time; he was so very worthy, and looking back on their evening she could remember no conversation at all on her part, merely a succession of 'really's' and 'fancy that's' and 'you don't say so's'. When he and his father had gone she gave Cousin Emma a potted version of her evening because she could see that the lady had no intention of allowing her to go to bed until she had done so, and then she went to Jonkheer van der Blocq's room to see if he had settled for the night. Somehow or other, he had contrived not to take his sleeping tablet, which necessitated her arguing gently with him for the best part of ten minutes, but when he had finally consented to do as she asked and she had turned his pillows and settled him nicely, he enquired after her evening, observing in no uncertain manner that he found Willem a dull fellow, which naturally had the effect of her replying that he had been a very interesting companion, that the dinner had been delicious, and that he had asked her out again.

'What did you talk about?' growled the old man.

'Oh, his work, naturally. And a girl he met while he was in hospital—he's very taken with her. He—he talked a lot about her.'

Jonkheer van der Blocq laughed until he had no breath. Mary Jane gave him a drink, told him severely that there was nothing to laugh about, wished him good night and presently went to bed herself. She hadn't mentioned to anyone that Fabian had been at the hotel too, and she didn't think she would.

He came the next morning while they were in church, and this time it was the Rolls parked outside the door when they returned. As they went in he came downstairs, wished them a pleasant good morning, agreed that a cup of coffee would be welcome and when Emma had disappeared kitchenwards to find someone to make it, turned to Mary Jane and invited her to enter the sitting room.

'I'll take my things upstairs first,' she told him coldly, and was frustrated by his instant offer to take her coat, which he tossed on to a chair.

'It can stay there for a moment,' he told her rather impatiently. 'I see you are wearing the new hat. It's pretty—so you found it.'

She gave him a frosty look and said witheringly, 'It wasn't difficult, it was on my head.'

The dark wings of his brows soared. 'Oh dear—I can see that I must apologise, my dear girl, and I do. I could make a flowery speech, but you would make mincemeat of it, so I'll just say that I'm sorry.'

She walked away from him into the sitting room, where she sat down, telling herself indignantly that she didn't care if he followed her or not. He took the chair opposite hers and stretched his long legs and studied her carefully.

'You wouldn't believe me if I say how charming you looked yesterday evening? he asked mildly.

'No.' She added nastily, 'You haven't a clue as to what I was wearing.'

His smile mocked her. 'Sea green, or would you call

277

it sea blue, something thin and silky. It had long sleeves with frills over your wrists and a frill under your chin and a row of buttons down the back of the bodice.'

She was astounded, but she managed to say with a tinge of sarcasm:

'A photographic eye, I see,' and then because her female curiosity had got the better of her good sense, 'The girl you were with was lovely.'

He picked a tiny thread from a well-tailored sleeve. 'Delightfully so. She wears a different wig every day of the week and the longest false eyelashes I have ever seen.'

Mary Jane turned a chuckle into a cough. 'And why not? It's the fashion. Besides, she would look gorgeous in anything she chose to put on.'

He agreed placidly. 'And you found William Trouw entertaining?' he asked suavely.

'We had a very pleasant evening,' she told him guardedly.

'A worthy young man,' went on her companion ruminatively. 'He would make a good husband—do you fancy him?'

She choked. 'Well, of all the things to say! I've been out with him once, and here you are, talking as though...'

He went on just as though she had never interrupted him. 'He has a good practice with his father, so he wouldn't be after your money, and I imagine he has all the attributes of a good husband—good-natured, no interest in drinking or betting, or girls, for that matter—a calm disposition, he...'

She ground her teeth. 'Be quiet! You may be my guardian, but you shan't talk like that. I'll marry whom I please and when I want to, and until then you can mind your own business!'

'From which outburst I conclude that Willem hasn't won your heart?'

She wanted to laugh, but she choked it back. 'No, he hasn't. As a matter of fact he spent quite a long time telling me about a girl he knew in hospital. I think he intends to marry her.'

'Ah, I wondered what it was that you found so interesting, though surely it was unkind of you to laugh so much during the recital?'

'I didn't...' she began, and stopped, because of course she had, so that Fabian should think she was having a lovely time. 'I enjoyed myself very much,' she muttered peevishly, and was glad to see Cousin Emma and Jaap with the coffee tray, coming into the room.

Fabian stayed for lunch, and his uncle insisted upon coming down to join them, contributing to the conversation with such gusto that Mary Jane feared for his blood pressure. But at least he was so tired after his meal that she had no difficulty in persuading him to take his customary nap, and when she had tucked him up and come downstairs again it was to find that Emma had allowed herself to be driven over to Doctor Trouw's house for tea. Which left her and Fabian. He was waiting for her in the hall and he sounded impatient.

'Shall we have a walk before tea?'

Mary Jane paused at the bottom of the staircase. 'Thank you, no. I have letters to write.'

'Which you can write at any time.' He came towards her. 'It's not often I'm here.'

'Oh—should I mind?'

'Don't be an impudent girl, and don't imagine it is

because I want your company,' he added quite violently. 'I had a letter from Mr North asking me to explain certain aspects of your inheritance to you, so I might just as well do it and take some exercise at the same time.'

'Charming!' observed Mary Jane, her eyes snapping with temper, 'and so good of you to fit me in with one of your more healthy activities.'

'And what,' he asked awfully, 'exactly do you mean by that remark?'

'Just exactly what I say. I'll come for half an hour—in that time you should be able to tell me whatever I'm supposed to know.'

She crossed the hall and picked up her coat, caught up her gloves and went to the pillow cupboard, rummaged around in its depths until she found a scarf, which she tied carelessly over her hair. 'Ready,' she said with a distinct snap.

They walked away from the village, into the teeth of a mean wind, while Fabian talked about stocks and shares and gilt-edged securities and capital gains tax, to all of which she lent only half an ear. As far as she could see she would have a perfectly adequate income whatever he and Mr North decided to do with her money. As long as she had sufficient to run the house and pay for Mrs Body and Lily and have some over to run the car and buy clothes ... She stopped suddenly and told him so.

'You are not only a tiresome girl, you are also a very ungrateful one,' Fabian informed her bitterly.

'I'm sorry—about being ungrateful, I mean, but I can't remember being tiresome—was it on any particular occasion?'

He sounded quite weary. 'You are tiresome all the

time,' he told her, which surprised her so much that she walked in silence until he observed that since she wished to return to Midwoude within half an hour, they had better go back. They didn't speak at all, and in the hall they parted. When Mary Jane came downstairs ten minutes later, it was to find that he had gone. She told herself with a little surge of rage that it was a good thing too, for when they were together they did nothing but disagree. She wandered across to the sitting room, telling herself again, this time out loud, that she was delighted, and added the hope that she wouldn't see him for simply ages.

But it wasn't simply ages, it was the following Wednesday, or rather three o'clock on Thursday morning. Jonkheer van der Blocq had had, for him, a very good day. They had played their usual game of cards, and she had helped him to bed, just a little worried because his colour was bad. But Doctor Trouw had called that afternoon, and although the old gentleman was failing rapidly now, he had seen no cause for immediate alarm. Mary Jane went to bed early, first taking another look at her patient. He was asleep, and there was nothing to justify her unease.

The peal of the bell wakened her. She bundled on her dressing gown, and not waiting to put her feet in slippers, ran across the dim landing. The old man was lying very much as she had left him, but now his colour was livid, although he said with his usual irascibility, 'I feel most peculiar—I want Fabian here at once.'

She murmured soothingly while she took a frighteningly weak pulse and studied his tired old face before she went to the telephone. It was quite wrong to ring up in front of the patient, but she didn't dare leave him. She rang Doctor Trouw first, with a suitably guarded request for him to come, and then dialled Fabian's number. His voice, calm and clear over the line, gave her the instant feeling that she didn't need to worry about anything because he was there—she forgot that they weren't on speaking terms, that he was arrogant and treated her like a tiresome child. She said simply, 'Oh, Fabian—will you come at once? Your uncle'—she paused, aware that the bed's occupant was listening—'would like to speak to you,' she finished.

'He's listening?'

'Yes.'

'I'll be with you in fifteen minutes. Get Trouw.'

'I have.'

'Good girl! Get Jaap up and tell him to open the gates and the door. Get Emma up too—no, wait—tell Jaap to do that. You stay with my uncle.'

She said, 'Yes, Fabian,' and put down the receiver. 'Fabian's on his way,' she told Jonkheer van der Blocq in a calm, reassuring voice. 'I'm to wake Jaap so that he can open the gates. Stay just as you are—I'll only be a few moments.'

Doctor Trouw came a few minutes later, and in response to the old gentleman's demand to be given something to keep him going, gave him an injection, told him to save his breath in the understanding voice of an old friend and went to Emma's room, where she could be heard crying very loudly.

Mary Jane pulled up a chair to the bedside, tucked her cold feet under her and took Jonkheer van der Blocq's hand in hers. 'Fabian won't be long,' she told him again, because she sensed that was what he wanted above anything else. She certainly was justified, because a moment later she heard the soft, powerful murmur of the Rolls' engine and the faint crunch of its tyres as Fabian stopped outside the front door.

He entered the room without haste, wearing a thick sweater and slacks and looking very wide awake. He said: 'Hullo, Uncle Georgius,' and nodded to Mary Jane, his dark, bright gaze taking in the dressing-gown, the plaited hair and her bare feet. He said kindly, 'What a girl you are for forgetting your slippers! Go and put them on, it's cold, and tell Trouw I'm here, will you. I don't suppose he heard me come, with the row Emma's making.'

His uncle made a weak, explosive sound. 'Silly woman,' he said, in a voice suddenly small, 'always crying —you'll keep an eye on her, Fabian?'

'Of course.' He lapsed into Dutch as Mary Jane reached the door.

Emma was in no state to be left alone; Mary Jane stayed with her as Doctor Trouw hurried across the landing, and was still with her when he came back to tell them that his patient was dead. It wasn't until poor Emma had had something to send her to sleep, and Mary Jane had tucked her up in bed, that she felt free to leave her.

The old house was very quiet; there was a murmur of voices coming from the kitchen, and still more voices behind the closed door of the small sitting room. She stood in the hall, wondering if she should go back to bed, a little uncertain as to what Doctor Trouw might expect of her. It was chilly in the hall and the tick-tock of the over-elaborate French grandfather clock dripped into the stillness with an oily sloth which she found intensely irritating. A cup of tea would have been nice, she thought despondently, and turned to go back upstairs just as the sitting room door opened and Fabian said: 'Ah, there you are. Come in—Jaap's bringing tea.' He glanced at her pale face. 'You look as though you need it. Cousin Emma's asleep?'

She nodded, then sat down in a chair by the still burning fire and drank her tea, listening to the two men talking and saying very little herself. When she had finished she got to her feet. 'Is there anything you would like me to do?' she asked.

Doctor Trouw shook his head. 'The district nurse will be here very shortly. Go to bed, Mary Jane, and get some sleep. I am most grateful to you for all you have done and I will ask you to do something else. Would you look after Emma for a few days? She has a very sensitive nature and I am afraid this will be too much for her—I will leave something for her, if you will give it when she wakes, and be round about lunch time to see how she is.'

She nodded, thinking that Cousin Emma would be even more difficult than her father, and went to the door which Fabian had opened for her. He followed her into the hall, shutting the door behind him, and she turned round tiredly to see what he wanted.

His voice was quiet. 'I know what you are thinking. We have imposed upon you and we have no right, but I too would be grateful if you would stay just for a little while and help Emma—she likes you and she needs you.'

She said shortly, 'Oh, that's all right. Of course I'll stay.'

He came nearer. 'You have had a lot to bear in the last few weeks, Mary Jane. Once I called you a tiresome girl. I apologise.' He bent and kissed her cheek with a gentleness which disturbed her more than any of the harsh words he had uttered in the past. She went upstairs, not answering his good night.

The next few days were a peculiar medley of intense activity, doing all the things Cousin Emma insisted should be done; receiving visitors, whose hushed voices and platitudes caused her to sit in floods of tears for hours after they had gone; going to Groningen to buy the black garments she considered essential and relating, seemingly endlessly, her father's perfections to Mary Jane, while crying herself sick again.

Mary Jane found it all a little difficult to stomach—father and daughter had hardly had a happy relationship while he was alive, now that he was dead he had somehow become a kind of saint. But she liked Emma, although she found her histrionics a little trying, and she did what she could to keep her as calm as possible, addressed countless envelopes and kept out of Fabian's way as much as possible.

He came frequently, but her quick ears, tuned to the gentle hum of the Rolls-Royce or the exuberant roar of the Jaguar, gave her warning enough to slip away while he was in the house. But one evening she had made the mistake of supposing that he had left the house; it was almost dinner time and there was no sound of voices from either of the sitting rooms. He must have gone, she decided, while she had been up in the attic, packing away Jonkheer van der Blocq's clothes until such time as his daughter found herself capable of deciding what to do with them. The small sitting room was dimly lit by the firelight and one lamp, and Freule van der Blocq was lying asleep on the sofa. Fabian was on one of the easy chairs, his legs thrust out before him, contemplating the ceiling, but he got up as Mary Jane started to leave the room as silently and quickly as she had entered it. Outside in the hall he demanded: 'Where have you been?'

'Upstairs in the attics, sorting your uncle's clothes.'

'Have you, by God? Surely there's someone else to do such work? And that was not what I meant. Where have you been? Whenever I come, I am conscious of your disappearing footsteps. Do you dislike me so much?'

She eyed him thoughtfully. 'I never think about it,' she said at length, not quite truthfully.

His expressive eyebrows rose. 'No? You thought I had gone?'

'Yes.'

He grinned. 'I'm staying to dinner, and now you're here there's no point in retreating, is there? We'll have a glass of sherry.'

She accompanied him to the big sitting room and sat down composedly while he poured their drinks. When he had settled himself near her he asked, 'When do you want to go home?'

'I should like to go as soon as the funeral is over. I understand that Emma is going away the day after—I could leave at the same time.' She sipped her sherry. 'If you would be kind enough to let me have some more money, I can see about getting my ticket.'

'No need. I shall take you with the car.'

She kept her voice reasonable. 'I don't want to go in your car. I'm quite capable of looking after myself, you know. Besides, you have your work.' She looked at him, saw his smouldering gaze bent upon her and added hastily, 'I'm very grateful, but I can't let you waste any more time on me.'

'Have I ever complained that I was wasting my time on you?'

'No—but one senses these things.'

He gave a crack of laughter. 'One might be mistaken. Would you feel better about it if I told you that I have to go over to England anyway within the next few days—I'm only offering you a lift.'

She said doubtfully, 'Really? Well, that's different, I'll be glad to go with you.'

She missed the gleam in his eyes. 'Tuesday, then. Cousin Emma will be fetched by her friends after breakfast. I'll come for you about four o'clock. I've a ward round to do in the morning and a couple of patients to see after that. We'll go from Rotterdam, I think, straight to Hull.' He thought for a minute. 'If we leave here after tea we shall have plenty of time to catch the ferry at Europort. If I'm not here by half past four, have tea and be ready to leave, will you?'

'Certainly.'

'You'll want to telephone Mrs Body.' He strolled across the room and picked up the receiver from the telephone on the delicate serpentine table between the windows. 'What is the number?'

It was nice to hear Mrs Body's motherly voice again. Mary Jane listened to her comfortable comments and felt a wave of homesickness sweep over her. It would be lovely to be home again. She told Mrs Body her news and heard that lady's voice asking if the dear doctor would be staying. Mary Jane hadn't thought about that. She repeated the enquiry and he turned to look at her. 'I began to think you weren't going to ask me,' he remarked mildly. 'A day or so, if I may.'

Mrs Body sighed in a satisfied manner when Mary Jane told her. 'That will be nice,' she said as she rang off, leaving Mary Jane wondering how much truth there was in that remark. Probably they would quarrel again before his visit was over, and there was nothing nice about that.

But at least they didn't quarrel that evening. By tacit consent, they allied to keep Cousin Emma interested and amused, and succeeded so well that she didn't cry once and went to bed quite cheerful. Mary Jane, quite tired herself, went to bed early too and closed her eyes on the thought that when Fabian wished, he could be a most agreeable companion.

She saw little of him until Tuesday, when Cousin Emma, vowing eternal thanks, was packed off to stay with her friends and Mary Jane found herself alone in the house except for Jaap and the cook. The morning passed slowly enough because she had nothing much to do but go for a walk, but after her solitary lunch she settled down with a book until four o'clock, when she did her face and hair once more, got Jaap to bring down her case and went to the window to watch for the car. It didn't come; it hadn't come by half past four either. She had her tea, punctuated by frequent visits to the window, and when she had finished, put on her outdoor things, made sure that she had everything with her, and sat down to wait. It was a quarter to six when the car's headlights lighted up the drive. She went into the hall to meet him, saying without any hint of the impatience she felt: 'You'd like a cup of tea, wouldn't you? I asked Jaap to be ready with one.'

'Good girl. I missed lunch—an emergency—I was called back to theatre.'

She was already on her way to the kitchen. 'I'll get some sandwiches.' She paused. 'I hope it was a success.'

'I think so—we shan't be certain for a couple of days.'

She nodded understandingly as she went, to return very soon with a tray of tea and buttered toast, sandwiches and cake. She poured the tea, gave him his toast and sat down again. Presently he said:

'You're very restful—not one reproach for being late, or missing the boat or where have I been.'

'Well, it wouldn't help much if I did, would it?' she wanted to know in a matter-of-fact voice. 'Besides, there's time enough, isn't there? The Rolls goes like a bomb, doesn't she, and the ferry doesn't leave until about midnight.'

'Sensible Miss Pettigrew! But I had planned a leisurely dinner on the way. Now it will have to be a hurried one.'

She smiled at him without malice. 'That won't matter much, will it? Now if I'd been the girl you were with the other night, that would be quite a different kettle of fish...'

He put down his cup slowly. 'You're a great one for the unvarnished truth, aren't you?'

She got up and went over to the big gilt-framed mirror at the opposite end of the room and twitched the beret to a more becoming angle.

'Seeing that we have to deal with each other until I'm thirty,' she said in a tranquil voice, 'we might as well be truthful with each other, even if nothing else.'

'Nothing else what?' He spoke sharply.

She went to pour him a second cup. 'Nothing,' she told him.

They set out shortly afterwards. It was a cold dark evening and the road was almost free of traffic and Fabian sent the car tearing along on the first stage of their journey. He showed no signs of tiredness but sat relaxed behind the wheel—it was a pity it wasn't light, he told her, for they were going to Rotterdam down the other side of the Ijsselmeer, and she would have been able to see a little more of Holland. Mary Jane agreed with him and they sat in silence as the Rolls ripped through the flat landscape. Only when they reached Alkmaar and slowed to go through its narrow streets did he say, 'I'm poor company. I'm sorry.'

'The case this afternoon?' she ventured, to be rewarded by his surprised, 'How did you guess? Would it bore you if I told you about it?'

She wasn't bored; she listened with interest and intelligence and asked the right questions in the right places. They were approaching Rotterdam when he said finally, 'Thank you for listening so well—I can't think of any other girl to whom I would have talked like that.'

She felt a little pang of pure pleasure and tried to think of something to say, but couldn't.

They had their dinner in haste at the Old Dutch restaurant, and Mary Jane, seeing how tired Fabian looked, did her utmost to keep the conversation of a nature which could provoke no difference of opinion between them, and succeeded so well that they boarded the ferry on the friendliest of terms.

The journey was uneventful but rough, but they were both too tired to bother about the weather. They met at breakfast and she was delighted to find that his humour was still a good one. Perhaps now that they wouldn't be seeing much of each other, he was prepared to unbend a little. She accompanied him down to the car deck, hoping that this pleasant state of affairs would last.

It didn't, at least only until they reached the Lakes, to receive a rapturous welcome from Mrs Body and

Lily and sit down to one of her excellent teas. They had barely begun the meal when Mary Jane stated rashly, 'I intend to buy a horse tomorrow.'

'No, you won't.' Fabian spoke unhurriedly and with cold finality.

She opened her eyes wide. 'Haven't I enough money?' she demanded.

'Don't make ridiculous statements like that—you have plenty of money. If you want a mount, I'll come with you, and you will allow me to choose the animal.'

'No, I won't! I can ride, you know I can.'

'Nevertheless, you will do as I ask, but before you start spending your money there are one or two details to attend to, I must ask you to come with me to the bank at Keswick, and Mr North will be coming here tomorrow morning. He will bring the last of the papers for you to sign, and as from then your income will be paid into your account each quarter. Should you need more money, you will have to advise me and I will advance it from the estate, should I consider it necessary.'

She boiled with rage. 'Consider it? It's ridiculous—it's like being a child, having to ask you for everything I want!'

He remained unmoved by her outburst. 'How inaccurate you are! You have more than sufficient to live on in comfort, and as long as you keep within your income, you will have no need to apply to me.'

She snorted, 'I should hope not—I'd rather be a pauper!'

'Even more inaccurate.'

There seemed no more to be said; she wasn't disposed to say that she was sorry and she could see that such an intention on his part hadn't even crossed his mind. He excused himself presently and she saw him cleaning the Rolls at the back of the house. From a distance he looked nice. He was a handsome man, she had to admit, and amusing when he wished to be, and kind; only, she told herself darkly, when one got to know him better did one discover what an ill-tempered, arrogant, unsympathetic ... She ran out of adjectives.

He stayed two more days, coldly polite, unfailingly courteous and as withdrawn as though they were complete strangers forced to share a small slice of life together. She told herself that she was glad to see him go as the Rolls went through the gate and disappeared down the road to Keswick. He hadn't turned round to wave, either, and he must have known that she was standing in the porch. His goodbye had been casual in the extreme and he had made no mention of their future meeting. Mary Jane stormed back into the house, very put out and banged the door behind her, telling Major in a loud angry voice that life would be heaven without him.

CHAPTER FIVE

IT was heaven for three or four days, during which Mary Jane explored the house from attic to cellar, examining with affection the small treasures her grandfather had possessed and which were now hers. She worked in the garden too, sweeping the leaves from the frosty ground, and went walking each day beside the lake with Major. It was cold now, and the snow had crept further down the mountains, but the sun still shone. She drove to Keswick, and to Carlisle to see Mr North, reflecting that it would have been marvellous weather for riding. But she had stubbornly refused to allow Fabian to choose a horse for her, and only after he had pressed the matter had she said that she wouldn't buy one at all if she couldn't have her own way; a decision she was regretting, for she had cut off her nose to spite her face, and a lot of good it had done her.

He hadn't even bothered to write to her—out of sight, out of mind, she muttered bitterly to herself, quite forgetting that she had hardly contributed to increase any desire on his part to have any more to do with her other than businesswise. It was that night, as she lay in bed very much awake, that she made the astonishing discovery that she actually missed him. She examined this from all angles and decided finally that it was because his extreme bossiness had imposed itself far too firmly upon her mind. Well, she was free of him now. She had a house of her own and what seemed to her to be quite a fortune—she could do exactly what she liked, whether he liked it or not—and she would too. She fell asleep making rather wild plans.

She found herself, as the days passed, filling them rather feverishly, quite often doing things which didn't need doing at all, taking walks which became increasingly longer, making excuses to get out the Mini and drive into Cockermouth or Keswick, and although she was happy she was lonely too, missing the rush and bustle of hospital life. In a few short weeks it would be Christmas and she wondered what to do about it. She hadn't a relation in the world whom she knew of and her friends were miles away in London, and what was more, they wouldn't be free over Christmas—nurses seldom were. She wondered what her grandfather and Mrs Body had done in previous years and went to ask that good lady, who chuckled gently and said:

'Well, Miss Mary Jane, not a great deal—your grandfather liked his turkey and his Christmas pudding, and his friends came in for a drink. When he was younger, he used to give a dinner party—even have a few of his closer friends to stay, but they've died or gone away. The last few years have been a bit quiet.' She looked a little wistful. 'I suppose you haven't any friends who could come—a few jolly young people?'

Mary Jane explained about nurses not getting holidays at Christmas and Mrs Body said: 'Well, there's Doctor Morris, and there's Commander Willis—he's a very old friend of your grandfather's, but Lily was telling me that he's not been so well lately...'

They stared at each other, empty of ideas and a little depressed. The sound of a car turning into the drive sent them both into the hall to peer out of the small window beside the front door. 'It'll be that nice Doctor van der Blocq,' breathed Mrs Body happily. 'Oh, how lovely if it is!'

Mary Jane was looking out of the window; if it was keen disapointment she felt when she saw that the car was a Ford Capri and the man getting out of it wasn't Fabian, she was quite unaware of it. The man was a stranger, young, fair and not very tall. He seemed to be in no hurry to ring the bell but stood staring at the house and then turned his attention to the garden. Only when he had looked his fill did he advance towards the door. As he rang the bell Mary Jane retreated to the sitting room, waving an urgent

294

hand at Mrs Body. She just had time to sit down in her grandfather's chair and take up the morning paper before the housekeeper, after the shortest of colloquies, put her head round the door. She looked surprised and excited.

'A young gentleman to see you, Miss Mary Jane. Mr Pettigrew from Canada.'

Mary Jane cast down the paper and goggled at her. 'Mr Pettigrew?' Enlightenment struck her. 'Do you suppose he's the cousin—the Canadian cousin—did he say?'

Mrs Body shook her head. 'He wants to see you.'

Mary Jane went into the hall. The young man was standing by the wall table, one of the Georgian candlesticks which rested upon it in his hands, examining it carefully.

She frowned. Even if he were a relation, it was hardly good manners to examine the silver for hallmarks the moment he entered the house. She said coolly, a question in her voice: 'Good morning?'

He put the candlestick down without any trace of embarrassment and crossed the hall, smiling at her, and she found herself smiling back at him, although her first impression of him hadn't been a good one. When he spoke it was with a rich Canadian accent.

'You must think I've got an infernal cheek...' He paused and widened his smile, and Mary Jane, a little on her guard now, allowed her own to fade, but this didn't deter him from continuing: 'I'm a Pettigrew—Mervyn John Pettigrew. My grandfather was your grandfather's cousin—he talked a lot about him when he was alive.' He put a hand into his pocket and withdrew a passport. 'I don't expect you to take me on trust—take a look at this.' And as she stretched out a hand to take it, 'You're Mary Jane, aren't you? I know all about you too.'

She glanced at the passport and gave it back, studying his face. She could see no family likeness, but probably there wouldn't be any; his mother had been a Canadian; he might take after her side of the family. She said quietly, 'How do you do? Why are you here?'

'We get the English papers—I saw a notice of my great-uncle's death. I had a holiday owing to me, so I decided to fly over and look you up.' He smiled again —he smiled too much, she thought irritably. 'My old man's dead—died two years ago. Mother died when I was a boy, and I'm the only Pettigrew left at home, so I thought I'd look you up.' He gave her a searching glance. 'I don't blame you for not quite believing me, despite the passport. If you'd give me ten minutes, though, I could tell you enough about the family to convince you.'

He had light eyes, a little too close together, but his look was direct enough. Mary Jane said on an impulse, 'Come in—I was just going to have coffee. Will you have a cup with me?'

She was bound to admit, at the end of ten minutes, that he must be a genuine cousin. After all, her grandfather had told her often enough that the nephew in Canada had a son—this would be he; he knew too much about the family to be anything else. And when he produced some letters written by her grandfather to his own father, there could be no further doubt. True, he didn't give them to her to read, but he showed her the address and the signature at the end, explaining, 'Great-uncle was very fond of my grandfather, you know—he was always making plans to visit him. He never did, of course, but he had a real affection for him—Dad was always talking about him too. Have you still got Major?'

Her last misgivings left her. She said with cautious friendliness:

'Yes—he's eleven, though, and getting a bit slow. He's in the kitchen with Mrs Body. Would you like to stay to lunch? Are you passing through or staying somewhere here?'

He accepted the invitation with an open pleasure which won her over completely. 'I'm touring around, having a look at all the places the old man told me about. I'm staying at Keswick and very comfortable.'

'Did you bring your car?' She corrected herself. 'No, of course you couldn't if you flew.'

'I've rented one.' And when he added nothing further she suggested that they should walk down to the lake. Their stroll was an unqualified success, partly because Mary Jane, who wasn't used to men—younger men, at any rate—taking any notice of her, found that not only did her companion listen to her when she spoke, but implied in his replies that she was worth listening to as well, and the glances he gave her along with the replies gave her the pleasant feeling that perhaps she wasn't quite as plain a girl as she had believed. It was a pity, she reflected, while the young man waxed enthusiastic over the scenery, that Fabian wasn't with them so that he could see for himself that not everyone shared his opinion of her. The horrid word tiresome flashed through her mind; it was amazing how it still rankled. A vivid picture of his face—austere, faintly mocking and handsome—floated before her mind's eye. She dismissed it and turned to answer Mervyn Pettigrew's eager questions about the house and its history.

She told him all she knew, studying him anew as she did so. He had good looks, she conceded, spoiled a little by the eyes and a mouth too small—and perhaps his chin lacked determination, although, as she quickly reminded herself, after several weeks of Fabian's resolute features, she was probably unfairly influenced, but these were small faults in an otherwise pleasing countenance. She judged him to be twenty-five or six, thick-set for his height and age. His clothes were right—country tweeds and well-polished shoes. On the whole she was prepared to reverse her first hasty impression of him, and admit that he might be rather nice. It was certainly pleasant to have someone of her own age to talk to; over lunch he told her about his home in Canada, volunteering the information that he was an executive in a vast business complex somewhere near Winnipeg, that he was a bachelor and lived in the house where he had been born—an oldish, comfortable house, by all accounts, with plenty of ground around it. He rode each day, he told her, getting up early so that he could take some exercise before breakfast and going to the office. 'Do you ride?' he wanted to know.

Mary Jane frowned. 'Yes. I haven't a mount, thought. I—I've a guardian who wouldn't allow me to choose a horse for myself; otherwise I would have had one days ago.'

Her cousin looked sympathetic. 'Don't think I'm interfering,' he begged her, 'but why not tell me about it? Perhaps there's some way ... surely he can't stop you...' He waved a hand. 'This is all yours, isn't it? and I suppose Great-uncle left you enough to live on in plenty of comfort, and you're over twenty-one.' He added hastily, 'At least, I suppose you are.'

He was very well informed, she thought vaguely; he knew so much. 'I'm twenty-two.' She hesitated; the temptation to confide in someone was very great, and he was family. 'It's a little complicated,' she went on, and proceeded to tell him a little about Fabian and the conditions of her grandfather's will. She was strictly fair about Fabian. He was, she supposed, a good guardian and quite to be trusted with her money, she didn't want her companion to be in any doubt about that, and she was careful not to go into any details about her inheritance—indeed, when she had finished she wasn't sure if she should have mentioned it at all, but Mervyn had seemed very sympathetic and she was further reassured by his brief, vague reply before he changed the subject completely.

He left soon after that and when she asked him if he would like to come again, agreed that he would. 'But not for a few days,' he told her. 'I have some business to do, in Carlisle—friends I promised to look up for someone back home, but I'll call and see you again when I get back.'

She watched him go with some regret; he had helped to pass the day, it had been pleasant to talk to someone and have company for lunch. She went along to the kitchen where Mrs Body was sitting in the shabby, comfortable armchair she had used ever since Mary Jane could remember, and asked that lady what she thought of their visitor.

'He seems nice enough,' said Mrs Body, 'very friendly too. Is he coming again?'

'He said he would.' Mary Jane picked up one of the jam tarts the housekeeper had put to cool on the kitchen table and ate it.

'You'll get fat,' declared Mrs Body, 'picking and

stealing between meals. Where's he from?'

Mary Jane ate another tart and told her.

'Why did he come?'

Mary Jane explained that too and then asked a little worriedly, 'Don't you like him, Mrs Body?'

'I've no reason to dislike him, but I don't know him, do I? I'm not quick to take a fancy to anyone.'

'You liked Mr van der Blocq . . .'

'That's different. Now if you take Major for a quick walk, I'll have tea ready by the time you get back.'

'Let's have it here,' begged Mary Jane, and went off obediently with the dog.

Mervyn didn't came for five days, during which time Mary Jane thought of him quite a lot while she busied herself about the house and the garden, writing letters to her friends at Pope's and answering a long dramatic letter from Cousin Emma, who, it seemed, had quite recovered from her father's death and was engaged in refurbishing her wardrobe—several pages were devoted to the outfits she had bought and intended to buy, to the exclusion of all other news. Fabian wasn't mentioned, nor had he written. That he was a busy man, Mary Jane was well aware, but he could surely have telephoned? But that took time, especially if he needed every free minute he had in order to take pretty girls out . . . she was aware that she was being unfair to him, but he could have taken some notice. When she wrote her Christmas cards, she sent him one too, and although sorely tempted to put a note in with it, she didn't do so.

She was in the kitchen helping Mrs Body and Lily with the Christmas puddings when Mervyn arrived. He apologised for disturbing her, offered her a box of chocolates with disarming diffidence and invited her out to lunch. 'There's a place in Cockermouth,' he told her, 'where we could eat, and I wondered if you would help me choose one or two things to take home with me—presents, you know.'

She felt faint dismay. 'You're not going back to Canada before Christmas?'

'I haven't any reason for staying longer.'

'What a pity! I was going to invite you to spend Christmas Day here.'

He didn't answer at once and he had turned his head away as he replied:

'That's a sufficiently good reason for me to cancel my flight, Mary Jane.' He turned and gave her a long, steady look. 'I've thought of you a good deal. When I came to England I decided to come and look you up, because you were family—but now I keep thinking of all kinds of excuses to keep me here.'

Mary Jane listened to him, enchanted. No one—no young man, that was—had ever talked like that to her before. All of a sudden she felt beautiful, sought after, and dripping with charm; it was a pleasant sensation. She smiled widely at him and said a little breathlessly, 'Well, don't go until after Christmas—it's only ten days.' They stared at each other in silence and then she said, 'I'll go and put on my coat—there's a fire in the sitting room, I won't be a minute.'

It was the first of several such expeditions. They would return after their shopping and have tea, and then, later, dinner, to return to the sitting room fire and talk until Mervyn got up to go about ten o'clock. He was an amusing talker, preferring to tell her about his own life than ask her questions about her own, although sometimes she would find that, almost without knowing it, she was answering questions she had hardly noticed about the house and its contents and whether she had enough to run it properly and if her capital was in safe hands. She told him about Mr North, assuring him that he had been the family solicitor for years and was very much to be depended upon.

'Oh, is that the North who lives in Keswick?' he asked carelessly.

'Is there one in Keswick? No, Carlisle—Lowther Street. The firm's been there for ever.'

He had made no comment and had gone on to talk about something else.

He got up to go soon after and she walked with him to the door. As he put on his coat he said, 'I've some business to see to in the morning—a call to Winnipeg. May I come after lunch and take you out to tea?'

She nodded happily and he kissed her lightly on the cheek as she opened the door. It took her a long while to go to sleep that night; it was a pity that her excited thoughts of Mervyn were interlarded with unsolicited ones of Fabian.

She felt a little shy when he arrived the next afternoon, but it seemed that he felt no such thing; he kissed her again, a good deal more thoroughly this time, and told her gaily to get her coat and drove her into Keswick, where they had tea, bought a few things Mrs Body had need of, and drove home again. It was dark already, although it was barely four o'clock, for the mountains had swallowed up what light there had been, only the water of the lake gave back a dim reflection. It would be cold later on, but they didn't care. They roasted chestnuts by a blazing fire and ate their dinner together, and after Mervyn had gone, with yet another kiss, Mary Jane had skipped into the kitchen, her plain face alight. Mrs Body looked up as she went in, asked Lily to take some more logs to the sitting room and when she had gone, observed, 'You're happy, Miss Mary Jane.' Her kind eyes were sharp. 'Has he proposed?'

Mary Jane flung her arms round Mrs Body's ample waist. 'Oh, Mrs Body, do you think he's going to? No one has ever proposed to me before.'

'Which is no good reason for accepting him,' counselled her companion shrewdly.

Mary Jane knitted her fine pale brows. Mrs Body's remark was a sensible one, but it didn't fit in with her own reckless mood. 'Oh, I know that,' she declared gaily, 'but we get on so well and he's such a dear—you know, thoughtful and interested in the house and careful of me—making sure that my future's secure and all the rest of it.' She laughed. 'He actually wanted me to take out an insurance policy!'

Mrs Body said quickly, 'You didn't take any notice of that?'

'Well, I couldn't even if I'd wanted to, Mr van der Blocq sees to all that, but I didn't bother to tell Mervyn . . . What shall I give him for Christmas?'

Mrs Body made one or two uninspired suggestions, adding, 'And that nice Doctor van der Blocq, what are you sending him?'

'Why, nothing,' said Mary Jane. 'He's got everything in the world, you know.' She danced off again to take Major for his bedtime trot around the garden.

It was several days later, when they were out walking on the hills, heavily wrapped against the cold, that Mervyn let fall that he had met someone who had a roan for sale, sixteen hands, with plenty of spirit but good-tempered with it. 'I know you promised this guardian of yours not to buy a horse, but if you gave me an open cheque, I could buy it for you. I'm not a bad judge and I dare say I could strike a good bargain.'

Mary Jane paused on the slope they were working their way down. 'Well, I'm not sure—I should love it, but Fabian did say that I wasn't to buy one...'

'Yes, but don't you think that he said that because he wasn't here to give you his advice? Probably he was afraid that you might be tricked out of your money—you know how unscrupulous some people are—but surely if I picked out a good mount for you, he wouldn't raise any objection?'

Put like that, it had a ring of reasonableness. Besides, Fabian probably wouldn't come again for months—she would never get a horse of her own. She said thoughtfully: 'All right, I'll give you a cheque. Will you see to it for me, please? I'm sure Fabian won't mind.'

The words sounded curiously false in her own ears; Fabian would mind. He would mind on principle, because he was her guardian and considered that she shouldn't do anything at all without first asking his permission. Indignation swelled her bosom and gave way to a feeling of sneaking relief because he wouldn't know anyway.

The horse arrived two days later, a nice beast who went to his stable quietly enough, although he had a rolling eye. Mervyn explained that the animal was a little nervous but would settle down in a day or so. He told her what he had paid for him too, a price which rather shocked her, but when she ventured: 'Isn't that rather a lot?' she was met with a chilly surprise.

'I had to haggle to get him at that price, but if you

could have done better...' He left the rest of the sentence in mid-air, where it hung between them like a small, disturbing cloud. It evaporated during the day, but she made a mental note that Mervyn was touchy about money and she would have to remember that.

It was Christmas Eve the following day, and Mervyn had said that he wouldn't be out until the afternoon, but he had kissed her warmly as he had said it and she hadn't really minded because she had planned to go riding—just a short canter across the fields by the lake, to see how Prince went. The morning was bright and clear and still very cold as she saddled him and led him out of the stable. He was still nervous, dancing along beside her, shying at every stone, and although she wasn't nervous herself, she could see that she would have to go carefully; he was a great deal more spirited than Mervyn had led her to believe. Perhaps in Canada they were used to horses that bucked and shied at every blade of grass. She had him away from the house by now, walking him across the meadow towards the water, she coaxed him to a standstill with some difficulty and was preparing to mount when Fabian spoke very quietly somewhere behind her.

'Don't, Mary Jane, I beg of you.' He was beside her now and had taken the reins into his own hands while she stared up at him speechlessly, a little pale in the face and with a most peculiar tumult of feeling inside her. He was pale too, but all he said was: 'He's not the horse for you—I told you to wait until I could find you something suitable. You broke your promise...'

'I didn't,' she said quickly, 'Mervyn bought him.'

She missed the sudden fire in his dark eyes. 'Mervyn?' repeated Fabian softly. 'Let us go back to the house and you shall tell me about—er—Mervyn!'

He began to lead Prince back to his stable and she, perforce, walked with him and waited while he saw to the animal, and then accompanied him into the house, to find Mrs Body, beaming with delight, hurrying with coffee and some of her mince pies.

'I knew you would come, Doctor dear,' she told him happily, 'with Christmas tomorrow.' She put down the tray and went to the door. 'I've the nicest piece of beef in the oven ready for your lunch.'

She went out of the room and Mary Jane said with polite haste, 'I hope you'll stay to lunch.' She busied herself with pouring coffee and didn't look at him. His clipped 'thank you' sounded coldly on her ears.

After a lengthening silence during which she sought for and discarded a number of conversational openings, Fabian said, 'And now if you would be good enough to explain about this horse.' He spoke in tones which brooked no hindrance; she explained at some length and in a muddled fashion which in the end left her with no alternative but to tell him about Mervyn too. He heard her out, no expression upon his calm, handsome features, and saying nothing, so that when she had finished she was forced to ask: 'Well?'

He raised his eyebrows. 'My dear Mary Jane, what am I expected to say? I haven't met this cousin yet, although I shall be delighted to do so, even if only to point out to him that I find his taste in horseflesh a little on the inexperienced side.'

Her gentle eyes flashed. 'Pooh! You only say that because you didn't pick Prince yourself.'

He ignored this. 'And what did you pay for him?'

She was a truthful girl, so she told him, waiting for his expected comment on the excessive price, but he said nothing, staring at her with narrowed eyes. Presently he said, 'Not a local animal, I fancy.' He sounded so casual that she let out a sigh of relief. 'No, Mervyn told me he had heard of him from someone he knew in Keswick.'

'Is that all you know?' She sensed the mockery in his voice and bristled as he continued, 'Surely you have the receipt and the bill of sale?'

'Mervyn will let me have them,' she protested, feeling guilty because she hadn't given the matter a thought. 'How is your cousin?'

If she had hoped to change the conversation she was unlucky. 'Very well, thank you. And when is Mervyn coming to see you again?'

She muttered, 'This afternoon,' and fidgeted under his look.

'Excellent. I shall enjoy meeting him. Had you planned anything? I shan't be inconveniencing you in any way?' His cold politeness chilled her. He got up. 'By the way, Prince has a slight limp in his left hind leg—you will agree with me that it should be attended to at once? I know it's Christmas Eve, but I'll see what I can do.'

He went out of the room, leaving Mary Jane with her mouth open in surprise. She hadn't noticed any limp, though now that she came to think about it, Prince had stumbled once or twice. She wouldn't be riding for a day or two; it might be a good idea to get it looked at.

Fabian came back presently and she asked, 'Did you find a vet?'

He strolled over to the window and stood half turned away from her, looking out on to the wintry morning. He said at length, 'Yes—he'll see what he can do some time today.'

'It's not serious?'

He turned to look at her across the pleasant room. 'No, but I don't think you should ride him, though. Now tell me, how are you managing? Have you sufficient money?'

They spent the remainder of the morning in a businesslike fashion, and over lunch they kept to commonplaces while she wondered silently why he was so abstracted in his manner. Once or twice she found him staring at her in an odd fashion, with an expression which she couldn't understand, and indeed, he was so unlike his usual cool, arrogant self that she began to feel quite uncomfortable. And asking questions hadn't helped either, for she had tried that with singularly little success, in fact he had remarked after one such probe into what he had been doing: 'I have never known you take such an interest in my life—should I feel flattered?'

She felt as uncomfortable as she knew she looked. 'No, of course not, but I haven't seen you for several weeks. I just wanted to—to hear what you've been doing.'

His eyes held a gleam in their depths. 'Then I am flattered. Tell me, what are your plans for Christmas?'

'Well, nothing much. Mervyn's coming for Christmas Day—after church, you know, and I expect he'll stay until after dinner, and on Boxing Day some of Grandfather's friends are coming for a drink. Mervyn will be coming to lunch again, but he says he can't stay to meet Doctor Morris, he's got some people to see. It's a pity, because Doctor Morris knew his father, I believe.'

Fabian leaned back in his chair. 'A great pity,' he commented in a dry voice. 'It sounds very pleasant.'

'And you?' she asked politely, and then struck by a sudden thought, added in tones of the utmost apprehension, 'You're not staying for Christmas, are you?'

Somehow the thought of Mervyn and Fabian together filled her with an uneasiness she knew was quite unjustified; she closed her eyes on the vivid picture her mind had conjured up of Fabian blighting Mervyn's cheerful talk with his damping politeness.

His companion's face remained unaltered in its blandness. 'I wasn't aware that I had been asked. Set your mind at ease, Mary Jane, I shall be leaving within an hour or so.'

'Oh well, that's all right,' she exclaimed, so relieved that she hardly realised what she had said. 'Do you mind sitting here while I see if lunch is ready? There's some sherry on the window table, do help yourself.'

She went out of the room, humming cheerfully. If Fabian was going so soon, he and Mervyn would only have to meet for a very short time, perhaps not at all.

Her optimism was ill-founded. They had barely finished Mrs Body's excellent lunch when Mervyn drove up, parked the car in front of the door, and walked in. To say that he was surprised was too mild a way of putting it—Fabian had put his car in the garage; there had been no hint of anyone else being in the house, so Mervyn came breezing into the sitting room, to stop short just inside the door, looking so disconcerted at the sight of Fabian lounging in a chair by the fire that he could say nothing. It was Mary Jane who plunged into speech.

'Mervyn—hullo. Fabian, this is Mervyn Pettigrew, my—my cousin from Winnipeg. Jonkheer van der Blocq, my guardian.'

Fabian had risen and advanced to meet Mervyn,

309

saying in a suave voice which somehow disturbed Mary Jane: 'Ah, Mr Pettigrew, Mary Jane has been telling me about you. I'm glad to have this opportunity of meeting you.'

He smiled, but his eyes were cold, and before Mervyn could say anything he went on: 'You must tell me about your home—Canada is a place I have often wished to visit. Your home is in Winnipeg? In the city itself or outside?' He waved Mervyn to a chair. 'Sit down, my dear fellow, and tell me about it.'

The conversation was in his hands; Mary Jane sat helplessly listening to Mervyn answering her guardian's questions, and even when she made attempts to change the conversation, she was frustrated by Fabian's blandly polite pause while she did so, only to have him resume his remorseless cross-examination again. Quite fed up, she suggested an early cup of tea because then Fabian might remember that he was leaving shortly ... She was half way to the door when she heard a car, voices and some sort of commotion; she got to the window in time to see a horse-box and a Land-Rover disappearing down the drive. Prince's head was just visible.

She cut ruthlessly into Mervyn's description of the grain harvest. 'They've taken Prince!' she uttered, and turned to look at Fabian, who returned her startled gaze with a placid unsurprised face. 'I mentioned it,' he reminded her mildly.

'Yes, I know—but I didn't know he was going. Where is he going to?'

'The vet has taken him into his stables. A very good man, I believe.'

'Prince? The horse I bought for Mary Jane?' Mervyn's voice sounded strained. 'What's wrong with him?'

'A limp—the near hind leg, my dear fellow. Nothing much, probably he did it after you saw him. A splendid animal, I must congratulate you on your choice. Which reminds me, Mary Jane couldn't remember from whom she had bought him—you have the papers on you, I daresay.'

Mervyn searched his pockets. His face was a little pale, he looked harassed. 'I've left them at the hotel,' he muttered. 'I quite intended to bring them—I must remember tomorrow.'

'Of no consequence.' Fabian's voice had a silkiness which struck unpleasantly upon Mary Jane's ears as she came back into the room. 'What did you pay?'

Mervyn answered before she had a chance to remind Fabian that she had already told him, and rather to her surprise, Fabian merely nodded his head, remarked that the price of horseflesh had risen out of all bounds, and went on to say that doubtless such a splendid beast would be well known in the district. 'I must go along and see his owner,' he observed casually, 'and see if he has anything as good. Where did you say he lived?'

Mary Jane watched the hunted look on Mervyn's face and wondered about it, and when he said at length that he couldn't exactly remember, helpfully suggested the names of some of the local breeders, to all of which Mervyn answered rather shortly that none of them was correct. At last, goaded by her excessive helpfulness, he said, 'It wasn't a breeder—just someone selling privately.'

'Ah,' Fabian's voice was still hatefully silky. 'Doubtless one of the small estates around here—I should have no difficulty in finding him.'

There was no knowing what Mervyn would have

replied to this if Mrs Body hadn't come in at that minute with the tea tray. Mary Jane poured tea and oil upon what she felt might be troubled waters if she allowed the two men to go on long enough, but she need not have bothered, for Fabian seemed to have lost interest in Prince and his former owner. He was talking, much more freely than he usually did, she thought, uneasily, about the house and it contents, which, he assured Mervyn in a manner quite unlike his own somewhat reserved one, were by no means without value and likely to become more so. 'A very nice little property,' he said as he got up to go, 'worth quite a considerable sum in the market today.'

He was about to shake hands with Mary Jane when Mervyn spoke.

'I may not see you again—I hadn't intended to say anything just yet, but as you are here ... I want to marry Mary Jane—I understand from her that she needs permission from you before she can marry. Well, I should like it now.'

This speech, uttered in urgent tones, had the effect of silencing Mary Jane completely, although it had no such effect upon her guardian, who remarked airily, 'My dear chap, why didn't you mention this earlier? Now I am forced to leave on most urgent business, and you can quite understand that I'm not prepared to give my consent until we have had a little talk about your prospects and so on. But I imagine that you will be here for another week or so? I'll endeavour to come and see you at the earliest opportunity.'

He glanced at Mary Jane, his face empty of expression. 'I'm sure that you both have a great deal to talk about. Goodbye, Mary Jane. I have no need to wish you a happy Christmas, have I—but I do, just the same.'

He took her hand, and she stared up into his face, completely out of her depth, filled with the ridiculous wish that he wouldn't go away, but stay for Christmas. She whispered some sort of reply and stayed in the middle of the room, watching him walk away.

Mervyn talked a lot after Fabian had gone. He talked about their future together and how he had been wanting to tell her that he loved her for several days. 'We'll get married after Christmas,' he urged her. 'There's no reason why we should wait, is there? I can move in here...'

She was surprised at that. 'But won't you have to go back to Winnipeg? What about your work? Do you want to give up your job there? and if you come here to live you'll have to get something else. Wouldn't it be better if I came to Winnipeg?'

He was adamant that that wouldn't do. 'You would be homesick,' he told her, 'and this will be a marvellous home for us both—we'll get another car, and a boat—something fast.'

She agreed happily, in a rose-coloured future, not quite real. She asked him, 'And your income? Is it enough for us to live on?'

'Oh, don't worry your little head about that,' he assured her, and kissed her. 'We'll go into all that when we're married.'

'But I don't suppose Fabian will let me get married until all that's sorted out. He takes his duties very seriously.'

Mervyn caught her hands in his. 'Look, darling, why do we wait for him? If we get married he can't do anything about it, can he? He's far too busy a man to get involved in our business—besides, he'll be glad to be rid of this guardianship—that is, unless he's feathering his own nest with your money.'

Mary Jane felt a sudden fierce rush of sheer rage. 'That's a beastly thing to say!' she said loudly. 'Fabian is the most honest man alive, he wouldn't touch a penny that wasn't his—besides, he's frightfully rich.'

Mervyn apologised at once, turning it into a joke, but the sour taste of it stayed with her for the rest of the evening, despite his gay talk, although she found it hard to resist his charm. He would be a delightful husband, she assured herself, and how lucky she was that he had appeared out of the blue to fall in love with her and want to marry her. She wished him a warm good night, all her small qualms forgotten, and went along to find Mrs Body making last-minute preparations for the following day while Lily stood at the sink cleaning the vegetables. Mary Jane drew up a chair to the table and began to blanch a bowl of almonds standing on it.

'He's gone,' said Mrs Body sadly.

'Just this minute, but he'll be back for lunch tomorrow.'

Mrs Body thumped the stuffing she was making with quite unnecessary vigour. 'Not him,' she sounded aggrieved, 'Doctor van der Blocq, and I'd like to know where he's going to spend his Christmas.'

Mary Jane, her mouth full of almonds, said indistinctly, 'Holland, I suppose.'

The housekeeper gave her an impatient look. 'Now, Miss Mary Jane, you know as well as I do that he can't get back all that way by tomorrow morning—not with the car, he can't. What are you about not to think of that? It fair bothered me to see him driving off alone this afternoon—didn't you give him a thought?'

'Yes—no—I had something else to think about. Mrs

314

Body, darling Mrs Body, I'm going to be married!'

'To that Mr Pettigrew? Well, I suppose it was to be expected, though how he could allow you to ride that wild animal I can't think. I never was so pleased to see the animal go again—he should have known better. Good thing dear Doctor van der Blocq came along like he did.'

'Oh, Mrs Body, aren't you pleased?' Mary Jane sounded as forlorn as she suddenly felt. 'I thought you would be—I'm not going to be an old maid after all.'

Mrs Body rallied. 'Of course I'm pleased, my dear, there's nothing I'd like better than to see you wed. But Canada's a long way off.'

Mary Jane reached over the table and kissed her housekeeper and friend on the cheek. 'But I'm not going there—Mervyn suggested that he should move in here just as soon as we're married.'

'And Doctor van der Blocq—does he know?'

'Oh yes, Mervyn told him this afternoon, and Fabian said he'd come back very shortly and they'd have a talk—about money and things.' She got up. 'I'm going to get something to drink—we'll toast Christmas before we go to bed.'

She went to sleep almost at once, thinking about the perfect future she was going to have with Mervyn, but she didn't dream of him, she dreamed of Fabian, driving his car endlessly through a lonely Christmas. She remembered it when she wakened in the morning and it became real somehow when Mrs Body brought her her early tea and laid a small package on the bed.

'A Happy Christmas, Miss Mary Jane,' she said, 'and the dear doctor asked me to be sure and give you this first thing in the morning.'

There was a velvet box inside the wrapping paper,

and in the box was a brooch, a true lovers' knot in rose diamonds, exquisitely beautiful. Mary Jane stared at it for a long time because it somehow seemed to be part and parcel of her dreams, its sparkle, a little blurred because of the sudden tears in her eyes, tears because she hadn't given him anything at all—she hadn't even invited him for Christmas. She remembered with shame that she had let him see her relief when he had told her that he was going away again. He must have said that because he was too proud a man to say anything else. She wondered forlornly where he had gone.

CHAPTER SIX

DOWNSTAIRS, Mary Jane found a delicately painted porcelain bowl on the breakfast table, filled with a gorgeous medley of tulips, hyacinths and dwarf iris. She sniffed their perfume delightedly and looked for a card. They would be from Mervyn, of course. She wandered into the kitchen to wish the others the compliments of the season, exclaiming: 'Those heavenly flowers—I wonder where he got them this time of year?'

Mrs Body dished bacon and eggs before replying. 'Brought them all the way from Holland, he did—made me promise to look after them and put them on the table first thing in the morning. It's a lovely bowl—ever so old. He gave us presents too, but we haven't opened them yet.'

Mary Jane remembered her remorse before she had gone to sleep, and it came crowding back into her head now—even if the flowers and the brooch had only been a gesture from a guardian to his ward, they had been gifts, and she had been horribly unkind. Once more she wondered where he had gone and if he had expected to stay. She pushed the thought away and with it the faint regret that the flowers hadn't been from Mervyn, even the brooch, although possibly he couldn't have afforded that. It struck her anew that he had never talked about money to her at all, only sketched in a vague background, leaving her to suppose that he was comfortably off. She sighed, for she was a romantic girl and had always cherished the idea that a man in love went to any lengths to please his girl-friend, and yet it had been Fabian, not Mervyn who was so in love with her, who had taken care that there would be presents waiting for her when she got up on Christmas morning. She ate her breakfast thoughtfully and then went, with Mrs Body and Lily, to church. Mrs Body and Lily wore the new leather gloves Fabian had given them, and Mary Jane wore the brooch.

They had a drink when they got back and then got the lunch ready together. Mrs Body and Lily had friends to share theirs, so Mary Jane laid the table in the dining room for herself and Mervyn. By the time he arrived she was feeling gay and lighthearted, having spent a good deal of the morning persuading herself that Fabian had only called in on his way to somewhere and wouldn't have stayed even if she had asked him.

She had bought Mervyn a picture, a landscape by a local artist of some repute. She gave it to him when he arrived and watched while he unwrapped it, admired it and then laid it on the table in the window. There

317

was an awkward pause until he said, 'I had no idea what to get you—we'll go together and find something later on.'

She made excuses for him—perhaps in Canada they didn't set much store by Christmas—but surely he could have brought a few flowers? She wasn't a greedy girl, only hurt because she had expected that because he loved her, he would have wanted to express that love with some small gift. She stifled the hurt and smiled at him. 'That will be nice,' she agreed. 'And now what about a drink before lunch?'

The bowl of flowers was on the table; he couldn't help but see it. He commented idly upon it, remarking that it looked a valuable piece.

'I don't know about that,' she said uncertainly. 'Fabian sent it.'

He frowned. 'Now that we're going to be married,' he stated categorically, 'I'm not sure that I like you receiving valuable gifts from him, even if he is your guardian.'

She flushed a little and said with a spurt of temper, 'Why ever not? As you said, he is my guardian, and what harm is there in giving a girl flowers? We do it a lot in England—for birthdays and Christmas.'

It was his turn to get angry. 'I don't like it,' he reiterated stubbornly. 'Before you know where you are he'll be giving you something really valuable—jewellery—bought with your money, no doubt.'

'I hope you'll apologize for that.' Mary Jane's voice was quiet, but it shook a little. 'I thought I had made it plain to you that Fabian wouldn't touch a penny of my money—he's my guardian, not a thief,' she added defiantly. 'He gave me this brooch.'

Mervyn stared at it across the table. Presently he

said sullenly:

'Oh, all right, I'm sorry I said it—I didn't mean it, you have to make allowances for a man being jealous when he's in love.' His eyes were still glued to the brooch. 'It looks very expensive—I thought it was something you had inherited from your grandfather.'

He smiled at her. 'I'm a brute behaving like this on Christmas Day, darling. I'm sorry—I suppose I'm a bit on edge. I want to marry you, you see, as soon as possible, and I can't think of anything else but that. I promise I'll make it up to you when we're married.'

He was charming for the rest of the day; she basked in his admiration and listened happily to the delightful things he said, knowing right at the back of her mind that most of them were grossly exaggerated if not completely untrue. No one had ever told her before that she was pretty, nor had they spared more than one glance upon her eyes, which Mervyn declared were quite remarkably lovely; her common sense, buried in a haze of wishful thinking, told her that. But no one had ever been in love with her before, she had no yardstick by which to measure him. She allowed herself to believe every word and squashed her common sense, almost squashing her resolve to wait for Fabian's permission before they married. It was tempting, especially when Mervyn showed her the special licence he had bought, sure that she would give in when she saw it. But she still refused and put his sulky silence down to disappointment on his part.

During the following few days he had become a little difficult, and once or twice, when she was alone and quiet, a small voice deep inside her wanted to know if she really loved him or was she just being swept off her feet because she had never been in love or loved before. She buried the thought under a host of more pleasant ones and scoffed at her doubts.

But they stayed; she asked Mrs Body about them, and that dear soul looked troubled even while she spoke reassuringly. 'And wait until the dear doctor comes,' she counselled. 'It can't be long now.'

It was Old Year's Day when Fabian came. Mary Jane had expected Mervyn to lunch; she had spent most of the morning helping Mrs Body in the kitchen because Lily had gone home for the day and now she sat at the desk in one of the sitting room windows, writing thank-you letters, and keeping an eye on the drive and the road beyond. It had turned cold once more, there were a few snowflakes falling and the frost had been heavy the night before. She had put on a new dress, a dark green pinafore with a matching crêpe blouse under it, and had pinned the diamond brooch into it. She had done her hair with more patience than usual too, but it was getting a little untidy again, for she had a habit of running her hand through it while she was writing and it was two hours since she had done it. She was shocked when she saw the time; it was past one o'clock—something must have delayed Mervyn, and she couldn't think what. She resolved to wait another half an hour and applied herself to her letters again, but only for a few minutes, for a car turned into the drive and she got to her feet and ran to the door without bothering to look out of the window.

It was the Rolls, and Fabian who got out of it. He came in slowly, looking tired, and the sight of his shadowed face stirred a desire deep inside her to help him. But Fabian wasn't a man to accept help or admit tiredness, so she said instead, 'Hullo, how nice to see you, and just in time for lunch—it's a bit late, because I'm expecting Mervyn. You'll be able to talk to him.'

'We have had our talk, and he won't be coming.'

He stood in the open doorway, towering over her, his face expressionless, staring down at her, making no effort to move or take off his coat.

Mary Jane gave him a puzzled look. 'Why isn't he coming? He particularly wanted to see you—he's got a special licence.' She bit her lip and went on in a cold little voice, 'Where did you see him?'

'In Keswick.' He paused. 'I have to talk to you, Mary Jane.'

'He's ill—hurt? Oh, Fabian, do tell me quickly!'

'It's neither. If we could go somewhere?'

'Yes, of course, and you must have something, you look tired to death.'

He smiled grimly. 'When I have finished what I have to say and you still want me to remain perhaps you will ask me then.' He sounded suddenly impatient. 'The sitting room?'

He didn't sit down, but walked over to the window and then turned to face her. 'Mervyn isn't coming. He won't be coming again. He has left Keswick and is already on his way to catch his plane, back to Canada.'

She felt the blood leave her cheeks. 'I don't believe you—he loves me.'

'I wouldn't lie to you, Mary Jane. He was no good, my dear girl—you are such an innocent.' He sighed. 'Oh, he was your cousin all right, always borrowing money from your grandfather, like his father before him, an undischarged bankrupt with not a penny to his name, who came to hear of your grandfather's death and saw a chance of easy money. And how much easier could it have been?' His voice took on a mocking, angry note. 'You, a little bored already, with a house of your own and money—quite a lot of money...'

She interrupted him, almost stammering. 'He had no idea—I never told him.'

'No? But he tricked old Mr North into telling him how much the estate was worth. I suppose you told him where North lived?' And when she nodded miserably: 'I thought so. And Prince—how could you have been so feather-witted, Mary Jane? Did you not wonder why he never showed you the papers connected with the sale, or the receipt? Why, I smelled a rat the moment you said—or were you so infatuated with him that you couldn't be sensible any more? Do you know what he paid for Prince? Exactly half the amount he told you. He had the rest; he hired a car in your name too—I paid the bill just now, and the hotel—he owed several weeks' bills and told them that you would pay.' He thrust an impatient hand into a pocket and tossed some papers at her. 'There, see for yourself.'

She left them to drift to the floor. 'How—how did you find out all this?' She tried to speak in a normal voice, but it came out in a miserable whisper.

'I asked around—it wasn't difficult—and then I flew to Winnipeg and made some enquiries.'

'You went to all that trouble?' She had her voice nicely under control now, but the effort to hold back the tears was getting beyond her. She said in a sudden burst: 'Did it matter? He's the only man who has ever asked me to marry him, do you know that? He said he loved me and now you've spoiled it all—I believe you want me to go on living here for ever and ever—I hate you, I hate you, I wish I'd never set eyes on you!' She hiccoughed and choked, then took a breath, for she

322

had by no means finished. Her heart, she most truly believed at that moment, was broken, and nothing mattered any more. All she wanted to do was to hurt the man standing so silently before her; his very quiet made her feelings all the hotter. But the words tumbling off her tongue were stilled by the entrance of Mrs Body with a loaded tray, who after one sharp glance at Mary Jane addressed herself to Fabian.

'I saw the car, Doctor dear, and I said to myself, "He'll be cold and hungry, I'll be bound," so here's coffee and sandwiches, and a Happy New Year to you.' She poured the coffee. 'And where did you spend Christmas, if I might ask?'

'Oh, in Keswick, Mrs Body. I had business there.'

'But why didn't you stay here? If Miss Mary Jane had known...'

'That had been my hope.' He smiled at her with great charm, and Mrs Body, quite overcome, exclaimed, 'You mean to say you came for Christmas and we never even gave you a good Christmas dinner?'

'It didn't matter. As it turned out I had a good deal to do. Thank you for the coffee.'

'Well, you look as though you need it, and no mistake, Doctor dear—worn out, you are. Have you come from Holland?'

He shook his head. 'Canada.'

Mrs Body was no fool. She said, 'Lor' bless my soul! I always knew...' She shot another look at Mary Jane, standing like a statue, taking no part in the conversation, and went out of the room, shutting the door very gently.

Fabian had made no attempt to drink his coffee, and when Mary Jane turned her back upon him he watched her for a few moments and then said softly:

'Mary Jane,' and when she didn't answer: 'I'm sorry, but I had to do it. I couldn't see you throw yourself away on a wastrel and ruin your whole life.' He paused. 'Do you want me to stay?'

She didn't turn round, only shook her head. She heard him cross the room and then the hall, and presently the front door was opened and shut again, and the Rolls murmured its way down the drive. By straining her ears Mary Jane could hear it going down the road, back to Keswick and, she guessed miserably, Holland. He wouldn't come again. There was no need to hold the tears back any longer; she flopped into the nearest chair and cried her eyes out, and when Mrs Body came back, sobbed out the whole sorry story to her, to be comforted and scolded a little and comforted again. 'And that poor man,' said Mrs Body, 'gone again without a bite to eat inside him, and him such a great man.'

'He can starve!' said Mary Jane savagely into Mrs Body's ample bosom.

'Now, now, dearie, that's no way to talk. I never said so, but I didn't fancy you marrying that Mr Pettigrew —far too glib, I found him. I know your heart's broken, but it'll mend, my dear, and you'll think differently later on, and when Mr Right pops the question you'll have forgotten all this.'

'But there isn't a Mr Right!' wailed Mary Jane.

'I'm not so sure about that,' said Mrs Body bracingly, and smiled to herself over the tousled brown head on her shoulder.

But despite Mrs Body's comforting words, Mary Jane found the days which followed hard to live through; she walked herself into a state of exhaustion, going over and over in her mind all that had happened, forcing herself to face the truth—that Mervyn hadn't loved her at all, only her money and her home, seeing her as an easy way to live in comfort for the rest of his life. Just as Fabian had said. She told herself that she would get over it, just as Mrs Body had told her, but in the meantime she was utterly miserable, not least of all because Mervyn hadn't written. He could have at least wished her goodbye—but then she hadn't said goodbye to Fabian either, had she? She had let him walk out of the house, cold and tired and hungry; even if she hated him—and of course she did —she had been pretty mean herself.

By the end of the week she wasn't eating much, nor was she sleeping; her mood was ripe for the letter from Pope's which arrived after a particularly bad night. It was from Miss Shepherd, telling her that there was a severe 'flu epidemic in London, the hospital was half-staffed and overflowing with patients, and how did Mary Jane feel like helping out on a temporary basis for a week or so?

Mary Jane went straight to the telephone, packed a bag, hugged Mrs Body and Lily goodbye and got into the Mini. She would only be gone for a week or so, but the prospect of having some hard work before her was just what she needed. She drove down the motorway, still unhappy, it was true, but finding life bearable once more.

It was amazing to her that she could slip back into life at Pope's with such ease, and still more amazing that it should be Women's Surgical to which she was sent, because the regular staff nurse was herself down with 'flu. Mary Jane went on duty a few hours after her arrival to find Sister Thompson sitting in her office, drumming impatient fingers on the desk while she harangued a part-time staff nurse whom she obviously didn't like; she didn't like Mary Jane either, but at least they knew each other, a fact she pointed out somewhat acidly before giving her a dozen and one things to do. Mary Jane, impervious to her bad temper, and relieved to have so much on her hands that she had no time to think, went into the ward, to be greeted happily by several nurses she had known. The ward was heavy and full with beds down the centre and cases going to theatre, to return requiring expert care and nursing. Sister Thompson sailed up and down between the beds, giving orders to anyone who was within earshot, complaining bitterly that there were no good nurses any more, and what was the world coming to—a purely rhetorical question which none of her harassed staff had neither the time nor the inclination to answer, at least not out loud.

Mary Jane, worn out after her hard day, slept as she hadn't slept for nights, and what was more, ate her breakfast the next morning. Despite her hard work, a faint colour had crept into her white face and the hollows under her eyes, while still there, weren't quite so noticeable. She was off duty in the afternoon, the day was cold and grey and the staff nurses' sitting room in the Home looked bleak—there were several of her friends off duty too, so she rounded them up and they went in a cheerful bunch to Swan and Edgar's where they had tea before embarking on a quick inspection of the January sales. She went back to the ward refreshed, and because Sister Thompson was off duty that evening, the work went better than it usually did. She went off duty that evening with the pleasant feeling that at least she had done a good day's work and slept soundly in consequence.

The days slid by, each one packed with work and the small petty annoyances which went with it. Mary Jane found little time to think of anything but drips, pre-meds, closed drainage and the preparation of emergency cases for theatre, and at night she fell into bed and was asleep before she had time to shed one single tear over her broken romance with Mervyn. Just once or twice, when she was in theatre with a patient, she was reminded of Fabian, because the operating theatre was his world; it surprised her that in place of the rage which had possessed her against him, there was now only a dull feeling, almost a numbness. Beneath the mass of bewildered thoughts and memories she had expected him to write to her despite the manner of his going, but nothing came, only letters from Mrs Body, detailing carefully the day-to-day life at home. She had hoped for a letter from Mervyn too, against all her better judgement, but as the days went by and she realised that he wasn't going to write, she knew that that was the best thing. He had never loved her, and she had been a fool to have imagined he did. He would never have left in that craven fashion if he had had even a spark of feeling for her, and certainly nothing Fabian could have said would have deterred him from at least explaining to her. She sighed; it was a pity she didn't like Fabian, for quite obviously he had done his best for her, though in an arrogant fashion and with a total disregard of her feelings for which she would never forgive him.

With each day she found that she was recovering slowly. It was no good moaning over the past, and she had much to be thankful for; a home, enough money, kind Mrs Body and the willing Lily. She would go back to them soon and pick up the threads of her life where Fabian had so ruthlessly broken them off. She would have to find something to do, of course; Red Cross, part-time nursing, something of that sort. And she could sail and ride—only she hadn't a horse, and unless Fabian came to see her again, she was unlikely to have one. Perhaps she would have to wait until she was thirty and free to do as she wished. Her thoughts were interrupted by Sister Thompson's sour voice, enquiring of her if she intended to be all day making up that operation bed and how about Mrs Daw's premed? And Mary Jane, who had already given it, said 'Yes, Sister,' in a mechanical way and went to see how the last case back from theatre was doing.

Op days were always extra busy. Sister Thompson went off duty after lunch and the atmosphere of the ward brightened perceptively even though an emergency appendix was admitted, followed by a severely lacerated hand. Mary Jane slogged up and down the ward, a little untidy now but still cheerful though a thought tired. She was going out that evening with some of her friends; there was a film which was supposed to be marvellous, but the way she felt by teatime, she didn't really care if she saw it or not, though probably once she was there she would enjoy it, and anything was better than sitting and thinking.

She was almost through giving the report to Sister Thompson before she went off duty when she was interrupted by the telephone. Sister Thompson lifted a pompous hand for silence and addressed the instrument with her usual severity, although this softened slightly when she discovered that the speaker was Miss Shepherd. She put down the receiver with a strong air of disapproval, observed: 'Matron'—she still called Miss Shepherd Matron because she didn't agree with all the new-fangled titles everyone had been given by the Salmon Scheme—'Matron,' she repeated, 'wishes to see you in her office as soon as possible. First, however, you will finish the report.'

Mary Jane, luckily at the tail end of her recital, made short work of the rest of it, wished her superior good night, waved to such of the patients who were in a fit state to notice, and started off down the corridors and staircases which separated her from Miss Shepherd's office. The hospital was fairly quiet except for the distant clatter of dishes denoting the advent of patients' suppers. She met no one and paused only long enough to fling open the door of Men's Medical where one of her friends worked, acquaint that young lady with the tidings that she might be late and they had better go on without her, and then tear on once more. The office was at the end of a short passage. Mary Jane knocked on the door, watched the red light above it turn to green, and went in.

Miss Shepherd was sitting at her desk and Fabian was standing in the middle of the room with his hands in his pockets, contemplating a very bad portrait of the first governor of Pope's. He took his eyes from it, however, as Mary Jane entered and met her startled gaze. She went red and then white, opened her mouth to speak, clamped it shut and turned for the door, quite forgetful of Miss Shepherd. It was that lady's calm voice which recalled her to her senses.

'Ah, there you are, Staff Nurse. Your guardian is most anxious to speak to you,' she smiled across the room at him as she spoke. 'I'm sure you will want to hear what he has to say.'

'No,' said Mary Jane baldly, 'I wouldn't.' She looked at Fabian. 'Why should you want to see me? I can't imagine any good reason...' She stopped because he was looking at her so oddly, and Miss Shepherd said smoothly:

'All the same, I think you might like a little talk.' She got up and went to the door and Fabian opened it for her with a smile. 'I have a short round to make, ten minutes or so. I daresay that will be long enough.'

She had gone. Fabian leaned against the door, watching Mary Jane, who, very conscious of his gaze, stared in her turn at the portrait on the wall.

'I had no intention of seeing you for some time,' Fabian began coolly, 'this is purely to oblige Cousin Emma. I did a thyroidectomy on her a week ago—she is doing very well, but now she insists that she won't return home unless you are there to look after her. I telephoned you, of course, but Mrs Body, although she knew you were here, had no idea how long you would be staying. Miss Shepherd tells me that she can let you go immediately.'

'There are plenty of nurses in Holland,' said Mary Jane flatly, while she thought with sudden longing of the old house in Midwoude and even more longingly of Fabian's great house by the canal. 'I don't want to go,' she added for good measure.

He chose to ignore this. 'Emma likes you—more, she has an affection for you, she feels that she will never make a complete recovery unless you are there to help her. And it is important that she recovers completely, for Trouw has asked her to marry him and although she longs to do so, she says that she will refuse him unless she is quite well again. And I think that you are the one to convince her.'

Womanlike, Mary Jane had fastened on the piece of news which aroused her interest most. 'Married? How marvellous! Oh, I am glad, and of course she must marry Doctor Trouw. I always thought ... she must be very happy.'

Her voice died away because she herself should have been feeling very happy too, married by now, surely—instead of which, she was standing here in Miss Shepherd's office listening to Fabian's calm demands on her time and energy. She said in a husky little voice, à propos of nothing at all:

'I haven't a horse—what happened to Prince?'

Fabian made a sudden movement and then was still again. 'I know. Prince is now owned by the vet. I believe he's very content and they suit each other very well.' He began to walk towards her. 'Mary Jane, I told you that I had no intention of coming to see you, for I am only too well aware of your feelings towards me—you made them abundantly clear—but I am fond of Cousin Emma and I want her to be happy; she has spent a great deal of her life looking after Uncle Georgius—very inadequately, I must admit, but she did her best. And now happiness is within her reach and unless we help her, her stubbornness is likely to ruin everything.' His voice roughened. 'And you need entertain no fears that I shall be under your feet. When I come to see Cousin Emma it will be as her surgeon, not as your guardian. In future any meetings we may have shall be strictly on a business footing, I promise you that.'

For some unaccountable reason her heart sank at his words, for despite his indifference towards her, she had come reluctantly to regard him as someone to whom she could turn. She knew now, standing so close to him in the austere little room, that she had always been aware of him somewhere in the background, ready to help her if she needed help, and despite their dislike of each other he never had and never would let her down.

She was horrified to find her eyes filling with tears. They spilled down her cheeks and she wiped them away quickly, miserably aware that she looked quite hideous when she wept. But she was too proud to turn her face away. 'I'll come because Cousin Emma wants me,' she told him, 'not because you asked me.'

'I hardly expected that.' His voice was remote, as was his expression. They stared at each other in silence for a few seconds and Mary Jane, watching his calm face, felt a keen urge to talk to him, to tell him how she felt. She blew her nose and wiped away the last tear and would have embarked on heaven knew what kind of speech, only she was interrupted by the return of Miss Shepherd, who sat down at her desk and asked pleasantly, 'Well, all settled, I hope?'

'Indeed yes, Miss Shepherd. You did say that my ward could leave immediately?'

'Of course. We are very grateful to the girls who came back to help us, but we wouldn't dream of keeping them a moment longer than necessary—Staff Nurse Pettigrew would have been going in a day or two, in any case.'

'Splendid!' He turned to Mary Jane. 'I'll send your tickets to the front lodge, shall I? Could you be ready to leave tomorrow evening?'

She was surprised. She had taken it for granted that she would be with him; that he would take her back to Holland. She was on the point of saying so and prevented herself from doing so just in time, for of course he would have no wish for her company and and she had no wish for his. Her voice was as cool as his own had been. 'Yes, I can.'

'You have enough money?'

'Yes.'

There was a little pause until Miss Shepherd said briskly, 'Well, that seems to be settled, doesn't it? I won't keep you, Staff Nurse—you are off duty, I believe.'

Mary Jane said that yes, she was. She thanked Miss Shepherd, said goodbye in a cold voice to Fabian and went through the door he was holding open for her. It shut behind her, a fact which disappointed her; she had half expected him to follow her out. She even loitered down the corridor, so that, if he wished, he would have ample time to catch her up. He did no such thing, so rather put out, she went off to the Home.

Her friends had gone, leaving a note saying that they would wait outside the cinema until seven o'clock and after that it would be just too bad. Her watch said twenty minutes to the hour; to bath, change, catch a bus to Leicester Square and arrive at seven o'clock was an impossibility. She would spend the evening writing to Mrs Body and packing her few things. She tore off her cap and flung it on the bed, flung off her apron and belt too and was about to give her uniform dress the same rough treatment when there was a knock on the door.

'Oh, come in,' she called crossly, ripping pins out of her hair, and turned to see Fabian standing in the doorway. She forgot that they were barely on speaking terms, that she hated him, that he was arrogant and always had his own way. 'For heaven's sake,' she breathed, 'you can't be here! This is the Nurses' Home —it's private . . .' She waved an agitated hand at him. 'Men don't come upstairs—there's a little room by the front door . . .'

'For boy-friends?' he wanted to know. 'But I'm not a boy-friend, Mary Jane.' He sounded serious, but she could have sworn that he was laughing. 'There was no one downstairs, you see, so I looked in the Warden's office and found your room number.'

'You've got a nerve!' she told him fiercely, still whispering. 'Go away!'

'Of course, if you'll have dinner with me.'

She tossed a curtain of honey-brown hair over her shoulders. 'No, I won't,' she said tersely, then gasped as he came in. 'Supposing the Warden comes along?' she begged him. 'Do go—I'll get into trouble and—and you'll lose your reputation.'

She gave a small shriek at the great roar of laughter he gave. 'Oh, please, Fabian,' she said, quite humbly.

He went to the door at once. 'Half an hour,' he told her. 'I'll be in the—er—boy-friends' room, and don't try and give me the slip. Possibly you will find the situation easier if I assure you that I'm not asking you out for any other reason than that of expediency. I'm leaving England in a few hours and I should like to tell you about Emma before I go, it will be easier for you when you arrive.'

She joined him in half an hour exactly, wearing the new clothes she had bought for herself because she had wanted to look nice for Mervyn—a burgundy red coat with its matching dress, a red velvet cap on her pale brown hair, expensive gloves and handbag and suede boots with leather cuffs. She was thankful that she had found time to pack them when she left home to go to Pope's, for she had nothing much else with her—a skirt, a handful of sweaters and her sheepskin jacket which she had flung into the back of the Mini.

They dined at a nearby restaurant, and it wasn't until he had ordered and they were sipping their drinks that he abandoned the polite, meaningless conversation with which he had engaged her during their drive from Pope's. She had answered him in monosyllables, fighting a feeling of security and content, induced, she had no doubt, by the comfort of the Rolls and the anticipation of a delicious meal.

'You are sure that you have enough money?' he wanted to know again.

She mentioned the amount she had and he raised his eyebrows in surprise. 'My dear girl, you will be with Emma for at least two weeks, that's barely enough to keep you in tights.'

'How do you know I wear tights?' she demanded.

His lips twitched. 'I don't live in a monastery. I'll see that there's some money with your ticket. You had better travel to the Hoek by the night boat from Harwich. Someone will meet you there and drive you up to Midwoude. Emma is still in hospital, I should like you to be there when she is fetched home—that will be arranged. You'll need some overalls or something similar for a few days. What size are you?'

'Twelve,' she told him. She had no idea that he was such a practical man.

He eyed her thoughtfully. 'Twelve what?' His voice was bland.

'Well, that's my size—the number of inches I am.'

'Vital statistics?' and she saw the twinkle in his eyes and said severely: 'Yes.'

He made a note. 'Must I guess?' he asked mildly. 'Thirty-four, twenty-two, thirty-five or six—inches, of course. Is that near enough?' and when she nodded, speechless, he went on pleasantly: 'Now, as to Emma

—I did a sub-total on her. She has needed it for a year or more, but she always refused—you know how thyroidtoxicosis cases refuse treatment. Besides, I think she felt that she would be letting Uncle Georgius down in some way, but now the way seemed clear for an operation; it was Trouw who persuaded her. It is all very successful, but she doesn't believe it yet—I think you will be of great help in convincing her. Besides, you can encourage her to make plans for her wedding.' He stopped, staring at her, his eyes hooded, and she felt her cheeks go white.

'That was unpardonable of me, Mary Jane, I'm sorry.' He looked away from her strained face and continued in an impersonal voice, 'She has made a satisfactory recovery—a sore throat and hoarseness, of course. She's on digitalin and Lugol's iodine, and there are several more days to go with her antibiotic.' He added, 'She's a terrible patient. If you decide to change your mind, I shall quite understand.'

'I haven't changed my mind.'

'I didn't think you would.' He smiled at her and beckoned the waiter. 'The chocolate gateau is delicious here, would you care to try it?'

They were halfway through it before he spoke again. 'Mary Jane, you shall have your horse. I'll go over to the Lakes as soon as I can spare the time and find a good mount for you.' He shot her a lightning glance. 'You need not worry, I won't expect an invitation to stay.'

She didn't look at him. 'That sounds like a bribe.'

She wished she hadn't said it, for he at once became remote and haughty and faintly impatient. 'Don't talk nonsense,' he told her sharply. 'And now if you will listen carefully, I will finish telling you about Emma's treatment.'

The rest of the evening was businesslike in the extreme, for the talk was of such a professional nature that they might have been on a ward round at Pope's. He took her back without loss of time after dinner and wished her goodbye at the hospital gate with the air of a man who had concluded a satisfactory deal and now wanted to forget about it for pleasanter things.

'He's so unpredictable,' said Mary Jane, talking to herself as she went through the hospital to the Home, and a harassed night nurse hurrying in the opposite direction flung over her shoulder, 'They all are, ducky.'

Mary Jane left the following evening, her ticket and more money than she could possibly spend safely in her handbag, what clothes she had stowed in her case. She had wished Sister Thompson goodbye and had been told, to her surprise, that she was no worse than all the other girls who thought they were staff nurses, and if she chose to return at any future date, she, Sister Thompson, would personally ask Miss Shepherd if she could be posted to Women's Surgical ward. Mary Jane, overwhelmed by this treat for the future, thanked her nicely, took a brief farewell of such of her friends as were about and climbed into her taxi, reflecting that even if life wasn't treating her as kindly as it might, at least she had no time to sit and repine. When the friendly taxi-driver asked her if she was going on holiday she told him, 'Work,' adding to puzzle him, 'Work is the great cure of all the maladies and miseries that ever beset mankind.'

He grinned at her. 'Have it your own way, miss.'

CHAPTER SEVEN

It was Doctor Trouw who met the boat at the Hoek van Holland, and Mary Jane, a little wan after a rough crossing, was delighted to see him, although the delight was tinged with disappointment—probably, she told herself bracingly as she responded to the doctor's friendly greeting, because she was tired and, for some reason, lonely. She would feel better when she reached Midwoude, where she had no doubt her days would be filled.

Doctor Trouw had a Citroën, large and beautifully kept. She sat beside him responding suitably to his pleased speculation upon his hoped-for marriage to Cousin Emma. 'We have always been fond of each other,' he told her gruffly, 'and now that my wife is dead...' He paused. 'I feel that life still has much to offer.' He coughed. 'Of course, we are neither of us in the first flush of youth.'

'I don't see that that matters at all,' said Mary Jane with sincerity. 'There's not much point in getting married unless you're sure that you're going to be happy, and that could happen at any age. I'd rather wait for years and be certain.'

Her companion looked pleased and plunged into plans for the future; she suspected that he was really thinking aloud for the pure pleasure of it—which left her free to consider what she had just said. If she had married Mervyn would he have been the right man? Unbidden, the thought that she hadn't liked him when she had first seen him crossed her mind, to be instantly dismissed—he might have treated her badly, but that was no reason for her feelings to change, or was it? If she had loved him, surely her feelings wouldn't have changed. What did she feel for him now, anyway? Dislike—indifference? She wasn't sure any more, she wasn't even sure now that she had ever loved him. It was all very bewildering and a relief when Doctor Trouw stopped for coffee.

They reached Midwoude just before noon, to be welcomed by Jaap, and Doctor Trouw didn't wait—he had some cases to see, he explained, but he would be back at two o'clock, if she could manage in the meantime.

She and Jaap managed very well, each speaking their own language and understanding the other very well in spite of it. She had the same room as she had had previously and he took her case up for her, telling her that lunch would be in half an hour and leaving her to unpack, do her face and tidy her hair. She did this slowly, savouring the peace and quiet and comfort around her. After that afternoon, when Cousin Emma was home again, she wouldn't be quite so free, so she might as well make the most of her leisure now.

The hospital at Groningen was large and imposing with a medical school attached. Doctor Trouw skirted the main building, and halfway down a side turning ran the car under a stone archway and into an inner courtyard, where he parked the car. Mary Jane, getting out, guessed it to be the sanctum of the senior staff of the hospital and knew she was right when she saw the Rolls in a far corner. They entered the hospital through a small door which led to a short dark passage which spilled into a wide corridor with splendid doors lining its walls, and scented with the faint unmistakable smell of hospital cleanliness. It was also very quiet. The consultants would gather somewhere behind these richly sombre walls, as would the hospital board, and V.I.P.s visiting the hospital would no doubt drink their coffee, cocooned in its hushed affluence. All hospitals are alike, Mary Jane decided, treading carefully in Doctor Trouw's wake.

He opened a door almost at the end of the corridor and gave her a kindly prod. The room was large, its centre taken up by an oblong table hedged in by a symposium of straight-backed chairs. There were other chairs in the room, easy ones, grouped round small tables, and the air was thick with cigar smoke. It seemed to her that the room was full of men—large, well-groomed men, every single one of whom turned to look at her. In actual fact there were a bare dozen, senior members of the hospital medical staff who had just risen after a meeting.

'Over in the far corner,' said Doctor Trouw in her ear, and began to steer her to where Fabian was standing. He had his back to them, talking to two other men, but he turned and saw them and came to meet them. He looked, thought Mary Jane a trifle wildly, exactly what he was; a highly successful surgeon with plenty of money, plenty of brains and so much self-confidence that he could afford to look as though he had neither. She felt depressed and a little shy of him, for he seemed a stranger, and her reply to his pleasant 'Hullo, Mary Jane' was stiff and brief. But he seemed not to notice that; enquiring after her journey, whether she had slept and if she felt herself capable of undertaking the care of Emma within the hour. She told him yes, checking an impulse to address him as sir, and with a perception which took her by surprise he remarked:

'We all look rather—er—stuffy, I suspect. Whatever you do, don't address me as sir.'

She smiled at that. 'Not stuffy,' she assured him. 'It's just that you all look so exactly like consultants, and so many of you together is a bit overpowering.'

The two men laughed as they ushered her to the door again, pausing on the way to introduce her to various gentlemen who would have gone on talking for some time if Fabian hadn't reminded them that they were expected elsewhere. They traversed the corridor once more, this time to a lift. It was a small lift, and with Doctor Trouw's bulk beside her and Fabian taking up what space there remained, she felt somewhat crowded, and more so, for the two men carried on a conversation above her head, only ceasing as the lift purred to a halt, to smile down at her for all the world as though they had just remembered that she was there.

They stepped out into another wide corridor, this time lighted from the windows running its whole length and lined on one side by doors, each numbered, each with its red warning light above the glass peephole in its centre. They entered the first of these to find Cousin Emma sitting in a chair, dressed and waiting, and if Mary Jane had been in any doubt as to Fabian's sincerity when he had told her how much his cousin needed her, it could now be squashed. Cousin Emma uttered a welcoming cry, enfolded her against a fur-clad, scented bosom and began a eulogy upon Mary Jane's virtues which caused her face to go very red indeed.

'I knew you would come!' breathed Emma. 'I said to Fabian, "If Mary Jane doesn't come, I shall make no effort to recover from this dreadful operation."' She

341

paused, allowed Mary Jane to assume the upright and swept aside her mink coat.

'The scar,' she invited dramatically. 'Look at the scar—is it not dreadful? How can a maimed woman accept an offer of marriage with such a blemish?'

Mary Jane considered the hair-fine red line drawn so exactly across the base of her patient's throat. 'You won't be able to see it in three months' time,' she pronounced. 'Even now it's hard to see unless one stares—and who's going to stare? All you need to do is to get a handful of necklaces which will fit over it exactly—we'll do that, one for each outfit.'

She smiled at Cousin Emma, her eyes kind, unheedful of the two men standing close by.

'I feel better already,' declaimed Emma, and smiled with all the graciousness of some famous film star. 'I'm ready.'

Fabian drove her back in the Rolls and Mary Jane followed behind with Doctor Trouw in the Citroën, giving all the right answers to her companion's happy soliloquising. He would be, she considered, exactly right for Cousin Emma, for he obviously worshipped the ground she trod upon, while being under no illusion regarding her tendency to dramatise every situation. She asked: 'When do you hope to get married, Doctor Trouw?'

'Well, there is no reason why we shouldn't marry within a week or so. All the preliminaries are attended to—I persuaded her to become *ondertrouwt* before she went into hospital. Perhaps you could persuade her?' He looked at her hopefully. 'She is a sensitive woman,' he explained, just as though Mary Jane wasn't already aware of it, 'and prone to a good deal of dejection. Once we are married, I believe that can be cured.'

He turned the car in through the open gates and pulled up beside the Rolls. 'Willem is home,' he told Mary Jane as they got out. 'I daresay he will be over one day to see you.'

'How nice,' said Mary Jane, not meaning it—she foresaw a busy time ahead, acting as confidante to father and son while each confided their romantic problems to her. She sighed soundlessly and followed him into the house.

She had said almost nothing to Fabian, nor he to her, nor did he attempt to speak to her before he left very shortly afterwards. He had told her, she recalled, that he would be his cousin's surgeon when he called and not her guardian, now it seemed he had every intention of keeping his word. She answered his brief nod as he went with something of a pang and went to make Cousin Emma comfortable.

It proved an easier task than she had supposed. For one thing the operation had been a success; in place of the emotional, overwrought woman she had been, Cousin Emma had become quieter; her feverish gaiety and sudden outbursts of tears had been most effectively banished. She was still rather tearful, but that was post-operative weakness and would disappear with time. In the meanwhile, Mary Jane kept her company, saw to her pills and tablets, cared for her tenderly, talked clothes, reassured her at least twice a day that the scar was almost invisible, and coaxed her to eat her meals. And when Fabian came, as he did each day, she met him with a politely friendly face, answered his questions with the right amount of professional exactitude, commented upon the weather, which was bitterly cold once more, listened carefully to any instructions he chose to give her, and then retired to a corner of the room, to resume her knitting. Only when he got up to go did she put it down—thankfully, as it happened, because she wasn't all that good at it, and walk to the door with him and see him out of the house. It was on the fifth day after her arrival that he paused on the steps and turned round to face her.

'Have you recovered?' he wanted to know coolly. 'Though perhaps I'm foolish to ask such a question, for you're not likely to tell me, are you?'

'No, I'm not,' she replied in an outraged voice, her eyes no higher than his waistcoat. She spoilt this by adding: 'It's not your business, anyway.'

He grinned. 'Who said it was? Willem Trouw was asking about you yesterday. He doesn't know about your broken romance and he's having difficulties with his own love life. I believe you might console each other.'

Mary Jane was furious, so furious that for a moment the words she wanted to say couldn't be said. At last: 'You're abominable—how dare you say such things? You're cruel and heartless!' She tried to shut the door in his face, but he took it from her and held it open.

'Probably I am,' he agreed, 'but only when I consider it necessary.' He bent suddenly and before she could turn her head, kissed her mouth. Then he shut the door gently in her surprised face.

Willem came over that very afternoon, and remembering Fabian's words, she was hard put to it to be civil to him; supposing Fabian had said the same sort of thing to Willem? Perhaps men didn't confide in each other, but to be on the safe side she refused Willem's invitation to go out with him that evening, doing it so nicely that he could always ask again if he wanted to.

She had been there more than a week when Fabian, on one of his daily visits, mentioned casually that the continuous frost had made it possible to skate on the lake. 'Do you skate?' he wanted to know.

They were in the little sitting room, Cousin Emma in an easy chair, leafing through a pile of fashion magazines, Mary Jane determinedly knitting. She bent her head over it now, rather crossly picking up the stitches she had dropped, and became even crosser when Fabian remarked:

'I think you are not a good knitter, for you are always unpicking or dropping stitches or tangling your wool.'

He was right, of course; she had been working away at the same few inches for days, for the pattern always came wrong. Probably she would tear it off the needles and jump on it one day. Now she left the dropped stitches and knitted the rest of the row, briskly and quite wrongly, just to let him see how mistaken he was. It was a pity that he laughed.

'There are skates in the attic,' Cousin Emma informed anyone who cared to listen. 'I shall not skate, naturally, but you, Mary Jane, must do so if you wish. It is a splendid exercise and Willem could come over and teach you if you aren't good at it.' She added complacently, 'I'm very good, myself.' She glanced at her cousin. 'What do you think, Fabian?'

Mary Jane wasn't sure how it happened. All she knew was that within minutes she had agreed—or had she?—to spend the following afternoon skating with Willem. It would be so convenient, said Emma, because Doctor Trouw was coming over to discuss wedding plans with her, and Willem could come with him.

They would stay to tea, of course, and Mary Jane might like to make that delicious cake they had had a few days ago—Cook wouldn't mind.

Mary Jane replied suitably, doggedly knitting. But in the hall she said to Fabian: 'I don't particularly wish to skate with Willem, and I should be much obliged if you would mind your own business when it comes to my free time...'

He put on his car coat and caught up his gloves. 'My dear girl, have I annoyed you?' His voice was bland, he was smiling a little. 'Perhaps you have other plans —other young men you prefer to skate with?'

He was still smiling, but his eyes were curiously intent.

'Don't be ridiculous, you know I haven't.' She went on gruffly: 'When can I go home? Emma is almost well.'

He was pulling on his gloves and didn't look at her. 'No one would wish to keep you here against your will, Mary Jane, but I think that Emma would be broken-hearted if you should wish to go home before her wedding.'

'Will they marry soon?'

'I imagine so. Are you homesick?'

She raised puzzled eyes to his. 'No—at least, I don't think so. I—I don't know. I feel unsettled.'

He put a compelling finger under her chin. 'Unhappy?' His voice was gentle. And when she shook her head, 'The truth is that you are still in a mist of dreams, are you not? But they will go, and you will find that reality is a great deal better.'

He went away and she stood in the lobby watching the Rolls being expertly driven down the frozen drive and away down the road. Sometimes he was so nice, she thought wistfully, wondering what exactly he had meant.

She went skating with Willem when he came because there was nothing she could do about it—he arrived with his father, his plans laid for an afternoon on the ice with her. He had even borrowed some skates, and despite everything, she enjoyed herself. The lake was crowded, the bright colours of the children's anoraks lent the scene colour under the grey sky, their shrill, excited voices sounding clearly on the thin winter air. Willem was a good skater, if unspectacular. They went up and down sedately while he told her about the girl he wanted to marry and who didn't seem to want to marry him. 'I can't think why,' he told her unhappily. 'We're such good friends.'

'Sweep her off her feet,' advised Mary Jane. 'I don't know much about it, but I think girls like that. You could try—you know what I mean, be a bit bossy.'

'But I couldn't—she's so sure of what she wants, at least she seems to be.'

Mary Jane executed a rather clumsy turn. 'There, you see? Probably she doesn't know her own mind. Where is she now?'

They were going down the length of the lake again. 'As a matter of fact she's in Groningen.'

'Today? This afternoon?' Mary Jane came to such an abrupt halt that she almost lost her balance. 'What could be better? Go and fetch her here, make her put on skates and rush up and down with her until she's worn out—show her who's master.' She gave him a push. 'Go on, Willem—she'll be thrilled!'

'You think so?' He sounded undecided and she reiterated: 'Oh, go on, do!'

'But what about you?'

'I'm all right here. If I'm not back by dark you can come and fetch me.'

'Really? You don't think I'm being—being not friendly towards you, Mary Jane?'

'No, Willem. It's because we're friends that we can make this plan.' She started off, waving gaily. 'Have fun!'

She didn't look round, but when she turned and came back, he had gone.

The afternoon darkened early and became colder, but she, skating with more enthusiasm than skill, glowed with warmth; she had on her sheepskin jacket and a scarf tied tightly over her bun of hair, and she had stuffed her slacks into a pair of Cousin Emma's boots—they were too big, but they did well enough, as did the thick knitted mitts Jaap had found for her. Her ordinary little face was pink with pleasure and exercise, her eyes sparkled; that she was alone didn't matter at all, because there were so many people around her, enjoying themselves too. She skated to the end of the lake and then, the wind behind her, came belting back. There were fewer people now; the children were leaving, and there was more room. She was almost at the end when she saw Fabian some way ahead, right in her path. Even in the gathering dusk there was no mistaking his tall, solid figure. She began to slow down, for, most annoyingly, he hadn't moved. She was still going quite fast when she reached him, but he stayed where he was, putting out a large arm to bring her to a standstill.

'Whoops!' said Mary Jane, breathless. 'I thought I was going to knock you over—you should have moved.'

He was still holding her. 'No need. I weigh fifteen stone or thereabouts, and I doubt if you're much more than eight.' He laughed down at her. 'You show a fine turn of speed, though I don't think much of your style.'

'Oh, style—I enjoy myself.'

He had turned her round and they were skating, hands linked, back down the lake. Presently he asked, 'Where is Willem?'

'He's gone to Groningen to meet his girl-friend.'

'I thought he was spending the afternoon with you?'

'Oh, we started off together, then he started telling me about her and really, he was so fainthearted, I thought I'd better encourage him to go after her.'

'So you gave him some advice?'

'That's right. Have you the afternoon off?'

'More or less, but I must go home shortly. Will you come and have tea with me? Willem is presumably occupied with his girl, and Cousin Emma and Trouw will be engrossed with each other. That leaves us.'

She considered. 'Well, tea would be nice—but won't they wonder where I am?'

'I'll let them know. Shall we race to the end—you can have twenty yards' start.'

She did her best, but he overtook her halfway there, and then dropped back to skate beside her until they reached the bank, where they took off their skates and walked through the bare trees to where he had parked the car.

His house was warm and inviting, just as she had remembered it. They had tea in a small, cosily furnished room with a bright fire burning and lamps casting a soft glow over the well-polished tables which held them. And the tea was delicious—anchovy toast, sandwiches and miniature cream puffs. Mary Jane, with a healthy appetite from her skating, ate with the pleasure of a hungry child. She was halfway through the sandwiches when she exclaimed, 'We haven't telephoned Midwoude—do you think we should?'

Fabian got up at once. 'I suppose I can't persuade you to stay to dinner?'

She refused at once very nicely and was at once sorry that she had done so, because she would very much have liked to spend the evening with him. She told herself urgently that it was foolish to be charmed by him just because he was being such good company—besides, there was Mervyn. She pulled herself up with the reflection that there wasn't Mervyn; she owed nothing to him, neither loyalty to his memory or anything else; not, said her heart, even love, for it hadn't been love, only a plain girl's reaction to being admired....

'You're looking very thoughtful,' remarked Fabian and sat down again. 'You said you wanted to go home—will you agree to stay until Emma is married as I asked you? I think the wedding will be very soon, probably we shall hear something when we go back presently.'

She spoke at random to fill the silence between them: 'This is a lovely house.'

'You like it? it needs a family—children—in it. You like children, Mary Jane?'

'Yes.' She was unconsciously wistful as they lapsed into silence once more. She had abandoned her confused thinking, and it seemed a good thing; she needed peace and quiet to sort herself out, and Fabian's presence had the effect of confusing her still further. She wasn't even sure what she wanted any more—only one thing was clear, he didn't mind if she returned home; she had watched his face when she had

350

told him that she wanted to go and its expression hadn't changed at all. Not meaning to say it, she asked: 'When I go home, will you need to visit me again?'

His casual, 'Oh, I think not; everything is arranged very satisfactorily. If you should need my services you can always write or telephone,' daunted her, but she tried again.

'But what about the horse?'

'I asked the vet to keep an eye open—he'll let me know when he finds something worth while.'

She said, 'Oh, how nice,' in a small forlorn voice, aware that she had been using the horse as a line of communication, as it were, and Fabian had cut the line. She got to her feet. 'I think I should be getting back,' and when he got to his feet with unflattering speed, 'You said we wouldn't meet—that you would only be Emma's surgeon—I forgot that this afternoon. Did you?'

His dark eyes rested briefly on hers. 'No, I hadn't forgotten, Mary Jane, but there is such a thing as a truce, is there not?'

He fetched her outdoor things and they went out to the car. A good thing, she thought savagely as she got in, that she hadn't accepted his invitation to dinner— uttered out of politeness, no doubt, for he was obviously longing to be rid of her. Telling herself that it didn't matter in the least, she kept up a steady flow of chat as he drove her back to Midwoude, her voice a little high and brittle.

But he seemed in no hurry to be rid of her company or anyone else's when they reached the house. Cousin Emma and Doctor Trouw were in the sitting room, the tea things still spread around them, deep in wedding plans. They would be married, declared Emma, with a suitable touch of the dramatic, in four days' time—the *burgermeester* of Midwoude had promised to perform the ceremony in the early afternoon at the Gemeentehuis, and afterwards they would cross the street for a short ceremony in church. 'And you will come, Mary Jane, because you have been so kind and good...' the ready tears sprang to her eyes, 'and when you marry I shall come to your wedding.'

'How nice,' said Mary Jane briefly. 'Tell me, what will you wear?'

Her companion was instantly diverted and the two ladies became absorbed in the bridal outfit. They were still engrossed in this interesting topic when the gentlemen wandered off to the other side of the room to have a drink, and when after a few minutes Fabian said that he must go, he did no more than pass a careless remark about their pleasant afternoon before he took himself off.

There was no time for anything but the wedding preparations during the next day or so. Cousin Emma, fully recovered from her operation, plunged into a maelstrom of activity with Mary Jane doing her best to hold her back a little. Recovered she might be and in the happy position of having others to attend to her every want, she still needed to rest. Mary Jane gently bullied her on to the chaise-longue in her bedroom each afternoon and by dint of guile and cunning, kept her there until Doctor Trouw called at tea-time. Fabian came too, but only for a few minutes, to check his cousin's progress, although on the day previous to the wedding he remained long enough to tell Mary Jane that should she wish, he would arrange for her to travel home on the day after the wedding. 'But time enough to let me know,' he assured her carelessly. 'There are few people travelling at this time of year, it will only be a question of a few telephone calls.' He had nodded cheerfully at her and added, 'I shall see you at the wedding, no doubt.'

Getting Cousin Emma to the Gemeentehuis proved a nerve-shattering business. Not only was she excited and happy, she was tearful too, and when almost dressed declared that she looked a complete guy, that her shoes pinched and that her scar was so conspicuous that she really hadn't the courage to go through with the ceremony. It was fortunate that her bridegroom— come, as Dutch custom dictated, to fetch his bride to their wedding—had brought with him his wedding gift, a string of pearls which exactly covered the off-ending blemish. Mary Jane, rather pink and excited herself, left them thankfully together and hurried to the front door. Jaap was to drive her to the village and she was already a little late. He wasn't there, but Fabian was, strolling up and down the hall in morning clothes whose elegance quite dazzled her.

'There you are,' he remarked. 'I sent Jaap on, you're coming with me.' He stood looking at her. 'Now that is a new hat,' he decided, 'and a very pretty one.'

Mary Jane gave him a doubtful look. The hat had taken a good deal of thought and she hadn't had all that time to escape from Cousin Emma. It matched her coat exactly, a melusine with a sideways-tilted brim ending in a frou-frou of chiffon. Not at all her sort of hat, but after all, it was a wedding and one was allowed some licence. It added elegance to her ordinary face too and gave it a glow which almost amounted to prettiness.

'Someone told you,' she accused him.

353

'No, indeed not,' he laughed at her, 'and it really is pretty.'

She wished that he would say that she was pretty too, although that would be nonsense, but he didn't say anything else, but tucked her into the Rolls beside him and drove off to the Gemeentehuis, a small, very old building, ringed around now with a number of cars and little groups of people from the village. Inside, Fabian found her a seat at the back before he went to take his place with his family in the front row. The ceremony was short and quite incomprehensible to her, but the service in the church was more to her taste, for she was able to follow it easily. And when it was over she watched the bride and groom and their families, correctly paired, walk down the aisle to the door of the church. She knew none of them, save for Fabian and Willem. They looked, she considered, a little haughty, very well dressed and faintly awe-inspiring, although the younger members of the party were gay and smiling and enjoying themselves. Willem, she was glad to see, had his girl with him—at least, she hoped it was his girl. He certainly looked happy enough, and Fabian—Fabian was escorting a truly formidable lady of advanced years, just behind the bridal pair.

She waited until almost everyone had gone and made her way to the door, looking for Jaap. He was nowhere to be seen. There were still several groups of people lingering around the porch, but they were all strangers to her. She supposed she would have to walk. She frowned—how like Fabian to forget all about her; she wished she hadn't come, he was horrible, thoughtless, thoroughly beastly ... He touched her arm, smiling at her, so that she felt guilty, and felt even more so when he said, 'I knew you would have the sense to wait until I came for you—Great-aunt Corina isn't to be hurried. Come on.'

She travelled back sitting with the old lady, who wasn't haughty at all, while a large young man, whom Fabian introduced as Dirk—a cousin—squeezed in beside them. Fabian introduced the girl sitting beside him too—a blue-eyed creature wrapped in furs. Her name was Monique, and even though he said she was a cousin, Mary Jane didn't take to her. She was still pondering the strength of her feelings about this when they arrived at the house.

The vast drawing room had been got ready for the reception, with a long table and a number of smaller ones grouped around it. Mary Jane, seated between Dirk and an elderly uncle of the bride, found that she was expected to make a good meal. She went from champagne cocktails to lobster meuniere, from venison steaks to chocolate profiteroles, each with its accompanying wine. It was a relief to hear from Dirk that a wedding cake wasn't customary, for what with the wine and champagne and the warmth of the room, she began to feel a little lightheaded. Even the haughty members of the family didn't seem haughty any more, indeed, those she had spoken to had been charming to her. She glanced round her. Everyone looked very happy, but then marriages were happy occasions, although if she married she would want a quiet one with just a few friends. The corners of her gentle mouth turned down; the sooner she stopped thinking that romantic nonsense, the better. She turned to Dirk, who was quite amusing although a little young, she considered, and when he asked her if he might take her out to supper that evening, she re-

fused with a charm which drew from him a regretful
smile and a promise to ask her again the very next
time they met. It seemed pointless to tell him that she
was going back to England the next day, she laugh-
ingly agreed and listened with all her attention while
he told her about his ambition to be as good a surgeon
as his cousin Fabian.

The guests began to leave as soon as the bridal pair
had gone; car after car slid away into the winter darkness until there were only a very few left, their owners
delaying their departure for a last-minute chat or waiting for each other. Mary Jane felt rather lost; the
drawing room was in the hands of the caterers, under
the sharp eye of Jaap, being returned to its usual
stately perfection. Sientje was in the kitchen, the daily
maid had gone long ago. Mary Jane stood in the hall,
remembering how cheerfully Fabian had asked 'Tomorrow?' when she had asked him on the way to the
wedding if he would arrange for her to travel home.
'I'll send the tickets here to you,' he had told her casually, 'in plenty of time for you to catch the boat train
from Groningen. Jaap will drive you to the station.'

Now she wondered if that was to be his goodbye. She
had helped him when he had asked her to; her own
affairs were in order, there was nothing more for him
to do; did he intend to drop their uneasy acquaintance completely? Just as well, perhaps, she mused, they
had never got on well. She wandered into the empty
sitting room and sat down by the window, staring out
into the dark evening, her mind full of useless regrets,
her fingers playing with the diamond brooch Fabian
had given her and which she had pinned to her coat.
She had written and thanked him for it. It had been a
long letter and she had tried very hard to show her

gratitude, but he had never answered it, or mentioned it—she wasn't sure if he had even noticed that she was wearing it today. She got up and strolled back into the hall, empty now. Not quite empty, though, for Fabian was there, sitting in the padded porter's chair by the door. He walked over to meet her and said easily, 'Hullo—I'm just off. You're fixed up for the evening, I hear. Dirk told me earlier that he intended taking you out to supper.' He smiled. 'He's good company, you'll enjoy yourself.'

'Oh, indeed I shall,' she assured him, her voice bright. How pleased he must feel, thinking that she was settled for the evening and that he need not bother ... 'I hope you have a pleasant evening too,' she assured him untruthfully, 'and thank you for seeing about the tickets. I'll say goodbye.'

She held out her hand and had it engulfed in his, and it became for an amazing few seconds of time the only tangible thing there; the hall was whirling around her head, her heart was beating itself into a frenzy because she had at that moment become aware of something—she didn't want to say goodbye to Fabian, she didn't want him to go, never again. She wanted him to stay for ever, because she was in love with him—she always had been. But why had she only just discovered it? And what was the use of knowing it now? For even as the knowledge hit her he had dropped her hand and was at the door. He went through it without looking back.

CHAPTER EIGHT

MARY Jane stood staring at the door for a few seconds, hoping that he might come back; that he had forgotten something; that he would ask her to go out with him that evening, Dirk or no Dirk. Anything, she cried soundlessly; a violent snowstorm which would make it impossible for him to drive away, something wrong with the Rolls, an urgent message so that she could run after him with good reason ... Nothing happened, the hall was empty and silent, there was a murmur of voices from the drawing room where there was still a good deal of activity, and from outside the crunch of the Rolls' wheels on the frozen ground. They sounded remote and final; she waited until she couldn't hear them any more and then went in search of Jaap.

If the old man was surprised at her decision to go to bed immediately, he didn't show it. They had become used to each other by now, so it wasn't too difficult to let him suppose that she had a headache and wanted nothing for the night. He wished her good night and went back to the caterers.

She slept badly and got up early, which she realized later had been a silly thing to do, for the morning stretched endlessly before her. She wouldn't be leaving until the late afternoon, and somehow the time had to be helped along. She spent some of it with Jaap and Sientje, but conversation was difficult anyway, and they had their work to do—they were to go on a short holiday and return to make the house ready for Cousin Emma and her husband, who had agreed to the happy arrangement of leaving his own house for his son's use and carrying on his practice from Midwoude. Mary Jane, sensing that much as Jaap and Sientje liked her, they wanted to get on with their chores, offered to clear away the silver and glass which had been got out for the wedding, and then went around freshening up the floral arrangements; probably Jaap would throw them out before he closed the house, but it gave her something to do. But even these self-imposed tasks came to an end, and she ate her lonely lunch as slowly as possible, hoping that Fabian would telephone; surely he would say goodbye? But as the minutes ticked by she was forced to the conclusion that he had no intention of doing so. Perhaps he would be at the station—if she could see him just once more before she went away ... She told herself it was foolish to build her hopes on flimsy wishes, a good walk would do her good and she had plenty of time. She went and got her coat, tied a scarf over her head, snatched up her gloves, and went in search of Jaap. He seemed a little uncertain about her desire to go out, but she could understand but little of what he said and she wasn't listening very hard; she wanted to get out and walk—as fast as possible, so that she might be too tired to think about Fabian. She made the old man understand that she would be back in good time for him to drive her to the station, and fled from the house before he could detain her longer.

The afternoon was bleak and frozen into stillness; the ground was of iron and she quickly discovered that it was slippery as well. She walked fast into an icy wind, down to the village, and when she looked at her watch and saw that she still had time to kill, she walked on, towards the path which led eventually to the lake. Here the bare trees gave some pretence of shelter even though the ground under her feet was rough and treacherously slithery, something she hardly noticed, trying as she was to outstrip her unhappiness, forcing herself to think only of her future in the house her grandfather had left her. She came in sight of the frozen water presently and paused to look at her watch again. She would have to return quite soon and she decided not to go any further.

There were people skating on the lake, turning the greyness of its surroundings into a gay carnival of sound and colour. Mary Jane drew a sighing breath, the memory of her afternoon with Fabian very vivid, then turned on her heel and started to retrace her steps along the path, and after a short distance, lured by the cheerful sight of a robin sitting in a thicket, turned off it and wandered a little way, absurdly anxious to get a closer view of the bird. But he flew just ahead of her so that when she finally retraced her steps the path was hidden. She hurried a little, anxious to find it again because it would never do to lose the boat train. She didn't notice the upended root under her foot—she tripped, lost her balance on the smooth ice, and fell, aware of the searing pain in the back of her head as it struck a nearby tree.

It was like coming up through layers of grey smoke; she was almost through them when she heard Fabian's voice saying 'God almighty!' and it sounded like a prayer. With a tremendous effort she opened her eyes and focused them upon him. He looked strange, for he was in his theatre gown and cap and a mask, pulled down under his chin.

'You sound as though you're praying,' she mumbled at him.

'I am,' and before she could say more: 'Don't talk.'

His voice was kind and firm, she obeyed it instantly and closed her tired eyes, listening to him talking to someone close by. He had taken her hand in his and the firm, cool grip was very reassuring; she allowed the soft grey smoke to envelop her once more.

When she wakened for the second time, the room was dimly lit by a shaded lamp in whose glow a nurse was sitting, her head bowed over a book. But when Mary Jane whispered, 'Hullo there,' she came over to the bed and said in English, 'You are awake, that is good.'

Mary Jane suffered her pulse to be taken, and in a voice which wasn't as strong as she could have wished said, 'I'll get up,' and was instantly hushed by the nurse's horrified face.

'No—it is four o'clock in the morning,' she remonstrated, 'and I must immediately call the Professor—he wishes to know when you wake, you understand? Therefore you will lie still, yes?'

Mary Jane started to sit up, thought better of it because of the pain at the back of her head and said weakly, 'Yes—but no one is to get up out of his bed just to come and look at me. I'm quite all right.'

'But the Professor is not in his bed,' explained the nurse gently. 'He is here, Miss Pettigrew, in the hospital, waiting for you to wake.'

She went to the telephone as she spoke and said something quietly into it, then came back to the bed. 'He comes,' she volunteered, 'and you will please lie still.'

He was there within a few minutes, this time in slacks and a sweater. To Mary Jane's still confused eyes he looked vast and forbidding and singularly remote, and the fact disappointed her so that when she spoke it was in a somewhat pettish voice. 'You stayed up all night—there was no need. I'm perfectly all right.' She frowned because her headache was quite bad. 'It was quite unnecessary.'

He said tolerantly, 'It's of no matter,' and took her wrist between his finger and thumb, taking her pulse. 'You feel better? Well enough to talk a little and tell me what happened?'

She blinked up at him. His face looked drawn and haggard in the dim light and she felt tender pity welling up inside her so that she could hardly speak. 'I'm sorry,' she managed, 'I mean I'm sorry you've had all this trouble.'

'I said it didn't matter. What happened?' His voice was quiet, impassive and very professional. He would expect sensible answers; she frowned in her efforts to be coherent and not waste his time.

'I went for a walk,' she explained at last. 'You see, I hadn't anything to do until it was time to leave. I went to the village and there was still lots of time—I went down the path between the trees to the lake. There was a robin, I went to look at him and I slipped and hit my head—I can remember the pain.' She stopped, thankful to have got it all out properly for him. 'I don't know how long I was there. Did I dream that I saw Jaap and it was very cold?'

Fabian had pulled up a chair to the side of the bed. 'No—you were cold, and it was Jaap who found you when he went to look for you because you hadn't gone back to the house and he was worried, only he didn't find you straight away because you were a little way from the path. You have a slight concussion—nothing serious, but you will stay here, lying quietly in bed, until I say otherwise. And you will do nothing, you understand?'

She muttered 'Um' because she was drowsy again, but she remembered to ask, 'Where's here?'

'The hospital in Groningen.' And she muttered again, 'Thank you very much,' because she was grateful to be there and wanted him to know it, but somehow her thoughts weren't easy to put into the right words. Forgetting that she had already said it once, she thanked him again. 'I'm such a nuisance and I am sorry.' A thought streaked through the fog of sleep which was engulfing her. 'I'm going home today,' she offered in a groggy voice.

'Yesterday—no, Mary Jane, you are not going home, not just yet. You will stay here until your headache has gone.'

She managed to open her heavy lids once more. 'I don't want...' she began, and met his dark eyes.

'You'll stay here,' he repeated quietly. 'Nurse will give you a drink and make you comfortable and you will go to sleep again.'

She was in no state to argue; she closed her eyes and listened to his voice as he spoke to the nurse, but he hadn't finished what he was saying before she was asleep again.

It was afternoon when next she woke, feeling almost herself, and this time there was a different nurse, a big, plump girl with a jolly face, whose English, while adequate, was peppered with peculiar grammar. She turned Mary Jane's pillow, gave her a drink of tea and went to the telephone.

Fabian was in his theatre gown again. He nodded briefly with a faint smile, took her pulse and, satisfied, said: 'Hullo, you're better. How about something to eat?'

She didn't answer him. 'You're busy in theatre,' she observed in a voice which still wasn't quite hers. 'What's the time?'

'Three o'clock in the afternoon.'

'Have you a long list?' She hadn't meant to ask, but she had to say something just to keep him there a little longer.

'Yes, but we're nearly through. How about tea and toast?'

She nodded and started to thank him, but sneezed instead. 'I've a cold,' she discovered.

'That's to be expected. The temperature was well below zero and you were half frozen. I'll see that you get something for it.'

She sneezed again and winced at the pain in her head. 'That's very kind of you,' she said meekly. 'I'm quite well excepting for a bit of a headache.'

He gave her a smile which he might have given to a child. 'I know. All the same, you will stay where you are until I say that you may get up.'

Mary Jane nodded and closed her eyes, not because she was sleepy any more, but because to look at him when she loved him so much was more than she could bear. When she opened them he had gone and the large cheerful nurse was standing by the bed with tea and toast on a tray.

It took two more days for her headache to go, and even though she felt better, the cold dragged on. Two days in which Fabian came and went, his visits brief and impersonal and kindly, during which he conferred with the nurse, made polite conversation with herself, read her notes and went away again. On the morning of the third day he was accompanied by a young man whom he introduced as his registrar, a good-looking, merry-faced young man, trying his hardest to copy his chief's every mannerism; something which might have amused Mary Jane ordinarily, but which struck her now as rather touching. He listened attentively while Fabian explained what had happened to her and agreed immediately when Fabian suggested that she might be ready to leave hospital. He stayed a little longer, talking to Mary Jane, and then at a word from Fabian, took himself off.

She had got up and dressed that morning and had been sitting by the window watching the busy court-yard below, but she turned round now to face Fabian. She had had a few minutes to pull herself together; she said in a matter-of-fact voice, 'I should like to go home tomorrow if you will allow it and it isn't too much trouble to arrange. I'm perfectly well again. Thank you for looking after me so well . . .'

He made a small, impatient sound. 'You will do nothing of the kind, that would be foolish, at least for the next few days. As soon as I consider you fit for travelling I will arrange your journey. In the mean-time you will come to my house—my housekeeper will look after you.'

She sat up very straight in her chair, which caused her to cough, sneeze and give herself a headache all at the same moment. Her voice was still a little thick with her cold when she spoke. 'I don't think I want to do that—it's very kind of you, but . . .'

'Why not?' he sounded amused.

'I've been quite enough trouble to you as it is.'

His ready agreement disconcerted her. 'Oh, indeed you have—you will be even more trouble if you don't do as I ask now. I shall be in Utrecht, and Mevrouw Hol will be delighted to have someone to fuss over while I am away. You shall go back to England when I return.'

Her reply was polite and wooden. If ever she had needed to convince herself of his indifference to her, she had the answer now. His obvious anxiety to get her off his hands even while he was treating her with such care and courtesy and arranging for her comfort, told her that, and he didn't care a rap for her ...

'What are you thinking?' he demanded.

'Oh, nothing, just—just that it will be nice to be home again. Are you going to Utrecht straight away?'

He was leaning against the wall, staring at her. 'To-night. You will be taken to my house tomorrow morning, Mevrouw Hol is expecting you. Her English is as fragmental as your Dutch; it will be good for both of you. She is a very kind woman, you will be happy with her. She has the same good qualities as your Mrs Body —to whom, by the way, I have written.'

Mary Jane was startled to think that she had quite forgotten to do that.

'Oh, I forgot—how stupid of me, I'm sorry.'

'You have had concussion,' he reminded her, and added with a little smile, 'And you have no reason to be apologetic about everything.'

She coloured painfully and just stopped herself in time from saying that she was sorry for that too. Instead she wished him a pleasant time in Utrecht, her quiet voice giving no clue to her imagination, already vividly at work on beautiful girls, dinners for two ... perhaps he had another house there. He strolled to the door, his eyes on her still.

'But of course I shall,' he told her. 'I always do.' He opened the door and turned round to say, 'We shall see each other before you go, I have no doubt.' With a careless nod he was gone, and presently, by craning her neck, she was able to see him crossing the courtyard below, Klaus Vliet, his registrar, beside him. She couldn't see them very clearly because she was crying.

She left the hospital the following day, just before noon, and was driven to Fabian's house by Klaus, who called to fetch her from her room in the private wing of the hospital, explaining that his chief had told him to do so—furthermore, he was to see her safely installed with Mevrouw Hol and call daily until such time as her guardian told him not to. Mary Jane, now she was up and about, was disappointed to find that she still had a headache, it made her irritable and she would have liked to have disputed this high-handed measure on Fabian's part, but she couldn't be bothered. She accepted the news without comment and closed her eyes against the dullness of the city streets.

But inside Fabian's house it wasn't dull at all, but gay with flowers and warm and welcoming. Mevrouw Hol was a dear; round and cosy and middle-aged with kind blue eyes and a motherly face. Mary Jane, whose headache had reached splitting point, took one look at her and burst into tears, to be instantly comforted, led to a chair by the fire in the sitting room where she had tea with Fabian, divested of her outdoor things, told not to worry, and given coffee while Klaus tactfully left them to fetch her case and carry it upstairs. He joined her for coffee presently, ignoring her blotched face, and when they had finished it, ordered her to lie down the minute she had eaten the lunch Mevrouw Hol was even then bringing to her on a tray. He gave her some tablets too, with strict instructions to take them as directed. 'And mind you do,' he warned her kindly, 'or the chief will have my head.' He got up.

'I'm going now, but I shall be here tomorrow morning to see how you are. Mevrouw has instructions to telephone if you feel at all under the weather.'

Mary Jane smiled shakily at him. 'You make me feel as though I were gold bullion at the very least!'

'Better than that,' he grinned, 'above rubies.' He lifted a hand. 'Be seeing you!'

She ate her lunch under Mevrouw Hol's watchful eye and went upstairs to lie down. Her room was at the back of the house, overlooking a very small paved courtyard, set around with tubs full of Algerian irises and wintersweet. The room was delightful, not very large and most daintily furnished in the Chippendale style with *Toile de Jouy* curtains in pink and a thick white carpet underfoot. She looked round her with some interest, for it didn't seem at all the kind of room Fabian would wish for in his home. She had always imagined that above stairs, the rooms would be furnished with spartan simplicity. She didn't know why she had thought that, perhaps because he was a bachelor, but of course, the house would have been furnished years ago, for everything was old and beautiful. As she closed her eyes she thought how nice it would be to live in the old house, nicer than her grandfather's even.

She felt much better the following morning. She had done nothing for the rest of the previous day, only rested and eaten her supper under Mevrouw Hol's kindly eye and gone to bed again, and now after a long night's rest she felt quite herself again, even her headache had gone.

Perhaps it was her peaceful surroundings, she thought, as she accompanied the housekeeper on a gentle tour of the kitchen regions, for it was peaceful;

back in the hall she stood still, listening to the rich tick-tock of the elaborate wall clock before wandering into the sitting room to sit, quite content, in one of the comfortable chairs, doing nothing. The sound of the great knocker on the front door roused her though and she got up to greet Klaus, who, after carrying out a conscientious questioning as to her state of health, joined her for coffee. He stayed for half an hour, talking gently about nothing in particular, and when he got up to go, promised to return the next day. When she assured him that this was quite unnecessary, he looked shocked and told her that he had been asked to do so by the chief and would on no account go against his wishes. Nor would he allow her to go out, not that day, at any rate.

'Well,' said Mary Jane, a little pettish, 'anyone would think that I had a subdural or a C.V.A. or something equally horrid. I only bumped my head...'

'And caught a cold,' he told her, laughing.

Two more days passed and she felt quite well again. Even her cold had cleared up and Klaus, looking her over carefully each morning, had to admit at last that he could find nothing wrong with her, a remark which caused her to ask: 'Well, when's Professor van der Blocq coming back?'

Klaus put down his coffee cup and looked at her in bewilderment. 'Coming back? But he has never been away.' His pleasant face cleared. 'Ah, you mean when does he come back to his house? Very soon, I should suppose, for I am able to give him a good account of you today, so surely he will now allow you to return to your home.' He grinned at her disarmingly. 'He is not of our generation, the chief—he holds old-fashioned views about things which we younger men think nothing of.'

She went a bright, angry pink. 'Don't talk as though he were an old man!' she said sharply. 'And I share his views.'

Klaus smiled ruefully. 'I see that I must beg your pardon, and I do so most sincerely. You must not think that I mock at the chief—he is a mighty man in surgery and a good man in his life and much liked and respected—I myself would wish to be like him.' He looked at her with curiosity. 'You knew, then, that he was living in the hospital until you are well enough to leave his house?'

'Of course.' Her voice, even to her own ears, sounded satisfyingly convincing. 'I am his ward, you know. It's like having a father . . .'

The absurdity of the remark struck her even as she made it. Fabian was no more like a father than the young man sitting opposite her. 'Well, not quite,' she conceded, 'but you know what I mean.'

He agreed politely, although she could see that he had little idea of what she meant; she wasn't certain herself. He got up to go presently, wishing her goodbye because he didn't expect to see her again, 'Although I daresay that you will visit your guardian from time to time,' he hazarded, 'and I expect to be here for some years.'

She gave him a smiling reply, longing for him to go so that she could have time to herself to think. To learn that Fabian had been in Groningen all the time she had been at his house, and had made no effort to come and see her, had been a shock she was just beginning to realize. Maybe he was old-fashioned in his views, she was herself, and she could respect him for them, but not even the most strait-laced member of the community could have seen any objection to him going to see her in his own house—or telephoning, for that matter—and surely he could have said something to her? There was only one possible explanation, he was quite indifferent to her; considered her a nuisance he felt obliged to suffer until she was fit to return home. It would have been nice to have confronted him with this, but then he might ask her how it was that she knew he had been in Groningen, and unless she could think of some brilliant lie, poor Klaus would get the blame for speaking out of turn. She allowed several possibilities, most of them highly impractical, to flit through her head before deciding regretfully that she was a poor liar in any case, and she would not have the nerve, not with Fabian's dark, penetrating gaze bent upon her, so she discarded them all to explore other possibilities.

She could run away—a phrase she hastily changed to beating a retreat—if she did that, it would save Fabian the necessity of arranging her journey and at the same time save her pride and allow him to see that she was quite able to look after herself. She didn't need his help, she told herself firmly, in future she would have nothing to do with him. Doubtless he would be delighted—had he not told her that she was tiresome to him? Mary Jane paced up and down the comfortable room, in a splendid rage which was almost, but not quite, strong enough to conceal her love for him. But for the time being, it served its purpose—she would write him a letter, thanking him for all he had done ... She began to plot, sitting before the fire in the pleasant room.

By lunch-time she had it all worked out, she would

leave that very afternoon. She wouldn't be able to take her case with her, but Klaus had said that she might go for a short walk if she had a mind to. He had told Mevrouw Hol this—it made it all very easy; she had her passport and plenty of money still, she could buy what she needed as she went, and this time she would fly—it would be quicker and she supposed that there would be several flights to London once she got to Schiphol. She ate her lunch on a wave of false excitement and over her coffee began the letter to Fabian.

Her pen was poised over the paper while she composed a few dignified sentences in her head when the door opened and he walked in. If he saw her startled jump and the guilty way she tried to hide her writing pad and pen, he said nothing.

'Young Vliet tells me you're quite recovered,' he began without preamble. 'I've arranged for you to travel home this evening.'

She gazed at him speechlessly, feeling dreadfully deflated after all her careful planning, and when she didn't speak, he went on, 'I expected you to express instant delight, instead of which you look flabbergasted and dreadfully guilty. What have you been doing?'

'Nothing—nothing at all.' Her voice came out in a protesting, earnest squeak. 'I'm surprised, that's all. I—I was—that is . . .' She remembered something. 'Did you have a nice time in Utrecht?'

'Yes. I see you're writing letters—leave them here and I'll see that they're posted.'

She was breathless. 'No—that is, they're not important—there's no need . . .' She tore the sheet across and crumpled it up very small and threw it on the fire. She had only got as far as 'Dear Fabian,' but she didn't want him to see even that. She sighed loudly without knowing it and said with a brightness born of relief, 'There, I can write all the letters I want to when I get home.'

Fabian had seated himself opposite her and was pouring himself the coffee which Mevrouw Hol had just brought in. 'Not to Mervyn, I hope?'

'Mervyn?' She stared at him, her mouth a little open. She had forgotten about Mervyn because there wasn't anyone else in the world while Fabian was there. 'Oh, Mervyn,' she said at last, 'no, of course not. I don't know where he is.' She stared at the hands in her lap. 'I don't want to know, either.'

'The temptation to say "I told you so" is very great, but I won't do that.' He put down his cup. 'The train leaves here about six o'clock—do you need anything or wish to go anywhere before you leave?'

He wanted her out of the way. She got to her feet and said coldly, 'No, thank you—I'll go and put a few things together...'

'Five minutes' work,' he was gently mocking, 'but it's as good an excuse as any, I imagine.' He went to the door and opened it for her. 'I shall be in the study if you should want anything,' he told her.

She made no attempt to pack her case when she reached her room; he was right, five minutes was more than enough time in which to cast her few things in and slam the lid. She sat down in the little bucket chair by the window and stared down into the little courtyard, not seeing it at all. It was a very good thing that she was going away, although perhaps not quite as she had planned. She should never have come in the first place, only Fabian had been so insistent. She allowed her thoughts to dwell briefly on Cousin Emma and Doctor Trouw and wondered if she would ever see them again—perhaps they would come and stay with her later on, then she would get news of Fabian. Although wasn't a clean break better? He had told her that her affairs were now in good order, anything which needed seeing to could be done by letter or through Mr North.

She got up and prowled round the room, touching its small treasures with a gentle finger—glass and porcelain and silver—Fabian had a lovely home and she would never forget it. Presently she sat down again and dozed off.

Mevrouw Hol wakened her for tea, bustling into the room, wanting to know if she felt well and was she cold, or would she like her tea in her room. Mary Jane shook her head to each question and went downstairs. There was no sign of Fabian; she ate her tea as she had always done, from a tray on the small table by the fire. He must have gone back to the hospital. She poured a second cup, wondering if he had left instructions as to how she was to get to the station.

She finished her tea and went back upstairs to ram her things into her case in a most untidy, uncaring fashion, not in the least like her usual neat ways, and, that done, went back downstairs and out to the kitchen where Mevrouw Hol was preparing dinner. Mary Jane watched her for a moment and asked in her frightful Dutch: 'People for dinner?' and when Mevrouw Hol nodded, felt a pang of pure envy and curiosity shoot through her. 'How many?' she wanted to know.

The housekeeper shot her a thoughtful glance. 'Three,' she said, 'two ladies and a gentleman.'

'Married?' asked Mary Jane before she could stop

herself.

Mevrouw Hol nodded, and Mary Jane, her imagination at work again, had a vivid mental picture of some distinguished couple, and—the crux of the whole matter—a beautiful girl—blonde, and wearing couture clothes, she decided, her imagination working overtime. She would have a disdainful look and Fabian would adore her. She got down from the edge of the table where she had perched herself. 'I'll get ready,' she said in her terrible Dutch.

She went downstairs at twenty to six, because Fabian had said that the train went at six o'clock, and perhaps she should get a taxi. She was hatted and coated and ready to leave and there was no sign of anyone. Fabian came out of his study as she reached the hall. He said briefly: 'I'll get your case,' and when he came downstairs again she ventured, 'Should I call a taxi—there's not much time.' She searched his tranquil face. 'I didn't know you'd come back,' she explained.

'I've been here all the afternoon—I had some work to do. If you're ready we'll go.'

'Oh—are you taking me to the station? I thought . . .'

'Never mind what you thought. Don't you agree that as your guardian the least I can do is to see you safely on the way to England?'

She had no answer to that but went in search of Mevrouw Hol, who shook her by the hand and wished her 'Tot ziens', adding a great deal in her own language which Mary Jane couldn't understand in the least.

The journey to the station was short, a matter of a few minutes, during which Mary Jane sought vainly for something to say. She couldn't believe that she was actually going—that perhaps she might not see Fabian again for a long time, perhaps never, for he had no reason to see her again.

She looked sideways at his calm profile and then at his gloved hands resting on the wheel. She loved him very much; she had no idea that loving someone could hurt so fiercely. She went with him silently into the station and on to the platform and found the train already there. She watched while Fabian spoke to the guard, took the tickets which he handed to her and thanked him in a small voice.

'There's a seat in the dining car reserved for you,' he told her. 'Someone will fetch you. The guard will see about a porter for you when you reach the Hoek. Just go on board, everything is arranged. There's a seat booked on the breakfast car from Harwich. Have you your headache tablets with you?'

'Yes, thank you, and thank you for taking so much trouble, Fabian.'

'You had better get in,' he advised her, and disappeared, to reappear within a few minutes with a bundle of magazines. 'Don't read too much,' he told her.

She lingered on the steps. 'I must owe you quite a bit—for the journey—shall I send it to you?'

'Don't bother. Mr North will settle with me.' He put out a hand. 'Goodbye, Mary Jane, have a good trip.'

She shook hands and answered him in a steady voice —how useful pride could be on occasion! She even added a few meaningless phrases, the sort of thing one says when one is bidding someone goodbye at a railway station. He dismissed them with a half smile and got out of the train. She watched him getting smaller and smaller as the train gathered speed and finally went round a curve, and then he was gone.

The journey was smooth and so well organised that she had no worries at all; it was as though an unseen Fabian was there, smoothing her path. She wondered to what trouble he had gone to have made everything so easy for her. It was a pity that his thoughtfulness was partly wasted, for she spent a wretched night and no amount of make-up could help the pallor of her face or the tell-tale puffiness of her eyelids. She arrived, thoroughly dispirited, at Liverpool Street station in the cold rain of the January morning, and the first person she saw was Mrs Body.

CHAPTER NINE

LATER, looking back on that morning, Mary Jane knew that she had reached the end of her tether by the time she had reached London, although she hadn't known it then, only felt an upsurge of relief and delight at the sight of Mrs Body in her sensible tweeds and best hat. She had almost fallen out of the train in her eagerness to get to her and fling herself at the older woman, and Mrs Body, standing foursquare amidst the hurrying passengers, had given her a motherly hug and sensibly made no remark about her miserable face, but had said merely that the dear doctor had been quite right to ask her to come to London, much though she disliked the place, for by all accounts Mary Jane had had a nasty bang on the head. She then hurried her into a taxi and on to the next train for home, and Mary Jane, exhausted by her feelings more than the rigours of the journey, slept most of the way.

She had been home for almost a week now, a week during which she had filled her days with chores around the house and long walks with a delighted Major trailing at her heels. Her evenings she spent chatting with Mrs Body, talking about the village and what had happened in it while she had been away, various household matters, and the state of the garden. Of Holland she spoke not at all, excepting to touch lightly upon the wedding and her fall, and to her relief neither Mrs Body nor Lily had displayed any curiosity as to what she had done while she was there, nor, after that one remark Mrs Body had made on Liverpool Street station, had Fabian been mentioned. It should have made it all the easier to erase him from her mind, but it did no such thing; she found herself thinking of him constantly, his face, with its remote expression and the little smile which so disconcerted her, floated before her eyes last thing at night, and was there waiting for her when she wakened in the morning; it was really very vexing.

She tried inviting a few of her grandfather's old friends in for drinks one evening and realised too late that they were deeply interested in her visits to Holland, and wanted to know all about that country, and what was more, about her guardian too. They discussed him at some length—very much to his advantage, she was quick to note—and old Mr North, when asked to add his opinion to those of the other elderly gentlemen present, observed that, in his judgement, Jonkheer van der Blocq was a man of integrity, very much to be trusted and the right man to solve any problem. 'That episode with Mr Mervyn Pettigrew, for example,' he began, and then coughed dryly. 'I beg your pardon, Mary Jane, I should not have mentioned him; doubtless your feelings on the matter are still painful.'

He smiled kindly at her, as did his companions, and she smiled gently back, happily conscious that her feelings weren't painful at all, at least not about Mervyn. 'It doesn't matter,' she assured them, 'I got over that some time ago.' She realised as she said it that it was only a few weeks since her heart had been broken and had mended itself so quickly. 'I made a mistake,' she said calmly. 'Luckily it was discovered in time.'

'Indeed yes, and solely due to your guardian's efforts. To travel to Canada when everyone was enjoying their Christmas showed great determination on his part. I feel that your future is in safe hands, my dear.'

The other gentlemen murmured agreement, and Mary Jane, busy playing hostess, wished with all her heart that what Mr North had said was true; there was nothing she would have liked better than to have had a safe future with Fabian, not quite such a one as her companions envisaged perhaps, but infinitely more interesting.

The next morning, urged on by a desire to do something, no matter what, she took the Mini to Carlisle and bought clothes. She really didn't need them; she had plenty of sensible tweeds and jersey dresses and several evening outfits which, as far as she could see, she couldn't hope to wear out, let alone wear. She had bought them when Mervyn had come to visit her. Now, speeding towards the shops, she decided that she loathed the sight of them; she would give them all away and buy something new.

Once having made this resolve, she found that nothing could stop her; several dresses she bought for the very good reason that they were pretty and she looked nice in them, even though she could think of no occasion when she might wear them. She balanced this foolishness by purchasing a couple of outfits which she could wear each day, and, her conscience salved, bought several pairs of shoes, expensive ones, quite unsuitable for the life she led, and undies, all colours of the rainbow.

She bought a red dressing gown for Mrs Body too, and more glamorous undies for Lily, who was going steady with the postman and was making vague plans for a wedding in the distant future.

She and Mrs Body and Lily spent an absorbing evening, inspecting her purchases, but later, when she was alone in her room, she hung the gay dresses away, wondering wistfully if she would ever wear them. It seemed unlikely, but it wasn't much good brooding over it. She closed the closet door upon them and got into bed, where she lay, composing a letter to Fabian, reminding him that she still hadn't got a horse to ride. The exercise kept her mind occupied for some time and although she knew that she would never write it, and certainly not send it, it gave her a kind of satisfaction. She should have said something about it in the short, stiff letter she had written to him when she arrived home, a conventional enough missive, thanking him for his thoughtful arrangement of her journey and his care of her while she had been in hospital. It had taken her a long time to write and she had wasted several sheets of notepaper before the composition had satisfied her. He hadn't answered it.

The weather, which had been almost springlike for a few days, worsened the next morning, with cold grey clouds covering the sky, a harsh wind whistling through the bare trees and a light powdering of snow covering the ground. A beastly day, thought Mary Jane, looking out of the window while she pulled on her slacks and two sweaters. She had promised Mrs Body and Lily most of the day off too, to attend a wedding in the village, and heaven knew what time they would get back; weddings were something of an event in their quiet community and the occasion of lengthy hospitality. With an eye to the worsening weather, Mary Jane saw them off after an early lunch and went back to the kitchen to wash up and set the tea tray. This done, she wandered into the sitting room. It looked inviting with a bright fire burning and Major snoozing before it, but there was a lot of the day to get through still; she decided on a walk, a long one down to the lake and along its shore for a few miles and then back over the hills, and if the weather got too bad she could always take to the road. It would get rid of the restlessness she felt, she told herself firmly, and went to put on an old mackintosh and gumboots.

They set off, she and Major, ten minutes later—it was no day for a walk, but she was content to plod along in the teeth of the wind, thinking about Fabian, and Major was content to plod with her.

They got back home at the end of a prematurely darkened afternoon—the snow had settled a little, despite the wind, and the daylight had almost gone. The cold had become pitiless. Mary Jane and Major, tired and longing for tea and the fire, turned in at the gate and hurried up the short drive. The house looked as cold as its surroundings; she wished she had left a lamp burning as a welcome, then she remembered as

381

she reached the door that she hadn't locked it behind her--not that that mattered, she had Major with her. But Major had other ideas; he had left her to go round the side of the house to the back door; years of training having fixed in his doggy mind that on wet days he had to go in through the garden porch.

She went in alone, pulling off her outdoor things as she went and casting them down anyhow. The hall was almost in darkness and she shivered, not from cold but because she was lonely and unhappy. She said quite loudly in a miserable voice: 'Oh, Fabian!' and came to a sudden shocked halt when he said from the dimness, 'Hullo, Mary Jane.'

She turned to stare at him dimly outlined against the sitting room door and heard his voice, very matter-of-fact, again. 'You left the door open.'

She nodded into the gloom, temporarily speechless, but presently she managed, 'Have you come about my horse?'

'No.'

She waited, but that seemed to be all that he was going to say, and suddenly unable to bear it any longer, she said in a voice a little too loud: 'Please will you go?'

'If you will give me a good reason—yes.'

She didn't feel quite herself. She supposed it was the shock of finding him there, but she seemed to have lost all control over her tongue.

'I've been very silly,' her voice was still too loud, but she didn't care. 'It's you I love. I think I've always loved you, but I didn't know—Mervyn was you, if you see what I mean.' She added, quite distraught: 'So please will you go away—now.' Her voice shook a little, her mouth felt dry. She urged: 'Please, Fabian.'

He made no movement. 'What a girl you are for missing the obvious,' he observed pleasantly. 'Why do you suppose I've come?'

She wasn't really listening, being completely taken up with the appalling realisation of her foolish and impetuous speech, but she supposed he expected an answer so she said, 'Oh, the horse—no, you said it wasn't, didn't you. Have I spent too much money? You could have written about that, there was no need for you to have come...'

He crossed the hall and took her in his arms. 'You're a silly girl,' he told her, and his voice was very tender. 'Of course there is a need. Only perhaps I have been silly too—you see, my darling, you are so young and I—I am forty.'

'Oh, what has that got to do with it?' she demanded quite crossly. 'You could be twenty or ninety; you'd still be Fabian, can't you see that?'

His arms tightened around her. 'I'll remember that,' he told her softly, 'my adorable Miss Pettigrew,' and when she would have spoken he drew her a little closer. 'Hush, my love—my darling love. I'm not sure when I fell in love with you, perhaps when we first met, although I wasn't aware of it—that came later, the night Uncle Georgius died and I opened the sitting-room door and you were on the stairs looking lost and unhappy. But after that you were never there, always disappearing when I came. I waited and waited, hoping that you would love me too, and then Mervyn turned up. I have never been so worried...'

'You didn't look worried,' Mary Jane pointed out.

'Perhaps I'm not very good at showing my feelings,' he told her, 'but I'll try now.' She was wrapped in his arms as though he would never let her go again—a state, she thought dreamily, to which she was happily resigned, and when he kissed her she had no more thoughts at all. Presently she said into his shoulder, 'I was going to run away, but you came back. I thought you didn't like me being in your house—that you wanted me to come back here.'

He loosed his hold a little so that he could see her face. 'My dearest darling, there was nothing I wanted more than to have you in my home, but you were my ward...'

'You let me go.' She frowned a little, staring up into his dark eyes. 'You arranged for me to go.'

'Because I knew that you would run away if I didn't —you see, my love, I know you better than you know yourself.' He pulled her quite roughly to him and kissed her thoroughly. 'I haven't been the best of guardians, but I shall be a very good husband,' he promised her, and kissed her again, very gently this time.

It was quite dark in the hall by now, and Major, fed up with waiting at the back door, pattered in and came to sit down beside them, thumping his tail on the floor. 'He wants his supper,' said Mary Jane in a dreamy voice.

'So do I, my darling girl.'

She wasn't dreamy any more. 'Oh, my darling Fabian, you're hungry! I'll cook something.' But when she would have slipped from his arms he held her fast. 'Not just yet...'

'We can't stay here all night—Mrs Body and Lily won't be back for ages—they've gone to a wedding.' She smiled up at him, quite content to stay where she was for ever.

'They shall come to ours, my darling.'

384

'Oh, Fabian!' She could hardly see his face although it was so close to her own, but that didn't matter, nothing mattered any more. Life had become blissfully perfect, stretching out before them for ever. She clasped her hands behind his neck and because she couldn't put her happiness into words, she said again, 'Oh, Fabian!' and kissed him.

Three
for a
Wedding

Phoebe agreed to take her sister's place on a special exchange assignment. She needed to escape a tepid, go-nowhere romance, and besides, work in the Dutch hospital would be challenging.

"He looked half-asleep," Sybil said, remembering her interview with the doctor in charge there. "I doubt if he even noticed I was a woman."

But Dr. Lucius van Someren was not as unobservant as he appeared!

CHAPTER ONE

PHOEBE BROOK, Night Sister on the medical block of St Gideon's hospital in one of the less salubrious quarters of London, raised a nicely kept hand to her cap, twitched it to a correct uprightness, and very quietly opened the swing doors into the women's medical ward. Her stealthy approach to the night nurse's desk might at first glance have seemed to be a desire to catch that young lady doing something she ought not; it was in actual fact, due to a heartfelt desire not to waken any of the patients. She had herself, when a student nurse, done her nights on the ward, and again when she was a staff nurse; she knew only too well that Women's Medical, once roused during the night hours, could become a hive of activity—cups of Horlicks, bedpans, pillows rearranged, even a whispered chat about Johnny failing his eleven-plus, and what would Sister do if she were his mum—so it wasn't surprising that the nurse sitting at the desk put down her knitting and got to her feet with equal stealth, at the same time casting a reproachful look at the clock. She was supposed to go to her dinner at midnight, and it was already half past, and that added on to the fact that she had been alone for the last hour, all of which thoughts Sister Brook read with ease and a good deal of sympathy, even though she had small chance of getting a meal herself. She whispered:

'Sorry, Nurse, I got held up on Men's Medical—a coronary. Come back in an hour.'

The nurse nodded, instantly sympathetic, thinking at the same time that nothing on earth would induce her to take a Night Sister's post once she had taken her finals, and why Sister Brook, with a face like hers, hadn't gone out and got herself a millionaire was beyond her understanding.

She crept to the door, leaving the subject of her thoughts to hang her cape on the chair and lay the pile of papers she had brought with her on the desk—the bed state, the off-duty rota, the bare bones of the report she would have to hand over to the Night Superintendent in the morning—she looked at them longingly, for it would be nice to get the tiresome things done before she left the ward, then she might have time to snatch a cup of tea and a sandwich. But first she must do a round. She went, soft-footed, past the first three beds, their occupants, recovering from their several ailments, snoring in the most satisfactory manner, but the occupant of the fourth bed was awake. Mrs Tripp was elderly and extremely tiresome at times, but the nursing staff bore with her because, having bullied the doctor into telling her just what was wrong with her, she was fighting the inevitable with so much gusto that Sir John South, the consultant in charge of her case, confided to his registrar that he wouldn't be at all surprised if she didn't outlive the lot of them out of sheer determination. Nonsense, of course; Mrs Tripp would never go home again to her ugly little red brick house in a back street near the hospital—she knew it and so did everyone else. The nursing staff indulged her every whim and took no notice when she showed no gratitude, which was why Sister Brook paused now and whispered: 'Hullo, Mrs Tripp—have you been awake long?'

'All night,' said Mrs Tripp mendaciously and in far too loud a voice so that Sister Brook was forced to shush her. 'And now I'm wide awake, ducky, I'll have a . . .'

Sister Brook was already taking off her cuffs, musing as she did so that on the few occasions when she had to relieve a nurse on a ward, she invariably found herself hard at work within a few minutes of taking over. She stole out to the sluice, collecting two more requests on the way, and as all three ladies fancied a hot milk drink to settle them again, it was the best part of twenty minutes before she was able to sit down at the desk.

She had just begun the bed state, which didn't tally as usual, when the doors were opened once more, this time by a young man in a white hospital coat, his stethoscope crammed in its pocket. He looked tired and rather untidy, but neither of these things could dim his slightly arrogant good looks. He took a seat on the edge of the desk, right on top of the bed state, and said:

'Hullo, Phoebe—good lord, haven't you got any nurses about tonight? I've been hunting you all over. That coronary, he's gone up to Intensive Care, so that lightens your burden a bit, doesn't it?'

She smiled at him; she was a beautiful girl, and when she smiled she was quite dazzling. Before he had met her, he had always scoffed at descriptions of girls with sapphires in their eyes and corn-coloured hair, but he had been forced to admit that he was wrong, because Phoebe had both, with the added bonus of a small straight nose and a mouth which curved sweetly, and although she wasn't above middle height, her figure was good if a little on the plump side. She was, he had to own, quite perfect; the one small fact that she was twenty-seven, three years older than himself, he did his best to ignore; he would have preferred it otherwise, but one couldn't have everything. . . . As soon as he had taken a couple more exams he would ask her to marry him. He hadn't intended to marry before he was thirty at least, with a fellowship and well up the ladder of success, but if he waited until then she would be thirty herself—a little old, although she would make a splendid wife for an ambitious young doctor, and looking at her now, she didn't look a day over twenty.

'Any chance of a cup of tea?' he wanted to know.

She didn't bother to tell him that she had missed her own midnight meal; that she would get a sketchy tea into the bargain. 'Yes—but you must be very quiet, I've only just got them all quiet again.' She got up. 'Keep an eye on the ward,' she begged, and slipped away to the kitchen.

She came back presently with two mugs, a thick slice of bread and butter atop each of them, and handed him his with a murmured: 'I haven't had my meal.'

'Poor old girl—I'll take you out for a good nosh on your nights off.'

'I can't, Jack, I'm going home. Sybil's got a week's holiday, and I haven't seen her for ages.'

Sybil was her younger sister, twenty-three and so like her that people who didn't know them well occasionally confused their identities, which was partly why Sybil, when she decided to be a nurse too, had gone to another training school—a London hospital and not very far away from St Gideon's—but what with studying for her finals and Phoebe being on night duty, they saw very little of each other. Soon it would be easier, Phoebe thought, taking a great bite out of her bread and butter, for Sybil had sat her hospital finals and the last of the State exams had been that morning. When she had qualified, as she would, for she was a clever girl, they would put their heads together and decide what they would do. The world, as the Principal Nursing Officer had told Phoebe when she had offered her the post of Night Sister, was her oyster. That had been three years ago and she still hadn't opened her particular oyster—there were jobs enough, but she had wanted to stay near Sybil until she was qualified. Now perhaps they would go abroad together.

Her train of thought was interrupted by her companion, who put down his mug, squeezed her hand and went out of the ward. Phoebe watched him go, the smile she had given him replaced by a tiny frown. He was going to ask her to marry him—she was aware of that and she didn't know what to do about it. She liked him very much, they got on well together—too well, she thought shrewdly—they had similar tastes and ideals, but surely, she asked herself for the hundredth time, there was more to it than that? And shouldn't she know if she loved him? Was this all that love was, a mild pleasure in someone's company, a sharing of tastes, a gentle acceptance of being a doctor's wife for the rest of her days—for Jack, she felt sure, would expect her to be just that and nothing more, she would never be allowed to steal the scene. Would her heart break if she never saw him again, or if, for that matter, he were to start taking some other girl out for a change? She was older than he; she had pointed this out to him on several occasions, and more than that, being a soft-hearted girl she had never allowed the thought that she found him very young upon occasion take root in her mind.

The hour ticked away. She solved the bed state, puzzled out the off duty for another two weeks, and was dealing with old Mrs Grey, who was a diabetic and showing all the signs and symptoms of a hyperglycaemic coma, when Nurse Small came back. They dealt with it together, then Phoebe, gathering up her papers and whispering instructions as to where she would be if she was wanted again, went silently from the ward, down the long corridor, chilly now in the small hours of an April morning, and into the office which was hers during the night when she had the time to sit in it. She had barely sat down when her bleep started up—Children's this time, and could she go at once because Baby Crocker had started a nasty laryngeal stridor. She had to get Jack up after a while; he came to the ward in slacks and a sweater over his pyjamas, and they worked on the child together, and when he finally went, half an hour later, she walked down the corridor with him, starting on her overdue rounds once more. At the end of the corridor, where he went through the door leading to the resident's quarters, he gave her a quick kiss, said 'See you' and disappeared, leaving her to make her way to Men's Medical on the ground floor, musing, as she went, on the fact that although his kiss had been pleasant, it hadn't thrilled her at all, and surely it should?

The early morning scurry gave her little time to think about herself. Fortified by a pot of strong tea, she did her morning rounds, giving a hand where it was wanted and then retiring to her office to write the report and presently to take it along to her daytime colleague before paying her final visit to the Night Super. A night like any other, she thought, yawning her way to breakfast, where Sadie Thorne, Night Sister on the Surgical side, was already waiting for her. Night Super was there too, a kindly, middle-aged woman, whose nights were filled with paper work and an occasional sortie into which ward was in difficulties. She was good at her job and well liked, for she never failed to find help for a ward when it was needed and had been known to roll up her own sleeves and make beds when there was no one else available. But normally, unless there was dire emergency in some part of the hospital, or a 'flu epidemic among the nurses, she did her work unseen, supported by Phoebe and Sadie and Joan Dawson, the Night Theatre Sister. She looked up from her post now as Phoebe sat down, wished her good morning just as though they hadn't seen each other less than an hour since, and went back to her letters, while Phoebe made inroads on her breakfast, thinking contentedly that in another twenty-four hours' time she would be going home. She caught Sadie's eye now and grinned at her.

'One more night,' she declared.

'Lucky you. Going home?'

Phoebe nodded. 'With Sybil—she's got a week off and goes back to night duty.'

Night Super looked up briefly. 'I hear she did very well in her hospitals.'

'Yes, Miss Dean. I don't know how well, but I hope she's in the running for one of the prizes.'

'Like her sister,' murmured the Night Super, and Phoebe, who had gained the gold medal of her year, went a becoming pink.

She packed her overnight bag before she went to bed, because on the following morning there would be barely time for her to tear into her clothes and catch the train. Then she washed her hair, and overcome by sleep, got into bed with it hanging like a damp golden curtain round her shoulders.

The night was fairly easy—the usual mild scares, the usual emergency admission, and hubbub on the children's ward, because one of its small inmates was discovered to be covered in spots. Phoebe, called on the telephone by an urgent voice, made her way there as quickly as she could, sighing. It was early in the night, she still had her rounds to make.

The child was a new patient, admitted just as the day staff were handing over thankfully to their night colleagues, and not particularly ill. She was popped into a cot while the more urgent cases were attended to, presently she would be bathed, her hair washed, and tucked up for the night.

Phoebe, looking quite breathtakingly beautiful in her dark blue uniform, trod quietly down the ward with a nod to the nurses to get on with what they were doing and not mind her. The child was sitting on a blanket in its cot, eating a biscuit. It looked pale and undernourished and was, like so many of the children who were admitted, too small, too thin and lacklustre as to eye—not through lack of money, Phoebe knew, but through the parents' neglect; good-natured and unthinking, but still neglect. She smiled at the elderly little face, said brightly, 'Hullo, chick, what's your name?' and at the same time peered with an expert eye at the spots.

There were a great many of them, and when she peeped beneath the little flannel nightshirt there were a great many more. She straightened up and spoke to the nurse who had joined her. 'Fleas,' she said softly, so that no one would hear save her companion. 'Infected too. A mild Savlon bath, Nurse, usual hair treatment and keep a sharp eye open. Give her a milk drink and let me know if she doesn't settle. She's a bronchitis, isn't she? She'll be seen in the morning, but if you're worried let me know.' She turned away and then came back to say in a low voice: 'And wear a gown.' Her lovely eyes twinkled at the nurse, who smiled back. 'And I might as well do a round now I'm here, mightn't I?'

The night went smoothly after that. She was accustomed to, and indeed expected, the diabetic comas, coronaries and relapses which occurred during the course of it. She dealt with them as they arose with a calm patience and a sense of humour which endeared her to the rest of the night staff. She even had time for a quick cup of tea before she went to give her report.

She arrived at Waterloo with a couple of minutes to spare. There was no sign of Sybil—she would be on the train, a long train, and only its front carriages went to Salisbury; she jumped into the nearest door and started walking along the corridor. Her sister was in the front coach, sitting in an empty compartment with her feet comfortably on the seat opposite her, reading a glossy magazine. She was very like Phoebe, but her good looks were a little more vivid, her eyes a shade paler and her voice, when she spoke, just a tone higher.

'Hullo, Phoebe darling, here by the skin of your teeth, I see. How are you—it's ages since we saw each other.' She was putting Phoebe's bag on the rack as she spoke, now she pushed her gently into a window seat. 'Here, put your feet up and have a nap. We can talk later. I'll wake you in good time.'

And Phoebe, now that she had caught her train and greeted her sister, did just as Sybil suggested; in two minutes she was asleep. She wakened, much refreshed, at the touch on her arm and sat up, did her face, tidied her hair and drank the coffee Sybil had got for her, then said contritely: 'What a wretch I am—I quite forgot. How about the hospitals?'

Sybil grinned engagingly. 'The Gold Medal, ducky! I couldn't let you be the only one in the family with one, could I? I don't get the State results for six weeks, but I don't care whether I pass or not.' She looked secretive and mischievous at the same time, but when Phoebe said: 'Do tell—something exciting?' all she would say was: 'I'll tell you later, when there's no hurry. Look!'

The carriage door was flung open and a horde of people surged in, making conversation impossible. The train shuddered, gave a sigh as though it disliked the idea of leaving the station, and continued on its way. At Shaftesbury, they got out; they lived in a small village close to Sturminster Newton, but Aunt Martha, who had moved in to look after them when their mother had died, and stayed on when their father died a few years later, liked to come and fetch them in the second-hand Austin which they had all three bought between them. She was on the platform now, in her tweed skirt and her twin-set, a felt hat of impeccable origin wedged on her almost black hair, only lightly streaked with grey despite her fifty-odd years. It framed her austere good looks and gave colour to her pale face, which broke into a smile as she saw them. She greeted them both with equal affection and walked them briskly to where the car was parked, telling Sybil to sit in front with her so that Phoebe, if she felt so inclined, could continue her nap undisturbed in the back.

Which she did without loss of time, waking after a blissful fifteen minutes to find that they were already going through East Orchard; at the next village, named, inevitably, West Orchard, they would turn off on to a side road which would bring them to Magdalen Provost, where they lived—a very small village indeed, which Phoebe had declared on several occasions to have more letters to its name than it had houses. It was a charming place, only a mile or so from the main road, and yet it had remained peacefully behind the times; even motor cars and the twice daily bus had failed to bring it up to date, and by some miracle it had remained undiscovered by weekend househunters looking for a holiday cottage, probably because it was so well hidden, awkward to get at, and in winter, impossible to get out of or into by car or bus because it lay snug between two hills rising steeply on either side, carrying a road whose gradient was more than enough for a would-be commuter.

Aunt Martha rattled down the hill and stopped in the centre of the village where the church, surrounded by a sprinkling of houses, the pub and the post office and village stores which were actually housed in old Mrs Deed's front room, stood. Phoebe's home stood a little apart from the rest, surrounded by a stone wall which enclosed a fair-sized, rather unkempt garden. The house itself wasn't large, but roomy enough, and she loved it dearly; she and Sybil had spent a happy childhood here with their parents, their father, a scientist of some repute, pursuing his engrossing occupation while their mother gardened and kept house and rode round the countryside on the rather fiery horse her husband had given her. Both girls rode too, but neither of them were with their mother when she was thrown and killed while they were still at school, and their father, considerably older than his wife, had died a few years later.

Aunt Martha drew up with a flourish before the door and they all went inside. It was a little shabby but not poorly so; the furniture was old and well cared for and even if the curtains and carpets were rather faded, there was some nice Georgian silver on the sideboard in the dining room. Phoebe, now wide awake, helped bring in the cases and then went upstairs to change into slacks and shirt before joining Aunt Martha in the kitchen for coffee, regaling that lady with the latest hospital news as they drank it, but when Sybil joined them, the talk, naturally enough, centred around her and her success. It wasn't for a few minutes that Phoebe came to the conclusion that it was she and their aunt who were excited about the results and not Sybil herself. She wondered uneasily why this was and whether it had something to do with whatever it was Sybil was going to tell her. Prompted by this thought, she asked:

'Shall we go for a walk after lunch, Syb?' and the uneasiness grew at the almost guilty look her sister gave her as she agreed.

They went to their favourite haunt—a copse well away from the road, with a clearing near its edge where a fallen tree caught the spring sun. They squatted comfortably on it and Phoebe said: 'Now, Sybil, let's have it. Is it something to do with St Elmer's or about your exams?'

Her sister didn't look at her. 'No—no, of course not —at least ... Phoebe, I'm giving in my notice at the end of the week.'

Phoebe felt the uneasiness she had been trying to ignore stir, but all she said was: 'Why, love?'

'I'm going to get married.'

The uneasiness exploded like a bomb inside her. 'Yes, dear? Who to?'

'Nick Trent, he's the Medical Registrar. He's landed a marvellous job at that new hospital in Southampton. We're going to marry in two months' time—he gets a flat with the job and there's no reason for us to wait.'

'No, of course not, darling. What a wonderful surprise—I'm still getting over it.' Phoebe's voice was warm but bewildered. They had discussed the future quite often during the past six months or so and Sybil had never so much as hinted. . . . They both went out a good deal, she had even mentioned Jack in a vague way, but she had always taken it for granted that the two of them would share a year together, perhaps in some post abroad. Sybil had known that, just as she had known that Phoebe had stayed at St Gideon's, waiting for her to finish her training. She asked in a voice which betrayed none of these thoughts: 'What's he like, your Nick?'

'I knew you'd be on my side, darling Phoebe.' Sybil told her at some length about Nick and added: 'He wanted to meet you and Aunt Martha. I thought we might fix a weekend—your next nights off, perhaps.'

'Yes, of course.'

'He's got a car—we could all come down together.'

Phoebe smiled. 'Nice—I shall be able to snore on the back seat,' and then, quietly: 'There's something else, isn't there, Syb?'

'Oh, Phoebe darling, yes, and I don't know what to do unless you'll help me. You see, a few weeks ago I was chosen to take a job in Holland . . .'

Phoebe had her head bowed over the tree-trunk, watching a spider at work. She said placidly: 'Yes, dear—go on.'

'Well, it's some scheme or other cooked up between St Elmer's and some hospital or other in Delft—there's a professor type who specialises in fibrocystitis—he's over here doing some research with old Professor Forbes, and the scheme is for a nurse from Delft to come over here and me to go there for two months. But first I'm supposed to go to the hospital where he's working—you know that children's hospital where they've got a special wing—the idea being that I shall be so used to his ways that it won't matter where I

401

work. I thought it would be fun and I said I would, and then Nick ... we want to get married.'

'Of course, but you could get married afterwards, dear. It would only be a few months—not long.'

Her young sister gave her a smouldering glance. 'Yes, it is,' she declared. 'I won't!'

'Well, tell your people at hospital that it's all off.'

'I can't—all the papers and things are signed and the hospital in Delft has made all the arrangements. Phoebe, will you go instead of me?'

'Will I *what*?' uttered Phoebe in a shocked voice.

'Go instead of me.'

'How can I possibly? It couldn't be done—it's absurd—they'd find out.'

'You know you're dying to leave and get off night duty and try something else for a change. Well, here's your chance.'

'But I'm not you.'

'Near enough, no one need know. No one's ever seen us at the children's hospital, nor in Delft, have they? Even if they had, we're so alike.'

'I thought you said the Dutch doctor had seen you?'

'Pooh, him—he looked half asleep; I don't think he even looked at me, and we were only together for a couple of minutes, and I hardly spoke.' She added persuasively: 'Do, darling Phoebe! It sounds mad, doesn't it? but no one's being harmed and it's not really so silly. And don't worry about the man, I doubt if he even noticed that I was a girl.' She sounded scornful.

'He sounds ghastly—I suppose he speaks English?'

'So well that you know he's not,' explained her sister, 'and he's got those vague good manners. . . .'

'I'll not do it,' said Phoebe, and was horrified when Sybil burst into tears.

'Oh, dear,' she wailed through her sobs, 'now I don't know what I'll do—at least, I do. I shall run away and hide until Nick goes to Southampton and we'll get married in one of those pokey register offices and n-no one will come to the w-wedding!'

Phoebe sat watching her sister's lovely face. Even while she cried she was beautiful and very appealing and she loved her dearly—besides, she had promised her father that she would look after her. She said now: 'Don't cry, love—I'll do it. I think it's crazy and I'm not sure that if I'm caught I shan't get sent to prison, but it's only for a couple of months and if you don't go someone else will, so it might as well be me. Only promise me that you'll have a proper wedding, the sort Mother and Father would have liked you to have. And are you sure about Nick? I mean really sure—it's for the rest of your life.'

Sybil smiled at her through her tears. 'Oh, Phoebe, I'm sure—I can't explain, but when you love someone like I love Nick, you'll know. You're a darling! We'll fix it all up while we're here, shall we? Just you and me—Nick doesn't know, I was so excited and happy I forgot to tell him and when I thought about it later I couldn't. And Aunt Martha...'

'We won't tell anyone at all,' said Phoebe. Now that she was resigned to the madcap scheme she found herself positively enjoying the prospect of a change of scene. 'I'm quite mad to do it, of course. Now begin at the beginning and tell me exactly what it's all about. Are you sure this doctor didn't get a good look at you?'

'Him? Lord, no, Phoebe. I told you, he's the sleepy kind, eyes half shut—I should think that half the time he forgets where he is. You'll be able to twist him round your little finger.'

'What's his name?'

Sybil looked vague. 'I can't remember. I'll find out for you, and the name of the hospital and where he lives and anything else I'm supposed to know.'

'Which reminds me—I don't know an awful lot about fibrocystic disease—hasn't it got another name?'

'Mucoviscidosis, and you can forget it. The treatment hasn't changed much in the last year or so and you know quite enough about it—I remember telling me about several cases you had on the Children's Unit. . . .'

'Three years ago,' murmured Phoebe.

'Yes, well . . . I'll bring you up to date, and what does it matter anyway, for the whole idea is that I—you should be seconded to this hospital so that you can learn all about this man's new ideas.'

'And afterwards? Am I supposed to go back to St Elmer's and spread the good news around?—then we are in the apple cart.'

'No, nothing like that. I'm free to do what I like when I come back from Holland. As far as St Elmer's goes, they think I'm giving in my notice so's I can get a job somewhere else when I get back to England.'

'My passport,' hazarded Phoebe suddenly. 'Supposing this man sees it? Or don't we travel together when we go?'

'Oh, yes, that's all been arranged, but remember the British and the non-British split up when they get to the Customs. Anyway, he's hardly likely to breathe over your shoulder, he's not that sort.'

'He sounds a dead bore,' Phoebe said slowly. 'I'm not sure . . .'

'You promised—besides, there are bound to be other people around—housemen and so forth.' She paused. 'I say, there's nothing serious between you and Jack, is there?'

Phoebe shook her head and said thoughtfully: 'And if there was, this is just what's needed to speed things up—I can't quite make up my mind. . . .'

'Then don't,' said Sybil swiftly. 'Phoebe love, if it were the real thing, you wouldn't even stop to think—you'd know.' She grinned and got up. 'You see, this is just what you need, away from it all you'll have time to decide.'

Phoebe got to her feet. 'Perhaps you're right, love. Now tell me, you and your Nick, when do you want to get married?'

They spent the rest of their walk happily discussing wedding plans and clothes. Phoebe had a little money saved, but Sybil none at all.

'Well, that doesn't matter,' declared Phoebe. 'There's enough to buy you some decent clothes and pay for the wedding,' and when Sybil protested: 'I'm not likely to marry first, am I?' she wanted to know soberly, and then broke off to exclaim: 'Look—three magpies, they must have been eavesdropping. What is it now? One for anger, two for mirth, three for a wedding . . .'

They giggled happily and walked home arm-in-arm.

By the time Phoebe returned to St Gideon's from her nights off, she and Sybil had their plans laid, the first step of which was for her to resign immediately. It would work out very well, they had discovered; she would be due nights off before she left, time to go home, explain to Aunt Martha that she had taken a job with this Dutch doctor and would be going to Holland, collect the uniform Sybil's hospital were allowing her to keep until she returned to England, and make her way to the children's hospital, where, according to Sybil, she was expected. The one important point to remember was that for the time being, she was Sybil and not Phoebe.

She went to the office to resign on the morning after her return, to the utter amazement of the Chief Nursing Officer. She was a nice woman, interested in her staff and anxious to know what Phoebe intended to do—something, of course, which Phoebe was unable to tell her, for most of the big hospitals knew each other's business and probably the exchange scheme at St Elmer's was already common property. Miss Bates would hear sooner or later via the hospital grapevine, that Sybil had left to get married, probably she already knew that she had been seconded for the scheme, she wasn't above putting two and two together and making five.

'I haven't quite decided,' Phoebe told her, playing safe. 'I think I shall have a month or two's holiday at home.'

If Miss Bates considered this a curious statement from a member of her staff whom she knew for a fact depended upon her job for her bread and butter, she forbore from saying so. She thought Phoebe a nice girl, clever and remarkably beautiful. She hoped that she would marry, because she deserved something better than living out her life between hospital walls. Miss Bates was aware, just as the rest of the hospital, that the Medical Registrar fancied Night Sister Brook, but she was an astute woman, she thought that the affair was lukewarm and Sister Brook, despite her calm disposition, was not a lukewarm person. She sighed to herself, assured Phoebe that she would always be glad to see her back on the staff should she change her mind, and hoped that she would enjoy her holiday.

Phoebe didn't see Jack during her first night's duty; he had gone on a few days' leave and wouldn't be back for two more days—something for which she was thankful, for it seemed a good idea to let the hospital know that she was leaving first. The news would filter through to him when he got back and he would have time to get used to the idea before they encountered each other, as they were bound to do.

They met over the bed of a young girl three nights later—an overdose and ill; there was no time to say anything to each other, for the patient took all their attention, and when he left, almost an hour later, he gave her some instructions to pass on to the nurses, and walked away. Ten minutes later Phoebe left the ward herself. She had done her first round, thank heaven, so she could spare ten minutes for a cup of coffee. She opened the door of her office at the same time as the junior nurse on the ward arrived with the tray and she took it from her with a word of thanks, noting with a sinking heart that there were two cups on it—presumably Jack intended to have a cup with her. She pushed the door open and found him inside, standing by the desk, glowering.

He said at once; 'I'm told you're leaving. Rather sudden, isn't it?'

Phoebe sat down, poured coffee for them both and opened the biscuit tin before she answered him. 'Yes, Jack. I—I made up my mind while I was on nights off. Sybil's leaving too.'

He looked slightly mollified. 'Oh—you're off together somewhere, I suppose. For how long?'

'No—I've decided to have a little holiday, staying with relatives.' The idea had just that minute popped into her head and she hated lying to him, but after all, it wasn't his business. 'I feel unsettled.'

He stirred his coffee endlessly, looking at it intently. 'Yes, well, I suppose if you feel you must—I shall miss you, Phoebe, but I daresay you'll be ready to come back by the time I decide to marry. I shall ask you then.' He glanced up briefly. 'Everything has to be just as I want it first.'

That jarred. Was she not important enough to him —more important—than the set pattern he had laid out for them both, and without first finding out if she wanted it that way? She could see it all—the engagement when he was suitably qualified and had his feet on the first rung of the consultant's ladder, the wedding, the suitable home, suitably furnished, all the things that any girl would want, so why did she feel so rebellious?

It was all too tepid, she decided. It would be nice to be swept off her feet, to be so madly loved that the more mundane things of life didn't matter, to rush off to the nearest church without thought of the right sort of wedding. She passed him the sugar and sipped her coffee. If Nick could marry Sybil on his registrar's pay and find it wonderful, why couldn't Jack feel the same way? She began to understand a little of what Sybil had meant about loving someone, and she knew at that moment that she would never love Jack—like him, yes, even be fond of him, but that wasn't at all the same thing.

She said quietly: 'Jack, I can't stop you doing that, but I don't think it's going to be any use.' She stared at him over the rim of her mug, her lovely eyes troubled.

'I'll be the best judge of that,' he told her a shade pompously, 'and until then I prefer not to discuss it.'

He was as good as his word; they discussed the patient they had just left until, with a huffy good night, he went away.

She should mind, Phoebe told herself when she was alone. She had closed the door on a settled future, and just for a moment she was a little scared; she was twenty-seven, not very young any more, and although she could have married half a dozen times in the last few years, that was of no consolation to her now. She sighed and pulled the bed state towards her. It seemed likely that she was going to be an old maid.

CHAPTER TWO

A MONTH later, on her way to Magdalen Provost, St Gideon's behind her, the doubtful future before her, Phoebe reflected that everything had gone very well—there had been no snags, no one had wanted to know anything, no awkward questions had been asked. Sybil had already left and was at home making plans for her wedding to Nick, whom Phoebe considered to be all that could be desired as a brother-in-law. Sybil was going to be happy; now that she had met him Phoebe had to admit that in Sybil's place, she would have done exactly as she had done. Even Aunt Martha had accepted everything calmly—she had liked Nick too, had been generous in her offers of help to the bride, and was entering into the pleasurable excitement of a wedding in the family with a great deal more zest than Phoebe had supposed she would. And as for her own future, when she had told her aunt what she intended doing, without bringing Sybil's part into it at all, the older lady had wholly endorsed her plans.

'It's high time you had a change,' she stated approvingly, 'it sounds a most interesting scheme and you'll enjoy a change of scene. What did Jack have to say?'

Phoebe had told her rather worriedly and added: 'I feel guilty, Aunt, but honestly, I didn't let him think that I . . . I don't think I encouraged him at all; we just sort of liked being together.'

'Well, my dear,' her aunt had said briskly, 'there's a good deal more to being in love than liking each other's company, and I'm sure you know that. Have you been able to convince him, or does he still think you might change your mind?'

'I told him I wouldn't do that.'

She remembered the conversation now, sitting in the train, and wondered what would happen if she suddenly discovered that she had made a mistake and was in love with Jack after all, and then dismissed the idea because they had known each other for a year or more and surely by now she would have some other feeling for him other than one of friendship. She decided not to think about it any more—not, in fact, to think of anything very deeply, but to take each day as it came, at least until she returned to England.

It was Nick and Sybil who met her at Shaftesbury, for Nick was spending a day or so at Magdalen Provost before taking Sybil to meet his parents. They discussed the wedding as he drove his car, a Saab, rather too fast but very skilfully, in the direction of the village, but presently he interrupted to ask: 'Phoebe, what's the name of this man you're going to work for? I've an idea I know something about him.'

'Oh, good,' said Phoebe lightly, 'because I don't—his name's van Someren.'

Nick tore past an articulated wagon at a speed which made her wince. 'I knew his name rang a bell,' her future relative told her cheerfully. 'Old van Someren—met him at one of those get-togethers. . . .'

'Then you can tell me something about him,' said Phoebe firmly.

'Don't know anything—surely your people have given you all the gen?'

'Oh, I don't mean that. How old is he, and is he nice, and is he married?'

They were going down the hill into the village at a speed which could if necessary, take them through it and up the other side. 'Good lord, I don't know—

thirty, forty, I suppose—and what do you mean by nice? To look at, his morals, his work?'

'Just ... oh, never mind, you tiresome thing. You're not much help. There's ten years between thirty and forty, but perhaps you haven't noticed.'

Nick laughed and brought the car to a sudden halt outside the house. 'Poor Phoebe—I'd have taken a photo of him if I'd known. Tell you one thing, though, I'm sure someone told me that he's got a boy, so he must be married.' He turned in his seat to look at her. 'When do you go, tomorrow?'

'On an afternoon train. I said I'd arrive at the hospital in the evening.'

'We'll take you in to Shaftesbury—we'd go the whole way, but we've still got to see the parson about this and that.' They were all out of the car by now, loitering towards the door. 'You'll be at the wedding, won't you?'

It was Sybil who answered for her. 'Of course she will. I know I'm not having any bridesmaids, but Phoebe's going to be there,' she turned to her sister, 'and you'd better be in something eye-catching, darling.'

'It's your day, Syb. I thought of wearing dove grey—that's if Doctor van Someren allows me to come.'

'You'll have days off—all you have to do is save them up and tell him you have to attend a wedding. Anyway, didn't I read somewhere that the Dutch set great store on family gatherings? Of course you'll be able to come.'

She sounded so worried that Phoebe said reassuringly: 'Don't you worry, I wouldn't miss it for the world.'

They went indoors then, to Aunt Martha, busy in a kitchen which smelled deliciously of something roast-

412

ing in the oven, and no one mentioned the Dutch doctor again.

Twenty-four hours never went so quickly. Phoebe, joining the queue at Waterloo station for a taxi, felt as though she hadn't been home at all. She would miss going down to Magdalen Provost and she doubted very much if she would get another opportunity of a weekend before she left England. She had quite forgotten to ask Sybil the arrangements for her off-duty, but surely she would manage a day or two before she left the children's hospital. She got out of the taxi, paid the man and rang the visitors bell of the Nurses' Home. If anyone wanted to see her so late in the day, the warden would doubtless give her the message. But there was only a request that she should present herself at the Principal Officer's office at nine o'clock the next morning, and when she stated simply that she was Nurse Brook, the warden hadn't wanted to know any more than that, but took her up to a rather pleasant little room, offered her a warm drink and wished her good night. So far, so good, Phoebe told her reflection in the mirror, and went to bed and slept soundly.

The Principal Nursing Officer was brisk and busy. As Phoebe went into the room she said: 'Ah, yes, Nurse Brook. Splendid. Will you go along to the Children's Unit and they'll put you in the picture—I'm sure it has already been made clear to you that this scheme is housed here temporarily, and it's run quite separately from the hospital itself. Anything you want to know, there will be someone you can ask there.'

She smiled quite kindly in dismissal and pulled a pile of papers towards her, and Phoebe, murmuring suitably, got herself out of the office, sighing with relief that it had all been so easy, aware at the same time that she should be feeling guilty and failing to do so because she remembered Sybil's happy face.

The Children's Unit was across the yard. Supposedly there was another way to it under cover, but she couldn't see it and it was a lovely sunny day and she welcomed the chance to be out of doors, if only for a minute or two. The door stood open on to the usual tiled, austere entrance, a staircase ascending from it on one side, a row of doors lining its other wall. On the one marked 'Doctor van Someren' she knocked, for it seemed good sense to get to the heart of the matter at once. No one answered, so she opened the door and went inside. It was a small room and rather dreary, with a large desk with its swivel chair, shelves full of books and papers and two more chairs, hard and uncomfortable, ranged against one wall. Phoebe, who had seen many such offices, wasn't unduly depressed at this unwelcoming scene, however. Hospitals, she had learned over the years, were not run for the comfort of their staff. There was an inner door, too. She crossed the room and tapped on it and a woman's voice said 'Come in.' It was an exact copy of the room she had just left, only smaller, and had the additions of a typewriter and a woman using it. She wasn't young any more and rather plain, but she looked nice and when Phoebe said: 'I'm Nurse Brook and I'm not at all sure where I'm supposed to be,' she smiled in a friendly fashion.

'Here,' she answered cheerfully, 'if you like to go back to the other room, I'll see if Doctor van Someren is available. I expect you want to start work at once.'

She went back with Phoebe to the doctor's room, waved a hand at one of the chairs and disappeared. Phoebe sat for perhaps ten seconds, but it was far too splendid a day not to go to the window and look out. It was too high for her to see much; obviously whoever had built the place had considered it unnecessary for the occupants to refresh themselves with a glimpse of the outside world. But by standing on tiptoe she was able to see quite a pretty garden, so unexpected that she opened the bottom sash in order to examine it with greater ease.

She didn't hear the door open. When she turned round at last, she had no idea how long the man had been standing there. She frowned a little and went a faint pink because it was hardly the way she would want an interview to begin, with her leaning out of the window, showing a great deal more leg than she considered dignified for a Ward Sister—but then she wasn't a Ward Sister—she really would have to remember. . . . And he wasn't in the least like the picture Sybil had painted of him. He was a big, broad-shouldered man and very tall, something her sister had forgotten to mention, and she, for that matter, had forgotten to ask. His hair was the colour of straw which she thought could be streaked with grey; it was impossible to tell until she got really close to him. And she was deeply astonished to find him good-looking in a beaky-nosed fashion, with a firm mouth which looked anything but dreamy, and there was nothing vague about the piercing blue gaze bent upon her at the moment.

'Miss Brook,' his voice was deep, 'Miss Sybil Brook?'

She advanced from the window. 'Yes, I'm Miss Brook,' she informed him pleasantly, pleased that she didn't have to tell a downright fib so soon in the conversation. There would be time enough for that; she only hoped that she wouldn't get confused. . . . 'You're Doctor van Someren, I expect. How do you do?' She held out her small capable hand and had it gripped in a gentle vice. For one startled moment she wondered if

415

he could be the same man whom Sybil had seen, and then knew that it was; his face had become placid, his eyelids drooping over eyes which seemed half asleep, his whole manner vague.

'Er—yes, how do you do?' He smiled at her. 'I think it would be best if I were to take you to the ward—you can talk to Sister Jones, and later there will be some notes and so on which I should like you to study.' He went over to the desk and picked up a small notebook and put it in his pocket, saying as he did so: 'I'm sometimes a little absentminded. . . . I shall be doing a ward round in an hour, I should like you to be there, please.'

He sat down at the desk and began to open a pile of letters stacked tidily before him, quite absorbed in the task, so that after a few minutes Phoebe ventured to ask: 'Shall I go to the ward now, sir?'

He looked up and studied her carefully, just as though he had never set eyes on her before. 'Ah—Miss Brook, Miss Sybil Brook,' he reminded himself. 'I really do apologise. We'll go at once.'

Following him out of the room and up the stairs Phoebe could understand why Sybil had described him as vague—all to the good; she saw little reason for him to discover that she wasn't Sybil; she doubted if he had really looked at her, not after that first disconcerting stare.

Sister Jones was expecting her, and to Phoebe's relief turned out to be a girl of about her own age, with a cheerful grin and soft Welsh voice which had a tendency to stammer. She greeted the doctor with a friendly respect and Phoebe was a little surprised to hear him address her as Lottie. She hoped he wasn't in the habit of addressing his nursing staff by their christian names, for not only would she find it difficult to answer to Sybil, she discovered at that moment that she had no wish to tell him a fib. He was too nice—an opinion presently endorsed when he did his ward round; he was kind too and his little patients adored him.

There were ten children in the ward, most of them up and about, full of life and filled, too, with a capacity for enjoyment which fibrocystics seemed to possess as a kind of bonus over and above a child's normal capacity to enjoy itself. They were bright too, with an intelligence beyond their years, as though they were being allowed to crowd as much as possible into a life which would possibly be shortened. The small boy Doctor van Someren was examining at that moment was thin and pale, but he laughed a good deal at the doctor's little jokes, discussed the cricket scores and wanted to know who Phoebe was. The doctor told him briefly and went on: 'And now, how about that tipping and tapping, Peter?'

A question which called forth a good deal of sheepish glances and mutterings on Peter's part. He didn't like hanging over his bed, being thumped by a nurse at six o'clock in the morning, he said so now with considerable vigour, and everyone laughed, but instead of leaving it at that, Phoebe was glad to see the doctor sit down on the side of the bed once more and patiently explain just why it was good for Peter to hang head downwards the minute he woke up each morning. Having made his point Doctor van Someren strolled towards the next bed, murmuring as he went:

'What a sad thing it is that this illness is so difficult to tackle.' He looked at Phoebe as he spoke and seemed to expect an answer, so she said: 'Yes, it is, but I'm afraid I don't know enough about it to pass any opinion.'

417

'A refreshing observation,' he said surprisingly. 'I find, during the course of my work, that there are a distressing number of people who have a great deal too much opinion and very little sense. I fancy that you have plenty of sense, Nurse Brook.' He nodded at her in a kindly way, sat down on the next bed and became instantly absorbed in its occupant. Phoebe, standing close behind him, found herself wondering how old he was. She had been right, there was quite a lot of grey mixed in with the straw-coloured hair. She guessed forty, but a moment later when he turned his head to speak to Sister Jones, and she could study his face, she decided that he was a good deal younger than that.

She had been a little disturbed to find that she was to go to Delft in ten days' time, for she had imagined that it would be longer than that, as it wasn't very long in which to get to know the doctor and his methods, and now she very much doubted if she would be able to get home again before she went, for Sister Jones had explained at some length that it was hoped that she would take her days off singly because the time was too short for her to miss even two days together; there was so much for her to learn. She had agreed because there was nothing else she could do, and in any case she would be going home for the wedding—she dragged her thoughts away from that interesting topic and applied herself to what the doctor was saying. He had some interesting theories and a compelling way of talking about them which held one's attention; by the end of the day she found herself deeply interested, both in the man and his ideas, and was a little surprised to find that the ward seemed very empty without him, rather like a room without its furniture, and yet he was a quiet man, there was nothing flamboyant about him—indeed, when he wasn't

418

actually engaged in his work, he was positively retiring.

In her room, after a friendly cup of tea with the other staff nurses, Phoebe undressed slowly, thinking about him, and when she was finally ready for bed she didn't go to sleep immediately, but sat up against the pillows, her golden hair cascading round her shoulders, her lovely face, devoid of the small amount of make-up she used, creased in a thoughtful frown. It wasn't turning out a bit as she had expected—she had expected to feel regrets, even guilt, but she didn't feel either, only a faint excitement and a certainty that she was going to enjoy every minute of Sybil's scheme.

Her feelings were strengthened during the next ten days; it seemed strange to be a staff nurse again, but Sister Jones was a dear and the other nurses were pleasant to work with. There was plenty of work on the ward, for Doctor van Someren was a man who expected his orders to be carried out to the letter, and it was sometimes hard and exacting. He had given Phoebe a number of books to read, some of them written by himself, and she couldn't help but be impressed by the string of letters after his name. He was undoubtedly clever, which might account for his moments of vagueness and for his habit of staring at her, which at first she had found a little trying until she decided that he was probably deep in thought and wasn't even aware of her.

She was to spend five nights on duty, because there was a good deal to do at night and he wanted her to be conversant with that as well, and to her surprise Doctor van Someren had himself suggested that she should have two days off afterwards so that she could go home before returning to London to meet him for the journey. He had offered no information about the trip. She supposed they would travel by train and cross from Harwich, and although she would have liked to know very much, she hadn't liked to ask him because he had appeared so preoccupied when he had told her; he had moved away even as he was speaking, his registrar and housemen circling around him like satellites round their sun.

Phoebe hadn't been best pleased about going on nights, although she didn't care to admit to herself that the main reason for this was because she wouldn't see Doctor van Someren—and she liked seeing him, even though he was a married man and never seemed to see her at all. Apparently he had no eyes for women, however lovely—unlike his Registrar and George the houseman, both of whom found her company very much to their liking. She sighed and wondered, not for the first time, what his wife was like, then pushed the ward doors open, ready to take the day report from Sister Jones on her first night on. Life seemed strangely-dissatisfying.

The children took a lot of settling; she and Rawlings, the student nurse on with her, were still hard at it when Doctor van Someren came quietly into the ward. Phoebe laid the little girl carefully on to the pillows stacked behind her, conscious that her heart was beating a good deal faster than it should do.

'Any trouble?' he asked quietly, and she shook her head and smiled at him because it was so nice to see him unexpectedly.

'No, thank you, sir. They're very good, but we've still got two more to see to.' She was apologetic because it was almost nine o'clock, but he made no sign of having heard her, only stood looking down on the child, comfortable and sleepy now, and presently he went away.

He came each night, conveying without words that his visits were simply because he liked the children and not because he had doubts as to his nurses' ability. And in the small hours of the night—her third night on, when Andrew, the ten-year-old in the corner bed, died, he was there again, with his registrar and Night Sister. But Phoebe noticed none of them, doing what she had to do with a heavy heart, and later, when there was no more to be done, going into the kitchen on some excuse or other because if she didn't shed some of the tears her throat would burst. She neither saw nor heard Doctor van Someren; it was his apologetic little cough which caused her to spin round to face him. She said wildly: 'You see, I'll be no good for your scheme —I can't bear it when this happens—he was so little.'

She wiped the back of her hand across her eyes to blot the tears, and despite them, her lovely face was quite undimmed.

The doctor said nothing for a moment, but crossed to the table, ladled tea into the pot, lifted the boiling water from the gas ring and made the tea. 'On the contrary, you will be very good, because you feel deeply about it.' He looked at her and in a voice suddenly harsh, asked: 'And how do you suppose I feel?'

She sniffled, 'Awful. I'm sorry.' She began to gather mugs on to a tray. 'I mean I'm sorry because I'm being a fool, and I'm sorry for you too, because this happens despite all you do.'

He took the tray from her. 'You are kind, Miss Brook, but the boot is on the other foot—soon we shall win our battle, you know.' He kicked open the door. 'And now dry your eyes and have a cup of your English tea—I should warn you that in Holland our tea is not as you make it, but our coffee is genuine coffee, which is more than I can say for the abomination I am offered here.' He smiled at her and she found herself smiling back at him; he really was nice—absent-minded, perhaps, a little pedantic and, she fancied, old-fashioned in his views, but definitely nice.

But the sadder side of her work was seldom in the ascendant—there was a good deal of fun with the children too, and the nurses, under Sister Jones' rules, were a happy crowd. And over and above that, Doctor van Someren's enthusiasm spilled itself over the lot of them, so that very soon Phoebe found herself looking forward to going to Holland, where, so Sister Jones told her, his work was having a steady success—no spectacular results, just a slow, sure improvement in his little patients. She found herself wishing that she, in her small way, would be able to help him to attain his goal.

There was a party on the ward—a farewell party for Doctor van Someren—on her last night on duty. She got up an hour or so earlier than usual and went along to help with the peeling of oranges, the dishing out of ice-cream and the wiping of sticky hands. It was noisy and cheerful and it would have been even greater fun if various important people to do with the hospital hadn't been there too, to take up the guest of honour's time and attention. All the same, he found the time to wish each child goodbye and then crossed the ward to thank Phoebe for her help and to hope that the children would settle.

'They will give you a little trouble, perhaps,' he hazarded, 'and strictly speaking it is not good for them, but they must have their fun, don't you agree, Miss Brook?'

She nodded understandingly, aware as he was that during the early part of the night there would be a great deal of chatter and requests for drinks of water, and little tempers as well as tears, but they would sleep eventually and they had loved every minute of it. She looked around her, reflecting how strange it was that a few paper hats and balloons could create a party for a child.

He turned away. 'I shall see you here at seven o'clock in the evening, on the day after tomorrow,' he reminded her, and before she could ask how they were to go to Holland, he had gone, large and quiet, and very quickly.

She spent two busy days at home; there was a great deal she would have liked to discuss with Sybil, but somehow Aunt Martha always seemed to be with them, and beyond a few safe commonplaces about her work, she could say very little. Only when they had gone to bed, Sybil had come along to her room and sat on the bed and demanded to know if everything was all right.

Phoebe nodded. 'I think so—you were quite right, Doctor van Someren is absentminded, but only sometimes. He's a splendid doctor though. I expected him to be older—he seems older than he really is, I think, but only when he's worried. I like the work....'

Sybil interrupted her happily. 'There, didn't I say that it was a good thing when you agreed to go instead of me? And I bet you're far better at it than I should ever be. How are you going to Holland?'

'I don't know—I've been told to go to the hospital tomorrow evening at seven o'clock, that's all. What clothes shall I take?'

It was well after midnight before this knotty problem was solved to their entire satisfaction. Phoebe, remembering the doctor's gentle remark that he hoped that she wouldn't have too much luggage, decided to take one case, a small overnight bag and her handbag —a stout leather one capable of holding everything she was likely to need en route. The overnight bag she stuffed with night things, and as many undies as she could cram into it, and the case she packed under Sybil's critical eye with uncrushable cotton dresses, sandals, two colourful swimsuits, a sleeveless jersey dress in a pleasing shade of blue, a very simple dress in strawberry pink silk and, as a concession to a kindly fate, a pastel patterned party dress which could be rolled into a ball if necessary and still look perfection itself.

This task done, she felt free to wish her sister good night and go to bed herself. Not that she slept for several hours; her mind was too full of her job, and woven in and out of her more prosaic thoughts was the ever-recurring reflection that she was pleased that she would be seeing a good deal more of Doctor van Someren during the next few weeks.

The morning was taken up with last-minute chores and a discussion about the wedding, coupled with a strong reminder from Aunt Martha to make very sure that she returned home for it. She was thinking how best to settle this matter when her taxi drew up outside the hospital entrance and she stepped out. There was no one about. Through the glass doors she could see the head porter's back as he trod ponderously in the direction of the covered way at the back of the hall—perhaps she should go after him and find out.... She actually had her hand on the door when Doctor van Someren said from behind her:

'Good evening, Miss Brook. You are rested, I hope? If you would come with me?'

It annoyed her that she felt flustered. She wished him a good evening in her turn in a rather cool voice and followed him to the hospital car park.

They stopped beside a claret-coloured Jaguar XJ12 and she tried to conceal her surprise, but her tongue was too quick for her. 'My goodness,' she exclaimed, 'is this yours?'

He looked faintly surprised. 'Yes—you didn't tell me that you disliked travelling by car. It is the simplest way. . . .'

'Oh, I don't—I love it. Only she's so splendid and she took my breath—I didn't expect . . . And I'm sure it's the simplest way, only I don't know which way that is.'

He put down her case and bag the better to give her his full attention. 'Did I not tell you how we should be travelling?'

She shook her head.

'Dear me—you must forgive me. By car, of course. We shall load it on to the Harwich boat and drive to Delft from the Hoek when we land in the morning. You are a good sailor?'

'Yes—though I've only crossed to Calais twice. We nearly always went by plane, and I loathed it.'

'We?' he prompted her gently.

'My mother and father and s . . .' she stopped just in time, 'me,' she added lamely, and felt her cheeks warm, but he didn't seem to notice and she drew a relieved breath. How fortunate it was that he wasn't an observant man, only with his patients. He picked up her case and put it in the boot, already packed with books and cases and boxes—no wonder he had hoped that she wouldn't bring too much luggage with her.

It was extraordinary how many times during their journey to Harwich that she had to stop to think before she replied to his casual questions. She hadn't realised before how often one mentioned one's family during the course of even the most ordinary conversation; she seemed to be continually fobbing him off with questions of her own about his work, their journey, details of the hospital where she would be working—anything, in fact, but her own home life. It was a relief when he slid the car to a halt in the Customs shed, a relief tempered with regret, though, because he was a most agreeable companion and she had found herself wishing that she could have told him all about Sybil and Nick, and her own part in the deception they were playing upon him. When she had consented to take Sybil's place she hadn't thought much about the other people involved; now she found that it mattered quite a lot to her.

They had a meal on board and Phoebe talked feverishly about a dozen subjects, taking care not to mention her home or her family, and the doctor made polite comments upon her sometimes rather wild statements, and didn't appear to be aware of the fact that she repeated herself upon occasion, but as soon as they had had their coffee, he observed pleasantly: 'I expect you would like to go to your cabin, Miss Brook,' and stood up as he said it, so that there was nothing else for her to do. Besides, he had a briefcase with him; he was already opening it when she looked back on her way out of the restaurant.

Possibly, she thought crossly, he had been dying for her to go for hours past. She undressed slowly and hung her oatmeal-coloured dress and jacket carefully away so that they would be creaseless and fresh in the morning. 'Not that it would matter,' she told herself, getting crosser. 'If I wore hot pants and a see-through blouse he wouldn't notice!'

She lay down on her bunk, determined not to go to sleep so that she would be able to tell him that she had spent an uncomfortable night—no, not uncomfortable, she corrected herself—it was a delightful cabin, far more luxurious than she had expected, certainly first class and on the promenade deck. It surprised her that the hospital authorities were willing to spend so much money on a nurse. She would have been just as comfortable sharing a cabin with another girl, although she doubted if she would have had the cheerful services of the stewardess who promised tea at six o'clock and begged her to ring her bell should she require anything further. With difficulty Phoebe brought her sleepy mind back to Doctor van Someren; it would be nice if she were to see a great deal of him in hospital—presumably she would be working on one of his wards, but perhaps he would leave the actual instruction to one of the more junior members of his team. She frowned at the idea and went to sleep.

She slept all night and, much refreshed by her tea, dressed, did her face and hair with care and went along to join the doctor for breakfast, looking as though she had slept the clock round and spent several leisurely hours over her toilette. His eyes, very bright beneath the arched colourless brows, swept over her and then blinked lazily. He wished her a good morning, hoped she had slept well and begged her to sit down to breakfast, something she was only too glad to do. Coffee and toast would be delightful, but the ship seemed to be a hive of activity and they had already docked; perhaps he hadn't noticed. She mentioned it diffidently, to be instantly reassured by his easy: 'I have a theory that it is quicker to be last off the ship.' A remark which, it turned out, was perfectly true, for by the time they had finished, the last of the passengers were leaving the ship and the Jaguar was swinging in mid-air, on its way to dry land.

There was no delay in the Customs shed but a good deal of talk in Dutch, which sounded like so much nonsense in her ears, so that she didn't pay attention but stood looking about her. She was recalled from this absorbing pastime by Doctor van Someren's voice and she turned at once to answer him and in the same split second was aware that he had called her Phoebe and she had responded. She felt the colour leave her face and then flood back, washing her from neck to forehead with a delicate pink. She would have liked to have said something—anything, but her brain, like her tongue, was frozen. It was the doctor who spoke.

'Very interesting. I have been wanting to do that since we met.' His voice was thoughtful, but she could have sworn that he was secretly amused. He turned away to speak to a porter and she followed him to where the car stood waiting in the cobbled yard beyond the station. It was only after she had got into it and he had taken the seat beside her that she asked in a small voice: 'How did you know my name?' and then: 'Are you going to send me back?'

He didn't look at her. 'Your sister mentioned you, and no—why should I? You are an admirable nurse, obviously far more experienced than you wished me to believe. I don't know the reason for the deception, but I imagine it was a sufficiently good one.'

'When did you find out?'

He sounded surprised. 'When we met, naturally.'

She faltered a little. 'But Sybil and I are so alike, people can never tell us apart, only when we're together, or—or they look at us properly.'

'And your sister decided that I hadn't studied her for a sufficient length of time to make your substitution risky. You are not in the least like her.'

They were already out of the town, tearing along

428

the highway, but she really hadn't noticed that. She opened her mouth to refute this opinion, but he went on smoothly: 'No, don't argue, Miss Phoebe Brook. I'm not prepared to enlarge upon that at the moment, you will have to take my word for it.'

Phoebe stared out at the flat countryside without seeing any of it.

'I'm very sorry,' she told him stiffly, and thought how inadequate it was to say that. She was sorry and ashamed and furious with herself for playing a trick on him. 'It was a rotten thing to do. At the time, when Sybil—when I arranged to do it, it seemed O.K. I hadn't met you then,' she added naïvely, and failed to see his slow smile and the gleam in his eyes.

He gave the Jag her head. 'Do you care to tell me about it? But only if you wish. . . .'

She felt quite sick. 'It's the least I can do.' She stared miserably at a group of black and white cows bunched round a man in the middle of a field as green and flat as a billiard table. 'I'm the one to blame,' she began, faintly aggressive in case he should argue the point, and when he didn't: 'You see, Sybil wants to get married—quite soon. . . .' She was reminded of something. 'I should like to save up my days off and go home for the wedding, though I don't suppose you have anything to do with the nurses' off duty.'

They were in the heavy early morning traffic now and approaching a town. 'Is that Delft?' she wanted to know.

'Yes, it is. I have nothing to do with the nurses' off duty,' he was laughing silently again and she frowned, 'but I imagine I might be able to bring my influence to bear.'

To her surprise he edged the car into the slow lane and then into the lay-by ahead of them, switched off the engine and turned to look at her intently. 'Perhaps if I were to ask you a few questions it would be easier for both of us.' He didn't wait for her to answer him. 'Supposing you tell me where you were working to begin with. You are older than your sister,' he shot her a hooded glance, 'and I think that you have held a more responsible post. . . .'

She choked on pricked vanity—did she look such an old hag, then? Very much on her dignity, she said stiffly: 'I was Night Sister at St Gideon's—the medical block. I'm twenty-seven, since you make such a point of it. . . .' She paused because he had made a sound suspiciously like a chuckle. 'I will explain exactly what happened. . . .'

She did so, concisely and with a brevity which did justice to her years of giving accurate reports without loss of time. When she had finished she stole a look at him, but he was staring ahead, his profile, with its forceful nose and solid chin, looked stern. Perhaps he was going to send her back after all. She conceded that she deserved it. But all he said in a mild voice was: 'Good, that's cleared the air, then,' started the car again and allowed it to purr back into the stream of fast-moving traffic. 'The hospital is in the heart of the city. It's not new—there is a very splendid one, you must go over it while you are here—but the one in which you will work is very old indeed and although we have everything we require, it is dark and awkward. But the children are happy and that is the main thing. You will be on a sixteen-bedded ward of fibrocystics, but all the research work is done at the new hospital—St Jacobus.'

She found her voice. 'What's the hospital called—the one where I shall be?'

'St Bonifacius. You'll find that most of the staff

speak English, and as for the children, I have discovered long ago that they will respond to any language provided it is spoken in the right tone of voice. Besides, there are a number of words which are so similar in both languages that I have no doubt you will get by.'

She hoped it would be as easy as it sounded. They were going slowly now through the compact little city, its winding streets lined with old houses, some of them so narrow that there was only room for a front door and a window, some so broad and solid that they should have been surrounded by parklands of their own. The streets were intersected by canals linked by narrow white bridges. She had the impression that she would be lost immediately she set foot outside the hospital door.

The silence had lasted a long time. Phoebe asked in a polite voice:

'Is the hospital a medical school? Were you a student here?'

'No—at Leyden, a few miles away, but my home is in Delft—has been for very many years. I took over the practice from my father. Now I devote almost all my time to fibrocystics.'

He turned the car into a narrow cobbled street where there were no pavements and barely room for the car. 'A short cut,' he explained, 'but when you go walking, I advise you to keep to the main streets until you know your way around.'

Nothing was further from her intention than to go roaming off with nothing but a foreign tongue in her head and a poor sense of direction, but there seemed no point in mentioning it to him. She said like an obedient child: 'No, I won't, sir,' and remained silent while he eased the Jaguar through high gates leading to a paved courtyard where several cars were parked and an ambulance was discharging its patient through a heavy door strong enough to have withstood a siege.

Her companion came to a gentle and accurate halt between the ambulance and a large Citroën, and got out. He had her door open before she could reach for it, saying easily: 'Your luggage will be seen to,' and led her briskly through the hospital entrance, where he spoke to the porter before turning to her and saying: 'I hope you will be happy while you are here with us.'

His tone was formal enough, but his smile was so kind that she found herself saying: 'I'm so sorry—the only way I can make you believe that is by working hard, and I promise you I will.'

He took her hand. 'I know you will, and if it is any comfort to you, Phoebe, I am not sorry and I can see no reason for you to be, either.'

She stared up into his face. Such a kind man, she thought confusedly, and perhaps people took advantage of his kindness—she hoped his wife looked after him. He didn't let go of her hand, and when she heard footsteps advancing towards them from the back of the square hall, she was glad of its firm reassuring grip. The footsteps belonged to a rather dumpy little woman in a dark grey uniform with a prim white collar.

The doctor held out his other hand, saying pleasantly in English.

'Directrice, how nice to see you again—here is our English nurse, Miss Brook. I leave her in your capable hands.' He smiled a little vaguely at them, murmured goodbye and went out of the door again, and Phoebe, still feeling his hand on hers, smiled uncertainly at the little lady before her.

CHAPTER THREE

THE rest of the day was exciting, tiring and somewhat frustrating; everything was just a little different. She had accompanied the Directrice to her office, drunk coffee and listened to the details of the life she would lead while she was in the hospital, given in a fluent though sometimes quaint English; her salary, her off duty—which the Ward Sister would discuss with her— the length of hours she would work, the advisability of getting herself a dictionary at the first convenient moment. . . . Full of undigested information, she was handed over to the Nurses' Home warden, a white-overalled, elderly woman who walked her through a great many corridors and small passages, an odd staircase or two and through a door in a wall which opened into a modern hallway. That at least, thought Phoebe, was exactly the same as the hall in the Nurses' Home at St Gideon's. Apparently hospital decorators the world over had the same unimaginative ideas about dark varnished wood and pale green walls. But her room, when she reached it, was pleasant, with a gay bedspread and curtains and a cheerful rug. Left to herself, she unpacked, changed into her uniform and mindful of her instructions, found her way back to the hospital and into Zaal Drie.

Zaal Drie was really three smallish wards, connected to each other by means of archways driven into the ancient walls of the hospital, the only evidence of the building's great age, for the beds, furniture and furnishings were modern and brightly coloured. There were flowers too and some budgerigars adding their

433

tiny voices to the cheerful din, for it was already mid-morning and those children who were up were having lessons at a centre table in the first ward. They paused in whatever it was they were reciting under the direction of their young teacher and turned to stare at Phoebe, who stared back, wondering what she should do next—a problem solved for her; a small door beside her opened and the Ward Sister came out.

Doctor van Someren had told her that everyone would speak English, but she hadn't expected quite the degree of fluency she was encountering. Zuster Witsma addressed her in welcoming tones: 'Ah, our English *Zuster*! We are all glad that you are here, and we wish you a happy stay. Come, we will have coffee and then I will show you round. Doctor van Someren tells me that you are—are *bijdehand*,' she tried again, '*handig*', and Phoebe said quickly, 'Oh, I think you must mean handy.'

Zuster Witsma smiled. She had a round, friendly face and Phoebe guessed her to be about her own age. 'That you can do all things,' she explained happily as she offered Phoebe a mug of coffee across her desk. 'Now I will tell you all—day duty first, and then night duty every four weeks—one week. We work from seven in the morning until three o'clock on one day and on the other day from two o'clock until ten in the evening. The night nurses do duty from nine in the evening until half past seven in the morning. You find the hours strange, yes? But they work very well, you will see,' she nodded her head encouragingly. 'There is always much to do for the children; they depend on us to keep them happy too, and Doctor van Someren will not have that they are treated as sick. Even when they are very ill he does not like that they should know, only then we put them into the last ward—but never

434

until there is nothing more to do, you understand.' Her blue eyes surveyed Phoebe. 'You are very pretty.'

'Thank you,' Phoebe smiled at the other girl, liking her, finding herself looking forward to the weeks of work ahead. 'Where would you like me to start?'

The rest of the morning passed on wings; at midday she went down to the basement, through a labyrinth of passages and odd stairs, with some of the other nurses, and ate her dinner with them in a long dark room with a row of small windows at one end, and listened to the chatter going on around her, wishing she could understand at least some of it, although everyone was very kind. Some of the nurses spoke good English, all had a smattering, and they took care to include her in their conversations when they could. She went back to the ward presently, to do the medicine round with Zuster Witsma and be shown the mechanism of admitting a patient, which was exactly the same as in an English hospital, and then to be initiated into the mysteries of writing the report, finally to be told kindly that she might go off duty. 'There will be things you wish to do,' said Zuster Witsma in a friendly voice, 'and perhaps a little walk, no? Tomorrow at two o'clock you will come again.'

Phoebe went off duty, conscious of a keen disappointment because she had seen no sign of Doctor van Someren; there had been a young doctor, who, before doing his round, had been introduced as Doctor Pontier, the Registrar. There were two other house doctors, he told her gravely, whom she would meet in due course, and he and they would be glad to help her in any way they could. He had smiled at her, openly admiring of her good looks, and had said with a flattering eagerness that he hoped that he would see more of her soon. She dismissed him from her thoughts as soon as she reached her room; it was already past three o'clock; she had intended to write a letter home, now she had the far better idea of telephoning. She changed out of her uniform and hurried out of the hospital and was on the point of opening its front door when a pretty blonde girl, also on her way out, stopped. 'The English nurse?' she asked cheerfully. 'You would like that I go with you and show the way?'

Her name was Petra—Petra Smit. She was, she told Phoebe rapidly in fluent, ungrammatical English, a trained nurse working on the surgical ward. 'We all hear about you,' she informed Phoebe gaily, 'we hope that you will like us.'

Phoebe assured her that she would and went on to explain that she wanted to telephone. Half way through her explanation she put her hand to her mouth. 'Money!' she exclaimed. 'What a twit I am—I haven't any Dutch money. I never thought to change it before I left and then I didn't think about it. . . .'

'Easy,' said her companion. 'The banks are closed, you understand, but there is a shop—they will take your English money.'

Phoebe got her money, and armed with it and still in the faithful Petra's company, she went to the Post Office where her companion, with pressing business of her own, left her, giving her instructions as to how to get back to the hospital before she did so, instructions which Phoebe immediately forgot in the excitement of speaking to Aunt Martha. But it was a small town, she told herself unworriedly as she strolled along in the warm sunshine, and when she saw a tea-room on the corner of two narrow streets, she went in, took a table in one of its windows, watching the people and bicycles crossing and re-crossing the complexity of canals and bridges while she drank her tea and then applied herself to the street map Petra had thoughtfully bought for her. Refreshed, she set off on a voyage of discovery—the Prinsenhof, she soon discovered, was a useful centre from which to find her way. She had peered into no more than half the shops around it when the city clocks reminded her that it was five o'clock and supper at the hospital was only an hour away. She loitered along, peering down the narrow streets and along the canals, each lined with houses, some built into the water itself. They were narrow and old, their gabled roofs rising sharply, each with its tiny window at the very top—she longed to explore one of them.

She played tennis after supper. Somewhere at the back of the hospital a hard court had been made in the square of ground around which the greater part of the building was built. Someone lent her a racquet, the evening was bright and still warm, and they were evenly matched. The four of them stood, getting their breaths before they played a final set, and Phoebe peered up at the windows around them, wondering which belonged to Zaal Drie. She had given up hope of finding it when a movement at one of the windows caught her eyes. Doctor van Someren was standing there, watching them. She looked away quickly and when they began the next set, her play, to her vexation, was indifferent, but at the end of the game, when she stole another look, he had gone. It was no comfort to her that she played quite brilliantly during the next game.

She admitted to disappointment when she didn't see him during the following day either, for he had done a round, Zuster Witsma told her, that morning, and although the Registrar came during the afternoon, bringing one of the housemen with him, and both young gentlemen made themselves very pleasant to her, she went down to her supper quite put out. That this was a foolish attitude on her part she was the first to admit. There was no reason why the doctor should make a point of seeing her; she had come to learn his methods—just as easily learned from Zuster Witsma and the medical staff—and he was, moreover, an important man in his own world—he had, to coin a phrase, other fish to fry.

She went back after supper and set about settling the children for the night. They were tired now, but some of them, despite this, were determined to stay awake as long as possible and tired though they were, couldn't settle. She thumped up pillows, rearranged bedclothes, squeezed oranges and as a last resort with one small boy, Dirk, who had worked himself into quite a state, lifted him out of his bed and sat him on her knee, and because she could think of nothing else to do, began to talk to him in English. That he couldn't understand a word didn't seem to matter; her voice was soothing and gentle, presently he chuckled, tucked his lint-fair head into her shoulder, and forgetting to wail, stared up at her with huge blue eyes. She tucked him a little closer; he was one of the ones who wasn't going to get well, so the Registrar had told her; he had been in hospital for almost a year, on and off, and Doctor van Someren had done wonders but it was a losing battle, although, he had hastened to add, several of the children went home much improved. One day they would cure all the children, he had said determinedly, and Phoebe, recalling Doctor van Someren's absorbed face when he was on his ward round, found herself agreeing, for she imagined him to be a quietly persistent man who didn't take no for an answer.

She winked a gorgeous long-lashed eye at Dirk and looked up to see the man she was thinking about standing beside them. She hadn't heard him come into the ward, probably because she hadn't expected him. She was still deciding what to say when he said 'Hullo, Phoebe,' and added something in his own language, and when she asked in a whisper what it was he had said he shook his head and smiled. 'All alone?' he asked.

'Yes, but only for a short time—Zuster Witsma's gone to supper and the night staff will be here shortly.'

He sat down on the edge of Dirk's bed. 'You think you will like it here?'

She nodded. 'Yes, very much—I felt a bit lost yesterday and today. . . .' There was faint reproach in her voice although she was unaware of it, but he must have heard it, for he said at once: 'I do a good deal of work at Leyden—the Medical School is there, as you know, but I contrive to come here at least once a day, twice if necessary—sometimes more often. I must confess I like working here, although a more out-of-date place would be hard to find.'

'But it's beautifully equipped.'

He nodded a little absently, staring ahead of him and frowning. Presently he asked: 'You're comfortable in the Nurses' Home? I'm afraid you can't qualify for the Sisters' quarters.'

She flushed. 'That's quite all right. I knew I'd be working as a staff nurse. I don't deserve it anyway. My room is very comfortable and everyone is kind to me.'

He got to his feet, took the sleepy Dirk from her and laid him in his bed. His good night was abrupt and she stared after his broad back in surprise, wondering if she had said something to annoy him.

She was on duty at seven o'clock the next morning,

and when Zuster Witsma came on at eight, she did the medicine round with her again, studied a case history with an eye to Doctor van Someren's methods, and then listened to the Ward Sister's painstaking explanations of the smallest detail to do with running the ward before going down to the dining room for her coffee. She was half way through the ward door when Zuster Witsma called her back.

'A little talk about your journey home for your sister's wedding,' she said kindly. 'Doctor van Someren has asked me to arrange that you have a sufficiency of free days—for such an important family event it is necessary that you have the maximum.' She led the way into her office, waved Phoebe to a chair and sat down at her desk. 'It is easy,' she went on, refreshing her memory from the odds and ends of forms, notebooks and folders before her. 'You will do the night duty—seven nights, and then you will have five nights in which to make your trip.'

She beamed across at Phoebe and Phoebe beamed back because she had been worrying as to how she should ask for the time off. Apparently Doctor van Someren wasn't so forgetful after all! 'That will be lovely,' she agreed. 'It's in a few weeks' time. . . .'

'Just right; by then you will know the ward routine and you will have learned a little of Dutch, yes?'

Phoebe echoed the yes and hoped she would. It sounded an awful language, but perhaps by then she would have picked up an odd word or two—surely if everyone around her could speak at least a little English, she could do the same with Dutch. She remembered the dictionary in her uniform pocket and promised herself a little steady work with it each day.

She went to coffee then, wondering why Doctor van Someren hadn't seen fit to tell her that she would be

440

able to go home—perhaps he considered it hardly his business; she was not a very important cog in the wheel of his scheme, and there was no reason for him to put himself out.

She was free that afternoon, she went out into the early June sun, determined to see as much as possible. Her guide book told her to go to the Markt, with its fourteenth-century New Church and its Town Hall, but although she started off in that direction, she quickly became diverted by a great many other things equally interesting. Shops for a start, little streets with old crooked houses which looked half forgotten, canals lined with trees and behind them, gracious houses with narrow flat fronts and heaven knows what treasures behind their solid doors. She strolled along, looking almost fragile in her sugar pink cotton dress, oblivious of the admiring glances cast at her as she walked. She had stopped to listen to a street organ when a bunch of small boys came tearing along, on their way home from school, she supposed, stepping prudently against the wall to give them room on the narrow pavement. But they stopped, pushing and shoving and fighting as small boys will, hemming her in entirely, so that she came in for more than her share of kicks and blows. Phoebe tucked her handbag under her arm for greater safety and, conscious of sore shins and trodden-on feet, gave vent to her feelings.

'Oh, move on, do!' she apostrophised them loudly. 'Quarrelsome brats, why don't you kick each other's shins instead of mine?'

Naturally no one took any notice, at least, none of them except one small boy of about eight who had just fetched her an unintentional blow with his school satchel—its buckle had etched a weal above her wrist. They stared at each other for a long moment and she realised with a shock that he had understood what she had said. He put his tongue out at her, shouted something at his companions, and they all made off together—a good thing, she thought crossly, for her own tongue had itched to retort in kind.

The weal was still very much in evidence when she went on duty the following morning. Zuster Witsma, clucking sympathetically, cleaned it up, but nothing could disguise the nasty bruise around it. She had told everyone that she had bumped into something and left it at that, and when Doctor van Someren, with his registrar and a posse of students entered the ward, she took care to keep her hands behind her back, just in case he might, for no reason at all, want to know how she had come by it, and she had no intention of telling him—she might never see the little boy again, but that was no reason to tell on him.

It was unfortunate that during the round she should be asked to get one of the children ready for examination, for the bruise, although she did her best to conceal it, was very much in evidence; but it wasn't until the round was over, the students bunched at the ward doors, the Registrar standing a little apart and Doctor van Someren standing in the middle of the ward having a few words with Sister, that Phoebe, hanging up charts and tidying beds and buttoning pyjama jackets, saw Zuster Witsma look across the ward in her direction and then walk towards her. She was smiling largely, as though she were the bearer of splendid news. 'Doctor van Someren wishes to speak to you—in the office. Go quickly, Nurse Brook, he is not to be kept waiting.'

Phoebe saw no reason to go quickly; it smacked of being back at school, summoned to the Head because she had been naughty, and as usual, caught at it. The thought put her in mind of the little boy; for some reason his angry face with its thatch of fair hair had stayed in her memory. She pushed open the door, feeling faintly angry herself.

Doctor van Someren was standing by the narrow window, his hands in his pockets, his attention apparently taken by the blank brick wall which was all the view there was, but he turned round as she went in and said without preamble: 'Ah, yes—you have a bruise on your arm. Why?'

And there's a silly question, thought Phoebe pertly. 'Something hit it,' she told him, the pertness in her voice.

He glanced at his watch and frowned. 'Do not waste my time, I beg of you, Miss Phoebe Brook; I am responsible for your person while you are here. I wish to be certain that the—er—something was reasonably clean.' He raised his eyes to her face. 'I am indifferent as to its cause; I have no wish to pry. . . .'

Phoebe could feel her annoyance melting away. She caught at the shreds of it and said a little tartly: 'I'm quite capable of looking after myself, and you have no reason to worry, it was only a school s—the buckle of a bag—someone quite accidentally swung it against my arm. It's as clean as a whistle.'

He was staring at her with a kind of alert thoughtfulness which she found strangely disconcerting; just as though he had remembered something and was putting two and two together.

'Yes? Very well—but please take care; you are not to be replaced.'

She inched to the door. Of course she could be replaced, she knew of half a dozen nurses of her acquaintance who would jump at the chance of her job. She opened her mouth to say something, she wasn't sure what, but it didn't matter because he spoke first.

'Tomorrow you have a day off. I think that you should see the hospital at Leyden—the research department where I do most of my work. I have arranged with Zuster Witsma to bring you there in the afternoon.' He looked suddenly vague. 'Thank you, Nurse.'

She got herself out of the room, hardly knowing whether to be annoyed or laugh. Here he was, arranging her day off for her without a by-your-leave. Presumably she was supposed to be so mad keen on her work that she would welcome its spilling over into her free time. Upon thinking about it she was quite glad to have her day arranged for her; she had hardly had the time to plan any expeditions herself, and to tell the truth she was diffident about going around on her own until she had found out about buses and trains and the easiest way to get about.

Later that day, when she was off duty, she found her way to the V.V.V., a kind of tourist information centre which supplied leaflets and maps in a great many languages. Here she collected as many as possible about Leyden and went to bed early to study them in peace and quiet, and in the morning, making a leisurely dressing gown breakfast while her uniformed companions gobbled and swallowed against time, she contrived to add to what she had learned by asking a few questions about the hospital at Leyden. She sauntered back upstairs, sorting the facts from some of the more frivolous answers she had been given—the Medical School sounded interesting. She began to look forward to her afternoon, but in the meantime the morning stretched before her in delightful idleness. She dressed and wandered out into the bright morning, intent on finding somewhere pleasant for coffee while she decided how to spend the time before midday dinner.

444

She went, finally, to Reyndorp's Prinsenhof, where the prices rather took her breath away although the surroundings were worth every penny, and then went to look at Tetar van Elven Museum and afterwards, by way of light relief, window-shopped, a delightful pastime which culminated in the buying of a French silk scarf which she didn't really need but which was just too lovely to pass by.

They were to leave for Leyden directly after lunch, so that Phoebe spent half an hour before then changing her dress and attending to her face and hair. She chose the sugar pink cotton again because it seemed rather an occasion and crowned her bright head with a natural straw hat with a small upturned brim, and got out her nicest sandals and handbag. She was glad that she had done this when she saw Zuster Witsma waiting for her in her Daf. She had dressed for the occasion too—in blue and white; they made rather a nice pair, Phoebe considered as she got in beside her. The drive to Leyden was a short one of only a few miles, but Mies Witsma was a shocking driver so that the distance seemed twice that length. Phoebe made conversation in a voice which only shook slightly when they missed a bus by a hairsbreadth and again when Mies, seeing a dog about to cross the road, shot across into the path of the oncoming cars, causing a good deal of horn-blowing and squeaking of brakes. It was a decided relief when they entered Leyden and slowed down, and when they entered the Rapenburg, its quiet waters reflecting the great buildings on either side of it, Phoebe forgot about her companion's erratic driving and looked about her, trying to identify them as Zuster Witsma pointed them out—something which did her driving no good at all.

They had gone through the gates of the Medical

School and were about to enter its door when Phoebe said: 'You do look nice—I hope you don't mind me saying so. . . .'

The girl beside her turned a beaming face tinged with shy embarrassment. 'You think? I wish to be chic today—I hope he will think as you do. . . .'

Phoebe was conscious of a peculiar sensation of doubt deep inside her—who was this *he*? Surely not Doctor van Someren? At the idea the feeling, now tinged with a slight peevishness, became stronger. She longed to ask and would have done so, but they were in the entrance hall by now and a young man was bearing down upon them.

He shook hands with Zuster Witsma, uttered a few words, presumably of welcome, and then turned to Phoebe, shook her hand too and said: 'Van Loon,' and she, wishing to be civil, told him: 'I'm Phoebe Brook,' then remembered that she was Sybil, or didn't that matter any more?

They walked the length of the hall while the young man, in quite beautiful English, explained that he was one of Doctor van Someren's team and had been sent to meet them, and when they fetched up before a massive mahogany door he tapped importantly and threw it open.

Phoebe hadn't known what she expected to see, certainly not Doctor van Someren stretched out in a comfortable chair by one of the long windows, fast asleep. The young man, not in the least put out, stepped forward, tapped him briskly on the shoulder and murmured deferentially, whereupon he opened his eyes and got to his feet and advanced to greet them, his manner imperturbable. Mies Witsma shook hands first, talking animatedly and at some length, and Phoebe watched narrowly, deciding that the doctor was certainly not

446

the *he* her companion had mentioned. This filled her with such pleasure that it showed on her face and her host remarked: 'You look as though you had just made a delightful discovery—nothing to do with me taking a nap, I hope?'

She laughed. 'No, of course not—it seems an awful shame to wake you up, though. I'm sorry.'

He shrugged his great shoulders. 'It is a pleasure to wake and find you—and Zuster Witsma—here.' He looked over his shoulder to where the young man was deep in conversation with her. 'Van Loon,' he said easily, 'be a good chap and let Doctor Lagemaat know that we are ready, will you? And I will see you to-morrow as usual.'

Van Loon said, 'Yes, sir,' and then, 'Good-day, ladies, it has been a pleasure,' and cast a lingering look at Phoebe as he hurried away, to be replaced in no time at all by a very tall, very thin man, soberly dressed in dark grey and a rather dreary tie, but his face was pleasant and good-looking too in a blunt-featured way, and Phoebe, watching with quickening interest, saw at once that this was the one who was to be dazzled by the blue and white outfit. Zuster Witsma went pink as he came in and greeted him with the extreme casualness of manner which, to Phoebe at least, was all the proof she needed. He had smiled nicely at her as he crossed the room; he smiled nicely at her too as Doctor van Someren introduced him, but he went back immediately to the Dutch girl.

'We will go,' said Doctor van Someren, breaking into her speculations. 'Arie, you will accompany Mies, will you not? and I will go with Miss Brook so that she misses nothing of what is to be seen.'

There was a great deal to be seen, and all very interesting too. Phoebe had never been keen on research, but she had to admit that it was a fascinating subject. The path lab engaged her attention too; she spent some considerable time peering down a microscope while the doctor patiently explained what she was looking at. When she finally got to her feet there was no sign of the others—they were alone at one end of the vast place and there was no one within earshot.

'Oh, dear,' said Phoebe, 'I've held everything up, haven't I? I'm sorry—I've kept everyone waiting.'

The doctor's voice sounded amused. 'My dear good girl, do you really suppose the other two have any idea as to what we are doing, or where we are? I credited you with an eye sharp enough to see that.'

She smiled at him and a dimple showed itself briefly. 'Oh, yes, I did, but I thought perhaps it was just me. Isn't that nice? She's such a dear and he looks rather a sweetie, only I don't like his tie.'

He let out a great shout of laughter. 'Do your suitors stand or fall by virtue of the ties they choose?' he wanted to know.

'I haven't got any s...' She stopped, remembering Jack.

'What's his name?' enquired her companion with an intentness quite at variance with his usual placid manner, and she found herself answering obediently: 'Jack—only he's not my—my suitor, not really, just persistent.'

They walked out of the path lab and started down a long wide corridor.

'Will he be at the wedding?' her companion wanted to know, and his voice was very soft.

'No—yes, I don't know.' She gave him a bewildered look and encountered his eyes; the gleam in them left her even more bewildered and strangely excited. She turned her head away and said, a little breathless.

'Where are we going now?'

'The small museum attached to the school—some fascinating things there—and we have just time. . . .'

Phoebe peeped at him. He resembled himself again, not the exciting man who had stared at her so strangely a moment ago. She said primly: 'I hope we haven't taken up too much of your time.'

He flung open a door and started down a steep flight of steps beside her. 'No.' He opened the door at the bottom and ushered her into the museum. Mies Witsma and his colleague Arie were there, staring at an old engraving of some medieval gentleman having his leg amputated and, from the look on his face, taking grave exception to it. Phoebe doubted if either of them saw that, though; they looked up with the slightly bewildered air of people who have been interrupted unnecessarily but are too polite to say so, and her companion must have seen that too, for he made no attempt to join them, merely saying: 'We'll see you both in five minutes in the front hall,' and led her away in the opposite direction.

'I can't possibly see all this in five minutes,' began Phoebe.

'No—but I want my tea. I'll show you the most important exhibits, you shall come again and see the rest.'

She was hurried from one case to the next and whisked through the door again with her impressions nicely muddled and feeling hurt because he seemed in such a hurry to finish their tour. There was a great deal she hadn't seen, she felt sure—what about the wards and theatres and . . .

'Tea!' boomed Doctor van Someren from somewhere above her, and hurried her along more passages until they emerged in the front hall once more. The other two were there already. 'Coming with us?' he asked them. 'Arie, you take the Daf, I'll take Phoebe with me.' He started down the steps, his hand firmly on her arm.

'I haven't said goodbye,' she protested.

'Quite useless,' he told her cheerfully, 'and unnecessary. You will see them very shortly. Come along.'

'Where to?'

He stopped short. 'Did I not invite you? No, I see that I didn't. You are all coming to tea at my house.'

'At your house?' She was aware that her conversation lacked sparkle, but he was going a little fast for her.

'Yes, of course—why not?'

He was crossing the courtyard to where the Jaguar waited sleekly, and she found herself forced to trot in order to keep up with him.

'I'm not sure that I should,' she essayed. 'It's such a great waste of your time, and whatever will your wife think if you bring hordes of people back for tea?'

'Not hordes,' he corrected her, 'three, and I have no wife.'

She got into the car because he had opened its door and obviously expected her to, pity and sympathy swelling inside her—poor man, so he was a widower, or divorced—although she couldn't think how any woman in her right senses would want to let a man like him go once she had him.... What a life it must be for him, bringing up a small boy. Someone had told her that children didn't go to boarding school in Holland—perhaps there was a governess. She stifled a pang of disquiet at the thought; someone young and pretty, who might catch her companion unawares and marry him. Her reflections were interrupted by his quiet voice: 'Who told you that I was married?'

'Someone in England—at least, they didn't say that you were married, but that you had a son.' She turned to smile at him and encountered a faintly mocking smile.

'Hardly the same thing,' he murmured, and before she could recover: 'Did you enjoy this afternoon?'

She flushed, sensing his gentle snub. 'Very much,' she told him politely, and went on to enlarge upon the things she had seen until they were back in Delft where Doctor van Someren stopped the car in one of the narrow streets bordering a tree-lined canal, sending her heart into her mouth as they came to a halt, the car's elegant nose poised over the dark water.

'How often do cars get driven into the canals?' Her voice was tart to cover her fright.

He shrugged. 'Daily—we have an excellent rescue service, though.'

Which made her laugh as she got out to inspect the houses crowding on either side of the canal. She had wandered down that very street only that morning; it pleased her mightily that he was leading the way to one of them—a narrow house, five stories high, with a semi-basement and a double step leading to its front door. Inside the hall was cool and quiet and dim but not gloomy, for above their heads she could see a circular window set in the roof, towards which the narrow staircase wound, its carved balustrade forming a narrow spiral at each ascending gallery. The room they entered was cool too, the furniture old and simple and very beautiful, highlighted by the silver in a display cabinet against one wall and the paintings on its white walls. Phoebe halted in the middle of the room and said in a pleased voice:

'That's a Quaker chest, isn't it?' and then bit her lip because she had sounded rude, but her companion looked pleased.

'Yes—isn't it delightful? And how nice that you know it for what it is. You like old things?'

'Very much. I came past these houses this morning and longed to see inside them, and now I am—I can't believe my good luck.' She smiled, her sapphire eyes sparkling, and he said quickly: 'In that case . . .'

He got no further, for the door opened and Zuster Witsma and Doctor Lagemaat came in, followed almost immediately by a pleasant-faced woman whom Phoebe took to be the housekeeper, bearing a tray of tea things. She had hardly closed the door behind her when it was opened again and a small boy came in— the boy who had put his tongue out at her. He shot her a look of horrified surprise and ran across the room to Doctor van Someren, who had apparently not seen the look and said easily in English: 'Hullo, Paul—you must speak English for a little while, for we have a guest for tea—from England. Come and be introduced.'

Phoebe offered a hand and smiled. Little boys were, after all, little boys and what was a rude gesture between friends, but although he shook her hand and said how do you do with perfect good manners, the look he shot at her for the second time was far from friendly, rather was it suspicious and wary. She made a few random remarks to cover what she felt to be an awkward pause and was thankful when Paul went to talk to Mies Witsma and Doctor Lagemaat, with whom, she noted, he appeared to be on the best of terms. They had tea then, and everyone talked a great deal save for her host, who spoke so little she wondered if he were in danger of falling asleep again; apparently not, for the moment the meal was finished he sent Paul away to get on with his homework and offered to show

452

her the house.

The next hour was a delight, for her host's idea of showing her round was to let her roam at will, merely opening and shutting doors as required, supplying the history of anything she enquired about, and putting into her hands some of his more delicate treasures for her to admire more closely. The size of the house surprised her, for it had great depth, with three rooms, one behind the other on the ground floor and some enchanting passages running haphazardly from the galleries above. There was a walled garden too, sloping down to another, smaller canal at the back of the house; it had a small jetty and a rowing boat, and at Phoebe's questioning look, the doctor said: 'Paul's—it's a safer way of getting around than the streets.'

She nodded, wondering about him and Paul. The boy was devoted to him, she had seen that at once, and the doctor seemed equally fond of Paul, but surely they didn't see much of each other? The doctor was engrossed in his work—ward rounds, teaching rounds, lectures, research work—there was no end to it; there couldn't be much time in which to be with the boy. 'He must have a lot of friends,' she ventured.

They were standing side by side, looking down into the dark water, highlighted here and there by the late afternoon sun. Her companion didn't answer this remark, instead he flung an arm around her shoulders. 'I hope you will be happy here,' he observed thoughtfully, and then to shock her into a gasp: 'You had met before, I gather.'

'Who?'

'Don't prevaricate, you're too sensible for that. You and Paul.' And when she didn't reply: 'Of course, this....' He took his arm away and lifted her hand to look at the still colourful bruise. 'A school satchel—

453

that was what you intended to say, was it not? Very nice of you not to—how do you say—split? Although of course you had no idea who he was.'

'None,' she said faintly.

'But you could have said something just now.'

Phoebe snatched her hand away. 'Who do you take me for?' she asked crossly. 'I'm not in the habit of telling tales, you can't have a very good opinion of me.'

'As to that, it is a subject which, for the moment, I am not prepared to discuss.'

She looked at him then. 'What do you mean? Is it because I pretended to be Sybil?'

He looked amused. 'What an enquiring mind you have! I hope you are satisfied with the arrangements made for your visit to your home?'

A snub which she ignored because she was suddenly stricken. 'Oh, I forgot to thank you—I'm so grateful, it's exactly right, and Zuster Witsma says it won't upset anything at all.' She added a little shyly: 'You must find it very silly of me to wish to go home so soon after I've arrived here, but they wanted to get married before Nick took up this new job . . .'

'Naturally,' he agreed lazily, 'I think . . .'

She wasn't to know what he thought; the housekeeper came down the garden and began to speak to him in an urgent voice. He listened without speaking, nodded, said to Phoebe: 'I'm sorry, I have to return to the hospital immediately,' and started to walk back to the house.

'One of ours?' hazarded Phoebe, trying to keep up.

He didn't slacken his pace. 'One of ours, dear girl. You will forgive me?'

She nodded and stopped trying to keep pace with him. 'Thank you for a pleasant afternoon,' she said swiftly, and he turned to smile at her as he went.

Indoors she found the other two sitting close together in the small sitting room which opened into the
garden. They had obviously been undisturbed for
some time, and when she told them that the doctor
had been called away and she would wait in the garden until they were ready to leave, they agreed with
such an unflattering readiness that she made haste to
go back to the garden. There was someone else there
now—Paul, sitting in his boat, doing something or
other to one of the oars.

She went and stood close by him and ignoring the
scowl on his little face, said coaxingly: 'You understand English very well, don't you, Paul, well enough
for you to understand me when I say that I should like
to be friends? I don't care a row of buttons about the
other afternoon, you know—indeed, I'd forgotten
about it. Couldn't we be friends?'

He didn't smile, but at least he seemed interested.
He was on the point of speaking when his eyes slid
past hers, watching someone coming down the garden.
Phoebe turned to see who it was—a girl, tall and dark
and magnificently eye-catching. She wasn't hurrying;
by the time she reached them Phoebe had the unpleasant feeling that she had been studied from head
to toes, assessed, and instantly disliked. Nonetheless,
the girl's manners were charming. 'You don't know
who I am, so I'll introduce myself—I should have been
home for tea, but I was held up by the traffic. I'm
Maureen Felman, Paul's governess. You're the English
nurse, aren't you? Lucius told me about you.'

'Lucius?' Phoebe forced her voice to friendliness.
'Do you mean Doctor van Someren?'

The girl laughed. 'I forgot—I've been here so long,
we've been Lucius and Maureen for years.'

Phoebe let that pass. 'My name's Phoebe Brook.

Your English is so good you must be . . .'

'My mother. I speak both languages fluently.' And Phoebe, already disliking her, disliked her still more for the smugness of her voice. 'Paul and I speak English when we're together—Lucius wants that.'

'Paul's English is very good,' observed Phoebe politely. 'Do you live here?'

'Not yet.' Maureen smiled as she spoke; the smile was smug too and Phoebe's dislike turned to instant hate. 'Lucius is a stickler for the conventions—I live here during the day, though, and while Paul's at school I act as secretary to Lucius and drive him around when he doesn't want to drive himself.'

Phoebe murmured a casual something; it would never do to let this girl think that she was even faintly interested in the doctor. All the same, she found it strange that he liked to be driven. He had struck her as a man who did his own driving, and what secretarial work was there for her to do? There was a secretary at the hospital, who did the ward rounds with him, she had seen that with her own eyes—was this girl hinting that she was something more to him than a secretary-cum-governess? She glanced at Paul and saw that he was watching her in a speculative way which caused her to say airily: 'It sounds a nice job. I hope we meet again before I go back to England.'

'Probably—Delft is small. You must come round one day and Paul shall practise his English on you.' She gave the little boy a malicious glance as she spoke and Phoebe had the uncomfortable feeling that she didn't like him—and she must be on very close terms with the doctor if she could invite people to his house. . . . She said sweetly: 'How nice. I shall look forward to that, and now I must go and find Zuster Witsma.'

That young lady was, in fact, advancing down the

garden at that very moment. She spoke coolly to Maureen, with warmth to Paul and swept Phoebe away. 'Doctor Lagemaat has to be back—we'll drop you off at St Jacobius as we go,' she explained.

They paused for a moment before they entered the house and looked back. Paul and his governess were standing watching them, and Maureen was laughing, they could hear the light mocking sound quite clearly.

In the car Mies turned in her seat to say: 'Not nice, that girl, but clever. Doctor van Someren thinks that she is a splendid governess and of such great help to him.' She snorted: 'He is so wrapped up in his work he can see nothing!'

Outside the hospital, when Doctor Lagemaat stopped the car, he turned to say to her: 'We must not bother you with our small differences of opinion, but we are old friends of Doctor van Someren, and I agree with Mies.' He smiled nicely at her. 'May I not call you Phoebe?'

'Oh, please,' said Phoebe instantly, and Mies chimed in: 'And you shall call me Mies—not in the hospital, of course, and him,' she nodded at Doctor Lagemaat, 'you shall call Arie. Thus we shall be friends!'

Phoebe, standing on the pavement, watching them drive away, felt a pleasant warmth. It was nice to make friends; it was nice, too, to know that Lucius van Someren had good friends too. She had a sudden urge to find out as much as possible about him.

CHAPTER FOUR

SHE had her opportunity the very next day, for in the morning, when Doctor van Someren had finished his teaching round, he clove his way through the circle of students to where she was standing behind Mies, and said: 'I have a few hours to spare this afternoon—you will be free, I take it? I should like you to visit the Hortus Botanicus behind the university, and should there be time to spare, another visit to the museum might not come amiss.'

Phoebe thanked him quietly, conscious of a pleasurable glow beneath her starched apron, and when he went on: 'At the entrance, then, at half past three,' she had a job not to smile widely with the pleasure she felt; instead she said soberly enough: 'Very well, sir,' and received a little grunt in reply as he wandered away. She watched him go down the ward; at the door he stopped to write in his notebook and she wondered what it could be—a reminder perhaps, about the afternoon's outing.

She was a little late, for it hadn't been possible to get off duty punctually and she had had to change much too quickly, so that she was totally dissatisfied with her appearance as she hurried to the hospital entrance. Nonetheless, she looked cool and fresh in her blue and white striped dress, and because it was unusually hot for the time of year, she had dispensed with stockings and put on a pair of blue sandals which exactly matched her shoulder bag. But if she had hoped for a word of appreciation from her companion she was to be disappointed; he gave her the briefest of greetings and hardly looked at her. They were free of Delft and well on the way to Leyden when he said: 'I'm sorry I had to leave you yesterday afternoon.'

'It didn't matter at all,' she assured him, 'especially as Wil is so much better today—it was for her you went, wasn't it?'

He nodded and she went on, choosing her words: 'I went back to the garden after you left, just for a little while—Paul was there, and then his governess came.'

'Maureen? Ah, yes, she mentioned that she had met you. She organises us—a most efficient girl.'

'And a very striking one,' remarked Phoebe, hoping he would go on talking about the wretched creature if she gave him a little encouragement. But she was frustrated by his: 'You can afford to be generous, Phoebe,' a remark which pinkened her cheeks with annoyance, because what might have been meant as a compliment had been uttered in a tone of voice which verged on mockery. The vague half thoughts she had had of putting a spoke in Maureen's wheel withered away under the sudden sideways glance he directed at her—not in the least absent-minded but very intent, as though he knew what was in her mind. The pink deepened and she looked out of the window and made an observation, stiffly, about the weather. She was sorry she had come, she told herself savagely, and how stupid of her to allow her interest to settle upon a man she was unlikely to see again once she had gone back to England and who was already quite satisfied with his life, and anyway, a small stern voice reminded her, was it quite sporting to try and attract his attention away from the glamorous Maureen? She had no opportunity of solving this interesting problem, because they had arrived at the Medical School once more and her companion was suggesting, in the mildest of voices, that she should get out of the car.

The next hour was a delight to her. They wandered round slowly, and Phoebe, naming each plant as they inspected it, was quite taken aback when Doctor van Someren exclaimed: 'Good heavens, girl, your Latin is excellent—are you a botanist as well as a nurse?'

She denied it, suddenly shy. 'Why, no—my father was, at least it was his hobby. We used to go for walks and he taught me a great deal.'

'Latin or botany?' he asked idly.

'Both, I suppose.'

'What profession had your father?'

She bent to examine a fine specimen of basil. 'He was a scientist.'

They had reached a fine old mulberry tree with a bench built around it. 'Let us sit,' suggested the doctor. 'The museum can wait until another day—you shall tell me about your father and something of yourself too, and I shall discover even more facets to your character.'

She was taken aback. 'Facets? Whatever for—I didn't know I had any.'

They were sitting side by side and the sunlight dribbled through the leaves on to her bright hair. He answered her quietly: 'Oh, you have a great many—you are intelligent for a start, you have a quick brain, you are kind, impulsive—you like your own way.' He went on, ignoring her gasp: 'I think you may have a nasty temper when you are roused. You are intensely curious. . . .'

'What about?' she demanded.

'Me,' he answered simply.

'I'm not,' she began, and he said sharply, 'and do I have to add another facet—a slight twisting of the truth?'

460

'Well, what if I am?' she snapped crossly. 'It's natural, and at least I haven't turned you into facets like a specimen under your microscope, sir.'

'Ah, yes—something I had forgotten to mention. Would you refrain from addressing me as sir? My name is Lucius; I do not propose that you should address me so in hospital, but surely when we are away from our work we might assume that we are friends. I am not so very much older than you, Phoebe.' And at her look of surprise: 'Thirty-four, and you are twenty-seven.'

'How you do harp on my age,' she protested. 'It's not nice to remind a woman how old she is.'

He lifted colourless eyebrows. 'Indeed? Have I offended you? I'm sorry.' He didn't look in the least sorry; he was laughing at her. After a moment she smiled reluctantly and he said instantly: 'That's better—don't you want to ask me any questions?'

She said without hesitation: 'Yes, of course I do, but it wouldn't be polite.'

His blue eyes twinkled. 'Try me, or shall I answer the first one for you? You wonder about Paul, do you not? He calls me Papa and you have been told that I have a son, and where, you ask yourself, is his wife—dead, divorced, run away with some other man who has no work to fill his days and more money than he knows what to do with?' He paused. 'Yes?'

'Yes,' said Phoebe, thinking how very good-looking he was.

'I have no wife—Paul is my adopted son. His parents—my friends—died in that Italian plane crash four or five years ago—perhaps you remember it? I am his godfather, he has no grandparents; it was right and natural that he should make his home with me.'

The flood of relief she felt quite shocked her. Not

stopping to think, she said: 'Oh, I thought—that is, I ...'

'I have no doubt you did,' he agreed suavely. 'I should have mentioned it to you before, but it slipped my memory.'

She disagreed quite fiercely. 'Oh, no, why should you? It's none of my business,' and felt irrationally disappointed at the casual shrug he gave in answer. They sat in silence then, the breeze stirring the tree above them, the air full of the varied hum of insects.

'All the live murmur of a summer's day,' uttered the doctor suddenly.

'Matthew Arnold,' Phoebe gave the information automatically and then laughed when he said: 'You are a difficult girl to impress—your knowledge of botany is more than satisfactory, so is your Latin, and now, when I quote an apt phrase, you cap it with its author.'

'Oh, I'm sorry—I didn't mean to—I wasn't trying to impress you or anything.' She added earnestly: 'As a matter of fact, I hardly know any.'

'No? I shall have to try and catch you out.' He gave her a long considering look which so disconcerted her that she suggested that they should finish their tour of the garden.

'You'll come back with me to tea?' he asked her as they got into the car later.

She hadn't expected that and it flustered her. 'Me? Well—I came yesterday.'

He shot the car with heart-stopping precision between a slow-moving lorry and a stationary baker's cart. 'I hadn't forgotten,' he told her mildly. 'I thought it would be pleasant for you to further your acquaintance with Maureen, and it's good for Paul to speak English as much as possible.'

'Why?'

'He wants to go to Oxford. His father and I were there, you see.'

Paul and Maureen were in the garden, sitting on the grass and although the boy ran to greet the doctor and give a hand to Phoebe, his governess made no effort to rise. Only when they had reached her she lifted her head and smiled at them with a casual hello and an offer to fetch the tea into the garden. 'It's so warm,' she explained. 'When Paul came out of school we decided that the garden was the only place to be. I hope you agree, Lucius?' She looked at the doctor, who said vaguely: 'Oh, yes—do whatever is fun for Paul,' and then to the small boy hanging on his arm: 'The rowlock is loose in the boat. Have you seen it? We'll fix it now.'

So Phoebe was left alone to sit on the grass and admire the view and the flowers and watch the two of them absorbed in their work, their lint-fair heads close together. But not for long, for the doctor looked up, said something to Paul and got out of the boat to cast himself down beside her.

'Forgive me, I thought Maureen was here.'

'If you remember she went into the house to fetch the tea tray.'

He looked surprised. 'Did she? Well, why not—it's just the day to have tea out here.'

Phoebe suppressed a smile. 'Don't let me hinder you from mending whatever it is,' she reminded him.

'Paul can manage on his own now, I showed him what to do.' He rolled over to look at her. 'What do you intend to do with your evening?'

She was aware of intense pleasure, although she kept her voice carefully casual. 'Why . . .' she began, but was interrupted by Maureen, calling gaily for the doctor to

463

go and carry the tray. He got to his feet with no sign of disappointment at not having had an answer, and by the time he had returned and they had settled to their tea, she could see that he had forgotten all about it.

Getting ready for bed that night, she decided that, from her point of view, the tea party had been a failure. Maureen had been charming, she had also been possessive towards the doctor—no, bossy, Phoebe corrected herself as she brushed her hair with unnecessary vigour. She had also managed, with diabolical sweetness, to put Phoebe in the wrong on several minor points during their conversation, and worse, made her out to be a little stupid as well. 'I hate her!' declared Phoebe a trifle wildly, and flung the brush across the room, which did it no good at all, but certainly relieved her pent-up feelings. And Paul had enjoyed her discomfiture too, staring at her with his sharp dark eyes. Only the doctor had been unaware, sitting there, making gentle talk and seeing to their wants. He was an exasperating man!

She went to the mirror and peered at her face without conceit; she was a very pretty girl, accustomed to being looked at at least twice, her voice was quiet and low, she neither giggled or laughed brassily. If she was a little shy, she took care to conceal it. There was nothing, she told her reflection, to which Doctor van Someren could take exception, if indeed he had ever taken the trouble to really look at her.

She got into bed. 'It's a pity nothing ever happens to me,' she told the ceiling, then closed her eyes and went to sleep, and Fate, who had overheard the remark, grinned impishly and went off to make her own arrangements.

It was a glorious morning and Phoebe was free until

two o'clock. There was a great deal of the small city she hadn't seen and she took herself off to the Convent of St Agatha, where William the Silent had met his death, and this expedition over, and with time to spare, she decided to wander round one or two of the narrow streets leading away from the prescribed route to the hospital. The houses here were small, their walls uneven with age, their windows small too and filled with flowerpots so that Phoebe was unable to catch a glimpse of their interiors. They were neatly kept, with fresh paint and sparkling windows and here and there a canary bird singing in its cage hung outside an upstairs window. She wandered on, knowing herself to be lost but not worried, because Delft wasn't large enough for her to remain so; she would soon find her way again. She was on the point of doing this when her eye was caught by a cul-de-sac, lined with very small houses indeed, its cobbled centre ornamented by a plane tree. It was very quiet there and although the houses looked well tended, she had the strong impression that the place was empty. She had walked down one side of it and was about to cross over to the other when the door of a house she was passing opened, revealing a very old lady.

Phoebe paused in her walk, smiled, essayed the 'Dag, mevrouw,' she had learned to say and prepared to move on, but a timid hand was laid on her arm and the old lady started to unburden herself at such length and with so much agitation that there was no use in Phoebe trying to stop her. When she at last came to an end they stood looking at each other in a puzzled way, Phoebe because she had no idea what the old lady wanted, the old lady because she was getting no response.

At length Phoebe said regretfully with a strong English accent: '*Niet verstaan,*' and then with a flash of inspiration asked: 'Help?'

The old lady nodded, muttered, '*Ja, ja, hulp!*', and drew Phoebe inside. In the small overfurnished, spotlessly clean front room was another old lady, lying on the floor, her eyes closed. Phoebe lost no time in taking her pulse, which was far too weak for her peace of mind, just as the pale old face was far too white, and her breathing was so shallow that there was almost no movement of the old-fashioned black bodice. She was unconscious, but Phoebe was sure it wasn't a coronary, not even a black-out, but the old lady was ill, without a doubt. She selected a beautifully embroidered satin cushion from an assortment on the stiff settee and placed it beneath the old lady's head, then mimed the need for a blanket, reflecting that ignorance of the Dutch language was putting her at a most appalling disadvantage. The blanket was fetched, she tucked her patient up carefully, took her pulse again, peered under the closed eyelids and then once more played her desperate charade to convince her companion that she would have to go for help. This, naturally enough, took time, but once she had made herself understood, Phoebe wasted no time. She shot through the front door and began to run in the general direction of the St Bonifacius hospital. Lucius van Someren would be doing his round, she was quite certain of that, for whatever else he forgot, he didn't forget his patients. She could explain to him quickly, far more quickly than trying to find a policeman, or for that matter, any passer-by—and there were none at that moment—and wasting time making herself understood.

She got there quicker than she had hoped, because she chanced her luck, taking what looked like a short cut down a narrow alley and arriving almost in the hospital yard. She didn't stop to wonder what everyone would think as she belted up the stairs and into the ward. She hardly noticed the surprised faces or the children's quickened interest, only Lucius' calm face and his quiet: 'You want me, Phoebe?'

She nodded, out of breath. 'There's an old lady,' she began, and prayed that he wouldn't waste time asking questions, 'in a little house in the Breegsteeg,' she knew her pronunciation was awful, but she was past caring. 'She's ill—unconscious. I don't think it's a coronary—there wasn't anyone, only another old lady, and I didn't know where to get help, so I came to you.' She looked at his grave, kind face and if she hadn't been so taken up with her errand, might have noticed the expression which passed over it. 'I'm sorry to interrupt the round.'

He asked no questions at all, but said something to Doctor Lagemaat who was with him and then: 'We'd better go and have a look, hadn't we?' and was off down the stairs, with Phoebe, still blown, trying to keep up with him.

In the car she repeated her apology, because to drag a consultant from his ward round—and now she came to think about it, there had been a crowd of students there, so it had been a teaching round—was hardly the thing. She added matter-of-factly: 'I'm sorry if you're annoyed ... it's not knowing the language.'

He made a sound which could have been a laugh as he inched the Jaguar through the busy streets with no sign of impatience while she, with something of an effort, held her hands quiet in her lap, thanking heaven that the journey was so short.

The old lady was at the door, looking more bewildered than ever; Doctor van Someren paused briefly to speak to her and went inside, Phoebe close

467

behind him, crowding into the small room. Presently, when he had made his examination, he said: 'You were right, it isn't a coronary—her skin's dry, she's very pale, not grey, just pale, and look at this.' He nodded at the bony arm he was holding. 'Malnutrition, general debility and anaemia, I should suppose, but I'll leave that for the medical side to confirm. Let's get her to hospital.'

Phoebe's lovely eyes asked a silent question.

'Yes, she'll get better—good food, rest, ferri. sulph. . .'

'And the other lady, what's to happen to her?'

He smiled fleetingly. 'Her younger sister, a mere eighty-two. We'll take her along with us and get the social workers busy.'

'Why are they alone? Where's everyone? Why haven't they enough money to . . .'

His smile widened. He said patiently: 'Not so fast! They're alone because everyone living in the *steeg* has gone on an outing, but our patient didn't feel up to it, so they stayed behind—presumably she collapsed.' He got to his feet. 'Now, let's get them to St Jacobus.'

They went in the car, Phoebe supporting the unconscious patient on the back seat, her sister, in her respectable, old-fashioned black coat and hat, sitting in front. Phoebe listened to her dry old voice, talking continuously now that relief had loosened her tongue and the doctor's calm tones had quietened her fright. She couldn't understand a word of what was being said, but she was quite confident that he would arrange everything to everyone's satisfaction. He certainly had instant attention at the hospital; with a brief direction that she was to stay in the waiting room with the old lady, he disappeared with the stretcher, a houseman, a couple of porters and a rather fierce-looking Sister. He didn't come back for twenty minutes, and Phoebe, looking up from her efforts to comfort her weeping companion, said, faintly accusing: 'She needs a nice cup of tea. . . .'

'Coffee,' he corrected her. 'We'll all have some, but first I must explain everything to her.' He took a chair and sat down by the old lady and began to talk to her. He sounded reassuring, and presently the old lady wiped her eyes, smiled a little and allowed him to help her to her feet. 'Now we'll go home,' he told Phoebe, 'and have that coffee and then take her back. She's to come and see her sister this afternoon—I've got someone to fetch her and take her back.' He paused. 'I suppose you're dying of curiosity—I'll explain it all to you later.'

She bristled. 'There's no need to put yourself out,' she said haughtily. Really, he was a most irritating man! Why had she ever rushed to him for help and dragged him away from his round and been so sure that he wouldn't be annoyed at the interruption? Vague notions about this floated at the back of her mind, but it was hardly the time to indulge in introspective thoughts. She got into the car with the old lady beside her, and was driven to the doctor's house.

It wasn't yet twelve o'clock. The hateful Maureen had told her that she spent her mornings in typing letters for the doctor, making appointments, filing correspondence and other secretarial duties. She had made it sound very important and Phoebe, despite herself, had been impressed, so that when the doctor opened the door and ushered them inside, she expected to hear the steady tap-tap of a typewriter, or failing that, the utter hush surrounding someone concentrating upon desk work. She heard neither—gales of laughter, the discordant thunder of a lesser-known pop group belting out a number on a record player, and the unmistakable clink of glasses were the sounds which assailed her astonished ears. But if she was astonished, her host was thunderstruck. His mouth thinned ominously, and it struck her suddenly that probably he had a shocking temper which he seldom allowed anyone to see. They weren't to see it now; after the barest pause, he led them to the sitting room, begged them to make themselves comfortable, pulled the bell rope with restrained violence and walked to the window to stare out into the street.

It was the housekeeper who answered it and Phoebe, who rather liked her, felt sorry for the surprise and discomfiture she was obviously experiencing. But her master ignored this, merely asking her to bring coffee, adding something else which Phoebe couldn't understand. Then he went and sat by the old lady and made gentle conversation.

But not for long; the door was opened presently and Maureen, rather pale, stood in the doorway, whereupon he got to his feet, saying in English: 'Ah, yes, Maureen—an explanation is due to me, I fancy—perhaps you will give it to me now.' He looked briefly at Phoebe. 'You will excuse me? And be good enough to pour the coffee when it comes.'

His voice, which he had neither raised nor quickened, was steely. Phoebe, feeling meanly delighted at Maureen's discomfiture, murmured suitably as she watched them leave the room together, then turned her attention to the old lady, who, unaware of any undercurrents, was smiling quite happily and, Phoebe very much feared, was about to embark upon an unintelligible conversation with her.

The coffee came. She attended to her companion's wants, poured herself a cup and listened to the sounds on the other side of the door—subdued voices, feet, a giggle quickly suppressed, and then utter silence. The visitors had gone. Somewhere in the house, behind one of the handsome doors, Doctor van Someren was with Maureen. Phoebe would dearly have loved to have been in a position to peer through the keyhole, or even eavesdrop.... She gathered her straying thoughts together, appalled at the depths to which she had sunk. She had been well brought up; such actions were despicable, she reminded herself, and applied herself to the pouring of second cups, then as the doctor came into the room, filled a cup for him too, and because his mouth was set so very grimly and no one spoke, she began a one-sided conversation to which neither of her companions replied. She was aware that she sounded chatty, but they couldn't sit there for ever, saying nothing.

'A lovely day,' she ventured, having exhausted the excellence of the coffee. 'How early summer is this year,' and then losing patience, she snapped: 'It's a pity I can't speak Dutch, for then at least this lady here would understand me and make some sort of a civil answer.'

The doctor smiled then. 'Poor Phoebe! You have my deepest admiration. Here you are, longing, no doubt, to indulge your curiosity and forcing yourself to discuss the weather. It must be agony for you.' His blue eyes studied her reflectively. 'We're going to take Juffrouw Leen here home.'

Having said which he addressed himself to his other guest, who got to her feet, looking quite cheerful, and accompanied him to the door.

Outside Phoebe said stiffly: 'Well, I'll be getting along—thanks for the coffee.'

'You will come with us Phoebe—please.'

She got into the car again, telling herself that she

was weak to do so, and when they arrived at the old lady's house, went inside, helped her off with her hat and coat and then waited patiently while Juffrouw Leen, possessing herself of the doctor's hand, began a long and voluble speech—thanking him, she supposed. Presently it was her own turn, but unlike the doctor, who had doubtless said something graceful, she was unable to do anything but smile. But Juffrouw Leen didn't seem to mind. She saw them off at the door, smiling and waving and quite happy again. Phoebe turned in her seat for a final farewell as they turned the corner of the *steeg* and Doctor van Someren said: 'The round will be finished. You're in time for your midday meal before you go on duty?'

'Yes, thank you. If you like to drop me off. . . .'

He took no notice. Perhaps he hadn't heard, for he went on: 'Juffrouw Leen will be all right—a social worker will call each day to make sure she can manage and someone is lined up to take her to and from the hospital.'

'Her sister—will she do?'

'I think so—the right diet, rest, care, and someone to keep an eye on them when she's back home.' He glanced at her and smiled. 'I'm afraid your off duty has been sadly curtailed.'

'It didn't matter—I was only pottering.'

He drew up before St Bonifacius. 'You enjoy that?'

She nodded. 'Very much—in a few days I shall go further afield. I want to see all I can.'

He didn't answer but got out and opened the car door and went inside with her, bade her a brief goodbye and went up the stairs to the ward, and Phoebe, because there was nothing better to do, went down to the dining room and ate her dinner.

She was off duty again the next morning and she

went along to see the old lady. There was someone with her—the district nurse, who had a smattering of English so that Phoebe was able to discover that the patient was doing quite well and that Juffrouw Leen was in good hands while her sister was in hospital. She stayed a while and had a cup of coffee with them, bade them a cheerful goodbye and made her way to the shops. She was coming out of Reynders, a piece of genuine blue Delftware tucked under her arm, when she came face to face with Maureen Felman, and before she could make up her mind whether to say a casual hallo and walk on, or stop and say a few polite words, Maureen had stopped, obviously intent on passing the time of day.

'Hullo,' she said coolly. 'I've been hearing all about you and your Nightingale act—I must say you don't look much like a do-gooder. Didn't you find it all a dead bore? Not that you'd be likely to say so.'

Phoebe eyed her thoughtfully. Here, she thought, was the enemy, although she wasn't quite sure why—and declaring war too.

'If I found it a dead bore,' she replied gently, 'I certainly wouldn't say so, but I didn't—I'm sure you would have done the same.'

Maureen smiled brilliantly. 'Not me—there are far too many old souls around as it is. I like life to be gay.' She stared at Phoebe and Phoebe looked back limpidly. 'You guessed that yesterday, I suppose.' Her eyes narrowed. 'Lucius never comes home before twelve o'clock—never—and yesterday, of all days . . . and you with him, all prunes and prisms! I could have managed him beautifully if you hadn't been there, looking as though butter wouldn't melt in your mouth. I was only having a few friends in for a drink—God knows life's dreary enough in that house.'

473

'You're rather rude,' Phoebe's voice had a decided edge to it, 'and I hardly know why, and what you choose to do while the doctor's away from home is really no concern of mine.' She smiled with charm. 'I dare say you're still feeling a bit scared—it must have been a nasty shock for you.' She allowed the smile to linger and watched Maureen's face tighten with ill temper. 'I must be going—it was interesting meeting you.'

She nodded and walked away briskly, thinking what a ghastly creature Maureen was and why, on the face of things, did the doctor put up with her. The thought that he might possibly be in love with her crossed her mind as it had done several times already, only now it refused to be dismissed. It remained, well damped down, for the rest of the day, affording her a good deal of disquiet.

It faded a little under the pressure of work during the next few days and even when she saw Doctor van Someren, it was always in the company of Mies Witsma or the other nurses, and their talk was entirely of the patients. It was the evening before her day off before she found herself alone with him; Zuster Witsma had gone to her supper, the ward was in the chaotic state which preceded the children's bedtime. Phoebe, with another nurse, was urging the more active and reluctant of her small patients to start undressing, supervising the washing of faces, the tidying of beds, the comforting of those who were feeling sorry for themselves and engaging, in her own peculiar, sparse Dutch, those who wished to talk in idle conversation. She had, naturally enough, become a little untidy during the carrying out of these tasks—her lovely hair was coming down, her nose shone, her apron was soaked with most of a glass of lemonade which a recalcitrant small boy had flung at her. Her pleasure at seeing him, therefore, was tinged with fears about her appearance, by no means allayed as he sauntered towards her, eyeing her with amusement.

'Fun and games?' he wanted to know gently.

'Bedtime,' she informed him succinctly. 'We don't reckon to look glamorous at this time of day. We're lucky if we get to supper in one piece.' She thrust in a hairpin with an impatient hand. 'Did you want to see someone?'

'You.'

She sternly curbed the tide of pleasure rising beneath her grubby apron. 'Oh? Well, it's not very easy, you can see that, can't you? And there are only two of us. Is it something you could say while I finish getting Piet into his pyjamas?' She was struck by a sudden and unpleasant thought. 'Do you want to tell me off about something?'

His eyes narrowed with laughter. 'I—tell you off? Why should I want to do that? By all means do whatever you need to do to Piet. You have a day off tomorrow, I believe. Paul has a holiday from school; I thought we might all go to the beach and swim—you do swim?'

She nodded, starry-eyed. 'Nothing spectacular, but I can keep myself from drowning. I'd love to come, but will Paul—that is, won't it spoil his day if I'm there?'

He looked surprised. 'I don't imagine so. Besides, you two girls can be company for each other if Paul and I want to go off together.'

'Yes, of course,' said Phoebe faintly. The idea of spending a day in Maureen's company didn't please her at all; on the other hand, she might find out more about her—and the doctor, and besides, this time Paul might be more friendly. She stared ahead of her, her sapphire eyes seeing nothing—her swimsuits were both rather dishy, and there was that nice towelling beach smock she hadn't intended to buy and had.

'You're not listening,' said Doctor van Someren, and Phoebe jumped guiltily.

'I beg your pardon—I was just … What did you say?'

'Ten o'clock, outside the entrance, and mind you're ready.' His voice changed and became businesslike, a little remote. 'And now I should like to take another look at that admission—Johanna—she's in the end ward, I take it.'

There wasn't much of the evening left by the time Phoebe had had supper. She washed her hair and changed her mind half a dozen times over what she should wear in the morning and then, too restless to go to bed, wrote a long letter home, touching lightly on the episode in Juffrouw Leen's house and not mentioning at all that she was to spend the day with Doctor van Someren on the morrow.

CHAPTER FIVE

DOCTOR VAN SOMEREN wasted no time in getting to Noordwijk-aan-Zee, and a good thing too, thought Phoebe, for when she had arrived at the hospital entrance at exactly ten o'clock it was to find the doctor at the wheel of the Jaguar with Paul beside him and Maureen, looking a perfect vision in a scarlet and white beach outfit which immediately made Phoebe feel dowdy. Sustaining a polite conversation with her companion on the back seat, even for so short a time, hardly improved her frame of mind. By the time they had arrived, parked the car in the grounds of the Hotel Rembrandt overlooking the sea, and had strolled to the beach, she was beginning to wish that she hadn't come—a wish which weakened under the spell of warm sunlight, a wide blue sky, a wide beach stretching away on either side of her and the inviting sea. They more than offset the doctor's coolly casual manner, Paul's bright stare and Maureen's sugary manner.

The doctor owned one of the gay little chalets set out where the dunes and the sand met, and the two girls went at once to change in the curtained alcove in its well-furnished interior. They emerged presently, in an atmosphere of artificial bonhomie, Maureen drawing all eyes in her scarlet bikini and white cap. It was some consolation to Phoebe that the doctor merely glanced at Maureen without much interest. He did the same to her, too, which she found disappointing, for while she made no effort to compete with her companion, she was aware that she made a pleasant enough picture in her sky-blue swimsuit. She wandered on down to the water's edge, leaving Maureen to wait for Paul and Lucius; the girl was obviously back in favour after whatever it was that had gone wrong when they had called at his house. Phoebe wandered slowly into the chilly water, wondering just how firmly entrenched the governess was in the doctor's household; she seemed full of confidence and very self-assured; he must like her very much, and although she hated to acknowledge it, probably he fancied her as well. She sighed and started to swim seawards.

She was a competent swimmer, no more. Within a few minutes she was overtaken by the other three, cleaving their various ways out to sea with an ease she frankly envied. The doctor had shouted something to her as he passed, but she hadn't heard what he had said and it didn't really matter. She called back brightly and swallowed so much water that she was forced to tread water while she coughed and spluttered. When she had her breath back she turned prudently for the shore; she had come quite a long way—too far, perhaps. She deliberately made her strokes slow and steady—she wasn't tired, only a little scared. All the same, her relief was very real when Lucius idled up beside her.

'Tired?' he asked.

'No—but I've not been quite as far as this before and I'm not sure how far I can go.'

He headed her off so that she found herself swimming parallel with the shore instead of towards it. 'In that case, we can stay as we are,' he told her, 'tell me if you get tired, I'll give you a hand.'

She applied herself to her swimming, happy that he had sought her company, sorry that it took up so much of her attention that she had little opportunity of doing anything else. All the same when he asked: 'Your plans are made for your trip home?' she was able to say: 'Yes, thank you—after my night duty—you remember?' She spoke cautiously, not quite happy about holding conversations in the North Sea while swimming.

She heard him grunt. 'You will fly?'

'Yes, in the morning—I shall be home during the afternoon.'

'You will meet all your friends?'

It was a question. 'Yes.'

'You have a great many. One in particular?'

She thought of Jack and hesitated. 'Not really. You asked me the other day.'

'I forget,' he said laconically, and then: 'Race you in!' and he allowed her to win.

They were lying on the sand, soaking up the sun, when Maureen and Paul joined them and Lucius asked the boy to go to the chalet and fetch the flask of coffee they had brought with them, but it was Maureen who suggested with an air of great friendliness that Phoebe might like to go with him. 'For he'll never manage the mugs as well,' she said gaily. As Phoebe got to her feet she watched the little smile on Maureen's face. It was amused and faintly contemptuous and she made no effort to hide it because Lucius was lying on his back with his eyes shut, and there was no need.

In the chalet they found the coffee and a tin of biscuits, and when Phoebe asked Paul where she should find the mugs, he shrugged his shoulders and turned his back, making for the door.

'There's no need to be rude,' she told him firmly. 'I asked a civil question and I deserve a civil answer.'

He shrugged his shoulders again and pointed to a

wall cupboard. 'They're there.'

She collected four, added spoons and asked: 'Paul, why do you dislike me?'

He stuck out his lower lip. 'I don't know you,' he muttered.

'No—and I don't know you, do I? But that's no reason to dislike a person.'

He gave her a flickering glance from his dark eyes. 'Maureen says you're . . .' He stopped, and she saw that he wasn't going to say anything more, but at least she had a clue. Heaven knew what the girl had told him. She said quietly: 'Let's go, shall we?'

They lunched at the hotel and later bathed again, but this time Lucius didn't come near her in the water, and yet he had been his usual kindly self at lunch and a very attentive host. She swam around for a little while, then went and lay on the sand waiting for the others, wondering when they would go back—after tea, she supposed, a meal which they took picnic fashion from a tray brought out from the hotel. It was still warm. Phoebe would have liked to have stayed where she was, soaking up the sun and dreaming, but instead she was forced to keep alert, answering Maureen's sly questions and parrying her remarks, sweetly made. 'Such a pity you don't have more time to swim—you poor thing, having to work so hard, you never have a chance to get good at anything, do you?' Her voice dripped kindness.

'No,' said Phoebe, her voice pleasant although she seethed, 'but it wouldn't make any difference. I'm far too cowardly.'

'Oh, never that! Cautious, perhaps—some people have no spirit of adventure. . . .'

Phoebe had thought Lucius to be asleep, he had been so quiet, but now he interrupted them. 'A remark which can hardly be applied to Phoebe. I doubt if she would have come to Holland otherwise.' He rolled over and looked at her and smiled lazily. 'You'll come back to dinner, Phoebe? It will be a pleasant end to a pleasant day.'

She thanked him nicely. Only his innate kindness and his beautiful manners had made him invite her, she felt sure, but the invitation gave her a badly needed uplift. 'I've only got my beach clothes with me,' she told him.

His unexpected: 'I like blue, it suits you,' took her quite by surprise and he went on: 'I'm sure none of us mind, and it will give me a good excuse to wear a shirt and slacks.'

He kept his word. When Phoebe went downstairs after making the best of her appearance in one of the beautiful bedrooms at the back of the house, it was to find him as informally dressed as she was so that she forgot the blue and white cotton shift she was wearing —forgot it until Maureen joined them. She, clever girl, had changed into an artlessly simple white dress which showed off her tan to perfection and made her look like some Greek goddess. She had brushed her dark hair until it gleamed and wore plain gold hoops as earrings, and on her bare feet she had gold kid sandals —she was wearing false eyelashes too, and Phoebe drew a thin trickle of comfort from the knowledge that her own, long and curling, were more than their equal. Secure in this knowledge, she was able to compliment Maureen upon her appearance in a serene manner before going to sit by Paul, whom she engaged in uneasy conversation until dinner was ready.

Because Paul was to dine with them, the meal had been put forward half an hour and they ate it in a room at the back of the house, filled with mellow old furniture, the table decked with fine china and silver worn paper-thin with age. The talk was general, and because Paul was with them, of a lighthearted nature. Phoebe, despite the presence of Maureen, enjoyed herself even though the boy avoided speaking to her and his governess, in a dozen subtle ways, allowed her to see just how firmly she was ensconced in the doctor's household. But Lucius at least made it his business to entertain her, so that her chagrin was all the more intense when, after dinner and when Paul had gone to bed, she suggested that she should go back to hospital and Lucius made no attempt to persuade her to stay, as he might well have done, for it was still early.

'I'll run you back,' he told her, and got to his feet with no sign of regret, and when she protested that she could walk the short distance, he took no notice at all but walked with her to the door while she bade Maureen good night.

They were halted at the door by that young lady's: 'Don't be long, will you, Lucius, and will you take me home? All that fresh air has made me too sleepy to be sociable tonight.'

Lucius had nodded without speaking and Phoebe got into the car beside him wondering what exactly Maureen had meant—was she in the habit of keeping him company in the evenings, or was she merely once more reminding Phoebe that she was firmly entrenched both in the doctor's home and his affections? She mulled it over while they drove to the hospital in silence. It was only when he stopped before its entrance that he spoke.

'I enjoyed our day. Perhaps we may do it again, Phoebe. I hope you enjoyed it too, though perhaps not as much as I.' He turned to look at her. 'I'm indebted to your sister for persuading you to take her place—we

482

might never have met.'

Phoebe sought for a suitable answer to this and could think of none. After a short silence, she came up with: 'I enjoyed myself very much, thank you, Doctor ...'

'Lucius.'

'Lucius.' She smiled at him. 'Good night.'

For answer he bent his head to kiss her, a gentle kiss on the corner of her mouth. 'I've been meaning to do that for some time,' he informed her, 'but I've such an infernal bad memory!' He got out of the car, opened her door and waited by it until the porter had opened the wicket in the door. She looked back and waved a little uncertainly and he raised a hand in casual salute. All the way over to the Home she was wondering if he was going to kiss Maureen good night too.

She woke the next morning to the realisation that she would be going on night duty that evening and she didn't particularly want to. It would mean that she wouldn't see anything of Lucius; consultants didn't do rounds at night, they had their registrars and housemen for that. Only upon very rare occasions or in some emergency did they appear on the wards, and that wasn't very often. She would have to resign herself to not seeing him at all and the idea didn't please her at all. She told herself what fun it had been trying to capture his attention; that it had been amusing even if not very successful, but at least he had noticed her a little and the detestable Maureen hadn't liked it. Presumably the doctor was old and wise enough to know what he was about, but Phoebe distrusted the governess as well as disliking her, nor did she think that she had a good influence upon Paul, despite her air of efficiency.

She wished she knew more about the fracas in his house, too, although Maureen had got back into his good graces quickly enough, surely a sign that he fancied her, for he had been very angry.... Phoebe reminded herself that she was very sorry for him. She frowned at her reflection as she pinned on her cap and repeated, out loud, that she was sorry for him for all the world as though she had contradicted herself. He was wrapped up in his work, unnoticing of the web Maureen was spinning for him—and Paul, would she be good to him? She thought not, for she wasn't the maternal type and the little boy badly needed mothering. She went down to breakfast and consumed her coffee and *boterham*, her head full of gloomy thoughts, not the least of which was that, counting her nights off, it would be a full two weeks before she would see Lucius again.

She was mistaken, for, coming off duty the next morning, yawning her head off and longing for her bed, she found him waiting at the head of the basement stairs.

'Five minutes,' he told her without preamble, and when she looked at him, bewildered. 'You'd better have a cup of coffee, we can breakfast after our swim.'

'Our swim?' she repeated stupidly, her eyes huge for want of sleep. 'Is this something you forgot to tell me, Doctor van Someren?'

He looked thoughtful. 'Possibly—you know what a head I have for remembering things, you must make allowances—anyway, I've told you now, haven't I?'

'I'm tired.'

'So am I,' he assured her. 'I've been up half the night. We need some exercise, so bustle up like a good girl. I'll be in the car.'

It was ridiculous, she told herself, half laughing,

half angry, as she tore off her uniform and flung on a cotton dress, pulled the pins out of her hair, brushed it perfunctorily, tired it back anyhow and raced downstairs, her swimsuit under her arm.

'Honestly,' she declared roundly as Lucius opened the Jaguar's door, 'I've not had time to do anything—I look a sight!'

'For sore eyes. Is that not what you say? You should wear your hair like that more often.'

'In a tangle?' she asked incredulously, 'and with nothing on my face—I feel awful.'

He was going slowly through the still quiet streets of Delft. 'At least you do not have to waste time putting on your eyelashes,' he observed mildly. 'Now shut your eyes and take a nap, I'll wake you when we get to Noordwijk.'

It was difficult to open her eyes; Phoebe felt his hand on her shoulder, but the urge to ignore it was very strong, but the hand was gently persistent, she woke up and found that he had parked the car in the hotel grounds again. 'Come on, lazybones,' he teased her gently as he helped her out of the car, put a key into her hand and said: 'Get undressed while I order breakfast,' and strolled away.

Once she had shaken off sleep she felt better, and by the time she was in her swimsuit she felt almost normal again. It was a lovely morning, cool enough to make her shiver a little as she came out of the chalet to find Lucius waiting for her.

She went to the water's edge, her toes curling under the chilly little waves, poking her hair unceremoniously into her cap, and he joined her there. She had barely tucked the last few stray curls away when he caught her briskly by the hand and ran her into the sea. The water was cold but not unkindly so. Phoebe gasped and laughed and finally swam, feeling her body glow and an energy she didn't know she possessed after a hard night's work.

'This is gorgeous—I could go on for ever!'

He made a wide circle round her, tearing through the water at a great rate before settling alongside her. 'You see? I knew you would feel better for it. We'll do this every morning while you're on night duty.'

He gave her a gentle shove in the direction of the beach.

'But your time?'

'There's always time to do the things one wishes to do, have you not discovered that?' He rolled over on to his back, paddling along slowly to keep pace with her earnest efforts. 'I don't start work until nine or half past, and we shall be back by then.'

'But Paul—won't you miss seeing him off to school?' she spluttered, her mouth full of water. 'And won't he mind!' she managed.

'We go our own ways in the morning—in the winter we breakfast together and during his holidays, of course. When he was quite a little boy we agreed about certain things. He understands that not having a mother he must accept that some things have to be different.'

Something in his voice warned her not to ask any more questions. When they reached the beach she said lightly: 'That was really marvellous—and how lovely it is with almost no one here.'

His eyes swept the empty expanse of sand. 'Just the two of us,' he agreed, and his eyes came to rest on hers. 'Lovely.' And something in his face made Phoebe say hastily, 'I'll go and change, I won't be a minute.'

They ate a gargantuan breakfast, sharing the hotel's large dining room with only a handful of people, for it was not yet nine o'clock. Phoebe, buttering toast with a lavish hand, observed: 'I could stay up all day, I feel so wide awake,' and had the remark greeted by a derisive chuckle from her companion.

'I'll check on that tomorrow morning,' he promised her, 'and now if you've finished . . .?'

An hour later, sitting up in bed, she felt so full of energy still that she decided that she wouldn't sleep; she would read for an hour or so and then get up and make a cup of tea. But she didn't open her book at once. She was wondering what Maureen would think, and possibly say, when she discovered that Lucius had taken her swimming and that the exercise was going to be repeated each morning until she went to England. Her satisfaction at the thought of Maureen's annoyance was tinged by regret at having to leave Delft, even for a few days. It would be lovely to see Sybil married, but she wished it could have been at some other time. She closed her eyes on the thought and slept.

She didn't wake until she was called at half past six and when she told Lucius that in the morning they laughed about it together. By the third morning she managed to have a cup of coffee on the ward, so as not to keep him waiting while she went to the dining room, and when they returned from their swim she changed into her cotton dress and sandals, put up her hair and went out to buy another beach outfit. She was coming out of the shop, a woefully expensive but eminently becoming ensemble dangling in its gay carrier bag, when she met Maureen—the last person she wished to see, for she was longing for her bed. The fine energy engendered by her swim was oozing slowly away and she was in no state to parry Maureen's clever thrusts, and she wasn't sure if her temper, now she was tired, would stand up to pinpricks. Maureen had stopped, so Phoebe braced herself.

But there was no need. The governess was pleasant, even friendly—she mentioned the early morning swim and gave her opinion that it was a splendid idea; she sympathised about the lack of time Phoebe had in which to enjoy herself while she was on night duty too. 'But you'll make up for that at your sister's wedding, won't you?' she suggested, laughing.

Phoebe tried to clear her sleep-laden wits. Maureen was behaving quite out of character and she wondered why. Besides, she was sure that she had never mentioned her trip to England to her. 'I didn't know I had told you,' she essayed.

'Oh, you didn't,' her companion agreed, 'but of course Lucius tells me everything—naturally.' Her dark eyes rested upon Phoebe's own blue sleepy ones. 'I know a great deal about you,' she laughed with a merriment which struck a discordant note in Phoebe's ear, 'so I shouldn't confide in Lucius if you want to keep any secrets from me.'

'I haven't any secrets,' said Phoebe flatly, then went a little pink. She certainly didn't want Maureen to know that she had taken Sybil's place, but surely Lucius...

The girl before her broke into her thoughts. 'No? Then you must be a paragon—I've got dozens.' Her glance slid to the package Phoebe was carrying. 'Shopping? It's a waste of time, my dear. Haven't you discovered that he doesn't notice—at least, not unless he's interested in the girl wearing them. Well, I must be off. 'Bye.'

Phoebe, despite her weariness, went over the conversation word by word before she finally went to sleep and decided that Maureen had wanted to make certain that she didn't trespass on her preserve—Lucius van Someren. 'And I wouldn't,' said Phoebe sleepily, 'if I were sure she loved him, but she doesn't.'

There was a message the next morning to say that Lucius wouldn't be able to take her swimming and just for a moment she wondered if it was Maureen's doing, but she didn't think Lucius would allow anyone to dictate to him about what he should do and what he shouldn't. And anyway, there was no sense in brooding over it. She accepted an invitation from two of the nurses to go with them and have coffee in the city and look at the shops, an occupation which filled the morning hours very satisfactorily and made her so tired that she fell asleep the moment her head touched the pillow.

She knew, the moment she opened the ward door that evening, that it was going to be a bad night—Zuster Witsma looked worried for a start, which was so unlike her that there had to be something wrong, and far too many children were wailing and calling out for attention, which was so unlike their usual sleepy high jinks that Phoebe asked at once:

'What's hit us?' and then remembered that Mies might not quite understand, for her English, though fluent, was strictly textbook. 'They're unhappy,' she substituted, and the Dutch girl said worriedly:

'Oh, Phoebe, such a day—and a nurse off sick. An infection, how do you say?'

'Bug,' supplied Phoebe unthinkingly.

'Bug? I thought that a bug was an insect.' Mies frowned because she was a stickler for getting her words right.

'It is, but it's what we call a virus infection—any infection—it's slang.'

'Ah,' Mies smiled faintly, 'now I have a new word.

There is a bug of the alimentary tract. . . .'

'D and V,' interposed Phoebe, and explained rapidly what it was.

'Exactly so—so horrid for the children and no rest for any of us all day. I'm afraid you will have a busy night, you and Zuster Pets—you will find gowns to wear in the treatment room and they are all on Mist. Kaolin and some of the worst are on Phenergan. Doctor van Someren thinks that it is not serious—twenty-four hours, perhaps a little longer. It plays havoc with the diets.'

Phoebe put down her cloak and bag, preparatory to taking the report, as Zuster Pets came into the office—a nice girl, large and rather slow but very patient and thorough. Phoebe and she exchanged a friendly hello and Phoebe thought how funny it was that a junior student nurse should be addressed as Zuster while she herself was called Nurse—an interesting point to take up with Lucius when next she saw him. Probably she wouldn't see him—she wrenched her mind away from that possibility and gave her attention to Zuster Witsma, painstakingly reading the report in both Dutch and English for the benefit of both of them.

She had been right about them being busy; it was almost midnight before the majority of the children, worn out and washed out, dropped off to sleep; only a handful of them remained awake, wretchedly ill and disposed to make the most of it. Phoebe went soft-footed up and down the wards, from bed to cot and back to bed again, feeling sorry for their occupants, for they were already fighting one disease, it was too bad that they had to endure this setback as well. Doctor Pontier had been in earlier in the evening, expressed satisfaction as to the small patients' conditions, amended some of the charts, drunk a hasty cup of coffee, invited Phoebe to go out to dinner with him when she returned from England, and went away with the earnest request that she should call him if she found it necessary.

He had barely closed the doors behind him when Night Sister arrived to do her round. She was a short, frankly outsize body, adored by the nurses. She had twinkling blue eyes, several chins, and had buried two husbands, and although she had none of her own she understood and liked children. Walking with a surprising lightness despite her ample proportions, she went from one child to the next, nodded her head in satisfaction and made her silent way from the ward, warning Phoebe to send Zuster Smit to her midnight meal, but on no account to leave the ward herself.

Alone in the ward, and all the children miraculously asleep, Phoebe settled down at the desk—they wouldn't stay quiet all night, but she had a short respite in which to chart temperatures and note the medicines she had given. She had done the first three or four when she became aware of footsteps on the stairs—unhurried and quiet—and she knew whose they were; she looked over her shoulder and Lucius was standing just inside the door.

Phoebe got up with the faintest of rustles from her gown and waited for him to reach the desk. He had been out, for he was in a dinner jacket, her imagination, always lively, pictured Maureen waiting outside in his car, looking glamorous, while she—— She glanced down at the voluminous folds of thick white cotton while she schooled her delightful features into a look of calm enquiry.

His voice was very quiet. 'Good evening, Nurse Brook—I'm glad to see that they've settled. They had us all a little worried today—were they very trouble-some?'

She spoke calmly, in a voice as soft as his. 'Oh, yes, very, but wouldn't we all be? They're worn out.'

He laughed soundlessly. 'And you?'

She gave him an austere look. 'Not in the least. Be-sides, I have Zuster Pets on with me, and she's a gem of a nurse.'

He looked interested. 'Is she now? We must keep an eye on her, since you say that.'

'For heaven's sake,' she uttered, 'that's only what I think . . . sir.'

'But I value your opinion, Phoebe, even when you call me sir in that repressive fashion.'

'I'm on duty,' she reminded him.

'Yes—unfortunately,' and when she gave him a questioning look: 'I'd like to take a look at Wil—and Jantje was a little off colour too.'

He took off his jacket and she tied him into a gown and went with him as he went to look at the children. When he had finished and was putting on his jacket again, he said very quietly: 'It's peaceful now—but it can't last all night. I don't envy you, even with the redoubtable Pets to be your right hand.' He smiled suddenly. 'Shall I stay and keep you company until she comes back, Phoebe?'

She couldn't see his face clearly in the dimness of the ward. She handed him a chart to initial and said in a steady, practical voice:

'You'll need to go to bed, you must have had a hard day.'

'A polite brush-off!' He sounded as though he were laughing.

'Oh, I didn't mean it to be,' she whispered anxi-ously. 'I'd love you to . . .' she stopped herself. 'I have a great deal of work to do,' she informed him sedately.

He nodded. 'A quarter to eight tomorrow morning,' he invited her. 'As it's Saturday, Paul will be coming too.'

'That will be nice, thank you,' and then, because she was unable to prevent herself, 'and Maureen?'

Lucius looked surprised. 'No—she doesn't live with us, you know. I have no idea at what time she gets up, but I imagine early rising isn't one of her strong points. She prefers her amusements to take place in the evening.'

He was standing very close to her; he had bent his head and kissed her and was at the door, his quiet, 'Good night, Phoebe,' a faint echoing whisper, before she moved.

She was a little late off duty in the morning and tired and faintly ill-tempered with it, but this feeling melted miraculously away as she got to the hospital entrance and saw the Jaguar standing waiting. It disappeared completely as Lucius opened the door for her and squeezed her in beside them, saying: 'You've had a wretched night, haven't you? Do you want to talk about it? I promise you I won't be bored, and Paul won't either.'

She smiled at the boy as the doctor started the car. 'Why, are you going to be a doctor too, Paul?'

He forgot to scowl, his face lighted with interest. 'I'm going to be a vet.'

'Oh, splendid,' said Phoebe with enthusiasm. 'I've an uncle who's a vet. I used to stay with him when I was a little girl; he let me help him, though I suppose I was never much use. Will you go to a veterinary college in Holland?'

He explained at great length and in great detail, and by the time they arrived on the beach, Phoebe thought that he had got over his dislike of her, but somehow, at some time, something went wrong to make him dislike her again, for in the middle of a laughing conversation with Lucius she looked up to find the boy's eyes fixed upon her with such suspicion and animosity that she was completely taken aback, lost the thread of what she was saying, and had to make some excuse for doing so, and although she continued to laugh and talk as before, the morning, for her at any rate, was spoilt. Her spirits were hardly improved by the doctor's careless statement that he would be going to Vienna for several days on the morrow, 'by which time you will be in England,' he reminded her cheerfully. 'And by the way, young van Loon will drive you to the airport,' and when she protested, he declared: 'He's been waiting to take you out ever since he met you. This will be the next best thing —he's a nice boy,' and his last remark capped her unsatisfactory morning: 'A little young for you, though.'

Tiredness and some feeling she didn't bother to analyse dissolved into a little spurt of temper. 'In that case, perhaps you'd better warn him not to go with me—there must be some middle-aged taxi-driver whom you might consider more suitable. I had planned to go by train.'

He had either not noticed her pettishness or chose to ignore it.

'Oh, lord, a ghastly journey—that's why I suggested to van Loon that he might take you. Much better go with him, Phoebe. Besides, he'll be so disappointed if you don't—you know what these young men are.'

'Do I?' Her voice was glacial.

He stopped the car outside the hospital and turned to look at her.

'I imagine that you have dealt kindly with dozens of

them.' He smiled with such charm that Phoebe found herself smiling back.

'If you're warning me not to gobble him up, I won't,' she assured him, and turned to say goodbye to Paul, sitting in the back of the car, and although he answered politely enough she could see that he disliked her still. She sighed a little, thanked the doctor for her trip, wished him a pleasant stay in Vienna, and got out of the car. She turned to wave before she went into the hospital, but they had already gone.

She felt lonely during the next few days; she told herself it was because she was tired from her night duty, and even though she went out each morning with one or other of the nurses, the days lagged sadly. It was a relief when she had gone on duty for the last time, packed her case and gone downstairs to meet young Doctor van Loon. At least he was delighted to see her, and made no secret of his admiration. Although she was tired and unaccountably despondent, she found herself enjoying the drive to Schipol; they parted like old friends when her flight was called and she left him vowing that he should take her out for the day when she returned.

The journey passed swiftly, for she had been up all night and slept a good deal, and when she wasn't sleeping, her mind was far too weary to allow her to think coherently, but at Shaftesbury, when she got out of the train and found Sybil and Nick waiting for her, her tiredness evaporated in the spate of news—the wedding, on the day after next, naturally took pride of place, and it wasn't until they were home, sitting round the table eating the belated tea Aunt Martha had prepared, that Sybil asked:

'Well, Phoebe, how's the scheme going? Is it fun?

495

Do you see much of the doctor and has he noticed you yet?' She laughed and Phoebe laughed with her, aware, to her annoyance, that her cheeks had turned a good deal pinker than usual.

'The scheme's fine,' she replied hastily. 'I love working there—the Ward Sister's about my age and we're good friends. Doctor van Someren comes each day, sometimes more often. He's nice.' As she said it she knew what an understatement that was, but for some reason she didn't want to talk about him; but the others did.

'And is he married?' Nick wanted to know, and Sybil chimed in. 'Yes, you said precious little about him in your letters.'

'Well——' began Phoebe, and went on hastily: 'No, he's not, but he's got an adopted son, Paul. He's almost nine and rather a dear, only he doesn't like me.'

'Why ever not?' asked Sybil. 'How funny—but you must have seen quite a lot of him, then.'

Phoebe made quite a business of buttering a scone. 'No, not really. I met him and then I went to the doctor's house with Zuster Witsma after we went to the botanical garden at Leyden. . . .'

'Who took you?'

She evaded her sister's eye. 'It was something I was supposed to see—part of the scheme. . . .'

'Who took you?' Sybil was nothing if not persistent.

'I went with Zuster Witsma—Doctor van Someren took me round.'

'Did he talk?'

'Yes, of course. He's a perfectly ordinary man.' She paused for a moment; he wasn't ordinary in the least, he was someone quite different. Phoebe dragged her attention back to what she was saying. 'We saw the museum too, it was very interesting.'

'What did he talk about?'

'Oh, the garden and plants and the hospital.' She looked down at her plate, remembering all the other things he had said.

'Charming—he sounds a bit dreary.'

'He's not,' said Phoebe sharply. 'He's a . . .' She stopped, not wanting to put her shadowy thought into words. 'I say, I've brought your wedding present with me, would you like to see it?'—a successful digression which sent everybody up to her room while she unpacked the Delftware coffee set and offered it to the happy pair.

She went to bed early, finding it pleasant to be in her own room again, so quiet and peaceful after the bustle of Delft and the noise from the wards. She went to sleep at once, but not before she had thought about Lucius and wondered where he was and what he was doing. It was too much to hope that he might miss her as she undoubtedly missed him. She slept on that not very happy thought.

There was too much to do the next day for anyone to have time to ask her any more questions. The wedding wasn't to be a large one, but even though they hadn't many relations, they had a great many friends, and Nick's family was a large one. They all drove over to Shaftesbury that evening, where his parents were staying for a couple of days. There were a round dozen for dinner and a very light-hearted meal it was, only broken up by Aunt Martha's firm decision that the bride required her beauty sleep.

Phoebe, waking early the next morning, went at once to her window. The weather had been unbelievably fine for weeks, and if it were to rain it would mean a last-minute rearranging of the buffet lunch which they were to have in the garden behind the house. But she need not have worried. The pale morning sky was clear and the sun, already bright, shone on to flower beds which really looked at their best. The roses were out too; the first buds of the Lady Seton had opened overnight, their pink the exact colour of the dress Phoebe had chosen to wear. She had a wide straw hat to go with it too, laden with matching roses—it was a beautiful hat and she looked nice in it. She found herself wishing that Doctor van Someren were there to see her in it.

She withdrew her head from the window, frowning a little. She was becoming obsessed by the man! She really must try to remember that however interesting she might find him, she wasn't likely to see him once she had left Delft, and that would be soon enough, she remembered with something like a shock as she went downstairs to the kitchen to make the morning tea.

The wedding went off brilliantly and was all that such an event should be. After it was all over and the bride and groom had left, the last of the guests gone and Aunt Martha had retired to her room, happy but worn out, Phoebe went into the garden and sat down in the still bright evening. It had been a wonderful day. Sybil had looked lovely and so very happy and everything had gone without a hitch—besides, it had been fun to meet old friends again, only she hadn't expected to see Jack there. She wondered who had invited him and then dismissed the thought as not worth bothering about. He had greeted her with an assurance which had annoyed her, as though he had only to raise his finger and she would come running.

She moved a little on the bench under the tree, smoothing the silk of her dress with careful fingers; it wasn't until she had come face to face with Jack that she had known that she really didn't care if she never saw him again. There was only one person she wanted to see—Lucius van Someren. She supposed, now that she allowed herself to think about it, that she had been in love with him all the time, only she hadn't been prepared to admit it. She sighed and got up and strolled down a garden path and, careless of her fine dress, leaned over the low stone wall at its end. There was Maureen to consider—it was impossible to tell from Lucius' manner what he felt about the girl, and as for herself, he had shown nothing but a pleasant friendliness towards her. And the dice were loaded against her, for Paul hated her and he and Maureen were a formidable barrier between her and the doctor. She felt helpless and hopeless out there in the darkening garden. The only thing which buoyed her up was the fact that she would be seeing him again in a couple of days.

She started walking back to the house, telling herself with a certain amount of force that one never knew what lay around the corner.

CHAPTER SIX

As it happened, it was Doctor Pontier round the corner. He was waiting for Phoebe at Schipol, and she, who had passed the flight in an indulging of impossible daydreams in which Lucius had come to meet her with every sign of delight, had difficulty in schooling her face into an expression of pleased surprise at the sight of his registrar.

He took her case and walked her out to where his car stood waiting.

'The boss asked van Loon to pick you up,' he explained, 'but I tossed him for it.' He laughed and Phoebe, of necessity, laughed with him.

'What about the ward round?' she asked.

'Jan will stand in for me. I told the boss—he said it didn't matter to him who fetched you as long as someone did.'

She was aware of ruffled feelings. It was rather like being a parcel which had to be collected; so much for her half-formed plans and hopes! She had allowed herself to drift from one delightful dream to the next during the last couple of days, and a lot of good they were doing her—a little realism would be a good thing. She turned to her companion and said cheerfully: 'Well, it's jolly nice to see you. I was just a bit worried about getting to Delft, though I'm sure it's easy enough—but this is much nicer. I wonder when I'm expected on duty?'

He got into the car and started the engine. 'I rather think this afternoon—there's a staff nurse off sick, nothing much, but she could be cooking up something.

Mies will be glad to see you.'

Nice to be wanted, thought Phoebe, nice to fill a niche, even a humble one. Even nicer if Lucius wanted her back too. She resolutely put him out of her mind and entertained Doctor Pontier with some of the lighter aspects of Sybil's wedding.

She didn't see Lucius until the evening, when after a heavy afternoon's work, he came quietly on to the ward, Mies and Arie with him. She had already seen these two, of course, but there had been little time to say much, only Mies had found time to apologise for asking Phoebe to go straight on duty. She smiled at Phoebe as they came down the ward now, but it was Doctor van Someren who spoke, and his impersonal friendliness chilled the warmth she felt at seeing him again.

'Nurse Brook, we are more than glad to see you back again. I hope you had a pleasant time at your sister's wedding? You were fortunate to have such splendid weather.'

She murmured something unintelligible to this rather prosy remark, but, as he wasn't listening she might just as well have said nothing at all. 'Wil,' he went on immediately, 'I'm not too happy about the child. We changed the dosage, didn't we? But the chest infection doesn't respond—we had better try something else.' He turned to Arie Lagemaat and switched to Dutch, and Phoebe, called by one of the children, went to attend to his small wants. When she had finished, Lucius had gone.

She met Paul the next day. The weather had changed with ferocious suddenness to a grey sky, a fine continuous rain and a high wind, but Phoebe, restless and disappointed at Lucius's lack of interest in her return, decided to go out. There was still a great deal of Delft to see; she hadn't visited the Tetar van Elven Museum yet; she dragged on a raincoat and tied a scarf over her hair without bothering overmuch as to her appearance, and started out. She had hours of time, for she had got up early after a night of wakefulness, and she wasn't on until two o'clock.

She lingered in the museum, drinking the coffee she was offered when she had toured its treasures, and then, because there was no sign of the rain abating, started off once more, walking a little aimlessly, until she remembered that she hadn't had more than a hurried peep at the Oude Delft canal; she would walk its length and fill in the time until she was due back on duty. She was halfway along the street bordering it, when the urge to explore one of the narrow lanes branching from it sent her down the nearest, dim and cobbled and on this wet day, dreary. She had reached the right-angled bend near its end when she heard the running feet behind her. They sounded urgent and Phoebe stopped, glancing to right and left of her, conscious that her heart was beating faster. Probably it was someone taking a short cut in a hurry. But it was Paul, tearing round the corner and stopping short within a foot of her. She managed a calm 'Hullo, Paul,' and waited for him to speak.

When he did, she could hear the excitement in his voice. 'I saw you,' he told her, 'and I wondered if you wanted someone to show you the city.'

She was taken aback. 'That's nice of you, Paul—I've just been to the museum in the Koornmarkt and I've an hour to spare still. I wasn't really going anywhere —and shouldn't you be going home?'

He looked away from her. 'No, I—I came out of school early this morning. I could show you some really old houses, near here.' He sounded eager.

'They're mediaeval and not used any more.'

Phoebe hesitated. She had time to spare, it was true, and this was the first occasion upon which Paul had shown any real signs of wanting to be friends. She said quickly: 'All right—where do we go first?'

For a boy of his age, he knew his home city well. They went up one *steeg* and down the next while he pointed out the interesting points of the buildings surrounding them. At length Phoebe glanced at her watch.

'Heavens,' she exclaimed, 'a quarter of an hour left! I must go.'

'One more,' he begged. 'There's a warehouse along here, by the canal.' He led the way through a narrow alley to a cobbled street, a canal on one side, narrow houses, grey and anonymous with age, on the other. They were deserted, forlorn in the rain which pattered into the dark, sluggish water of the canal.

Phoebe shivered. 'My goodness—this all looks a bit gloomy! Surely there's nothing . . .'

But Paul had crossed to one of the warehouses and pushed its door open. 'It's empty,' he told her. 'I've been inside lots of times. The room on the top floor is marvellous—you should just see it.'

Phoebe glanced up at the steep gable above their heads. It looked a long way away. 'I don't think I want to,' she said. 'I'll take your word for it.'

She knew she had said the wrong thing the moment she finished speaking; he gave her a look of scorn and said: 'Chicken! I didn't know you were frightened.'

'I'm not frightened,' she protested vigorously, 'only I don't see the point of climbing all those stairs . . .'

Paul turned away, his shoulders hunched. He said coldly: 'You keep saying you want us to be friends, but you don't really.'

'Is that what you want? Just to prove my friendship —to climb some stairs and look at a room?' she asked robustly. 'O.K., five minutes, then.'

He went inside first and although it sounded empty and hollow, there was nothing unpleasant about the old house. He led the way rapidly up the creaking stairs to the first floor and then up successively narrow staircases to the landings above, until on the third landing there was only a narrow twisting staircase in the wall, its steps worn and uneven. Paul went first to open the small door at the top—a heavy door, Phoebe could see, with great bolts top and bottom. She went past the boy into the dimness beyond and found an empty room; it smelled musty and close and because the shutter was barred across the window on the outside, it was darker than it need have been. She rotated slowly, staring round her. 'Why,' she cried, 'there's nothing here . . .' and turned her head sharply and too late at the sound of the door shutting. Paul had gone; she listened to the bolts being shot with a kind of stunned surprise, but only for a moment. She ran over to the door and rapped on it.

'Paul—I know you're having a joke, but I really haven't time. Will you open the door? I shall have to run all the way to the hospital!'

His young voice sounded thin through the thick wood. 'It's not a joke—Maureen says you're a scheming woman, out to catch Papa—well, you can't now. You didn't think I could be clever, did you? I knew if I waited I'd catch you!'

Before she could draw astonished breath to reply to this speech, he had gone down the stairs. She could hear his feet, echoing hollowly as he went further and further away. When she heard the bang of the street door she gave up calling after him and leaned against

504

the door, trying to think of a way out. The door was fast enough, and far too thick to yield to a hairpin, even if she knew how to use it—besides, there were the bolts, they would surely need a crowbar. The shuttered window wasn't any good either. Phoebe tried shouting through it, but the glass was thick and set in small leaded panes. She peered at her watch and made out that it was already time for her to be on duty and cheered up a little; very soon someone would wonder where she was, but her heart sank when she remembered that she had told no one where she was going. All she could hope for was that Paul would relent and come back for her, or take fright and tell Lucius—or even Maureen—but would Maureen take the trouble to come and let her out? She thought not. It would have to be Paul, and no doubt when he got home and started to think about it, he would return. Having settled this to her satisfaction, she looked round for somewhere to sit. There was nowhere but the floor, so she took off her raincoat, folded it carefully and sat upon that, her head against the wall. Every ten minutes or so she got up and went to the window and shouted, for surely at some time during the day someone would pass along the street below. She told herself vigorously that of course they would and ignored the fact she and Paul hadn't met a soul. . . .

The time passed slowly. Phoebe occupied it by reciting such Dutch words as she had managed to learn, going over the various procedures Lucius favoured for his patients and by writing, in her head, an amusing letter home. Only presently it wasn't amusing; she was hungry and the dry air of the ill-ventilated room had made her thirsty. Besides, the complete stillness of the old house had become something tangible. Supposing it was used by tramps at night, or hippies? After all,

Paul had known of it, so others would too ... supposing someone came, how was she going to make them understand how she came to be there, locked in? It was a thought she decided not to pursue. She might as well relax and have a nap, she told herself firmly; it was broad daylight, and even if no one knew where to look for her, the police were very good at finding people, so she had absolutely no reason to panic. Probably at this very moment Paul was telling Lucius what he had done. She eased herself on the raincoat, her pretty brow wrinkled. Supposing he didn't—supposing he told Maureen, who appeared to have a strong influence on him, and she decided that they would do nothing about it? After all, it was her ill-chosen words that had put the idea into the boy's head.

Phoebe got up; it was time to shout again. She would, she promised herself, have a heart-to-heart talk with Maureen.

A little hoarse, she settled down again, rehearsing what she would say, and dozed off in the middle of it.

At the hospital, Zuster Witsma had at first been unperturbed at Phoebe's absence. She had gone straight on duty the day before without a word of complaint; probably she had fallen asleep over a book. But when half an hour had passed and there was still no sign of her, she sent over to the Home, only to discover that Phoebe was not to be found and that the hall porter, who had seen her go out that morning, was quite sure she hadn't returned. It seemed a good idea to consult the Directrice, and that good lady was on the ward, conferring with Mies, when Lucius walked on to the ward to collect some papers. The sight of him induced both ladies to tell him about it and the Directrice concluded: 'I find it strange, Doctor van Someren, that Nurse Brook should not return—she is not a young, silly girl even if she is ignorant of our language. I cannot imagine her allowing that to stand in the way of her telephoning or sending a message.' She added firmly: 'I shall try the other hospitals.'

The doctor had said nothing at all—indeed, he appeared so abstracted in his manner that she wondered if he had heard her, but apparently he had, for after a pause he said: 'Yes, do that, Directrice, but please do nothing more until you hear from me. I have an idea—probably I am wide of the mark, but somehow I think not. You will excuse me.'

For a man of such calm and deliberation, his speed as he drove through the Delft streets to his home was excessive. He wasted no time in entering his house either and strode through it to the sitting room where he found Maureen and Paul. The boy had a free afternoon from school; at lunchtime Maureen had assured the doctor that she would take advantage of it and give Paul a lesson in English reading. However, as he entered Paul was sprawled on the floor, playing half-heartedly with a model car, and his governess was stretched out on one of the sofas, deep in a glossy magazine. The doctor frowned as she started up, but when he spoke it was with abrupt courtesy.

'Maureen, I wish to talk to Paul—you will excuse us,' and as she went out of the room he turned to his adopted son.

Paul had got to his feet. He had gone a little white and he looked decidedly guilty—frightened, even. The doctor sighed. His fantastic idea was likely to prove correct, but he had to be sure. With no sign of anger he said:

'Paul, Phoebe hasn't returned to the hospital, and

507

she's more than two hours overdue. I have a hunch that you know where she is. You were scared about something at lunch, weren't you? and you ate nothing to speak of, and when I mentioned that she was back at work you looked—er—shall we say guilty?' He strolled across the room and stood looking out of the window, his back to the little boy. 'I'm right, am I not?'

Paul scuffed his sandals, his eyes on the carpet, and muttered something.

'Yes—well, you shall tell me about it later, but now I want to know where she is.'

He had turned round to face Paul, who shot him a quick look. Something in the doctor's calm voice made him answer immediately.

Lucius left his house without a word. Within seconds he was in his car again, taking short cuts to the old warehouses by the canal. He was still driving much too fast and his face was without expression.

Phoebe had awakened from her brief nap unrefreshed and with a feeling that the room had become smaller, stuffier and very hot while she had slept. She also felt frightened, a sensation she quelled as best she could by going to the window and shouting once again through the shutters; at least it was somethng to do. She had barely seated herself once more before she was on her feet. There was someone in the house, she had heard the door bang below and now the faint sound of footsteps upon the stairs. She opened her mouth to call out, then almost choked herself with the effort to hold her tongue; if it were someone who knew her, they would surely call to her.

Whoever it was, was coming very fast. She faced the door, scarcely breathing as the bolts were shot back with some force and Lucius walked in. The breath she had been holding escaped in a small sound like a whispered scream mixed in with a sigh of relief. The desire to rush at him and fling herself in his arms was overwhelming, but she suppressed it firmly—and a good thing too, for he looked quite unworried, leaning against the door in a casual fashion, as though he were quite in the habit of releasing those foolish enough to get themselves locked up in deserted warehouses, and thought nothing of it. Her relief was swamped by a splendid rage, so that when he said: 'Hullo, Phoebe—sorry about this,' in a placid voice, her temper was exacerbated so that had there been anything handy to throw at him, she would certainly have thrown it.

Deprived of this method of relieving her pent-up feelings, she said crossly: 'Pray don't mention it, it was hardly your fault.' She looked at him with glittering blue eyes. 'I had a nice sleep,' she informed him, and burst into tears.

His arms were comforting and his shoulder reassuring. Phoebe muttered into the fine cloth of his jacket: 'You could have called out—I-I thought you were a t-tramp or a h-hippy!'

A smile, sternly suppressed, trembled on the doctor's lips although his voice was warmly comforting. 'My poor girl, you must have been terrified. What would you have done?'

'I haven't a clue,' she sobbed.

He spoke softly into her hair. 'I find that hard to believe. You are a woman in a thousand, you would have handled the situation very well, I have no doubt, and probably had them showing you the nearest way to the hospital within minutes.'

She laughed then, and presently, her tears dried, she drew away from him. 'How did you know where I was?'

'Paul told me.'

She glanced at him warily and saw that he was watching her closely. It was most unlikely that the little boy would have told him what he had said to her. She said lightly: 'Aren't little boys awful with their pranks? Don't be hard on him, will you? He was joking—I expect he got scared and didn't know what to do.'

Lucius took a long time to answer. 'Possibly, but even a boy as young as Paul would know that he only had to come back here and let you out.'

She didn't meet his eye. 'Yes—well, thank you very much for coming. I'm afraid I've taken up your precious time.'

'There are things more precious.' He had gone to try the shutters and spoke over his shoulder.

'I'll go back to St Bonifacius at once, I'm hours late.'

'You'll come back with me to my house and have a meal. They were managing very well on the ward, they can continue to do so for another hour.'

Phoebe was shaking out her raincoat. 'I'd rather go back—that is, if you don't mind.'

'I do mind. Besides, Paul is at home, he will want to apologise to you.'

She was flustered and furious with herself for being so—she, who had the reputation of keeping her cool at all times. 'Some other time—it surely doesn't matter. . . .'

'Am I to infer that you have some reason for not wishing to meet Paul?' His voice was silky.

'Of course not. Whatever reason should there be?' She put on her raincoat and he crossed the room to help her, turning her round to button it as though she were a little girl.

'A nice cup of tea?' he suggested. 'I know I need

one—I had no idea that I could feel so anxious.'

'About me?' The words had popped out before she could stop them.

'About you.' His hands were on her shoulders and he kept them there. 'I'm responsible for you.'

'So you are,' Phoebe said flatly, feeling elation draining from her. How silly of her to have imagined that his anxiety would have been for any other reason. She said brightly: 'I'm ready. Shall we go?'

Paul and his governess were still in the sitting room, he still on the floor with a book on his knees although he wasn't reading it and she still on the sofa, holding a long glass in one hand and still idly turning the pages of the magazine. She put both glass and magazine down hastily and got to her feet. 'Heavens, how quick you were! We didn't expect you. .... Phoebe, you poor thing! I've been telling Paul what a little horror he is, he should be severely punished.'

Phoebe could sense Lucius' anger, although she wasn't certain against whom it was directed, so before he could speak she said: 'Heavens, why? Didn't you ever play pranks when you were small? I know I did, and what harm's been done? I'm perfectly all right —as a matter of fact, I had a sleep.'

Maureen looked at her narrowly. 'Weren't you the least bit frightened?'

'No,' Phoebe uttered the lie stoutly, 'why should I be in broad daylight? I was a bit worried about getting back on duty, that was all. What was there to be scared about, anyway?'

She avoided the doctor's eye as she spoke, aware that she was gabbling. It was a relief when he spoke, his voice unhurried. 'Maureen, will you be good enough to go and ask Else to make some sandwiches and a pot of tea—Phoebe has missed her lunch.'

She went reluctantly. It wasn't until she had disappeared from the room that he spoke again. 'Paul, will you come here and apologise to Phoebe.'

The boy came and stood before her, giving her a look of mingled appeal and dislike. When he had apologised she said quickly: 'That's all right, Paul. Actually, I enjoyed our morning together, we must do it again some time.' She turned to Lucius. 'Paul's got a marvellous knowledge of Delft and he's a first-rate guide.' She smiled at him, coaxing him to good humour, and was disappointed when his face remained grave. 'I take it that Paul locked you in for a joke?' he asked her.

She felt her cheeks redden. 'Yes, of course,' she spoke quite sharply, 'and I hope that now he's said he's sorry, we needn't say any more about it.'

'You're generous. Very well, we won't. I don't think he'll do such a thing again, will you, Paul?'

The boy shook his head. His sigh of relief sounded loud in the silence which followed the doctor's remark and which was only broken when Else came in to tell them that she had taken the tea into the small sitting room at the back of the hall.

On the surface at least, tea was a pleasant meal, although Phoebe was the only one to eat anything. She made thankful inroads into the sandwiches and Lucius drank his tea—largely, she felt, to put her at her ease. He talked too, making sure that they all took their share of the conversation, keeping to mundane topics so that any constraint which might still be lurking was stilled. When she got up to go, Phoebe found herself more at ease than she had ever felt before at the house, despite the niggling thought that there must be some reason for Paul's behaviour which she hadn't hit upon.

Lucius, it seemed, had to return to hospital too.

They spoke little on the short journey and in the hospital they parted company, he to go to the wards, she to the Home. She thanked Lucius briefly in the hall and was about to turn away when he dropped a hand on her shoulder to hold her still.

'Don't disappear again,' he begged her, 'my nerves won't stand it.'

Phoebe changed with the lightning speed of long practice and while she anchored her cap, pondered his remark. Intended as a joke, she concluded, and indeed, his impersonal friendly manner towards her when she got on the ward seemed to bear this out; not that they exchanged more than a few words, for she was instantly plunged into the ward work after a brief explanation to Mies and a slightly longer one to the Directrice. By the time she had the leisure to look around her, Lucius had gone.

She didn't see him for several days after that—they met on the ward, naturally, but never to speak about anything but ward matters. She had the impression that he was avoiding her, and rendered extra sensitive by her love, she made it easy for him to do so by keeping out of the way when he did a round and seeing to it that there was little chance of her being about when he paid his evening visits. She went out to dinner with Doctor Pontier, the cinema with Jan, the houseman, and if that were not sufficient to distract her interest, accepted an invitation to have supper with Mies.

Mies had the day off, the Dutch staff nurse had gone off duty at three o'clock, so Phoebe found herself in charge of the ward until ten o'clock—rather a late hour, she had ventured to point out to Mies, to go out to supper. But Mies had laughed and told her that she could sleep it off the next day, as then it would be her day off, so, while other nurses were getting ready for bed, Phoebe was wrestling with her hair, changing her clothes and re-doing her face, rather regretting that she had agreed to go. But Mies was nice and it would be fun to see her flat. She snatched up her handbag and raced downstairs to engage the porter in the difficult task of calling a taxi for her. He shook his head, however, smiled and gave her some lengthy explanation not one word of which could she understand. She tried again, getting very muddled, and was cut short by Lucius' voice behind her.

'Don't struggle with our abominable language any more, dear girl,' he begged her, half laughing. 'He's only telling you that you don't need a taxi. I'll take you—come along.'

Phoebe stayed just where she was. 'Thank you, but I couldn't possibly give you the trouble. I'm going to Mies, she told me to take a taxi. . . .'

He looked conscience-stricken. 'Oh, lord, my memory! I quite intended telling someone or other that I should be calling for you; didn't I?'

He looked at her with raised eyebrows.

'No,' said Phoebe, 'you didn't.'

'I'm going to Mies' flat too.' He added, 'For supper,' as if that clinched the matter.

'Oh, well, are you? It's kind of you!' She petered out, so delighted to be with him for the next hour or so that she was hardly aware of what she was saying. She smiled at the porter, cast a quick, shy look at Lucius and allowed herself to be led out to the Jaguar.

Mies lived close by, down one of the narrow streets leading off a busy main street. The house was old, its ground floor taken up by a bakery, the narrow door beside the shop leading directly on to an equally narrow and steep stairs. The flat was on the top floor, three flights up—two attics, cunningly brought up to date, the mod con tucked away where it couldn't spoil the charm of the old low-ceilinged rooms. Mies had furnished it with bits and pieces, but there were flowers everywhere, highlighting the white walls and the polished wood floor.

Phoebe was whisked away to the bedroom, where Mies exclaimed happily:

'I am so glad that you have come—this is a feast, a celebration, you understand. Arie and I are engaged.'

Phoebe kissed the happy excited face, wished the Dutch girl everything suitable to the occasion and followed her out to the sitting room where there was another round of hand-shaking and kissing, first by Mies and Arie and then by Lucius. For a man of such absent-minded habits, he kissed remarkably well, Phoebe thought confusedly.

'There isn't—that is, it's not me you have to congratulate,' she managed.

His blue eyes were very bright. 'I never lose a good opportunity,' he told her gravely. 'Besides, I also am to be congratulated.'

She studied his face. 'You're going to be married too?' she asked, and managed, with a fair amount of success, to smile at him.

'You are surprised? At the moment it is strictly a secret.' He let her go and went to open the champagne he had brought with him, and the next half hour or so passed in a good deal of lighthearted nonsense and gay talk. Presently, helping Mies fetch in the supper, Phoebe had a few minutes, away from Lucius, to pull herself together—something she achieved to such good effect that she was able, with the help of the champagne and her resolute common sense, to pass the evening in a very credible manner—a little brittle in her talk, perhaps, and her laugh a little too high-pitched, but that was surely better than bursting into tears.

She awoke late, made a sketchy breakfast and decided to go to Amsterdam for the day. It stretched before her, a vista of endless hours until she should see Lucius again. She would have to fill it somehow—just as she would have to fill all the days ahead of her, once she had returned to England. 'The sooner you get him out of your system, my girl,' she told her face as she made it up with care, 'the better.'

She was on her way out of the hospital when she bumped into the youthful van Loon, who said joyfully: 'I say, what luck meeting you like this, Miss Brook. I must bring specimens for Doctor van Someren, but it is also my day off—you will perhaps have coffee with me?'

Any port in a storm. Phoebe gave him a wide smile. 'I'd love to. I was just on my way to catch a train to Amsterdam; I've got a day off too.'

'You're free all day? What luck! May we not go together? I have my car with me. I could show you something of the city.' He grinned widely, 'I would be most happy.'

'What a lovely idea. I'd like that, only we must go Dutch.'

'Go Dutch?' He looked bewildered. 'But I am Dutch.'

Phoebe laughed. 'It's a saying—we use it in English. It means we each pay for ourselves. I won't come otherwise.'

'You do this often in England? This going Dutch?'

'Yes—it's a common practice.' She smiled persuasively. 'No one minds.'

'Then I will not mind also. You will wait here for me?'

He had a Fiat 500, not new; it made the most interesting noises which they occupied themselves in identifying as they drove along. Phoebe, listening to the vague bangings and clangings beneath them, wondered if she would get back safely, but it seemed unsporting to voice her doubts, for her companion was so obviously enjoying himself.

'How long have you had this car?' she wanted to know, and wasn't surprised to hear that he had bought it off another young medic for five hundred guilden, and that this was his first trip of any distance. He added happily that he considered it a lucky coincidence that he should have met her, so that she could enjoy it with him. Phoebe agreed in a hollow voice, her doubts as to whether they would reach Delft again supplanted by the more urgent one as to whether they would reach Amsterdam.

But they did, and what was more, Eddie, as he had begged her to call him, was lucky enough to find a parking place by one of the canals. He stopped the car within inches of the water and oblivious of her shattered nerves, invited her to get out, a request she obeyed with alacrity, to find Lucius watching them from the pavement.

He crossed the road immediately, wished her a good morning, gave the car a considered stare and remarked to van Loon: 'I was told you had bought this car from Muiselaar, but I hardly credited you with driving it.'

Eddie patted its scratched bonnet with pride. 'It goes like a bomb, sir,' he said simply.

'Yes, I was afraid of that.' Doctor van Someren made to move away and Phoebe, longing to ask him where he was going, watched him reach the pavement, only to turn round and come back again. 'I hope you have a pleasant time,' he observed. His eyes flickered over van

Loon, whose head was under the boot. 'You will enjoy being with someone nearer your own age. If by any chance this—er—heap should fall apart, be good enough to telephone the hospital and I will arrange for someone to collect you.'

He smiled briefly into her surprised face and once more regained the pavement, to disappear among the passers-by.

But nothing untoward happened. They spent a cheerful day together and although it was Eddie who decided where they should go, it was Phoebe who kept an eye on the money they spent and an eye on the clock too.

She treated him like a younger brother—a relationship which seemed to suit him very well—and they got on famously. He took her to the Dam Palace where they wandered round the state apartments, which Phoebe declared to be magnificent but dreadfully uncomfortable to live in; she was whisked across the Dam square to look at the War Memorial, treading their way among the hippies to do so, then to drink coffee at a nearby café and then be walked briskly through the city's busy streets to the Rijksmuseum to see the famous Night Watch. She would have liked a chance to do a little window-shopping, but Eddie, determined that she should be stuffed with culture, marched her remorselessly about the streets, in and out of museums, standing her on pavements to crane her pretty neck at the interesting variety of rooftops, taking it for granted that she would leap on and off trams at a word from him. It was fun; the *broodje met ham* which they stopped to eat at a snack bar, the rich cream confections they consumed with their tea during the afternoon, the postcards she bought to send home—she thanked him during the drive back—accomplished despite the bangs and rattles—refused his pressing offer to have dinner with him, and went early to bed, tired out.

She was off duty in the morning, and despite the drizzling rain, decided to go out. She was at the hospital entrance when the Jaguar drew up beside her and Lucius got out. She wished him a good morning and made to pass him, but he stopped her with: 'Wait a minute, Phoebe,' and joined her.

'I've half an hour to spare,' he told her easily. 'I feel like a walk, if you don't mind?' He gave her a sideways glance. 'You seem determined to stretch my nerves to breaking point.'

She stopped walking the better to look at him. 'I do? How?'

'That—er—car which van Loon drives is hardly safe. Do tell him when next you go out together that he is to borrow the Mini—he has only to ask.'

'But I don't suppose I shall see him again. . . .'

He raised disbelieving eyebrows. 'No? But one day is hardly sufficient in which to see the sights. You had arranged to go with him?'

Phoebe blinked. If she hadn't known the doctor so well she might have deluded herself that he was jealous. 'Of course not! He happened to meet me as I was on my way to catch a train to Amsterdam—he had some specimens of yours to deliver or something of the sort, but he had a day off too—he suggested that I went with him so that he could show me the sights.' She added as an afterthought, 'I didn't know about his car.'

She watched the little smile play around his mouth. 'I was mistaken. It seemed natural that you should spend as much of your free time as possible with someone of your own age.'

'You keep saying that,' she told him, quite put out. 'You know quite well that he's five years younger than I—anyway, I feel old enough to be his mother.'

'Which reminds me—it's Paul's ninth birthday tomorrow, so will you come to tea? You're off in the afternoon, are you not?'

She wondered how he knew that. 'I'd love to. Did he really invite me? I must get him a present. What are you giving him?'

'A wrist watch, but I'm still wondering what else to buy for him. Have you any suggestions?'

'Mice?'

He laughed. 'An unusual suggestion from a woman —perhaps you like them.'

'I do not, but little boys do—didn't you keep mice?'

'Yes, but I had a tolerant mother—I'm afraid Maureen would never cope with them.'

'But they're not much work, and Paul would look after them. What about a puppy?' she asked, knowing already that it was useless—the governess obviously had the last say in such matters. She fell silent as they walked slowly down a gloomy *steeg*, twisting itself between old houses which had long ago been beautiful but were now let out in rooms. She glanced at the door they were passing, noticing its lovely ruined carving, and at that moment it was flung open and a very small puppy was ejected by a heavy boot. Phoebe had scooped the pitiful object up, hammered on the door with an indignant fist and was actually confronting the dour-looking man who opened it before she was reminded that she would be unable to tell him just what she thought of him. She turned to her companion, her eyes ablaze with indignation, and he gave her a smiling shake of the head and began at once to engage the man in conversation. She couldn't under-

520

stand a word of it, but the man looked annoyed, frightened and then downright cowed, muttering answers to the questions the doctor was putting to him in his calm, commanding manner. It didn't surprise her in the least that the man, after one final mutter, banged the door and Lucius said on a laugh: 'I feel sure that you are about to tell me that this creature is an answer from heaven, although he is hardly the breed I would have chosen. But it really won't do, you know. Maureen refuses to live in the same house as tame mice, so she will most certainly not agree to a dog—and such a dog!'

Phoebe bit back the forceful things she wished to say about Maureen.

'Oh, please,' she entreated softly, 'couldn't you—just him, not the mice—I'm sure he's a dear little dog and Paul would love him. Look how sweet he is!'

A gross exaggeration, she was aware, as she studied the puny, shivering puppy tucked in her arms. He stared back at her hopefully and heaved a sigh which caused his ribs to start through his deplorable coat. She went on urgently: 'We can't let him go back to that awful man.'

'Set your mind at rest, I have rashly acquired him.'

'Oh, Lucius, you dear!' she burst out, and modified this rash remark with rather stiff thanks and an enquiry as to what was to happen to the animal.

The doctor sighed. 'It just so happens that I have a friend living close by,' he sounded amused and resigned at the same time. 'He is a vet—and don't, I beg of you, tell me that he is an answer from heaven too. I suggest that we take him along now and see what he makes of the little beast.'

They came out of the *steg* into the Koornmarkt and the vet's house was a bare minute's walk away. He was a man of Lucius' own age and almost as quiet, who listened to Phoebe's earnest explanations, examined the puppy carefully, gave it his opinion that it should do well with proper care and food and bore them both off to drink coffee with his wife while the puppy was taken off to be bathed.

When they left shortly after a brief visit to the now clean animal, Phoebe expressed the view that he was a handsome dog, despite his undernourished frame. She wondered, out loud, what sort of a dog he might be and was indignant when Lucius laughed.

'I shall buy him a collar and a lead,' she declared. 'They will make a birthday present for Paul.' She stopped and turned to look at Lucius. 'You are going to give him to Paul, aren't you?' she asked, suddenly anxious.

He took her arm. 'Of course, but on one condition, that you are at my house by four o'clock tomorrow, for I can see that I shall need all the support I can get when that animal makes his entry.'

CHAPTER SEVEN

THE tea party was in full swing when Phoebe arrived at the doctor's house the following afternoon. She was surprised to find quite a number of people in the sitting room. Two-thirds of them were children, which was to be expected, the remainder were older people—aunts, uncles and a fair sprinkling of guests whom she had already met or seen in or around the hospital—and of course Maureen. One glimpse of her, in a sleeveless green dress, her hair piled in a cluster of curls, silver sandals on her bare feet, was enough to make Phoebe thankful that she had taken extra pains with her own toilette and had put on a blue silk jersey dress which highlighted her eyes in a most satisfactory manner, and added blue kid sandals to match it. Her hair she had done as she always did, rather severely drawn back from her face, and she wore no jewellery at all. She greeted the doctor sustained by the knowledge that she looked as nice, if not nicer than the governess; the thought added a sparkle to her eye and a faint pink to her cheeks and Lucius, greeting her, paused to take a second look.

'And what have you been up to?' he wanted to know. 'You look—pleased with yourself.'

She looked at him with innocent eyes. 'Me? Nothing—I've been working all the morning.' She gave him a smile and crossed the room to wish Paul a happy birthday. 'And I've something for you, but I'll give it to you later,' she explained as Arie Lagemaat bore her off to a corner, where he produced tea and cake for her, saying: 'Mies told me to look out for you.'

'If I'd known, I would have changed my off duty so that she could have come—she has far more right to be here than I have.'

He smiled nicely. 'You're mistaken there. I'm waiting for the great moment.'

'Oh—do you know?'

He nodded and smiled as his eyes met her. 'I'm to tell Mies all about it later.'

'Do you think . . .?' she began, then caught sight of Mijnheer van Vliet, the vet, standing in the doorway. A moment later Lucius crossed the room to where Paul was standing with his own friends. He took the wicker box hesitantly, his eyes on the doctor's face, and then, at the small snuffling sound from it, opened it in a rush. He and the puppy eyed each other for a brief moment and then the boy lifted him out to hold him tight against his chest. 'Is he really for me, Papa?' he asked in a strained little voice.

'Yes, for you, Paul—your very own dog.'

Phoebe thought that Paul was going to burst into tears, but instead he said in an excited voice: 'Oh, Papa, thank you! He's so beautiful and so—so noble —I shall call him Rex.'

As he spoke his eyes slid past Lucius to where Maureen was standing. They held pleading and defiance, but she turned her head away as Lucius went on: 'He's been ill, so I'm afraid Oom Domus will have to take him back for a few more days, but you shall go and see him each day and we'll have him home just as soon as he's fit—and as to thanking me, Paul, it is Phoebe whom you should thank for it was she who begged me to have him—you see, someone had just thrown him out and she rescued him.'

Everyone looked at her so that she smiled in lunatic fashion and retreated as far as possible behind Arie, feeling a fool. But when Paul came across to her, the puppy still clutched close, she forgot about the others. 'You really like him, Paul? I thought he had the sweetest face and such soft eyes. He's going to be happy with you; you'll grow up together.' She produced her own present. 'I thought he might wear these just to begin with, until he's learned to obey you, you know.'

She undid the small parcel for him, because he had no intention of letting go of the dog, and watched while he exclaimed over the red collar and lead.

'I don't know much about dogs,' he told her gruffly as he thanked her.

'Something you'll learn very quickly as you go along,' she assured him comfortably, 'and I'm sure Mijnheer van Vliet will give you lots of good advice, and your papa too.' She stroked the puppy's black nose, 'I'm glad he's made you happy, Paul,' she said.

He turned to go back to his friends and then came close to her to whisper so that she had to bend down to hear what he was saying.

'I don't think you're a scheming woman at all—Maureen says I mustn't like you, but I do.'

She said nothing, fearful of breaking the first threads of a friendship which was still too fragile to risk breaking with a careless word. She left soon after that, after a quiet goodbye to Lucius and an exchange of polite words with Maureen, whom, she suspected, was very angry indeed, for as they parted Maureen said with deceptive friendliness: 'You and I must meet some time, Phoebe—I'm sure we have a great deal to say to each other.'

'I'm free on Thursday,' said Phoebe, if she had to grasp the nettle she might as well get it over with, 'can't we meet for tea?'

'My dear, I work, or had you forgotten? But I'll

think of something.'

Lucius saw her to the door. On its step he observed blandly: 'I had no idea that you and Maureen were such good friends,' and something in his voice made her look at him sharply, but there was nothing but polite interest in his face.

'We—we know each other very well,' she answered carefully.

He leaned against the heavy door. 'You surprise me. I had quite the reverse impression—which just shows you how unobservant I am.'

She smiled at him. 'Now it's my turn to say I had quite the reverse impression, despite your notebook.'

His hand went to his pocket. 'Good heavens—wait!' He was thumbing through it. 'I know I made a note— yes, here it is. Have I asked you to dine with me this evening? If not, I'm asking you now.'

She laughed. 'No, you didn't, and if I say yes, will you remember that I did?'

He stared down at her. 'Oh, yes, I shall remember. Thank you for making Paul's birthday such a happy one.'

'It wasn't me—you said yourself that it was an answer from heaven.'

He held her two hands in his, staring down at her, and she wondered what he was going to say. When he spoke she was disappointed.

'*Tot ziens*, then. I'll pick you up at the hospital at eight o'clock.'

It was on her way back that she began to wonder why he wasn't taking Maureen out that evening. She might have another engagement, but she was hardly likely to be pleased if he went off with someone else— perhaps he wasn't going to tell her; perhaps their understanding of each other was so complete that it just didn't matter. If she were Maureen, though, she wouldn't share Lucius with anyone, however platonically.

There was one dress in her wardrobe which she hadn't worn yet, a pastel patterned crêpe. She belted it around her slim waist, caught up a coat and went downstairs as the clock struck eight.

She hadn't given much thought as to where Lucius would take her, for she had been far too excited to think sensibly about anything, and the sight of him, standing on the hospital steps, smoking his pipe and exchanging the time of day with the porter on duty, most effectively splintered the cool she had struggled so hard to maintain.

As they got into the car, Lucius said, 'I thought we'd try Schevingenen—everyone goes there. It's a kind of Dutch Brighton, and if you don't pay it at least one visit, no one will believe you've been to Holland.'

They were out of Delft, streaking down the motorway towards den Haag and the coast, before she said diffidently: 'I thought you would be going out with Paul and Maureen—you know, for a birthday treat.'

He sounded as though he was laughing. 'I took Paul to lunch—Reyndorp's Prinsenhof, I expect you've been there? and we spent the evening at van Vliet's, getting acquainted with Rex. Paul has gone to bed a very happy little boy.'

'I'm glad,' said Phoebe, and wished he would mention Maureen, but he didn't. They entered into a lighthearted conversation about dogs which led, somehow, to talking about her home, and by the time he had parked the car outside the Corvette Restaurant, nothing mattered but the delightful fact that they were to spend the evening together.

It was a gay place and crowded and the menu was

527

enormous. She studied it, hoping for some clue from her companion. It was quickly forthcoming. 'I'm famished,' observed Lucius. 'Paul's idea of lunch is consistent with his age group—*pofferjes*, ice-cream and some mammoth sausage rolls—you see, on his birthday, he plays host and orders the food—I merely eat it.'

Phoebe laughed. 'It sounds frightful, but I expect he loved it and thought you did too.' She added helpfully, 'I'm hungry.'

He sighed with exaggerated relief. 'Good—let's have herring balls with our drinks and then oyster soup, duckling stuffed with apples, and finish with Gateau St Honoré?'

It sounded delicious, although she wasn't sure about the oysters; perhaps they would look different in soup, but by the time they had had their drinks and demolished the herring balls, she was prepared to like anything. Over their meal she found herself telling Lucius exactly why she had taken Sybil's place. 'I thought it was an awful thing to do at first,' she explained a little shyly, 'and then Sybil was so determined to leave, and all the arrangements had been made —and I was longing for a change.' Her voice, without her knowing it, was wistful.

'Ah, yes,' his voice was gentle, 'and to get away from someone, perhaps?'

The excellent Burgundy they had been drinking betrayed her. 'Well, yes, that too—though he did turn up at the wedding.'

Lucius lifted a hand to the waiter and sat back comfortably while the plates were changed. 'And does that mean that there will be more wedding bells?' His tone was so casual that she answered almost without thought.

'Heavens, no! It was just that he was put out because I didn't fall into his arms like a ripe plum.' She added ingenuously: 'I've forgotten what he looks like.'

'Yes?' he smiled. 'You're more of a peach than a plum, you know. One is sorry for the young man.' He speared a portion of duck. 'But you have another admirer, did you know?'

She kept her eyes on her plate. Maureen or not, had she at last made an impression on his vague abstraction?

'Paul,' he went on cheerfully. 'A bit of a slow starter, wasn't he? But now you're female number one in his world. Maureen had better look out.'

And so had I, thought Phoebe, but all she said was: 'How charming of him. I should like to be friends.'

'Nice of you, Phoebe, after that strange episode in the warehouse. I find it hard to imagine that he did it purely for fun—he must have had some reason.' His eyes searched hers across the table, and silently she agreed with him. Aloud she said comfortably: 'Oh, you know what boys are like, always up to something.' She looked around, desperate to get the conversation on to an impersonal level. 'What a delightful·place this is. I expect you come here often.'

His eyes twinkled. 'No—why should I? Only when I'm celebrating something.'

'Paul's birthday; it was kind of you to ask me.'

His lips twitched, but he said no more on the subject, but presently asked her how many more weeks she had in Holland.

'Three—less than that.' She forced her voice to sound cheerful, thinking with dismay that the time was indeed short, and a week of it night duty, too. For the first time for some weeks she wondered what she would do when she got back to England. She might have pursued this melancholy train of thought if her companion hadn't said to surprise her: 'The time has gone very slowly, but probably you haven't found it so.'

Phoebe stared at him, her pretty mouth slightly open. 'No—I haven't. It's all fresh for me and everything's strange, but I expect it's different for you—one nurse after the other coming for a few weeks and then going again. I forget I'm one of a number.'

He didn't answer, only turned as the waiter arrived at the table.

'Ah, here is the famous Gateau St Honoré,' he observed. 'I think it deserves a bottle of champagne, don't you?'

She was on the point of begging him to curb his extravagance, but when she caught the gleam in his eyes, she closed her mouth firmly. Only when the waiter had gone and they were drinking it did he ask her:

'And what were you on the point of saying, dear girl? I have the impression that you disapprove of champagne—surely not?'

'Of course I don't.' She hesitated and went rather red. 'I—I just thought it was—well, champagne is rather expensive—you know, it's for special occasions.'

'You don't consider this a special occasion?' he was teasing her now. 'Besides, let me set your mind at rest. I have quite enough money to drink champagne with every meal if I should wish to do anything so foolish.'

The red deepened; the knowledge vexed her. 'I beg your pardon,' she said stiffly, 'I had no intention of prying.'

'You're not prying,' he told her placidly. 'I volunteered the information, didn't I? I'm flattered that you were kind enough to consider my pocket—not many girls would.'

The blush which she had succeeded in quenching to some extent returned. 'That's unusual too,' he went on, 'a girl who blushes. Drink your champagne, we're going for a walk.'

They went first to the southern end of the promenade where the fishing harbour, packed with herring boats, lay under the clear evening sky. There was a great deal to see, at least for Phoebe, who found the fishermen's wives in their voluminous dresses and white caps quite fascinating. They lingered there while Lucius explained the variations of costume to her; he explained about the annual race by the herring boats to bring back the first herrings, too, and showing no sign of impatience, answered her fusillade of questions about one thing and another. And when she had seen enough, he took her arm and walked her back, the boulevard on one side, the firm, fine sand and the sea on the other, until they reached the lighthouse at the other end, pausing to examine the obelisk marking the exact spot where William had landed after the Napoleonic wars, and then walked back again.

It was a fine evening, pleasantly warm and fresh after the rain, and there were a great many people about, strolling along arm in arm, just as they were. Phoebe heaved a sigh of content because for the moment at any rate, she was happy, and although she told herself it was probably the champagne, she knew quite well that it was because she was with Lucius. And make the most of it, my girl, she admonished herself silently.

It was dark by the time they got back to the Kurhaus Hotel; strings of lights festooned the boulevard; the café and restaurants, still crowded, were ablaze with light too, and there was music everywhere. It seemed a fitting end to their evening to sit outside the restaurant, looking at the sea and drinking a final cup of coffee, and surprisingly, still with plenty to say to each other, although thinking about it later, Phoebe was forced to admit that she had done most of the talking.

It was midnight when they reached the hospital and when she began a little speech of thanks as they got out of the car Lucius stopped her with: 'No need of thanks, Phoebe. I haven't enjoyed myself so much for a long time—and I'm coming in—I want to have a look at Wil.'

But that didn't stop her from thanking him just the same, once they were in the hospital. The hall porter had his back to them, there was no one else about. Lucius heard her out, clamped her immovable with his hands on her shoulders and kissed her soundly. 'Go to bed,' he said, 'my delightful Miss Brook.'

She didn't see him at all the next day, and when Doctor Pontier came to do a round on the following morning, she asked with careful casualness where he was.

Her companion gave her a quick look. 'The boss is in den Haag,' he told her. 'Some international meeting or other—it lasts three days, I believe. He's there all day; doesn't get home until the evening and leaves again early each morning.'

She murmured something. Lucius hadn't said anything to her when they had been out together, but then, her common sense told her, why should he? She refused an invitation to the cinema, pleading a headache, and went off to cope with little Wil, who was poorly again.

She had just got off duty that afternoon and was on her way up to her room when the warden called after her that there was a young lady to see her. At least

Phoebe, understanding only a few words, guessed that was the message. She turned and went downstairs again; it would be Maureen, her instinct warned her—and it was. Phoebe, seeing her sitting there in the comfortable rather drab little sitting room she shared with the other staff nurses, regretted that she had had no warning of her visitor; she would have re-done her face at least and tidied her hair. She said: 'Hullo, Maureen,' and her visitor smiled from her chair and said slowly: 'Hullo. My dear, how frightfully worthy you look in that uniform, though I must say it's a bit ageing—perhaps you're just tired.'

Phoebe sat down in a small overstuffed chair, smiled her acknowledgement of this remark, and waited for Maureen to begin.

'This business with that damned dog—how clever of you, Phoebe. Did you hope to win Paul over to your side because you knew Lucius is soft about him? If you did, you're more of a fool than I thought. What did you hope to gain, I wonder? Lucius? Oh, I've seen your face when you look at him, so don't pretend that you're not interested. But it's no good, my dear, I've got him where I want him—I only have to whistle and he'll come; he and his home and his cars and his lovely bank balance. You see he thinks Paul adores me and he would do anything for the boy.'

'You'll have Paul too,' Phoebe said flatly.

'I've got him where I want him too, so hands off. I must say you've got a nerve, coming here and making doe's eyes at Lucius. And don't think that you've stolen a march on me with your dinners at Schevingenen and your birthday tea parties and your Florence Nightingale act....'

'How incredibly vulgar you are!' Phoebe spoke in a cool voice which quite hid her rage, bubbling away

533

inside her and threatening to burst out of her at any moment. 'And do you really suppose that I should listen to you? Why, you don't even like me, and that's good enough reason to take no notice of anything you say.' She got to her feet and walked to the door. 'I'm sorry for Lucius—and Paul.'

In her room she took off her uniform, had a bath and then sat on her bed, having a good cry, which, while playing havoc with her face, did her feelings a great deal of good. She had no intention of heeding Maureen, and what could the girl do anyway? She would have to wait for Lucius to ask her to marry him —Phoebe's heart gave a joyful little bound because he hadn't done that yet, and until then, if Lucius asked her to go out with him again, she would most certainly go. He might not be in love with her, but at least he enjoyed her company, even if she could delay Maureen's plans for another week or two. She closed her eyes on the awful vision of Maureen, married to Lucius—but Lucius might not have made up his mind; he was a deliberate man, not given to impulsive action, at least it was a straw to clutch at.

Phoebe dressed and went down to tea and, carried on the high tide of hope, went out and bought a new dress, something suitable for dinner or an evening out —green and silky and extremely becoming. It was a shocking price; she told herself she was a fool throwing money away on a forlorn hope, but she felt a great deal more cheerful as she left the shop.

She saw Paul the next morning, hurrying along the Koornmarkt. It amused her a little to see how cautiously he looked around him before he crossed the road to speak to her. 'I'm going to see Rex,' he told her. 'I suppose you wouldn't like to come with me?'

Phoebe agreed promptly. The vet's house was close

by, and she had half an hour to spare. She occupied the short journey with questions about the puppy and listened to the little boy's happy chatter—Rex was to come home in a day or so, he told her; his papa would be back by then to help him decide where the puppy should sleep and what he should eat and when he should go for his walk. There was no doubt about it, Paul was a changed child, and changed towards her too, for at the vet's door he said in an off-hand voice: 'I'm glad I met you. Maureen won't talk about him, you see, and Else hasn't much time, though she says she'll like to have a dog in the house.'

Mijnheer van Vliet was home. He took them through the surgery to his house where Rex was waiting for them, a very different dog from the miserable little creature she had picked up. He flung himself at Paul and watching them together, Phoebe could only hope that Maureen would relent and at least treat the puppy with kindness even if she disliked it. After all, it would be Paul who would be looking after the dog. She met the vet's eyes and smiled. 'They're made for each other, aren't they? I must go—I'm on duty in an hour.'

She was at the door when Paul ran up to her and said in a conspirator's voice: 'You won't tell Maureen about us coming here, will you?'

'No, dear, not if you don't want me to—anyway, I seldom see her, do I, so it's not very likely I should mention it. But why not, Paul? You're not afraid?'

He wouldn't answer her, but ran back to Rex, leaving her to wonder if Maureen had forbidden him to have anything to do with her, but surely that was a bit high-handed?

The following day was Mies' day off which meant that Phoebe would have charge of the ward from two o'clock until the night nurses came on duty. The ward was quiet when she took over. There was no one very ill, only little Wil, sitting in her cot, her small chest labouring, her face too thin and white. True, she looked no worse than she had done for several days, but Phoebe wasn't happy about her. She confided her opinion to the invaluable Zuster Pets, who, although she didn't know much about it, promised to keep a careful watch on the child.

But it was Phoebe who was there when, just at seven o'clock when the ward was at its busiest, little Wil collapsed. Doctor Pontier had been to see her at teatime and although he shared Phoebe's vague fears, he had been unable to find anything wrong. Phoebe decided that she was being over-anxious—all the same, she found herself taking a look at Wil at more and more frequent intervals. And lucky for her that she had, she muttered as she switched on the oxygen, plugged in the sucker and rang the emergency bell by the cot. There was no one in the end ward at that moment. When she heard someone behind her she said: 'Pets—keep the other children out and send for Doctor Pontier.'

'Will I do?' Lucius' voice was quiet. She looked over her shoulder at him, unable to keep the joy out of her face or her voice.

'Lucius,' she spoke his name instinctively, and then, remembering where she was, 'Wil has collapsed, sir, she's been off colour all day. Doctor Pontier came to see her at teatime, but he couldn't find anything—a slight temp, but she's had that on and off for a day or two.' She had put a thermometer under Wil's arm and she withdrew it now.

'Forty-point-two centigrade,' she told him, 'and a racing pulse.'

536

There was no need to tell him the respiration rate, he could see the small heaving chest for himself. He was already sitting on the cot, his stethoscope out, his hands moving quietly over the bony little body. Presently he looked up. 'You know what this is?' he asked.

'Empyema?' she ventured, and glowed at his appreciative nod.

'Good girl, yes—rapid symptoms, I must say, but I'll stake my reputation on it. Let's try an aspiration.'

Zuster Pets had arrived, solid and dependable. Lucius spoke to her and she went away again and he got off the cot and took off his jacket. 'I'll just scrub —stay here, Phoebe, and keep a sharp eye open. We'll need an X-ray—get someone to warn them. Ah, Pontier, just in time. . . .' He switched over to his own language and Phoebe, passing on the instructions he had given her, went back to her patient.

The X-ray confirmed the diagnosis; Wil would have to go to theatre and have the cavity drained of the pus which had accumulated there. Phoebe was kept busy for the next half hour getting the small creature ready for the small, vital operation, and when she had seen her safely theatrewards, the faithful Pets in attendance, she applied herself to the preparation of the drainage bottles, the making up of the cot and all the small paraphernalia needed for the night.

Wil was back, perched up against her pillows, when Lucius came in. After he had bent over his small patient he turned to Phoebe. 'Fortunately we were able to tackle it at once—I've rarely seen one with such urgent symptoms—in fact,' he grinned at her, 'I've rarely seen one.'

Phoebe folded a small blanket and hung it over the end of the cot.

'I'm so glad!'

'It was thanks to you, Phoebe. No, I know what you're going to say, but you were quick off the mark. Well, I'm off home, I told them I'd be back an hour ago. Pontier will keep an eye on things.'

He nodded and walked rapidly away, but halfway down the ward he came back again. 'I'm almost sure I've forgotten something—I'll telephone if it's anything important.'

It was Sunday the next day and Phoebe's day off again, and although she had no reason to get up early, she did, because lying in bed was too conducive to thought, and she didn't want to think. She made tea and nibbled toast, then sat on her bed, wondering what to do. The beach would be crowded and it wouldn't be much fun on her own, and the idea of a bus trip didn't appeal. She was looking at her guide book when Zuster Pets knocked on the door. 'There's a telephone call for you,' she declared. 'It's Doctor van Someren.'

Phoebe flew to the telephone. It was Wil, of course —something had gone wrong. She snatched up the receiver and said Hullo in a breathless voice.

'Hullo,' said Lucius in her ear. 'You sound terrified —what's the matter?'

'Wil,' she managed.

'Doing well. Tell me, did I invite you to spend the day with us?'

'No.'

'Ah, then that is what I forgot yesterday evening on the ward. Will you?'

'Well . . .' began Phoebe, disciplining her tongue not to shout an instant yes.

'Good—I'm taking Paul to Noordwijk for a swim, then I thought we might go for a run round for a while. Else has promised us a bumper tea when we get back.'

'Nice! I'd like to, thank you.' Maureen's brilliant image floated before her in the telephone box, but she dismissed it firmly. 'When shall I be ready?'

'Half an hour. We'll pick you up.'

Phoebe dressed like lightning, not bothering with make-up and tying her hair back with a ribbon to match the pink cotton. The half hour was up as she rammed her beach clothes into her shoulder bag.

Paul was sitting in the back with Rex on his knee and there was no sign of Maureen. Phoebe smiled widely at the three of them and got in beside Lucius, who leaned over her to shut the door, remarking: 'Paul was sure you would never be ready—half an hour isn't long.' His gaze swept over her and he smiled nicely. 'But you seem to have made good use of it.'

She flushed faintly and turned to ask Paul about Rex, and the journey to the beach was wholly taken up by a cheerful three-sided conversation about dogs and Rex in particular.

'Is he home for good?' Phoebe wanted to know.

Paul nodded happily. 'Yes, today—we've just fetched him. He'll have all day to get used to being with us before Maureen comes....' He broke off and Lucius said mildly:

'Oh, come now, old chap, Maureen will like him, you see if she doesn't, once he's a member of the family. He only needs to learn his manners—she'll be enchanted with him.'

An opinion to which Phoebe found herself unable to subscribe.

The day was an enormous success; it was still too early for the beach to be crowded. They swam, sunbathed, swam again, and then, after Phoebe had made coffee for them all in the chalet and Rex had renewed his energy with a bowl of milk, they got back into the car. An early lunch, Lucius decreed; they went back inland to Oegsgeest, to de Beukenhof, an inn standing in its own garden and renowned for its cooking. They ate splendidly—Boeuf Stroganoff and strawberries and cream—and Rex, on his best behaviour, sat under Paul's chair.

They went north after that, to Alkmaar and on to den Helder and across the Afsluitdijk, where Lucius, to please Paul, allowed the Jaguar to show a fine burst of speed. But once on the mainland again, he turned off the main road, idling along the dyke roads as far as Lemmer before taking to the main road again, to race across the Noord Oost polder to Kampen and Zwolle and eventually to the motorway to Amsterdam and Delft. Phoebe, trying to see everything at once and failing singularly, found the day passing too quickly. It had been perfect—Paul was friends at last, Maureen wasn't there with her barbed quips and sly jokes, and Lucius—Lucius was the perfect companion; even if she hadn't loved him she would have allowed him that. True, he was not a man to draw attention to himself in any way, but he had a dry humour which she found delightful and even in the traffic snarl-ups they encountered from time to time, he remained cool and placid, and when the road was free before then, he drove at speed with the same placid coolness. Phoebe sat beside him and thought how wonderful it would be to be married to him—an impossible dream. She shook her head free of it and, obedient to Paul's advice, gazed out of the window at a particularly picturesque windmill.

They had a sumptuous tea in the garden, sitting by the water, all of them talking a great deal and doing full justice to the sandwiches and cakes Else had provided. Phoebe was surprised at Lucius' lighthearted mood. Listening to his mild teasing, she wondered how she could ever have found him absent-minded and vague. Was this his true self, she hazarded, or had he been like this all the time and she hadn't noticed because she had started out expecting him to be exactly as Sybil had described him? She filled the tea cups again, reflecting that it really didn't matter; she loved him whatever he was.

She watched him carry the tea tray back into the house and longed to stay there, in the garden by the water, with the church bells ringing from a dozen churches and Rex snoring on Paul's knee, but she got to her feet as Lucius rejoined them, saying: 'I think I must be getting back—letter to write. . . .'

Such a silly excuse, but it would have to do. She failed to see his smile and found it disconcerting when he said at once: 'I'll drop you off—I want to go to St Bonifacius myself.'

It wasn't until he drew up outside its doors and they were walking up the steps together that he said: 'I'll be here at half past seven—will that suit you? We'll find somewhere quiet to have dinner.'

Phoebe stood on the top step, looking up at him, waiting for her heart to slow and give her the breath to speak. 'I'd like that,' she managed, and went across to the Home on wings, for wasn't there a new dress in the cupboard, waiting to be worn?

Before she went to sleep that night, she tried to recall every second of the evening and couldn't—there was too much to remember; the drive along the motorway to Arnhem, and the village—Scherpenzel, such a funny name—where in De Witte Hoelvoet, they had eaten their dinner, not one single item of which could she recall. They had lingered over their meal and it had been late when Lucius stopped the Jaguar outside the hospital once more, and despite her protests had walked into the quiet entrance hall with her and in the centre of its utter quiet, had taken her in his arms and kissed her, and this time he hadn't been in the least vague.

She lay in bed, fighting sleep, thinking about it, and when at last she allowed her eyes to close, she dreamed of him.

CHAPTER EIGHT

PHOEBE was due for night duty again at the end of the week, and that meant that in no time at all she would be going home. She began, halfheartedly, to think about the future; perhaps it would be a good idea to go right away—Australia perhaps, or Canada. She had always wanted to travel, but now that urge seemed to have left her and the prospect of doing so daunted her. But there were good nursing jobs to be had in either country, although even the other side of the world, she reflected sadly, wasn't far enough away for her to forget Lucius.

She hadn't seen him for two days now. He was at Leyden, Mies had told her, a member of the Board of Examiners at the Academisch Ziekenhuis, adding diffidently that her Arie hoped to be elected to that august body in a few years' time, which remark naturally led the conversation away from Lucius to the fascinating one of her own future.

'We shall marry quite soon,' Mies confided happily, digressing briefly to explain the laws governing marriage in the Netherlands. 'Arie has a good salary and a splendid job and there will be a flat for us. . . . I shall not work.' She eyed Phoebe speculatively. 'I do not understand how it is arranged, but why should you not take my place as Hoofd Zuster when I leave? You know the work well and you please Lucius, and if you take lessons you will soon learn Dutch—you are a clever girl.'

The prospect appalled Phoebe. It would be an impossibility to stay in Delft, seeing Lucius every day, but only as his Ward Sister, while Maureen... She shuddered delicately. She had done some hard thinking during the last few days; Maureen had told her that she had Lucius just where she wanted him, and although she didn't want to believe it, it was probably true. She was an attractive girl and she knew how to make herself charming, and almost certainly Lucius believed that Paul adored her. Phoebe sighed. How blind could a man be? And he had told her himself that he was going to get married; probably, she thought bitterly, he regarded her as an old friend to whom he could confide his plans.

She ground her excellent teeth and because she didn't want to hurt Mies' feelings, shook her head regretfully.

'It's a lovely idea,' she agreed mendaciously, 'but I don't think it would succeed. For one thing, there must be lots of Dutch nurses with better qualifications than I, who want the job, and for another I doubt if I could get a work permit for an unlimited period.'

Neither of which reasons were insurmountable, but they sounded authentic, because Mies nodded regretfully. 'That is so—a pity. And now that you are here, we will arrange your free days. I have had such a splendid idea. You have but a week of day duty when you come off nights. I will give you only two nights off, the others you shall add to your day off at the end of your last week, thus you will be able to go home three days earlier than you expect.'

She looked so pleased with herself that Phoebe could not but agree with an enthusiasm she didn't feel. She had no wish to go home three days earlier—three days during which she might see Lucius—she had, in fact, no wish to go home at all.

And not only was time growing short, but everything else seemed against her, for the very evening she went on night duty, the weather changed dramatically to a chilling rain and a fierce wind from the sea which, even if Lucius had suggested it, and he hadn't, would have put their morning swim out of the question. Phoebe's hope that the weather would clear in a day or so proved a forlorn one; if anything it became steadily worse, and her temper with it, largely because she never saw Lucius at all—not until her fourth night on duty, and then he was in Maureen's company.

Phoebe had had a busy night, the third of her week's work. She had gone to bed tired and dispirited and quite unable to sleep. After several hours, during which time her thoughts were of no consolation to her at all, she got up, made herself some tea, wrote a letter home and decided that since it was only six o'clock and she had several hours before she needed to go on duty, she might as well go out and post it. A walk would do her good, she told herself, bundling on her raincoat and knotting a scarf under her chin with no thought for her appearance. She was on her way back, feeling hollow-eyed and pale from lack of sleep, when the Jaguar slid past her with Lucius at the wheel and Maureen beside him.

Maureen had seen her. Before Phoebe could cross the road, Lucius, obedient to his companion's direction, pulled the car into the curb.

It was Maureen who opened the conversation. 'My word,' she said in a voice which dripped a bogus sympathy, 'you do look a wreck! Just look at her, Lucius— the poor thing should be in bed—red-rimmed eyes and no colour!'

Phoebe managed a smile in answer to this perfidious attack. 'Oh, we all look like this after a few nights,' she said in a slightly brittle voice. 'You should try it and see.'

Her smile was as brittle as her voice. Probably it looked grotesque on her pallid face—she didn't care; she included Lucius in it just to let him see how fabulous she felt. But it was a useless effort, for he leaned across Maureen and said: 'Phoebe, you look fagged out. Are you all right?'

Before she could reply Maureen's gay voice cut in: 'You look at least thirty, my dear! I had no idea that a few nights out of bed could play such havoc with a girl's looks. You poor dear, going to a hard night's work just as we're starting out to spend our evening...'

Phoebe suddenly didn't want to hear how they were going to spend their evening; there was a gap in the traffic. With a hasty: 'I must go, or I shall be late,' she fled across the street.

It was after ten o'clock when Lucius came into the ward. She hadn't expected him, naturally enough—indeed, her evening had been made wretched by the thought of him wining and dining Maureen at some fabulous place, drinking champagne and living it up. She and the student nurse had just finished clearing up the mess after one of the smaller children had been sick. She was going down the ward, wrapped in a plastic apron a good deal too large for her, pushing the runabout full of linen to be sluiced. She eyed him uncertainly, decided that to get rid of the runabout was more important than going to meet him and with a murmured: 'I won't be a moment, sir,' she made for the sluice door. He opened it for her and followed her inside, so that she paused in her tracks and exclaimed in a shocked voice: 'Oh, you mustn't come in here, sir!'

'Why not?' he asked lazily. 'Is it sacrosanct?'

Which despite herself, moved her to hushed laughter. 'Don't be ridiculous! It just isn't—isn't suitable for you. Who did you want to see?'

He shrugged wide shoulders. 'My patients—no hurry. Tell me, Phoebe, do you find night duty too much for you? You looked exhausted this evening. Maureen thought . . .'

It was too much! Phoebe hurled her noisome bundle into the sink and turned on the tap. 'How kind of her to concern herself—I daresay she pointed out my haggard looks with a wealth of detail. I only hope it didn't spoil your evening together.' She turned off the tap with quite unnecessary violence and turned to face him where he lounged against the tiled wall.

He spoke blandly. 'Well, perhaps night duty may not exhaust you, but it certainly sharpens your temper.' He put his hands in his pockets and crossed his legs comfortably. 'As it happens I spent the evening at home—with Paul—and when he had gone to bed, I went to my study and worked, and a good thing I did, it seems, for you appear to grudge me any amusement I may care to arrange for myself.'

There was a wicked gleam in his eye which she ignored. 'I don't!' she declared hotly. 'What about . . .' She was about to remind him of their evening at Schevingenen and the dinner they had had together, but instead she said with a haughtiness which sat ill on her unglamorous appearance: 'I'm not in the least interested in your private life,' and started to tear off her apron. It was a pity that she hadn't thought to take off her rubber gloves first. After watching her wrestling with an ever-tightening knot Lucius offered mildly: 'If you'll turn round, I'll do it.'

She stood, her back like a ramrod, while he worked

away at it, and when he had freed her he said in quite a different voice—impersonal, a little cool: 'Good. Now if I might take a quick look at this vomiting infant before I go . . .'

He went shortly afterwards, wishing her a pleasant good night, whistling softly as he went down the stairs. Phoebe, her pen poised over a chart, listened to his footsteps growing fainter and fainter. They seemed symbolic of the future; she closed her eyes on sudden tears and then opened them resolutely and began to write in her neat hand.

It was two mornings later, as she was on her way out for a morning walk before bed, that she was overtaken in the entrance hall by Mies, running and waving an envelope at her.

She thrust it at Phoebe and said, very out of breath: 'I remembered that you said that you would take a walk. These are reports for Doctor van Someren—they came by mistake to the ward, you understand, and he will not be here today—he is at Leyden, but he goes home, I think, and he can see them there. Please to hand them in at his house.' She smiled in her friendly fashion. 'It is no hardship for you to do this?'

'No hardship,' said Phoebe. He wouldn't be home, anyway, so it made no difference at all. She might encounter Maureen, but her mood was such that she really didn't care. Besides, she might just as well walk past his house as anywhere else.

It was another dreary day, but she hardly noticed the fine rain as she walked briskly through the streets, glad to be out in the fresh air after her hectic night, her mind empty of thought because she was tired. She took the shortest way, deciding to go and have coffee at the Prinsenkelder and then go straight back to bed and, she hoped, to sleep.

She could hear Rex yelping as she raised her hand to the heavy knocker on Lucius' door. She heard Maureen's high-pitched voice, shrill with fury, at the same time, and when no one came she tried the door. It opened under her hand and she went in.

Maureen was in the sitting room with her back to the door so that she didn't see Phoebe. She had the dog lead in her hand and cringing on the floor was the terrified Rex. As Phoebe paused in the doorway, appalled, she raised her arm to bring the lead down once more, but this time Phoebe, galvanised into sudden action, caught her arm from behind, wrenched the lead from her and threw it into the corner of the room.

'You're mad!' she declared incredulously, and turned her attention to the puppy. He was shivering, very frightened, and there was a cut over one of his boot-button eyes. He winced and yelped as she lifted him gently to try to discover if he were injured and was relieved to find that at least all four of his legs seemed normal; she had no idea how long Maureen had been beating him, but undoubtedly he was severely bruised, if nothing worse. She laid a soothing hand on his heaving little body and turned to speak to Maureen.

'You must be mad—whatever possessed you, to ill-treat something so small and defenceless—and to hurt Paul? Why did you do it?'

Maureen flung herself into a chair. 'Oh, shut up,' she said roughly. 'Just my filthy luck for Else to go out and leave the door unlocked. Another few minutes and the little brute would have been dead. Take it away, Miss do-gooder, and I'll think up some tale or other about it running away.'

'You'll break Paul's heart—he loves Rex.'

The other girl laughed. 'Don't be such a fool! Do you think I care about that kid's feelings? Do you imagine that I enjoy being a governess? You're so dim. It serves my purpose, that's all—it keeps me near Lucius.'

Phoebe had gone to sit in a chair with Rex on her lap, examining him more carefully; neither of them heard the street door open, and both of them were taken by surprise when Lucius came into the room, but it was Maureen who recovered first. She was out of her chair in a flash, exclaiming: 'Lucius—thank heaven you've come! I'm in such a state! Rex ran out of the door and got knocked down by a car—Else left the door ajar when she went out. Luckily Phoebe came along with some message or other—I've not had the time to ask her—she's looking to see if he's badly hurt.' This remarkable speech had the effect of rendering Phoebe speechless. She gave Maureen an incredulous look and turned to Lucius, but he wasn't looking at either of them; he was bending over the puppy, examining him in his turn. Phoebe, seething with unspoken words, bit them back; a row wouldn't help Rex, for it would waste time. She said quickly: 'I hope he's not badly hurt.'

'It's hard to tell, but I don't think so. Probably the edge of the pavement or a stone cut his eyelid; he must have been tossed clear. Did the car stop?' He glanced briefly at Maureen.

'No—I didn't actually see it happen, only heard the noise—poor little beast.' Her voice was warmly sympathetic as she started to cross the floor towards them. 'I'll take him round to the vet—I can take the Mini . . .'

Phoebe caught her breath. 'No,' she said more sharply than she intended, 'I'll take him. Mijnheer van Vliet's house is close by—I'll carry Rex.'

There was a short pause until Lucius said deliberately: 'Thank you, but I shall take him myself and I'll pick up Paul from school at midday and take him along to see how Rex is shaping.' He picked up the puppy and started for the door and paused to ask of Phoebe: 'Why did you come?'

'I was asked to deliver some reports. I put them on the table in the hall.'

He nodded: 'Thanks,' and shut the door quietly behind him. There was silence after he had gone. Presently Phoebe left the house too, not speaking at all to Maureen, for she could think of nothing that she could say which might improve matters, and if she uttered the things she wanted to, it would probably make things hard for Paul as well as Rex. Besides, there was the chance that Maureen, after such a narrow shave, might change her ways. Phoebe hurried through the rain, wondering if and how she should tell Lucius about it and would he believe her if she did? Maureen was a clever girl, she would be able to turn a situation, however adverse to herself, to good advantage. Phoebe decided to wait until she was on the point of leaving Holland—only a few days away now. She would tell Lucius then and it would be up to him to sort things out for himself. She had forgotten her coffee. She walked around the streets aimlessly and was on her way back to the hospital when she suddenly decided to go and see Mijnheer van Vliet.

He received her very kindly and led her at once to the room at the back of the surgery where the sick animals were housed. Rex, looking sorry for himself, was in a basket, still shivering, but he opened one eye and looked at her warily and essayed to wag his tail.

'How is he?' asked Phoebe anxiously.

'He'll recover,' the vet smiled at her. 'He's a tough

little chap—a few days and he'll be well again.' He added on a puzzled note: 'Only his injuries do not match up with a car accident. I am a little perplexed. . . .'

'Look,' said Phoebe earnestly, wondering why she hadn't thought of telling him in the first place, 'it wasn't a car. I know how it happened, but you mustn't tell anyone—you'll understand why.'

She plunged into her tale, and when she had finished, Mijnheer van Vliet nodded his head. 'So that is the story, and a shocking one, but I must tell you that I am not altogether surprised. For some reason Maureen promised—oh, a couple of years ago, that she would give Paul a puppy. Always there have been reasons why she has not done so—it is as if she punishes him by refusing his constant wish to have a dog— and now he has Rex, a dog which she has not given him, and she is angry. I do not understand, but I thank you for telling me. I will say nothing, of course, but I promise you that I will keep an eye on him— daily visits perhaps, a check-up each week, something —and until then I will keep him safe here with me.' He eyed her thoughtfully. 'You do not feel that you should tell Lucius?'

She blinked her beautiful eyes in deep thought. 'No —you see Lucius thinks that Maureen is kind and good for Paul and that he's fond of her, and perhaps that is the truth—I don't know. Besides,' she paused, seeking the right words, 'they have known each other a long time, Lucius and Maureen. They're—they're old friends.'

Mijnheer van Vliet growled deeply, coughed hugely and offered her coffee, making no comment. She refused the coffee, saying that she really would have to get back to the hospital and get some sleep, and after a final look at Rex, she walked back to the Home, too tired by now to think sensibly about anything, and as it turned out, too tired to sleep.

She went on duty looking distinctly haggard and not much caring. The ward was busy, there was a great deal to do, and it was almost one o'clock in the morning when she sat down at her desk in the now quiet ward and a few minutes later Lucius came, looking vast in the dim, shadowed surroundings. Phoebe got to her feet wearily and wished him good evening, and he said softly:

'Hullo, Phoebe—they're all O.K., aren't they? I came to see you to tell you that Rex is better. He's to stay with van Vliet for a day or two.'

'And Paul?'

'He was upset, but he feels better now he's seen him.' He leaned over and turned the desk lamp on to her face. 'You've not slept,' he stated baldly, and then, to take her breath: 'What was wrong this morning?'

She faltered a little: 'Wrong? What do you mean?'

His voice was bland. 'You and Maureen. But I see you have no intention of telling me.'

'No.'

He nodded to himself. 'A little tiff, I suppose—you were tired, weren't you, and I daresay, short-tempered, and Maureen is no good with animals. She finds them a nuisance even when she wants to help them. I daresay you arrived just in time to prevent her having hysterics.'

Phoebe eyed him unsmilingly; he had called her short-tempered and somehow put her in the wrong. Well, let him find out for himself. 'You might say that,' she told him.

Lucius turned to go. 'Oh, Paul sent his love. He hopes you will go and see Rex.'

'Of course I will. Please give him my love.'

He lingered. 'You're friends at last. I wonder what stood in the way when you first met?'

She returned his thoughtful stare. 'I have no idea. Good night, sir.'

His lips twitched, he gave her a mocking smile. 'Good night, Nurse Brook.'

She went the following morning to see Rex and this time stayed for coffee with Mijnheer van Vliet and his wife. 'Rex is better,' the vet told her, 'but he's got some brutal weals on his back, poor little beast. He's on penicillin and he eats like a horse. Have you seen Lucius?'

'Yes—on the ward.'

'You didn't tell him?'

'No, and I don't intend to.' She got to her feet. 'Thank you for the coffee. May I come and see Rex again? When is he going home?'

Mijnheer van Vliet laughed. 'Tomorrow or the day after. Paul is longing to look after him and I find it hard to imagine that Maureen will repeat her actions.' He smiled grimly. 'If she does, then whatever you feel, I shall tell Lucius myself and he can find himself another governess.' He walked to the door with her. 'You will be back in England very soon, I understand. I am sorry to hear that; we shall miss you.'

Phoebe sped back to the hospital, wondering if Lucius would miss her too, or if he would forget about her going until she had gone and then wonder where she was.

She hoped that he would visit the ward that night, but this time it was Doctor Pontier. He wrote up a few charts, signed a couple of forms, asked her when she was leaving, hoped for the pleasure of taking her out before she did, and took himself off. He was a nice man, although he had a roving eye. Phoebe thought about him for perhaps ten seconds and then plunged back into her work.

She was late off duty in the morning. Everything had gone wrong—broken thermometers, cross children who refused to be washed, crosser ones who spat out their medicine and the cheerful ones who thought it fun to hide under the bedclothes and have a good romp before being hurried off to clean their teeth and wash their faces. Phoebe, a calm girl when it came to her work, took it all in good part, but by the time she left the ward she was tired enough to go straight to bed.

Breakfast, she promised herself as she went slowly to the dining room, and then a bath and bed. She had done the last night of her duty; she had two days off, so she would sleep until the afternoon, get up, have a walk and go back to bed again. The dining room was almost empty. Phoebe poured coffee, buttered some bread and sat down. She was half way through the coffee when she was told that there was someone to see her and it was urgent. She trailed up the stairs again—the ward had been all right when she left it. It wouldn't be Lucius in this weather; perhaps it was Rex—she hurried her lagging feet as she reached the entrance hall. Paul was there. He looked small and forlorn and wildly angry, and forgetting her tiredness Phoebe hurried to him.

'Paul—what's the matter? Rex?'

He stared at her for a moment and then began to pour out his tale, becoming quite incoherent and mixing Dutch and English together so that she was hard put to understand him. When he had finished she said in a calm voice: 'Let me get this straight, Paul—you stop me if I go wrong. Your father's away in England

555

—for how long? Two days. He fetched Rex back last night so that you should have him while he was away and this morning Maureen took him and shut him in the shed at the bottom of the garden, and made you go to school—how did she make you, my dear?'

Tears clogged his voice. 'She said it would be the worse for Rex if I didn't—that Papa had told her to do it, but I don't believe her. She's going to hurt him, I know she is.' He fixed her with a pleading eye. 'You must help me, please, Phoebe!'

'Yes, dear, of course I'll help you.'

His face brightened a little. 'You believe me, then?'

'Yes, of course I do. Where are Else and that girl who comes in the mornings?'

'Maureen told them they could have the day off. She does that when Papa's away—she tells them that he has said so, but he hasn't.'

She could well believe that. 'Any ideas?' she asked.

'Could we rescue Rex and run away, just till Papa comes home?'

She considered the idea. 'Is Maureen in the house?'

'Yes, she has friends in when Papa is away.'

She would! thought Phoebe savagely; there were a number of questions she was going to ask, but not now. 'So she wouldn't notice if we slipped into the garden?'

He was quick. 'From the canal. Oh, Phoebe, how clever you are! I can borrow Jan Schipper's boat, he lives a little further along—no one will see us, they'll be in the sitting room.'

'Good, though we must be careful. We'll go now, just as soon as I've changed.' She paused, struck by a thought. 'Where can we go to?'

Paul put a hand to his mouth, his eyes huge above it. 'I don't know,' he mumbled. 'Oom Domus—but he's going to den Haag.'

'Think of someone!' Phoebe besought him. 'Aunts, uncles, friends, an old nanny. . . .' He wouldn't know what an old nanny was—but he did.

He said at once: 'Papa's old nanny, Anna, she lives in Amsterdam, I know where. She loves him, she told me so.' He smiled. 'She'll help.'

Phoebe released a held breath. 'Good boy! Sit here and don't move. I'll be ten minutes.'

She was back in seven exactly, not perhaps looking her best, for she had flung on a cotton dress, belted her raincoat over it, concealed her untidy head under a scarf, caught up her shoulder bag, stuffed with a few necessities for the night and all the money she possessed, and raced downstairs again, full of false energy, her sapphire eyes blazing in a washed-out face.

'What about school?' she asked as they raced through the small back streets. When he told her simply that he hadn't been she forbore to say anything. Probably later on she would regret this whole business, but she could think of nothing else and she felt partly to blame because she hadn't told Lucius about the beating Rex had had. She thanked heaven silently that she had nights off and was free to do what she liked.

They came out into the street where Lucius lived, but at its other end, and Paul led her down a narrow dark path between two houses, opened the wooden door at its end and entered a garden. Phoebe hesitated.

'Paul,' she whispered, looking apprehensively over her shoulder at the house beyond the well-kept lawn, 'isn't this private?'

'It's Jan's home, and he's at school. No one will see us, and he won't mind.'

They had reached a small jetty, just like the one in Lucius' garden, and Paul got into the small boat tied to its side. Phoebe got in too; she wasn't sure about Dutch law, but she had a nasty feeling that they could be accused of stealing. 'Undo the rope,' Paul told her. He had the oars out and was already swinging the boat outwards. She did as she was bidden, recognising that he was leading the expedition for the moment, not she. She crouched opposite him, averting her eyes from the houses they were passing. Any moment now, she thought guiltily, some worthy citizen would fling open a window and cry the Dutch equivalent of 'Stop, thief!' But no one saw them. Paul shipped an oar and gentled the boat into the bank. They were there; Lucius' garden, bright with flowers, its beautifully tended lawn shining wetly in the rain, lay before them, and from the shed close at hand came a soft, hopeless whimper.

'I'll get him,' said Phoebe. 'Keep the boat close in, so we can run for it. If anyone comes you're to go on your own with Rex.' She pulled some notes from her bag. 'There, I expect this is enough to get you to Amsterdam.' She gave him a cheerful wink and stepped on to the jetty.

The shed door was fastened from the outside but not locked, which was a good thing because she had no idea what she would have done if that had been the case. Rex was tied up inside and whimpered joyfully when he saw her, but she said 'Hush!' in such an urgent voice that he kept quiet while she sawed through the rope with a pair of blunt garden shears. The simple task took an age. With her heart in her mouth Phoebe picked him up and made for the boat, and once there she had to put a hand over the puppy's muzzle to stop his ecstatic greeting of his young master.

'For heaven's sake,' she said, very much on edge, 'row—you can say hullo to each other presently.'

The return journey wasn't as bad as she had expected it would be; perhaps she was becoming inured to crime. She chuckled at the idea and Paul turned round to say: 'You are what Papa calls a good sport, I think, Phoebe.' Well, he wouldn't think that of her now. She handed the puppy to her companion and he asked: 'What do we do now?'

'The station,' she told him, 'and let's keep off the main streets.'

It was still early as they boarded an Amsterdam train, but the morning rush was over. They sat opposite each other, drinking coffee and eating the rolls Phoebe had bought and sharing them with the puppy. Finally, the last of the crumbs tidied away, Phoebe leaned forward.

'Now, Paul,' she said urgently, 'there are some things I must know.' And when he nodded, she went on: 'Tell me about Maureen, my dear.' She searched his solemn little face. 'There's something ... you have always been so careful to be obedient to her and yet I have the idea that you are afraid of her, but if that is so, why didn't you tell your papa?'

He took a deep breath. 'She said that if I did everything she said and—and liked her, she would buy me a puppy; she said it all depended on me whether I had him or not, because she would have to marry Papa before she could get him and if she went away and he had another governess for me she would be old and horrid and I'd never get a puppy of my own; she said,' he gulped, 'that if I said anything to Papa I'd never have anything, not as long as I lived.'

'Is that why you shut me up, Paul?'

He nodded. 'She said that you were a—a menace—

that you wanted to marry Papa. Do you?'

Phoebe stared back into his questioning eyes. 'Yes,' she said quietly, 'I do, but you need not worry, your Papa doesn't want to marry me.'

'She said you'd make him.'

She gave a lop-sided smile. 'How, I wonder? Even if I knew, I wouldn't do that, Paul.'

'She said you were a—a—canting hypocrite and a scheming old maid.' He smiled suddenly and endearingly. 'But she's wrong, you're not—I like you. She said I was to hate you, but I don't.' He looked, for a brief moment, forlorn. 'You're a little like my mama.'

She said steadily: 'Am I, dear? I think that's one of the nicest things anyone has ever said to me.' She smiled warmly at him. 'So now we know why Maureen was so angry that you have been given Rex—she has no hold on you any more.'

He didn't quite understand her. 'She said that Rex would die anyway because he was only a street dog, and when he did, she would buy me another, but only if she married Papa.'

'Oh, my dear,' cried Phoebe, 'I often wondered—most people have cats and dogs and a few tame mice or a hamster . . .'

His eyes sparkled. 'I like kittens too, but Maureen said they're not healthy.'

'Oh, pooh,' said Phoebe roundly. 'We've got cats and dogs and they're a great deal more healthy than some people I know.'

'Have you any mice?'

'Well, no—girls don't like mice, you know, but I can see that they make splendid pets for boys.'

She glanced out of the window and suddenly remembered where they were and what they were doing. 'We're almost in Amsterdam; you take Rex, and I'll

560

get a taxi.'

Anna lived in a long street called Overtoom. It was neither picturesque nor in a particularly good part of the city and in the rain any charm it might possess had been obliterated by the greyness of the sky and the dampness of its pavements, but to Phoebe it represented a solution, temporary at any rate, of their most pressing problems. She followed Paul down a flight of stone steps to Anna's front door, just below street level, and waited while he rang the bell.

There was no mistaking Anna when she opened the door, for she was exactly what anyone would imagine an old nanny to be, with bright blue eyes, extremely neat hair parted in the centre and gathered into a bun, and a small round person clothed in a black dress almost completely covered in an old-fashioned print pinny. At the sight of Paul she broke at once into delighted speech and after a minute Paul, remembering his manners, introduced them and said: 'Anna says we're to go inside.'

The rooms were very small and crowded with furniture, all very highly polished, and there was a lovely smell of coffee in the kitchen where Anna bade them sit down at the table. Over their elevenses Paul told his tale, and Phoebe, watching anxiously, was vastly relieved when at the end of it and after a few brisk remarks from Anna, Paul told her:

'Anna says we are to stay here until Papa comes back, and she's glad we came. You're to sleep on the landing, if you don't mind, because there's only one bedroom and I'm to sleep on the floor—I'll like that, and I'll have Rex.'

Phoebe eyed him tiredly. How resilient little boys were! She felt exhausted herself and said a little desperately: 'Will you tell Anna that I'll telephone your papa as soon as he gets back—in the afternoon. You'll be all right once he's home again, and Paul, do you think Anna would mind if I went to sleep for a little while? I can't keep my eyes open.'

'Oh, Phoebe, I forgot, you've been awake all night.' He addressed himself to the old lady, who peered across the table at Phoebe and nodded her head.

'You're to go to bed now,' Paul told her. 'Anna says you are a sensible girl but that you must have your sleep. You won't be too long?' He sounded wistful.

She shook her head, resolutely ignoring the longing to sleep the clock round. 'An hour or two. Paul, stay indoors, won't you? Is there a yard or something for Rex?'

'A little garden with a high wall,' he told her. She went up three or four steps leading out of the kitchen, guided by Anna, on to a small landing, bare save for a folding bed in one corner and a chair. She smiled sleepily at her kind hostess, tossed her things on to the chair, kicked off her shoes and curled up on the bed. She was asleep within seconds.

It was Paul who wakened her a few hours later, Rex still tucked under his arm. 'It's teatime,' he informed her. 'Didn't you undress? You must have been sleepy.'

Phoebe yawned, feeling heavy-eyed and hollow, fighting a desire to fall back on the bed again and sleep for ever. 'I was. I say, Paul, I want to wash—is there a bathroom?'

He shook his head. 'You use the kitchen sink. We won't look,' he added kindly as he went away. He was whistling cheerfully and a little off key and Phoebe smiled to herself. At least one of them was enjoying himself!

The remainder of the day passed surprisingly quickly. She tried out a little of her Dutch on Anna, and with Paul's help, they had quite a conversation, and even if they didn't understand each other very well, it didn't seem to matter. Anna, Phoebe could tell, was most definitely on their side, and Phoebe, waking in the night because the mattress wasn't all that comfortable, at least had the satisfaction of knowing that Anna approved of what she had done, she only hoped that Lucius would be of the same opinion.

CHAPTER NINE

THE rain had eased up in the morning and over their
simple breakfast Phoebe discovered that there was a
park behind Anna's flat—Vondel Park. It would be a
good place to go, she decided as she helped Anna with
the washing up. They had to spend the day somewhere
until it was time for her to telephone Lucius, and it
wasn't fair on Anna to fill her little home to overflowing with a high-spirited small boy and a puppy. They
set off presently, with a ball Anna had found from
somewhere or other, and strict instructions to be back
for their dinner at midday.

The park was pleasant, well laid out and almost
empty of people. They walked for a little while, Rex
lying snugly in Paul's arms, because, as Phoebe
pointed out in her sensible way, they would play ball
presently and he would want to join in and he ought
not to get too tired.

They had been tossing the ball to and fro for perhaps ten minutes when Paul gave a sudden shout,
hurled the ball wildly in the air and started to run
towards Phoebe, yelling as he came, his whole face
alight with happiness. She spun round, certain who it
was she would see—and she was right. Lucius, the ball
in his hand, was coming towards them over the grass.
He paused to put a hand briefly on Paul's shoulder as
they met and then came to a halt before her.

'Don't dare to be angry with him,' she said impul-
sively, then wished she hadn't spoken, because he was
indeed angry, but with her, not Paul. His words bore
this out, for when he spoke it was in a silky voice

which menaced her far more than a shout.

'I should like to wring your pretty neck,' he gritted. 'How dare you, Phoebe? Such a petty act, it wasn't worthy of you.'

She steadied her shaking mouth. 'But you're back a day too soon. . . .'

His eyes blazed. 'And how fortunate that I am—you had overlooked that possibility.' He smiled, not at all nicely. 'I am at a loss to discover why you should have done this—why should you wish to set Paul against Maureen? She telephoned me in great distress—she imagined that you were friendly towards her, so naturally she feels deeply hurt.'

Phoebe found her voice, keeping it low so that Paul, playing with Rex close by, shouldn't hear. 'Is that what she said?' She was surprised at the mildness of her tone; she felt as though she would blow sky-high with rage.

'Yes. When I returned last night I found a note from her asking me to telephone. She told me then that Paul had disappeared.'

'How did she know that I was with Paul?'

'She had the good sense to telephone the hospital and put two and two together.'

'And how,' went on Phoebe stubbornly, 'did you know where we were?'

'Van Vliet suggested I should try Anna—he remembered that Paul had been talking about her.' He added wearily, 'I tried everywhere else last night.'

'Is Maureen at your house?'

He raised his eyebrows. 'No—why do you ask? She will be there by the time we get back, I imagine. But don't worry, I have no intention of reproving you until we have got to the bottom of this in a rational manner, I'm sure that the three of us can discuss . . .'

'I won't,' said Phoebe, in far too loud a voice. 'I'll discuss nothing. You can think what you like, what do I care? You're so completely under that woman's thumb . . .' She stopped, choked and walked away very fast. By the time Lucius, with Paul and Rex, had arrived at Anna's house, she had dried her angry tears, composed her face and was ready with a polite refusal when he offered her a lift back to Delft. And when Paul, aware that something was not right in his little world, began his own muddled explanation, she bade him urgently to be quiet.

'Wait, my dear,' she besought him. 'It won't help now, and it doesn't matter any more, because your Papa is back home, don't you see? Besides, explaining things is so tedious.'

He eyed her. 'You've been crying. I'm sorry I shut you in that house.'

She bent and kissed him. 'I'm going to have a lovely day shopping,' she told him. 'If I see anything for Rex, I shall buy it.'

'The Bijenkorf has some tartan collars with a silver plate on them, for his name, you know—they put it on while you wait. . . .'

She smiled at him. 'Then that's what I'll get. Now go back to your father, Paul, he'll be waiting for you.'

He lingered by her. 'You'll come back, won't you? Won't you come with me to the door? You haven't said goodbye to Rex.'

Phoebe couldn't refuse him, so she tickled Rex under his chin, wished Paul a warm farewell and Lucius a glacial one, and went back to the landing, where she sat down on the bed, doing nothing until she heard the door close and knew that they had gone.

She waited a little while, trying to suppress the ridiculous hope that Lucius would come back, and when a half hour had gone by, and she knew that he wasn't going to, she tidied herself, stuffed her bag with her bits and pieces once more and went down to the kitchen to wish Anna goodbye.

The old lady was sitting at the table, knitting, but she got up when she saw Phoebe and without saying a word, drew her through a door into what must have been the parlour, seldom used and so stiffly furnished that it reminded Phoebe of a child's drawing. There was an old-fashioned sideboard against one wall, dominating the room and loaded with photos in heavy frames. Anna picked one up and handed it to Phoebe. It was Lucius as a small boy, leaning against his father's knee, a hand on his mother's arm. There was a baby too, invisible in a lacy shawl, and another small boy, younger than Lucius, sitting on the floor. She looked at Anna, who smiled and nodded and handed her a quite small photograph—Lucius in a student's gown, looking vaguely at the camera as though his thoughts were far away, and the last one, Lucius, older still, standing with a group of earnest-looking men outside the hospital. Phoebe gave that one back too and her companion put them carefully in their places and led her out again. At the door she took Phoebe's hand in her own and patted it, nodding her head in a satisfied way and murmuring to herself with an air of great content. Phoebe, not having the least idea what she was saying, could only nod and smile, and finally wish her goodbye.

The day stretched before her and she would have to fill it somehow. She would stay in Amsterdam until the evening and then go straight back to the Nurses' Home and to bed. She was on duty early the following morning, and in four days she would be able to go back home. She need not see Lucius again—there were ways of avoiding him on the ward. This firm resolution was instantly followed by a variety of reasons requiring her to seek him out. She could explain, she told herself, walking briskly along Ovetoom, and knew she never would. He had believed Maureen—he hadn't even asked her why they had come to Anna's, although to be fair, she hadn't given him much opportunity. She scowled fiercely and a meek-looking man coming towards her sidled past, looking quite apprehensive. 'Fool!' she said aloud, meaning herself, and found that she had arrived at the Leidseplein.

She wandered along, staring into the shops, stopping at a coffee bar, where she had hard work in repelling the advances of a cheerful young man who was apparently much taken with her looks. He told her so, in English, after she had informed him coldly that she couldn't understand Dutch. It took determination to shake him off. Phoebe plunged into Vroom and Dreesman, at the bottom of the Kalverstraat, going through its departments without seeing anything of them. By now they would be back in Delft. She pictured them sitting in his lovely house, discussing her; Maureen at her most charming, cleverly putting spokes in Paul's small, futile wheel. Well, it wasn't her business any more, only before she left Delft, she would go and see Mijnheer van Vliet and make sure that he did something about Rex—perhaps he could tell Lucius once she had gone—in the nicest possible way, of course.

Phoebe wandered on again and in company with dozens of other women, lunched in the balcony restaurant of the Bijenkorf. It was a nice store, she decided, so she would spend an hour or so exploring its departments, have tea, and then catch a train. It wouldn't matter if she went to bed early; heaven knew she was tired enough.

She was in the kitchenware department, studying a colourful display of saucepans, when she became aware that Lucius was standing beside her, so close that the sleeve of his jacket brushed her arm. A tide of feeling rushed over her; it was ridiculous that his presence beside her should have the power to melt all her carefully built-up resentment, her unhappiness even; to give her an overwhelming desire to cast herself into his arms, whatever he thought of her. Unable to bear it a moment longer, she snatched up a saucepan and studied it with all the interest of a good housewife on the lookout for a bargain. 'Go away!' she said fiercely.

She had lifted the lid and was peering inside when Lucius took it from her with the utmost gentleness and put it down.

'Phoebe, we must talk.' His voice was harsh and urgent.

She wasn't a girl to give in at the drop of a hat. She picked up a small steel object and gave it her full attention. He took that from her too. 'A hard-boiled egg slicer,' he remarked blandly. 'I imagine it to be a useful kitchen tool.'

'Hard-boiled eggs should be sliced by hand,' Phoebe snapped, aware that the conversation, such as it was, was leading them nowhere.

'Indeed? I'm sure you are right.' She thought she detected laughter in his voice now. 'May we talk?'

'No,' said Phoebe coldly. 'I've nothing to say to you.'

'Good, for I have a great deal to say to you.'

'I shan't listen,' she told him defiantly, and shot him a furious glance.

'Yes, you shall listen, my darling heart. I was angry this morning...'

Her mind registered the glorious fact that he had called her his darling heart even while she said in a voice squeaky with indignation: 'Angry? You wanted to wring my neck!'

'Your lovely neck,' he corrected her, 'and now listen to me so that you will understand why I was angry. When I got home and found Maureen's note and heard what she had to say on the telephone, I lost my temper—I don't often do that, Phoebe, but you see while I had been in England I had dreamed—oh, a great many dreams—of you, of course, and then when Maureen told me that you had made it up with this young doctor in England and pointed out that you were so very English and I was so very Dutch—and wrapped up in my work, and perhaps a little old—it seemed to me that I had dreamed too much.' He turned to look at her. 'It was like coming back to a nightmare—you gone, Paul gone. I could think of nothing else, and then I found you and I remembered the young doctor.'

'And you wanted to wring my neck—well, of all the...!' She paused: a saleswoman, a hawk-eyed, bustling woman, was peering at them from the other side of the saucepans, her dark eyes suspicious. She gave Phoebe a sharp glance and spoke to Lucius, who spoke to her in a smooth voice and actually made her laugh. When she had gone, Phoebe demanded:

'What did you say?'

'She suspected us of being shoplifters, I imagine. I told her that as a young wife, setting up house, you needed time to decide upon your purchases.'

Phoebe chuckled, quite forgetting that they were in the middle of a quarrel. 'Oh, Lucius, how could you? Now I'll have to buy something.'

'Buy anything you wish, my darling, only let me have my say. You see, Paul told me everything on the way back to Delft. I never knew, never even guessed—

why didn't you tell me? I can understand why Paul was afraid to tell me, but you—surely you could have said?'

She stared hard at a shelf loaded with frying pans, blinking back sudden tears. 'Maureen said that she was going to marry you and I didn't know if—if you loved her, so I couldn't say anything, could I?' She sniffed and looked at him and away again. 'Maureen said . . .' she began again.

'My dearest dear, have we not had enough of Maureen? You seem obsessed by her, which I assure you I am not. She was Paul's governess, that was all. I found her good at the job. I thought, heaven help me, that he liked her, that she was kind to him—that was why I allowed her to do much as she wished. It seemed to me that his happiness was more important than the unwelcome visitors she sometimes invited into my house, but once and for all, my darling, I must tell you that never once did I contemplate marrying her.'

He turned her round to face him and said gravely: 'I may be absent-minded and perhaps a little blind to what is going on around me, but there are some things of which I am very sure—my love for you, Phoebe; you are my life and my future. Do you suppose you could surmount the difficulties of marrying a Dutchman and bear with my occasional lapses of memory? Will you marry me, my darling?'

'How do you know I'm not going to marry Jack?'

'Paul told me.'

She leaned back a little against his arm and stared up into his face. 'But he doesn't know anything about him.'

'Naturally not, but you told Paul that you wanted to marry me.'

She drew an indignant breath. 'Well, really—the

little horror! Just wait until I see him!'

She felt Lucius shake with silent laughter. 'You won't get a word in edgeways, my dearest. He was so excited when I told him that I was coming back to fetch you. He babbled about kittens and mice, he even offered, once he has a cat or so to keep Rex company, to welcome a brother or sister into the family.'

'Oh, Lucius, darling Lucius, I'll marry you.' His arms tightened around her, his face was very close, but she held him away. 'No—no, just a minute, Lucius, I know we're not going to talk about Maureen any more, but where is she—did you see her—I ...'

'Gone. I had a talk with her when we got back, and she left the house for good, my darling. And now don't interrupt me again.'

'You can't—not here—people,' said Phoebe. He kissed her silent, and when presently she had her breath back and began: 'I don't think ...' he said comfortably: 'Quite right, my darling, there is no need,' and kissed her again.

In the car on the way to Delft she said shyly: 'I don't know anything about you, Lucius. Anna showed me some photos of you—have you a family?'

'A sister,' he told her, 'married to a Norwegian, a brother living in Canada. My parents are visiting him.'

'Oh—they live here, in Holland?'

'In Friesland—Father is a doctor too. They'll love you, my Phoebe.'

'I hope so. When will they be back?'

'Not for some months. We shall be an old married couple by then.' He drew up before his house and turned to smile at her. 'I told you that I had had dreams while I was in England; they seemed so real that I set about the business of getting a special licence. We can be married very soon, Phoebe.'